Where The Wind Blows

Life's Mysteries Unfold

June Hall

iUniverse, Inc.
New York Bloomington

Where The Wind Blows

Life's Mysteries Unfold

iUniverse books may be ordered through booksellers or by contacting:

iUniverse
1663 Liberty Drive
Bloomington, IN 47403
www.iuniverse.com
1-800-Authors (1-800-288-4677)

ISBN: 978-1-4401-0603-3 (pbk)
ISBN: 978-1-4401-0604-0 (ebk)

Printed in the United States of America

iUniverse rev. date: 12/9/2008

Dedication

This book is dedicated to my second hand family of wonderful sons and daughters. You have enriched my life and I love you so very dearly.

In Memory of Jesse M. Blackman

Comments

Do not use a dollar bill to measure the worth of a man.
June Hall

Nothing happens so bad that some good does not come from it.
Nora Fetters

ACKNOWLEDGEMENTS

Without the assistance from Laura Deck, Judy Prenovost, Lee Whittington and Clair Wesley, from our local library for their combined hours of research, plus the chambers of Commerce from San Angelo, Leaday and Concho, Texas. This work would never have reached fruition. The other sources were historical societies of Kansas, Montana, Wyoming, Utah, Colorado and volumes of input from the Railroad.

My heartfelt thanks go to Ardis Zidan for typing the lions share of pages but without the willingness and love of Lori Twiggs, Rod and Maryanne Collins, Kimberly and Virginia Kalin to complete the typing plus Pam O'Hara who so graciously assembled it, this book would not even exist.

My thanks to Ann Graham, Trina Huebler, Judy Michalek, and Mark Schechinger who's ears I have worn thin to transparency listening to one idea after the next. Without your encouragement I know I may never have finished this.

And an apology to my beautiful, patient, neglected twenty six pound cat, Missy. I love you everyone.

PREFACE

In 1957 while living only a few months in Montana, I was privileged to meet a gentleman whose name was Billy Good, he was still quite a character at age 92.

History will unfold as you read these accounts of his life. It begins in 1865 going through 1959 when he departed for a heavenly home at age 94.

Although third generation Pennsylvanians, the family left for Kansas in a covered wagon joining a group traveling across the Oregon Trail. At an early age Billy joined a cattle drive which became his occupation during his young adult years. So follow along through his adventures, trials and travels. Enjoy your trip.

Billy Good Characters

Billy Good	Age 11 through 94
Manter Good	Father of Billy, teacher, farmer, hardware store owner
Armilla Good	Mother of Billy, seamstress, gentle Christian homemaker
Sybil Good	Sister of Billy

Booth Gordon	Minister
Ira Fletcher	Teacher
Issac Foster	Teacher, second father figure
Matt Kimball	Neighbor, trail hand
Katie Harmond	Billy's sweetheart, wife
Marcia Mellon	Wealthy daughter of Pennsylvania industrialist
Miss Nora Ellen	Wonderful window revered by all
Lionel Longworth	Governor of Montana
Cartha Longworth	Daughter of Lionel, deceased, age four
Nelia Longworth	Adopted daughter of Lionel
Boots McGuiness	Trail hand
Starkey Blake	Trail hand
Lowell Pratt	Top hand
Elaina Pratt	Wife of Lowell
Tig Pratt	Son of Lowell and Elaina
Blaine Wilson	Veterinarian
Nolan Shank	Trail hand and married to teacher, Sara
Daylene Shank	Sister of Nolan, married to Matt Kimball
Marcellino DeBeaso	Trail Cook
Andrew Jackson Cox	"Ajax" trail boss
Clem Gabriel	Billy's best friend
Rand Blackwell	Trail hand
Reva Blackwell	Librarian, wife of Rand
Grant McMurray	Restaurant Owner
Ella May McMurray	Wife of Grant
Mitchell Hayes	Newspaper
Bertram Nutt	Optometrist

Nola Nutt	Wife of Bertam
Chrissy Sprow Nutt	Adopted daughter of Bertam and Nola
Fritz "Hard Knocks" Knox	Cattleman with cattle drive
Willie Bender	Saloon singer, wife of Fritz
Minerva Susan Watson	2nd wife of Lionel
Juanita Westinghouse	Daughter of Philidelphia tycoon
Davidean Westinghouse	1st wife of Lionel
Claire Dent	Attorney
Whitey Cobb	Sheriff
Adam Insley	Banker, bachelor friend of Manter
Carey Flinn	Town drunk
Sally Blake	Sister of Starkey
Ruth Romic	Owner/Manager rest home for men
Gus Romic	Uncle of Ruth, Billy's life long friend
Mason Philpot	Undertaker
Grady Miller	Local fisherman, friend of Lowell Pratt
Levi Guthrey	Trail hand who played mouth harp
Joe Sprow	Frail member of wagon train
Letishia Sprow	Joe's wife
Merry Christine Sprow	Joe and Lettie's daughter
Roscoe Peabody	Rough character in group
Beulah Peabody	Roscoe's wife
Sylvia Lee Peabody	Beautiful daughter of Roscoe and Beulah

BILLY GOOD

Part I

CHAPTER I

Pennsylvania weather is not known for its stability and today was no exception. Early April can be nasty or nice at the whim of the Almighty. On this particular day, God most surely was in a playful mood. The early morning started out cold and foggy but by mid morning the sun had burned through the fog. For a short time it appeared to be a forty to fifty degree start for the day and a man could go about his chores reasonably comfortable. However, before noon, the thunder clouds gathered themselves into a morbid looking disarray when the wind came up very suddenly. Someone up there unzipped the heavens and torrents of water poured from the sky at a slant, as the wind whipped the deluge past us, headed West.

Just as suddenly it stopped raining and hail came down like moth balls turning the earth white. The temperature plummeted by twenty degrees and sent people scattering for coats and scarves. Manter Good was in the livery stable with thoughts of getting over to Millie's home for supper. She had said hot biscuits, fried chicken, raisin pie and coffee were in the offer should he decide to close the store by 6:00.

It was now 4:15 p.m. and once again the sun was shining and the wind had subsided. Manter gathered up the buggy reins and clucked old Ted into a trot down the road to Millie's.

Armilla Hawks was a very pretty young lady with red hair and freckles. She was also handy with a needle, a fine cook, taught piano lessons and was in love with Manter. If the way to a man's heart really was through his stomach, she had every intention of feeding him well.

At the knock on the door she flipped up her unruly crown of auburn curls, wiped her hands on her apron, admonished her younger brother to behave and went mincing her way across the sitting room to greet Manter. He snitched a quick kiss and a pat on her bottom before she shut the door. Her face was red and he could not contain his mirth at her being so flustered.

"Hang your coat on the peg, Manter, I see you got caught in the cloud burst," she observed. "Not for long," he replied as he flung his cap on the hat stand.

"Any more news of the wagon train coming through?" she asked. Not today at least, he told her while pulling out a kitchen chair. The big black cat with four white feet came wandering over to get her usual attention when anyone would oblige. Boots was a stray who found a good home. That tail stood up like a periscope. With a swipe down the cats back and a pat on the head, Manter shew'd Boots on out of the way and sat down.

"Do you promise to cook like this after we are married?" he asked so unconcernedly, Millie dropped the spoon in her hand and, with a squeal, whirled around so fast she lost her balance. Realization sunk in; gathering up what composure she could muster, she grabbed at the back of the chair across from Manter and said with a grin, "that was a proposal I am to assume?"

"Well if I move in here with you and your brother otherwise, it might sully your reputation don't you think?" He tipped back on the legs of his chair and held out his arms. Millie flew around the table and landed quite unceremoniously in his lap. Brother Ned coming in from another room stopped in his tracks not knowing whether to go ahead or retreat.

3

Manter said, "Come here you young rascal! You're sixteen now and need to think about a job. How about working with me at the hardware store after school and Saturday?"

"Gee Millie, can I?" he asked excitedly.

"I don't see why not, Ned. Soon enough you will be on your own."

"Oh, how come?" Ned showed his surprise.

Manter tumbled Millie off his lap and said, "Meet your brother-in-law," while extending his hand. "She didn't say yes yet, but she will."

"Pretty sure of that, Manter Good," Millie retorted.

"You bet, who else wants that sassy red head as badly as me?" They both laughed and prepared to eat.

Ned and Millie's parents were dead three years now and Millie had taken in sewing to stay at home. That, with a small inheritance, had kept them well enough. In those days there were people leaving for the West quite regularly and were in need of garments necessary for travel, patch work quilts, comforters, and hand-me-downs altered or reconstructed.

The hardware store was busy and prosperous. It seemed there was no need for delay in wedding plans thus Manter and Millie were wed within the month of April, 1864.

A hard, cold wind settled over the Pennsylvania country side the night of January 20, 1865, when William Leroy Good made a howling entrance into this frozen world. At nine pounds, eight ounces, he could be quoted as a bouncing baby boy and would be followed in June of 1870 by a six pound sister fashioned exactly after her mother: auburn hair, blue eyes and dimples. She was the delight of the entire family!

By 1875 the Good family had decided to strike West with the next wagon train and prepared to sell their home and Manter's share of the hardware store. Other town residents also were gathering together making up several wagons adding to the line coming through. Again it was a blustery April morning that saw twelve wagons roll out of Pike Lake,

Pennsylvania, to be joined later by five more in Ohio. Starkey Blake and his sister, Sally, were in one of the covered wagons. Since Sally had owned her own business, a dress, shop, for a couple of years, she had fixed up the interior of the wagon quite comfortably. In time it became the gathering spot of many of the unmarried members going west. Starkey had never really became acquainted with work - to him it was among the unmentionable four letter words such as wind, rain, snow, hail heat, dust, cold, etc. He could rattle off these things that offended his sensibilities much to his delight, as he was of the opinion it was humor. That same level of intelligence had seen him through five or six jobs, thrown out of bars, fist fights, run-in's with two prospective father-in-laws who declared *that will never happen again* and it didn't.

Starkey was a goof-off. He lived for good times at others' expense; could charm one out of a dollar, a meal or a beer; sweet talked the ladies and was lazy by birth. Good looking in a rangy, rugged way, six foot one, blue black hair, beautiful teeth and had a gift with horses seldom seen by anyone. He was quite a contrast to his five foot, two inch chestnut colored hair, rather plain looking younger sister. She who thought idleness was an abomination unto the Lord and preached that sermon long and strong. He usually managed to duck out at the height of this vocal onslaught but he loved and admired his sister, who, to his thinking, could do no wrong. Woe unto any fellow foolish enough to even think of making a remark about her dowdiness.

It didn't take twenty four hours before Starkey was on a first name bases with "work" on the trail. Chopping wood was the devils idea and he knew in his gut he would surely parish if one more axe was doled out his way. Blisters and calluses were not known to him in his world but that was about to change on a grand scale. Little did he know then the truth of cattle herding!

Another couple who occupied a wagon on the trip was

Issac Foster and his widowed sister fondly referred to by everyone as Miss Nora Ellen. Issac was known as "Ike" and was admired by most for his gentlemanly ways and a bright mind. He figured at 43 he was entitled to indulge his dream of a school in the Mid-West territory of Kansas. Since his sister lived with him, it was only reasonable that she abandon her life style in Pennsylvania to accompany her teacher brother and to explain all that life could offer her. After living in one town all her life, her husband deceased and no children, one aim in her life was to be a missionary. That opportunity never showed its face but now she could do her God's work and will among those on the wagon train. She started a Sunday school for all the little folks, a sing-along on Wednesday evenings, became a counselor among those troubled by their choice and was adored by all.

Another fellow traveler from Pike Lake was Booth Gordon, a young minister with a desire to have his own church. He possibly would never have made this trip had not Miss Nora Ellen been on the trek.

In a small city of people that a wagon train becomes, people meet people - some times to their sorrow - sometimes to their surprise and blessing. It would take six months to reach the Kansas area they had set out for. New friends and relationships were formed and a few feuds popped up. Trouble with Indians and thieves did not help matters either.

Fritz Knox, known to all as Hard Knocks, was the wagon leader and a true blue cow man dead set on his own ranch. Honest to the core, he had some very unhappy experiences in his thirty years and decided that "Go West young man, go west" was good advice while he still fit the bill of being young. A tough hide and hard life had him in good stead as a wagon train boss. You conformed to the rules or else. "Else?" That some times meant you did not eat. Hard Knocks had been a Scout on a wagon train three years before, so knew the route, the trouble, water availability, where the trading posts were and where Willa Bender was, too. They had met on his last trip out and back. She was a jolly cut-up, a woman who never lacked for attention, she sang in a saloon in Jasper, Indiana and Hard Knocks just couldn't get that little blond haired vixen out of his head or heart. He swore to himself once he did get his own place in Kansas he was going back to collect his heart as it had stayed on the trail in Jasper. Since the miles from Pike Lake, Pennsylvania to Lawrence, Kansas, were a bit over 1100 miles, there was no time to waste.

There were rivers, springs and lakes plentiful. The valleys to the West and South were more than desirable, and winter on the open prairie not so desirable. Travel was not hampered by water problems. There was the Marais River that eventually flowed down from Loma, Montana confluence, the Wakarusa and Lawrence Rivers, the wide Missouri along the way, plus the huge Clinton Lake. Often times crossing the rivers did become a real problem, but with wits and ingenuity most catastrophes were avoided. On high banks the horses or oxen were unhooked and ropes allowed the wagons to slide down to the river bed below.

During a flash flood on the Ohio River the men were in a constant rush from wagon to wagon to keep everything upright. However, the Sprow family's team lost footing and, try as they might, the horses could not stay upright letting the wagon turn over.

Hard Knocks and several of the men not fighting their own teams rushed back to help salvage what they could unhitching the horses from the burden threatening to drag them down. Letty Sprow was pinned under a trunk when the wagon rolled over. She was screaming for help and such a chaotic mess followed that it was hard for Hard Knocks to shout orders to the men milling around in disorder.

"Sprow, get to the wagon and take four men with you! Tip it back on its wheels! Three others of you steady it as it hits the ground on the rebound. Someone go find the vet to look after

Letty since we ain't got no doctor with us. Bill, see to them horses - we can't afford to loose none at this early in the trip."

Blaine Wilson was a veterinarian from a farm community in Eastern Ohio who had joined the train when it came through his area. He was a large-boned, beefy built man in his forty's; without family or responsibilities. For some time he had "itchy foot disease", as the saying goes and now was as good a time as any to follow the trend and join a wagon train.

Blaine was already headed toward the wagon. "Wait up there!" he shouted.

"I'll steady the wagon on the other side, just don't drop it down. Get those ropes over and under the body and ease it down slow as you can."

A heavy wagon and slippery footing made a rough go of it. After the third attempt the wagon was erect. The horses were wild eyed and skitterish, making them difficult to handle.

"Get that dog away from the horses and where is Letty?" Blaine was trying to be in two places at once. Mr. Sprow was extracting his wife from the jumble inside the canvas covered wagon. Letty had a broken arm and several bruises. Other than being a nervous wreck, she was intact and sitting on a box near the river bank. The contents of their wagon was scattered helter-skelter, some carried away with the rushing water a mile downstream.

"Letty, come over here where I can get at your arm. Sprow, hold her tightly because I will need to pull that arm in place with a quick jerk or two and it will be painful." He gave a jerk on the word painful and Letty fainted swallowing a scream.

"Thank God she is out! Now someone get me something for a splint and some bandages before she comes to."

Miss Nora Ellen was ready with torn tea towel strips made from flour sacks and petroleum jelly should it be needed. Starkey handed Blaine two slates of wood he had ripped loose from a chicken crate and some twine he had on hand.

With all four helping they completed the project before

Letty regained consciousness and looked in alarm at the brace that had been concocted. Once the arm was in a sling and a swallow of laudanum took effect, Letty was just so grateful to everyone for saving what they could and all the help so unselfishly given, she began to cry.

This was the first of several mishaps along the way and the people on the train became like a big extended family. By evening things were calmed down and the fires stared for evening meals. These meals becoming more and more shared around the trestle table rather than the individual wagons. The children could run loose and live stock attended to, various dishes of food became staples and expected.

Daylene Shank was known to be an excellent cook and made her nightly corn pone, griddle cakes or flapjacks – it became her chore. Her brother, Nolan, hunted game along the way to stretch the food supply as well as provide fresh meat. Fishing was easy and plentiful and often the evening event for the older boys. Teenage girls were relieved of the baby sitting duties to have their free time as well. Couples made friends and, in general, things ran smoothly.

The Muskingum River was nearly flat and no source of great concern; but the next fly in the ointment was the heavy forest around Beer Point Lake. This meant delays due to the clearing required. After three days it was fairly easy going again. Below Cantrell Cliffs there were caves to explore near Lake Lagoon – Old Man Cave, Ash Cave - and an ancient rock house. These things were a joy and relief from the steady grind. But it was now mid May and temperatures were rising. They needed to start early, stop over to rest, and then restart by seven p.m. until ten p.m. This pattern was followed on hot days or moderated to fit the weather.

Sudden rain squalls hampered things now and then. They were welcomed until one day in July when along the Wabash River a thunder storm came up and hail pelted down so much it looked like snow. The animals were balking, chickens in an uproar, pandemonium set in and every hand was busy at one thing or another.

The weather is temperamental, hail stopped, wind died down, blue sky and sun reappeared and then it became hot enough to fry an egg on a flat rock. It was an exhausting day and supper time came early.

The next morning dawned cloudy which was a blessing. This day they came by an old Butterfield Overland stage station that had ended with the advent of the railroad in 1869. The station keeper still lived there and had a few horses and mules that people had left behind. He was so happy for company he made a nuisance of himself and was delighted to eat with the wagon people.

They could have remained three days before he ran dry of tales or became hoarse of throat. The next surprise was a group of Indians in Illinois territory. Grass ran sparse and prairie land is most unforgiving. Indians were not a welcome sight and I'm sure the opposite held true as well. With all the different types of people marching across "their" land, white folk were certainly an enigma as one group could be engaging and the next were corrupt. With little communication between them it was a hard way of life for both races. Letty and Joe were nearly back to their normal routine once repairs were made, supplies shared and her arm healing nicely. Then she discovered there was a baby on the way – the first one to be born in the new Kansas location.

Billy and his sister, Sybil, had learned to play checkers with their grandfather and also had a chess board, but Millie kept them busy looking for wild asparagus along the marshy areas when there were any, digging dandelions for greens and gathering wild onions. By the end of August, there were berries, crab apples and currants growing where homesteaders had lived and where a few people still hung on to their holdings. These times were not a bore for the Good children; Millie had insisted on some books in spite of the extra weight and read to her family on the long summer evenings.

Daylene and Nolan Shank had become close friends with the Good family and often times Sally Blake joined the women who were skilled seamstresses and worked on many items brought over to them for mending.

CHAPTER 2

In the second week of August, the wagons had reached the Mississippi River. Thankfully people heading over the trail going to various points east had told them of a new ferry float at Cairo crossing where the Ohio and Mississippi rivers joined. A few extra days here for supplies, to trade a few horses, attend a fair of sorts and a social held by some church women, with a dance afterwards. This was heavenly manna for them all. A few new acquaintances were made and two new members joined the train. Boots McGuinnes, the tall rangy red headed cut up and clown, fit in well and was everyone's friend. He and Matt Kimball who had been Manter and Millie Good's neighbor back in Pennsylvania, just hit it off and started talking ranching and cowboys. Each knew only a thimble full of the bragging they were doing but it made good listening fodder anyway.

"Boots," said Matt, "I'll lay ya two to one ya can't ride a horse one day without blisters on your rear." "Did you every see a steer in your lazy life?"

"Now lookie here, Matt, I can ride anything with hair on it," this from a fellow how had not even a speaking acquaintance with a horse, mule, or even a large dog. Boots whooped and hollered and slapped his hat against his leg. "We been out on the prairie so long at a time I plumb forgot what it was like to sleep on a mattress," he bragged.

Matt came back with some outrageous story about eating an armadillo and it would have been rejected by a tramp. "Them armadillo are so mean they are scarcely worth shooting. Rattlesnake! Now *there* is prairie chicken."

Both men slapped each other on the back and headed for a saloon. Next morning they were leaning up against the building when Nolan passed by.

"What you two up to so early?" he wanted to know. Nolan had his suspicions. "Drunk maybe?" he asked.

"Ah, nay – no setch. We out here holding up this building. See, we got our backs into it." With a great haw, haw, haw, and a slap on Matt's shoulder he started to move away.

"Don't DO that," Matt yipped. "You nearly discombobulated my arm!"

"Now what in tar nation does that word mean? You're always showing off," Boots said good naturedly. Off they headed for the wagons.

"Where you two been?" Starkey asked as he saw Matt and Boots shuffling along.

"We been to see the queen. Didn't find no mouse under her chair but we sure saw the hair of the dog. Roof of my mouth can prove it."

"If your going to the wagons it will take the rest of your life to get there at the rate you're moving right now." Starkey was a man born in overdrive and never got out of it.

That afternoon Ike Foster hiked into the village looking for school supplies. He had not packed many because of weight. He figured he could buy some closer to the final destination and save space for food and other necessities.

A big crowd was headed down the road on foot, out of curiosity he stopped a man and asked why the parade?

"Ain't no parade", was the offered information. "It's a funeral."

"Oh," said Ike. "Must have been a prominent figure by the

size of the mourners."

"Hell, no," said the man. "Meanest cuss this side the 'ole Mississippi. We all going to make sure he IS dead." With that startling piece of knowledge, Ike shook his head, put his hat back on and wondered at the type people he would soon be teaching. Trying to understand another, you haven't a clue about their inner regions. Some times you mis-read and it gnaws away at your pride, assuming you have any left.

Back at the wagons the two friends were hatching up more tall tales. They seemed to be absolute strangers to the truth.

"Hey Daylene you wanna go to the dance with us?" This from Boots.

With a shiver and mock horror she sweetly said, "Oh dear, I don't mean to be rude, but I'm fresh out of tolerance for fools." And with a quick shake of her hips she strode on to prepare dinner. Matt decided that falling in love was rather strenuous and said as much.

"Well, I'll be danged," Boots said. "Didn't know you *was* fallin in love." Does Daylene know?"

"I'll swear, Boots, a fish can go a longer time out of water than you can live without talking sense. Course she knows!"

Boots couldn't let it go. "You SURE she knows?" he demanded, his eyebrows had not settled into place after nearly pushing his hair line out of place.

Matt scuffed his left toe in the dust and made some inaudible grunt that was meant for a "yes". Boots was undone completely. He had remained unacquainted with responsibility all his natural life and for anyone to have just *one* girl seemed unthinkable. That usually led to a nose ring - this was too much.

"Now, when all did this take place?" he asked. I don't recollect you sparking No girls and sure not Nolan Shanks little sister. He'd have your ears for breakfast. Poor Matt looked as forlorn as stale bones. His quiet could be volcanic, may be best to just drop it, Boots decided.

The last day of August found the weary, dusty travelers and boned tired stock at the Lake of the Ozarks in Missouri. One more week and they would reach their destination. Except for Lettie's morning sickness, some head colds, sore feet, rattled nerves a few cantankerous older people and low supplies, all was going well.

Some of the women had dug up rose bushes and small trees from old homestead sites. A number of pieces of furniture and farm equipment that had been abandoned made its way among those who had space.

Billy's dog, Blue, had six pups that were a constant problem as they were into everything they could get at and Miss Nora Ellen had adopted a cat at the last river crossing. Boots was trying to tame a raccoon he caught, but the coon was definitely the boss.

During the last two days out from their hoped for destination they met a group of six wagons going south to Texas. Many stories were told of the stagecoach line – although it had been closed down in 1860, many buildings and signs of life remained along the route. It was a history lesson in the rough. The first two stage line attempts were unsatisfactory due to land conditions. The Jackass trail lasted one trip and Jim Birch who started it, drowned, when his ship sank off Cape Hatteras. The second attempt was John Butterfield's Oxbow route which also floundered; it added six hundred miles to the first route and was now two thousand eight hundred twelve miles and expected to be completed in twenty-five days.

John Butterfield, with a $600,000 government grant reassembled the equipment, horses and mules needed to build bridges and set up stations, dig wells, remove rocks from trails, etc. The next stage left Tipton, Missouri on September 2, 1858. In all there were one hundred thirty nine relay stations, eighteen hundred head of stock, two hundred fifty stages and a work force of eight hundred men. Each driver was responsible for sixty miles so he had a one hundred twenty mile round trip in twenty four hours - a very grueling schedule. In 1869 the transcontinental railroad finished the line and stagecoaches were no more. Such information is now legend.

Those stories were told and retold over the years as there were no newspapers available and travelers handed down the information they gathered along the way. It was really amazing how rapidly news did travel. Even then the coconut wireless was the best way to learn news.

Once the Kansas line was crossed the next town of any worth was Emporia. There the wagon train lost six wagons because the hardships were just too much and the women did not wish to go further. Salina was the haven of rest and the land between Emporia and Salina was reasonably unencumbered. Approximately one hundred and twenty miles more to travel so spirits were high.

Chapter 3

On September 9, 1878, the wagon train struggled into Salina's outskirts. Plenty of open land was a very welcome sight to buoy up weary travelers who mostly had decided regardless of land, weather, Indians, or wild animals they would roam never more. Matt and Boots of course made a dash for the nearest saloon for a drink of most anything but out right poison. They just knew they could spit cotton wads they were so dry. It naturally got them out of the work at hand as well.

Letty was four months pregnant and pretty much back to her old cheerful self after a very difficult first few months. Joe was so overly protective of her it had become a nuisance to most everyone, especially the women with children. They knew an expectant woman was no china doll.

For the next two weeks people were sorting out their belongings and doing mounds of laundry. Evenings were spent mending badly neglected clothing and making baby clothes. The men and animals had earned a couple of weeks rest and most of them did not offer too much resistance to that idea. Rest sounded just fine!

Soon enough it was time to think about purchases of land or seeking out available range land from homesteading days. Billy so badly wanted to go way out in the countryside, but school would start the following month and Millie wasn't keen on the solitary life. Being a friendly soul, she kept involved in local things in Pennsylvania and hoped to take up new ventures in this location as well. Sybil just wanted a friend to play with, her doll and to tag along after Billy which he could not tolerate very long at a time. Even fishing she wouldn't sit still or be quiet, which to him were the first and second books of a fishing Bible.

Manter started searching for a business opportunity to suit his abilities and skills. He headed for the bank where he met Adam Insley, a bachelor living alone. Before long they became dear and trusted friends. Manter was grateful for a friend with ambition and knowledge on numerous topics. These two spent many hours together that fall; Adam was helping build the Good's log cabin. Always grateful for a home cooked meal, he was often at the table Millie set.

By mid October, Manter had started a small hardware store, a trade he knew well, and was in business. He prospered rapidly as most of the wagon train people were not interested in a house in town but wanted their own land. They built cabins good enough to winter in planning to complete the buildings the next spring once weather allowed, before land clearing time.

Sooner or later that clown Boots McGuiness was bound to meet up with Carey Flinn. Carey was the town drunk with charming ways and a silver tongue that usually bought his liquor and got him out of trouble some of the time.

The Sheriff in Salina was Whitey Cobb, an easy going sort as long as you didn't rile his temper too much. The one thing he just couldn't abide was people who were egotists - but his tolerance of ignorance rated right up there along side egos. Dumb questions and foolish talk were not part of his daily program.

Things such as at the passing of a funeral procession, some one would ask him who it was – old Jake Pratt or whomever.

The fellow who asked the question would then remark, "Oh – did he die?" Whitey would grit his teeth and softly reply in his naturally serious way, "Why no – they are burying him alive."

Such foolishness he had no time for at all. Any spare time, which was mighty scarce, was usually spent on books. He loved history and could tell you about the Pony Express, stage coach routes, even some of the drivers, land grants where mines were or had been, the local caves which he avidly explored, the strata in the rocky ridge west of town or any number of things. Children used to go to him for their homework on geography or history as there was no library at that time.

Several members of the wagon train decided to live in town at least for the first year and search out near by areas for a permanent residence. The excitement and flurry of chopping trees, clearing a place for a house and the hub bub involved, just wasn't appealing. The spring time would be soon enough. So those with funds enough to winter in town, soon found other town people to mingle with. Some found employment and remained city dwellers altogether.

The nine families who chose to build helped each other as time allotted, several taking a half day or so to go help Joe. Letty wasn't much help with construction but kept the food and coffee ready for all who so generously had pitched in. One of these times when there was a festive mood and a new moon, Millie went to consult with the other helpers and their wives about an evening roundup of neighbors and an eat out. That idea was welcomed by all as a time of rest, some well earned good fun, and an opportunity to relax a bit. The women sent the children to locate other family members and then to prepare food to be set out on the trestle tables that had supported countless meals these past five months. Such events and nourishment had sustained them through many trails and hardships in their passage.

Brady Miller had been fishing that afternoon late and came

with a string of bass he had caught. Offering them proudly for his share of the food, he promptly declared it would be their first banquet. Years later it would still be remembered as the "dirt patch banquet".

Next Levi Guthrey, a fifty year old single traveler came wandering in with his fiddle and harmonica.

"I have some spuds to add," he said, "if someone will cook 'em. Got my music too."

Everyone was agreeable to this arrangement and so Levi joined the men who were standing, sitting or sprawled out to stretch weary backs and muscles.

Joe and Letty Sprow were told to just come help, don't worry about food as there would be plenty, there always was. Joe was poor in health, not really able to do much physically. The trip itself had been a real hardship on those two. Latisha known better as Letty, was a slight build but strong minded woman who was determined to get her husband into a different climate hoping the change in area would improve his health. So far nothing much had changed Joe except his attitude. He too had more interest in life and his surroundings. His mother had died of pneumonia when Joe was four and his father, already an alcoholic, became worse after his wife passed. He had no time or interest in little Joe, so his great Aunt Sophia Logan had reluctantly taken him in. Sophia was then in her fifty's and being saddled with a youngster was not her idea of a quiet old age. But after all blood was blood and one had their duty. Joe grew up frail and silent; Sophia could not and would not tolerate yelling, noisy young men. His interest in life became his pets and Pete Strong, a waif of the streets who had nothing and no principles to accompany the rest of his errant ways. Much to his sorrow, Joe was restricted from that relationship but he too realized it would come to no good end.

His interest in animals pleased Sophia and she would take in hurt, sick or abused strays that just seemed to gravitate toward Joe. There home and barn before long became the equivalent of a dog pound and housed every stray imaginable. It was not then known that fur and feathers were not a good idea for anyone with asthma. Letty lived three houses down the street from Joe and spent most free time with Joe and the menagerie. At eighteen they decided to marry, a choice Aunt Sophia admired. The young couple lived with her as Joe had no trade. They remained quite financially strapped except for Aunt Sophia's income. Upon her death they sold the place and joined the wagon train for Kansas.

Exactly what it was that drove Letty to pursue this trip even she didn't know, but here they were and Joe had perked up some. Now they had steady friends and help if needed, were looking for some type of enterprise Joe could handle and settle in. Events such as this banquet were opportunities to meet people, explore ideas and enjoy everyone.

How he happened to be among them Joe did not know, but he made the acquaintance of Mason Philpot, the town undertaker. Mason was a sturdy man, firm with his principles and lived alone. This meeting led to Joe and Letty living with Mason, and Joe learning a trade he could handle. God works in mysterious ways His wonders to perform.

Millie sent Sybil to locate Matt if he was around. Since Daylene had gone to work as a waitress in Salina at the "Kitchen" restaurant, Matt seemed to have a great deal to do in town. Boots said poor old Matt would go buy one nail at a time if it gave him an excuse to go to town. Grant and Ella Mae Murphy owned the one and only restaurant of choice. There were a couple of greasy spoon type and a Chinese eatery available, but that was about all the town could support so there was little choice.

Sybil reported back that Matt was on his way with Boots in tow. This news set Millie back a bit and started her wondering what pranks might upset an otherwise very pleasant evening.

The table was about half full of food, plates and necessities when Billy let out a shout. "Mama! Mama catch the cat! Old

Blue is chasing her your way." Too late, the cat jumped on the table to get away from the dog, and the dog raced circles around the table barking to tease the cat. Over the bread jumped the cat, landing on a stack of plates that slithered off to the ground; salt and pepper shakers and a butter dish followed. Blue stopped long enough to scarf down the butter and Levi grabbed the cat hissing and clawing until Levi set her down.

"I do believe Letty isn't the only pregnant one around here," he remarked. Sybil danced a jig of joy; Billy retrieved his dog; and Manter gathered up the mess on the ground. He took the cat and told Sybil to get Boots out of here. Just then Matt and Boots walked up with Boots stopping dead in his tracks.

"Gets Boots out of here," Matt said in utter astonishment.

"Now, what in heck did I do? I ain't done a thing, man, I just got here!" Boots knew he was the subject of much mischief and was rather proud of his spunky ways. He knew whatever had happened was not his doings this time. He just stood there completely confused.

Everyone but he and Matt started to laugh and whoop at his bewilderment. A few offered the opinion that now they had gotten even for his antics.

Millie swallowed another laugh and sputtered out, "Haven't you ever seen my cat?"

Boots thought about it a second or two and decided the answer was, "Maybe! Why?"

"She is black with white feet and her name is Boots; she is the creator of all this mess you see at the table."

Once that information was digested, Matt too started to laugh and slapped Boots on the shoulder and told him it was fine with him to share his name with a pussy cat so long as "he" didn't get with kittens. This started a boxing match between the two friends all in fun, and the evening resumed its jolly atmosphere.

The bread was fed to the chickens and Joe's two pet geese he brought along, the butter was replaced on a new plate, other dishes were rounded up, and the men got themselves busy building a bonfire around a very boisterous evening. Although the wagon crew's were approximately a half mile out from the town edge, the revelry going on, the music, hilarity and just clean fun were heard in Salina. Many of the permanent residents were pleased to realize the new neighbors were just good solid people of principle and morals. A good addition to their growing population.

The next week saw a good progress in the land clearing and the start of four more cabins.

Billy was growing not only tall, but strong and was a help in many ways with the structures of the cabins. The men soon learned who was best suited to which task. Manter made excellent shingles for roofing; Starkey turned out some remarkable cabinetry with his wood working tools; Ike Foster, the school teacher, could figure out square footage and measurements that saved precious time; and Nolan Shank was a first rate plank cutter, much to everyone's surprise – himself most of all.

Lowell Pratt settled into building fireplaces and rock chimneys. So it went – reasonably steady; mishaps occurred that were unexpected of course. Mason Philpot left his mortuary to lend a hand only to have a big log roll and break his left leg. He was glad he had enlisted Joe Sprow's help with coffins and undertaking services. Levi Guthrey mashed a thumb with a swing at a peg being held in place and you would think the world would end then and there.

He was screaming for Blaine and yelling his head off while running in circles. When Blaine came on the run from a hog pen delivering Luella's pigs, he expected to find Levi had an amputated hand or worse.

"Well how did you manage to do this now?" was Blaine's comment once he could get a hold of the mashed thumb.

"Settle down, Levi. That yelping would give gray hair to a bald man; I swear you are a grown baby."

"Fine!" says Levi, "Want me to stomp on your hand and see how it feels?"

"No, I need to get you padded and splinted. Here is some laudanum. Go get over there in the shade and sit you down. I'll be back as soon as I see to that pet sow of Mitchell Hayes. So far she burped out fourteen piglets but she don't look too good.

Levi nearly had apoplexy. "You delivered pigs and then fixed my hand! I'll probably be dead of some riggers or some disgusting ailment before morning. And what do you mean - she don't look so good? How in hell does a sow look 'cept like a hog?"

"Your mean she looks peaked or pale – good God I never heard of such as this. What do you mean Blaine?"

"No, of course not, you fool; she just might not make it and I'm afraid her bladder will rupture." Levi was the one who turned pale and regretted he even asked.

"Well," he drawled out, "give my regrets to Luella about her bladder predicament. By the way, how many pigs did ya say she got – fourteen? Now that must be some sort of record, ain't it?

"Don't really know, Levi, but she only has her table set for twelve so that will create a riot no doubt."

"There now, your thumb is all dressed up in its bandages and you can beg off work a day or so I expect. I need to go now." With this Blaine left on a trot to the Haye's farm half a mile or so out of town and about two hundred yards from the wagons.

The next catastrophe was when Carey Flinn, the town drunk, wandered in with some big yarn about his having been a contractor back in Ohio several years ago. Since the man seemed an absolute stranger to truth, no one paid much attention to him until he sat down on some window glass which broke, of course. Glass was a precious thing here and had to be brought in. You paid a good price for it. Since it was destined to go in a window in Grady Miller's home, Carey looked up to see Grady standing there with a smile on his face that would give you frost bite. Since he still had an axe in his hand, he pointed it toward town and said one word "git". Carey left, happy the axe had not parted him from his hair or worse. After the evening meal was finished and quiet had descended on the days work, Carey slipped back out in the moon light and quietly gathered up the broken pieces of window glass from where they had been tossed.

He did not wish to be caught for fear someone would be vicious as a mink and he just wasn't drunk enough to figure a way out. He felt more forlorn than stale bones, but he had a plan. The moon was pearly white with a scrap of clouds now and then; he needed to take advantage of those clouds. He had heard Grady's silence could be deadly.

Carey hopped back to the bar in town and wanted a drink, but Daylene said "NO". "Here is some coffee – stay decent for a while." He took a gulp and nearly passed out. "By damn, Daylene, where you boil this stuff! In a wash tub? It is so strong it would keep you up three days after you die! It ain't bad enough the pesky mosquitoes been tattooing the back of my neck for an hour and then lightning bugs cruising the night. It's enough to make me head feel like dry rot done set in."

Daylene wondered about Carey's family or even if he had one someplace. Any son was loved when small before he grew up a disappointment she supposed about now, near midnight she was about as relaxed as guitar strings and just wanted him to leave so she could close the place and go on home.

However, drunk or sober, Carey was so headstrong it was contrary to natural reasoning. Daylene was a happy, hard working young women who just naturally saw the best in people; then there was Carey. Only people like Daylene who loved life so greatly could be so outraged at its short comings.

Matt showed up to take Daylene home and Carey disappeared to what ever haunt he retreated to each night.

Matt observed the departure and ventured a guess at what time Carey would reappear. "Sometime before dawn I bet he is out to wakeup that rooster I hear about 4:30.am. Poor soul, he is just about so crooked he must cast a crooked shadow." By noon, Carey would again have a mouth that would make a leper septic.

Whitey Cobb was short on patience with Carey and told him one more time caught pan handling and he would no longer wonder where to sleep. The jail had good bunks.

Hard Knocks had made a deal with a group headed East to go scout for them and was telling Rand Blackwell about the trip. He was really looking forward to this trip because he intended to get married before he started back. He loved Willa Bender and that was that. The fact that she worked and sang in a saloon made not one wit of difference. This trip was good news and felt like a tonic. Indiana, I'm on my way!

This piece of news stirred up loneliness in Rand as his sweetheart was also in Indiana. Reva Thompson was a librarian and the love of his life. But since Rand was two thirds finished with his one room cabin and helping make Mortar for the fire place stone and bricks, he just could not leave in all honesty. Those people had taken him in to their homes, heart and confidence.

After much persuasion and downright begging, Hard Knocks agreed to bring Reva back with them if she would agree.

Rand nearly wrung his hand off in appreciation. "Thanks, Fritz," he said over and over. Knocks had so seldom heard his given name, he nearly didn't respond. "Well I'll be damned!" he said. "I've heard Knocks so much I near forgot it is Knox", he grinned.

The six wagons and Hard Knocks left on a Monday morning that held rumpled up clouds that had congealed into a solid overcast. The sky to the east let a few yellow ribbons of light peek out every now and then with a promise of better things to come. They had a patch of desert to cross before darkness closed in so it was best to get that out of the way the first day if possible. The desert looked like it was made of rough cast iron and a jumbled ocean of rocks and sand

The small gathering of well wishers scattered to their various chores and school was just letting out for recess so the students had missed the send off. Ira Fletcher had seen to that. There was a smell of frost in the air and the children were hard to settle down. The days of comfortable play were coming to a close far too soon. He had made a science of practicality and no nonsense, school was school and should be taken advantage of. He had a great influence on Billy Good and favored the boy somewhat. Here was potential in a good mind and curious nature all tucked away in a kind and gently boy turning into a young man.

"Billy," Mr. Fletcher called, "before you go home today I would like to speak with you." "O.K." came the answer back across the yard. "Now what you done?" Sybil wanted to know with concern in her voice. Billy was her idol and could do no wrong.

"Not anything I know of," was the bewildered reply from Billy. "He must have special work, I guess."

At close of the school day Billy approached Mr. Fletcher's desk with a question on his face. "Now Billy," Fletcher said, "Here are some history books from my own collection. You take care of them, please. I know you'll enjoy them. You might like to discuss them with Whitey Cobb if you like. The Sheriff is a good man; he knows and understands a great amount of the local history and times leading up to today. With your interest in things I imagine you will travel considerable in your time. You will see things make history, may even be a part of it one day. It would be good to start a journal even now, who knows one day, late in life, you may find even this trip and what seems natural today a history lesson for some one else to learn."

Ira stood up and handed three books to Billy, gave him a

fatherly pat on his shoulder and walked with him to the door.

Once home, Billy could hardly contain himself. Just bursting with pride he showed the treasured books to his mother and told of his personal time with his teacher. Millie was so overly pleased she had tears of joy.

"Billy, son, you heed his word and let me show you something." She went to the side pocket she had sewn on the canvas top of the wagon and pulled out a notebook she had been keeping her records in. "Here, son, you continue each day from now on just as I have. By my age you will have written your version of history also.

Grant and Ella Mae Murphy had been considering a new venture for some time now. After long discussions and prayer, they decided to open the restaurant each Sunday morning from 9:00 – 11:00 a.m. for Sunday school and church services, for any who wanted to come.

One of the late arrivals coming through was a minister by name of Booth Gordon. A very solemn natured man in his early forties intent on his purpose of having a church in what he expected to be the wilderness. Much to his delight he found an established community with little disorder at the time. When the cattle drives came it was a whole different story and his ears rang with tales of woo when that topic came up.

The Murphy's had asked Miss Nora Ellen's advice who in turn discussed it with Millie and Manter, all of whom were good solid Christian stock. Once all were in agreement, Manter went looking for Booth Gordon. The two men took a walk down along the river bank as Manter said he had a problem to solve so would Booth lend support. Oh course Booth would help, it was his calling.

They located a fallen tree and used it for a bench to sit and rest upon. It was a lovely fall day and the earth was still coated in its leaves of many colors. It covered this brown grey soil that served for the earth's poor flesh but looked like it would never raise a disturbance, let alone a crop. Such stony ground looked like the Earth's bones were poking through.

Booth remarked that all those stones were just a blessing and *that* Manter could not digest at all. But Booth saw them as chimneys and fireplace faces, leaving cleared land to plant and survive on; Manter saw hours of back breaking labor and piles of rocks. How true!

Booth said, in his soft voice, "Well, Manter, you mentioned a problem?"

"Yes, Booth, a few of us had an idea and we need to see how it sets up with you. The Murphy's, Miss Nora Ellen and ourselves was wondering if you would consider holding Sunday school class and church services on Sunday nine till eleven in the restaurant? Say Sunday school was nine to nine thirty, maybe, with time to change people and get set for services from ten to eleven, maybe? What do you think? No need to decide just now, we been without service on the trail for six months and no gathering place in Salina either."

"Murphy bought a piano from some folks going to join the Oregon Trail route to the West Coast," continued Manter. Millie Good can play the piano, and then there is Matt and Levi with their fiddle and harmonica. The other day I heard a guitar being strummed some where in town, but it shouldn't be difficult to locate whoever it is."

Manter got up a head of steam, igniting Booth to do the same and plans were set in motion for the opening of church services as soon as it could be arranged.

All this took place on Wednesday the third of October. Hammers, saws, axes chopping, horses pulling in logs and the sight of building were in full swing. The first killing frost had been three nights before and, although a few weeks of Indian summer were looked forward to, the work speeded up.

Locals had advised them over and over that because a day dawned crisp and sunny with azure blue skies, that October could lay down six inches of snow before night crept in on them. On prairie land it was not unheard of that October snow was there in April under several coats of ice, sleet, hail, rain and more snow. Winter got down to business once its mind was made up.

One old time person simply called Buck, would venture over once a week or more to just watch, comment and visit. No one seemed to know much about him. He looked as old as stone and was toothless as a turtle. He never had much to say, but when he did, it was worth listening to. He was clothed in respect and dignity and all the children loved him. Buck seemed to have a difficult time remembering that he was old. He had this ugly old dog that kept him company, but Buck didn't care that Sampson was so incredibly ugly and skin so tight he looked like he was forced into the wrong coat. Often times Buck and Sampson would follow Grady on his fishing trips once the day wore out. It was quiet company mostly. Even Billy would tag along now and then.

Once you could get Buck on a story you couldn't find an end to it without being rude. Mostly he spoke of his youthful days in the Kentucky coal mines and his dream of leaving there forever. The chance presented itself when he was in this 50's and he made his way across on a horse all alone. He had some hair rising stories that delighted Billy.

This was another item for his journal that further whet his appetite for seeing more country then Pennsylvania to Kansas.

When Billy related some of Uncle Buck's stories he felt in his heart the old man's imagination had blown a fuse but he kept it to himself. "Uncle" Buck was nearly part of the Good family so far as Billy was concerned.

Once a few children had followed Uncle Buck back to his shack home and were fascinated by all his trophies and keepsakes. One was a candle he saved just for Christmas, Billy insisted Millie go see it. No wonder it was a curiosity for the children; it no more resembled a candle than a tom cat. The candle stick had a six inch thick hairdo and was about as odd shaped as one could dream of. Millie sent over an oil lamp and a new candle. But Christmas day out came the weird one never the less.

On Halloween day there was a stir of excitement in town when two single wagons rolled in but only one family. The man was Roscoe Peabody, a mean looking and talking fellow about five foot four inches and one hundred and twenty pounds soaking wet. The woman was Beulah Peabody. Now there was a sight to behold! Beulah was about five foot ten inches and two hundred thirty pounds if she weighed an ounce, and was a loud, rough appearing person. With them was their adorable little blond, curly headed daughter; so prissy one was led to wonder if she had been kidnapped or stolen even. This little China doll was seven and a very precocious child. Her name was Sylvia Lee.

Roscoe Peabody handled the horses while Beulah handled the oxen. He was mean to the horses and Whitey stepped right up with a whip and said, "If you intend to stop here more than ten minutes, I suggest you get yourself an attitude adjustment, as folk here are civilized and not pert on the notion of trash invading our area." With that said he viciously snapped the whip about a hair's width from Roscoe's right ear. Beulah paid no mind to a word said; she might as well have been in England.

Sybil walked over and took the girl by the hand telling her she better stand back from the stock and stay with her.

"My name is Sylvia Lee, who are you?" With a big smile, Sybil told her her name and both girls started to laugh. "How old are you? I'm seven," said Sylvia Lee. "Me too!" squealed Sybil. "We will just be twins," Sybil said. She was so happy to have a friend and playmate.

Of course Casey had to show up in half a stupor and make a few observations. "That female looks like she could go bear hunting with a switch," he coughed and laughed at his own idea then added, "with that size and hips she looks like she could pull a cart like a Clydesdale." Then he added a couple of words decent people wouldn't even think of in a dark closet, let alone remark here in broad daylight.

By then Boot's curiosity could stand no more and he jostled his way up to see the new comers. He saw Sylvia Lee and Sybil – blond curls and red head side-by-side. "Who's the cute little blond belong to?" he asked Matt.

"Them what just arrived", he muttered.

"Well I'll be darned," said Boots." That cantankerous old ferret couldn't have fathered that angel. I'll bet her Mum has a few secrets tucked up her knickers." "What a dismal husband he must be." Boots pondered this a minute or two then decided he and Matt ought to go tell Daylene about the arrivals.

Daylene stepped outside and called the girls over to give them each a lollypop, this giving her a glance at the goings on. When she went back behind the bar she remarked to Matt she had visions of those two on into eternity, which was not inspiring in the least. Daylene said she thought that woman was possibly slower than weight loss but she bet that she was a workaholic too.

Roscoe stormed around a bit but settled down soon enough at sight of Whitey and that whip. He asked, in nearly a decent tone of voice, if the Sheriff "knowed where Silas Peabody's place was." Oh, now there, that made sense. Silas had passed on to his reward the year before and had left the acre of land, a dwelling of sorts, to his kin in Kentucky. Well, here they were at last.

"You just follow the East road out by the creek and turn south or right, about a mile along and you will see it," Whitey said.

He saw it and Roscoe was in a fit. The house looked like it had lived it's time and the work involved was not a joy to behold.

He seemed to regard youth as a violation of something

and yelled "wife" like it was a cuss word. He was so aghast at the sight of the building that Roscoe's chin threatened to sag down his neck.

Mitchell Hayes advertized the church service in the next newspaper and set the foundation for what later became the community church that moved into the old mercantile store when that store moved to the new building. The new mercantile building had gone-up during the summer the wagon train came through led by Fritz Knox who most people called Hard Knocks.

Most of the wagon people were now a part of Salina and had been a welcome addition with musicians, teachers, undertakers a veterinarian and other skills they brought to the community.

Sunday morning dawned brisk and clear. The Murphy's and Daylene opened at 6:30 to prepare coffee and breakfast for those who depended on them, by the written notice posted that food service would not be available from 8:30 until noon. The attendance was almost alarming in size. Some were first time goers to a church; some were curious; others were just grateful to have a service. One who showed up nearly filled the door and there stood Beulah Peabody and an immaculately dressed Sylvia Lee. A few murmurs and surprised expressions greeted her along with Booth Gordon's welcoming outstretched hand.

"We are so pleased to see you and your pretty little girl, Beulah. Won't you please sit down?" She chose a seat in the back near the door but Sylvia Lee ran up to sit with the Good's. Reverend Gordon had noticed a large canvas bag on the walk just outside and wondered where it belonged but made no comment.

Once the restaurant was full to over flowing, Reverend Gordon asked for quiet, gave the benediction, and asked Millie if she could play any hymns by ear as there wasn't any books or sheet music. Millie said, why yes, of course she could and hoped she remember them all the way through. Sylvia Lee stood up and turned around to face her mother. All she said was "Mamma." In the silence that followed, Beulah Peabody arose and asked if they had song books? No, there were only one or two people that had brought them along.

"Well, I done brought a pouch full from when our church burned up. Only saved a few but I brung 'em if you like." She lifted the canvas bag like it was full of feather and hefted them up on the bar. Such a welcome sight! The grateful members thanked her till she got flustered and sat down.

Once the attendees were seated and the music started, Reverend Gordon asked if anyone had a request, but Millie had already started playing Beulah's Land in honor of the giver of the books. Then the next surprise nearly stopped the music. Beulah Peabody stood up to sing with all the others, the volume quality she produced nearly shook the windows. Such a simply beautiful singing voice is seldom heard except in an opera. She was in a state of rapture, standing with her eyes closed and her head thrown back, she just simply belted out the song from the bottom of her heart. A few of the lady's had tears in their eyes and people begged her to do a few solos. Music was her escape from heart ache and hardships. Another fine addition to the community, the people decided.

Reverend Gordon had prepared a sermon he felt was appropriate for a first time gathering and altered it somewhat with blessed thanks to God for sending the Peabody's among them. With God's intervention, Booth felt confident Roscoe would see daylight, also, instead of mired in his world of ugly where he seemed not interested to leave.

"I am so pleased to see this congregation this morning. What a pleasure to have the music and hear the words of the hymn. Often times the music will get to people when words will not. Today I want to touch on several topics so if any of you brought a Bible let me turn to Psalm 63:10: my mouth shall praise you with joyful lips when I remember you from my bed and meditate on you in the night."

"'It is a wonderful thing to wake up with that rooster of Grady's and see another day. We need to give thanks for our rest and for all our blessings. But most of all, we need to be aware of what comes out of our mouths. The Bible says it is not what goes in our mouth that causes trouble, but what comes out of it."

"Words are powerful and can utter kindness or hate, be a blessing or a curse; carry laughter or sneers, but remember, always the devil works hard to set us up to get us upset. If you feel like you get up on the wrong side of the bed, don't start out being hateful or negative, just say, "Well, here I am, Lord. What are we going to do today? Set my feet on a path of goodwill, not destruction." You will even smile and feel better with that small conversation. Just because the Lord will run interference for you, doesn't mean you are not obligated to do your part, too. Open your eyes – it is a new day. The Lord has much to say about the mornings over and over. Yesterday died at midnight. If it wasn't satisfactory, set your mind to improve on it. The new day is a new start, a fresh opportunity. Some times we go to bed feeling hopeless and worn out but a good night's rest and a wake up call on your Faith, just works miracles. Say to yourself – I'll make it one more day and Thanks, God, for the morning.

Have any of you stopped to think how many disciples we have among us here? Yes, we do; I see those looks I'm getting from a few. Peter was a fisherman; we have a few. Then Jesus chose a doctor, a lawyer, a carpenter, a scholar, a tradesman, even a thief. We are well blessed with skilled people here. If the Disciples of Jesus day were out and about doing His work, look at the opportunity we have today with our lives.

Isaiah tells us how to eat and refuse bad things; how Jesus instructed planting seeds (of Faith) and reaping the harvest of rewards for our good works. Use it wisely; God won't support our gluttony when it is wrong for us. His answers to our prayers and requests is sometimes, "no". We need to see the other side of situations that are not pleasant and learn to forgive. The devil tells us "it is too hard; I'll do it later when I feel more forgiving." But we don't do it – ever. Too late is often the reward of that folly. We are to love one another as God loves us. Love believes the best of every person and often that seems to be a thankless task. Believe, my people, God win's your battle if you don't interfere and, believe me, God doesn't need your help. Do what is right and out smart the devil. Love is an action, not an emotion. God loves us unconditionally. We will see our payday. The Lord doesn't pay on Friday night, but He pays us just the same.

Once again it's our mouth that leads our way. Faith is a force in our lives; confess God out loud. When you complain you are opening the door for Satan. Trust in God's work and His ways. We don't need a wish bone, we need a backbone. Pray for your needs and give thanks; God is perfect, doesn't wear a hearing device. Don't let prayer be your last ditch effort. You will be amazed at the results. We give up to easy. In due time things will happen for our good as God gives us double for our trouble. You can pray boldly; He does not hold our sins against us. Things often take so much time we give up on God. That is not holding up your end of the bargain. Fill your time with little things; those get us our best harvest.

In Philippians 2:10 we are told to hold no grudges. If need be, you do the first apologizing. Hell shakes at the name of Jesus. Just sitting in church does not make you a Christian. You could sit in a hen house all day and not turn into a chicken, either. We need to be right with God and be born again. We need to be rooted and grounded in Christ to get us through the rough spots. Inspiration gets us revelation. You need to study your Bible too. To just read it is the first step, yes, and quote scripture is part of learning; but you won't get what you need by just wiping the dust off the cover on Sunday mornings. You can't get far in a parked buggy, you see.

Mark 11:23-26 stresses the need to treat others as we wish to be treated; it's a two-way street. If we don't forgive then neither will we be forgiven. Mark 20:29-32 says love God with all our being and our neighbor as our self. If we can live by these few rules and remember to say "Thy will be done, not "my will be done" we will grow in spirit and truth, be a better community and each of us go the extra mile with our time and attitude.

Remember the saying "people who pray together, stay together" and let the words of our mouth represent the good in our hearts. Let us pray, each to himself in his own way.

With bowed heads the people silently gave thanks for all they had and for neighbors, food and their blessings not even realized until now.

Booths asked Miss Nora Ellen to lead them in a closing prayer. Millie played the Doxology and their first service was complete. Although it was nearly eleven o'clock and time to clear the place for restaurant goers, people remained to talk to each other, offer help with the house building, congratulate Booth on a fine, down-to-earth message, and graciously accept Beulah Peabody into their midst.

Sundays were usually set aside by most people, the weather was threatening and each day grew closer to the predicted snowfall. Letty and Joe had emptied their wagon and were nearly settled in. The house was small so the pictures and furniture were struggling for space. Not willing to part with their things, Letty was doubling up in every corner and under the bed. Space needed to accommodate a cradle, also. Joe wondered if he could find a place for his fishing and hunting gear so he commandeered a couple of casket crates from Mason Philpot. One he used outside by the door as a trunk or chest for his things, it also served as a seat. The other one he stood on end and hinged the lid for a door which made a wardrobe of sorts. Letty was grateful for the addition of *furniture*, but knowing where it originated made her cringe. She only had about another five weeks before the baby was due and she needed to get things in order. Her cedar chest was now full of baby things the women had been sewing during the trip across the country and finished up in the cool of the evenings these past two months.

Joe was kept busy between his two jobs. He still helped Mason at the undertakers, and also helped Blaine when he needed assistance with his veterinarian duties. Actually, Joe was really happy for the first time in his life. He felt worth while and respected. Letty was a wonderful wife, although frail; his baby was on the way; he had an income that was earned; his health had improved; and the two room house was built and paid for. No man could want for more.

CHAPTER 4

"Joe – Joe – Hey Joe!" He roused up from the coffin crate bench and ran to meet Blaine. "What's the trouble?" Joe wanted to know.

"Come on and give me a hand, Joe," Blaine yelled down from the back of his horse. "Get yourself over to Murphy's. That great sow of his, that 500 lb. Luella hog, is having a time with birthing them pigs. She popped out fourteen when I had to go fix up Levi's thumb, but she is having a poor time of it."

"Fourteen pigs!" Joe shouted, "Never heard of such!" "Go on, I'm coming." That sow was a family member of the Murphy's. Ella Mae raised it from a baby and for a time it lived in the house. Then the back porch was its home and it had the run of the place until it got in her garden. Then it went to a fenced-up pen. Her only time away was to visit what Sybil Good called the "Daddy Sow", much to everyone's amusement. Luella had five litters and all good, healthy piglets.

This time, again, there were too many. She had two more, which made sixteen, and two were runts. Since Luella had the table set for twelve – this meant hand feeding four babies. Everyone in town knew of the baby pigs and since Ella Mae was at the restaurant from sun up to sun down, she would require help.

Millie asked Sylvia Lee's family if she could help Sybil with the feedings.

Roscoe said, yes, if he could get a free pig where upon his barge of a woman picked him up bodily and shook him like a dog. No words were exchanged. Roscoe disappeared to the dilapidated barn; Beulah gave the girls a piece of cake and shooed them out the door. Millie just kept her peace and waited for Beulah to decide.

"Now, of course Sylvia Lee can help. Why I even still have her baby bottles; here you take them along." "I swear one day I may kill Roscoe but he gave me the only joy in life I have. I never ever expected to have a child and Sylvia Lee was sent from Heaven. One day Roscoe will get his comeuppance; until then he has to stay."

Millie was grateful to Beulah and went to collect the girls and head back the half mile to the Murphy's place. Daylene offered to help feed the orphaned pigs as did Grady, Boots and Matt. Millie made out a time chart so each would know whose turn it was. Luella's bladder did rupture just as Blaine had expected so there was to be no more pigs. Grant Murphy said, "Well then, no more Luella." I can't feed no 500 lb. sow for a pet." This caused uproar first, then a silent, non-speaking household for the next month.

Ella Mae demanded he take the sow to the next town to sell her as *there would be no butchering, ever, and you better believe it, too.*

As the pigs grew, they were ready to sell by February and a new girl pig was kept, but never made a pet of.

All the houses were finished before Thanksgiving and a big dinner for all of them was held at the school house. Weather did not permit them using the trestle table that had become a way of life.

Each had their say as to being grateful. Manter was grateful for a safe trip and family. Millie held out for shelter and friends. Billy was glad for his school teacher, his dog and the new house. Sybil was grateful for her Mama and her new friends. Booth was happy he had a church in the restaurant and hopes of a building in the spring. Matt was grateful for his place and a new start. Miss Nora Ellen was just happy for everything. Boots couldn't single any one thing. Starkey and Nolan agreed they had made a good move and grateful for it. Blaine was pleased he was doing well. Daylene was grateful for her job and announced she had agreed to marry Matt. He nearly fainted from shock and everyone laughed till they were sick. Mitchell Hayes was grateful his new newspaper equipment had arrived. Grant and Ella Mae had to be stopped or they would have gone on and on. Rand just hoped old Hard Knocks got back with his sweetheart or wife, whichever Willa would be when they got here and also prayed they had convinced Reva Thompson to accompany them, as she was his sweetheart. Whitey Cobb was grateful for a quiet town. Adam Insley was grateful to see the bank prosper. Sally Blake was happy for her growing business and brother Starkey finally maturing which brought on a round of laughter. Mason was grateful for Joe's help and that it was too bad folks had to die before he could meet them. (more laughing). Grady was happy his house was done. Levi was grateful his thumb was O.K. and Blaine hadn't killed him. Joe and Letty were just grateful for everything. Roscoe and Beulah were pleased to be accepted. Reverend Gordon asked the blessing and the first Thanksgiving in their new area was under way. Much socializing and reminiscing continued until nearly dark. When they opened the door to leave for their destinations, it was snowing.

CHAPTER 5

Shelter and lean-to's were rapidly constructed for more of the animals who, until now, had pretty much their own way. The older town people knew the routine and were prepared. For the next week it snowed off and on in spurts. There was some sun and a lot of wind. The blanket of leaves turned soggy and mud colored, sticking to the sole of one's shoes and tracking in a mess.

Issac Foster came down with the flu and asked Manter to fill in until he got back on his feet. Manter had been a school teacher back in Pennsylvania and said, yes, of course, he would substitute. That became a constant in Manter Good's life. If either Issac Foster or Ira Fletcher were absent, Manter filled in.

Billy missed his own teachers and made many trips to see Mr. Foster. He chopped wood, took soup Millie had prepared and did any chores he could help with. Since Billy and Sybil had begged Manter into buying one of Luella's pigs, he knew how to care for Mr. Foster's pig also. Issac had purchased several gunny sacks of corn from the feed store when he bought the pig so Billy would set and shell the corn and save the cobs.

One day Issac felt well enough to sit up a while, the flu had left him weak as poor tea and his only exercise had been a call from nature. He was watching Billy shell the corn and wondered at the way he was doing it.

"Billy, how did you come by the idea to shell one cob with another?" This is pretty clever and I'm sure it saves your finger skin as well." Papa does it this way. Here, see this new corn. Well, pull off the first empty cob you just finished and rub it against the open spaces you just made that loosen the next kernels to drop off. See, it is easy."

Issac took the offered ear of corn and the empty cob and tried it himself. It was slow work, but it *did* work. "Teacher being taught!" laughed Billy. "You never were a farmer were you?" he said.

"No son, I was raised in an orphanage and by God's great grace I was adopted by a couple with no children and raised in a good educated home. They are gone now and I truly miss them. That is the main reason for my coming west. I want to make a start for myself and a difference in the lives of other people's children.

Billy said he hoped one day he could also make a difference for other people. Issac said, "Well here you are helping me, so I'd say, you had a good start on your plan."

"By the way, Billy, why are you saving those empty cobs?" Issac had noticed them piled in a separate area.

"Oh, those are for Mama. I put yours by the stove in the kitchen," Billy told him.

"I usually throw them in the fireplace," Issac said.

"I know, but Mama stands them up on end in a tin can half full of kerosene, or coal oil is what these people here call it. Then she takes paper and wood chips or shavings and lays the soaked cob in the middle to start her fire.

"Now isn't that clever," observed Issac. "I guess I've had my lessons today and I believe I'm worn down and better go back to bed. Thank Millie for my supper you brought over."

"Mama didn't send it, Mr. Foster; Daylene brought it from the restaurant and Letty is fixing venison stew tomorrow from the scrap meat of that deer Nolan shot last week."

"Well now, I didn't realize all this fuss was going on." Isaac felt very humble.

"You have been pretty sick, Mr. Foster. The women uptown have been out to see you also. One lady even took your washing in to her place and changed your sheets with you still in them; *that beat all* Mama said.

The last of the twelve ears of corn were shelled, the pig fed, eggs gathered and stove banked so Billy called, "Goodnight, I'll be back tomorrow." He was glad for the coat they had brought from Pennsylvania. It got pretty cold there also.

Once home in their new house, he reported that Mr. Foster had gotten up about twenty minutes and was better. It was warm as he had a two room house whereas Billy's new home had three. Millie was just delighted with it. Manter could only wonder at Millie's excitement as she and her brother, Ned, had lived in an eight room, two story house in Pennsylvania. She gave up a lot to marry him and he knew it well. He was a most fortunate man. A lovely wife he adored and two fine children. He hoped the winter would be kind as they had a burden of work to tackle in the spring.

A happy squeal and running feet were coming toward the bedroom door. It woke Manter and Millie in a state of alarm

"Mama! Mama!" Sybil was squealing. "Come, get up." Boots has four kittens. She is in the wood box; not her box papa made. Oh, they are so little! Oh, they are so cute! But they can't see – all this in one breath.

Sure enough there was Boots with four tiny mites having their breakfast and Boots purring so loud she sounded like an engine. She looked happy and proud and had nearly washed the fur off those kittens. Not much got done this Saturday morning in the Good house.

"Well, Murphy found homes for fifteen pigs; we ought not to have any trouble with four cats," this from Manter. "But Papa can't we keep them?" Sybil was about to cry. Millie hugged her sweet little girl and told her, "Darling child, you know how much we love Boots." "Yes, Mama." "Well don't you suppose other families would like to love a kitty too?" We already have Boots and they may not have anything to love." This sounded alright to Sybil. "But not yet, Mama, they are too little."

"Let's see how big they are by Valentines Day. How about that?" Millie asked. About then Billy came in from milking Gertrude, their Jersey cow, and from feeding his pig.

"Oh, Billy, come see Boots. She had babies!" She was towing Billy by his coat tails so fast he nearly fell over. He winked at his father and whispered, "Why do you think I didn't build a fire before I went to milk?" They shared a secret smile while Billy made a fuss over the kittens. "Sybil, you need to stay out of the way long enough for us to transfer that cat family into her own bed and we can start the fire for breakfast." Billy tugged his little sister up off the floor while Millie gathered cat and kittens.

Manter asked the children if they knew Gertrude was going to be a mother in the spring. They didn't, but his brought on more smiles and giggles from Billy and his little red headed sister.

"I need to go out to Sylvia Lee's, Mama. I have to tell her about the kittens and Gertrude going to have a calf."

"Honey, it's too cold to walk that mile out and back; wait until Peabody's come in for groceries this afternoon." A better plan Billy thought as he was pretty sure Manter would suggest he take Sybil out there and he did not particularly like Roscoe Peabody. Nobody really did, but they loved Beulah and Sylvia Lee so Roscoe was accepted.

Someone knocked on the kitchen door, even without looking up Millie called, "Come on in, Starkey, food is almost ready." Manter got up to open the door for Starkey and asked if Starkey had brought over the barb wire or had just come over to fill up on flap jacks and ham.

In 1874 Joe Glidden made this sharp prickly thing he named barbed wire to keep the dogs out of his wife's garden. It caught on so rapidly that shipments were arriving everywhere there were people who had stock.

"Yep, that wire is out by the hog pen and pass me that ham, Billy. You may be a growing boy, but I'm a starvin' man."

"I'm going to collect Matt and Boots to string wire over at Joe and Letty's this afternoon. Starkey, you want to round up Nolan and let's try to get these four pig pens finished up and build a fence to keep those pesky geese in? I've been hearing coyotes in the middle of the night. Anyway, ole Blue and those geese don't seem to get along much. She chases them until they get mad and chase her instead. Truth be told it is down right amusing to watch that show. The geese usually win out!"

Billy passed down the platter of ham and asked, "Hey, Starkey, did Papa tell you Gertrude was going to have a calf about April?" "By then we will be short on feed so she picked a good time."

Starkey chewed a mouth full and nodded his head, "I figured as much. She was just a big calf herself when we left Pennsylvania but I swear she got fat on ground a lizard wouldn't survive on. You know, Manter, it was a good plan you had to build just one big barn for all the stock. It will be warmer with them altogether and one trip out feeds everyone's horses, cows and those six mules. One of them don't look too pert, did you notice? I wonder how old that mule is anyway?"

Sybil piped up with her two cents worth of knowledge and quite grown up she offered her opinion that, "Yes, Papa, it was really smart of you to make a home for all the animals. I gathered eggs yesterday and they were everywhere. Can you make a box for the chickens to lay their eggs in so I don't need to hunt so long?"

Starkey told her it was a good idea and she could help build it, but why not make four boxes side-by-side all in a row then if more then one hen wanted her own box at the time, she wouldn't have to stand in line. At that Millie left the table before she broke out laughing. Manter had to cough just then and excused himself. Billy looked startled. "Wait in line?" he said in a high pitched voice. Starkey winked at him and poked a finger across the table at Sybil who was still figuring out the egg nests.

Sybil roughed up her red hair while thinking this over and agreed to help build what ever it was.

December was not a kind time of year and the wind was vicious on this open plain. The men of the wagon train had mostly found work in town or were busy at their own places. There was extra furniture to build and some to repair. Joe was struggling with building a cradle for the baby, due anytime, and was determined to do it alone. His own accomplishment meant not just an ego trip, but pride he had done it for Letty.

On December twenty fourth, Letty awoke about dawn and shook Joe awake. "You better go get the Doc today," she said. "Not yet, stay with me, it may be a while." Beulah had to wait ten hours and Millie said the first pains could be false labor, so just help me up and we will just see."

By the time Letty had finished speaking; Joe was in his clothes and out the door. Letty was talking to thin air. In spite of it she just had to hold her belly and laugh"; this thought made her laugh all the more.

Joe reappeared in a few minutes and looked down right sheepish. "Letty, it is in the middle of the night. I think we ought to wait a bit, don't you?" he asked in such a sober way. Poor innocent Joe. She did love him so.

The crib was finished and made up with all the new pillows, blankets and a stack of diapers ready for the new arrival. The day was bitter cold and new snow drifts covered the landscape because of the wind. The minus numbers of "cold" were nearly past comprehension. If the wind would die down, you could manage. Instead, it seemed to blow the cold right through you.

It was a long day for Letty who was frail to begin with, but stout hearted and determined to not be any more worry to Joe than was necessary. Joe was a sight to behold; every two minutes he wrung his hands and promised God they would never, never, ever, ever have any more children if they both lived through this one. Letty had to laugh in spite of the intense pain she had not known was even possible.

About 4:00 in the afternoon Millie and Daylene came over with hot food and a bottle for Joe. Since he didn't drink liquor, it only took a couple of swallows to settle him down a while. Joe thought nature knew nothing about justice and this weather was not only not cooperating, it was indeed unjust.

Millie kept Joe busy with bringing in wood for the stove and extra water by the buckets full. With every moan from the bedroom, Joe suffered. By 6:00 there was a wail from the next room, Joe was just limp as a rag; he promised God once again, if everything was fine, they would never again go through this.

Daylene came through the door carrying a bundle about the size of a grown cat. Joe wanted to know about Letty first and then asked about the baby. "You have a beautiful baby girl," Daylene said with tears in her eyes. One day she too would have a family. Holding her bundle out to Joe, who looked scared to death, Daylene said, "Here, Joe, take her. I need to go help Millie."

Letty was totally exhausted but so happy she only wanted Joe and the baby with her. Millie and Daylene finished cleaning up the room, getting Letty into a fresh gown, washing her face, combing her hair and straightening her bed.

Millie took the baby from Joe who hadn't seemed to have moved a muscle or hardly even taken a breath. He hurried into Letty and nearly wept. Since they had been so sure the baby was a boy, they had not settled on a girl's name. Some one was at the door, just opened it and walked in shouting, "Merry Christmas everyone!" Beulah had not realized the baby had been born just now. Her trip in from their farm was to bring in a baby gift she had prepared for this event. Daylene motioned

Beulah into the bed room.

"Now then, Letty girl, what you got there?" Beulah demanded. "It's a girl, Beulah!" Joe announced at the top of his lungs.

"That is just a new little angel," Beulah declared. "I know how wonderful it is. When Sylvia Lee came along I felt like I could handle anything on earth." "What is her name?"

Letty and Joe exchanged a gentle smile and clasped hands. Joe said, "Beulah, you named her when you came bolting through the door. Beulah looked blank and asked, "What did I say?"

"You shouted Merry Christmas. It is Christmas Eve and we decided then and there the baby's name would be Merry Christine. What do you say to that?"

Beulah started to cry and kept repeating, "Bless you, bless you. Millie said it would be a good thing to use up that energy helping boil up all these towels, sheets and rags that had accompanied Merry Christine into this world. The three women went about the laundry task, sent Joe for more firewood and allowed Letty time to rest and hold her precious Christmas present sent from God. She thought of Mary and the baby Jesus and drifted off to sleep.

Matt had dug two holes and erected a "T" bar clothesline for Letty, once the house was built. The heavy digging and dust were hard on Joe's asthma. The clothesline was three lines wide and twelve feet long from the cross bar and had been a blessing to Letty. Right now Beulah was out in that weather hanging up the items the three women had washed.

Daylene said it was foolish. "They would freeze on the line and it was dark and who cared." But Beulah insisted all the wet clothes had to be out of the house; they couldn't be flung about in the house. In her way she was correct. By the time she came back in to warm up, collect her things and leave for home, the frozen laundry was clacking away on the clothes line.

By 8:00 the Sprow home was once again in order, food

prepared for the next day and coffee on the stove. The women said their goodbyes and started out in the stark cold of the night. They each had things yet to prepare for Christmas Day at their own homes.

Christmas morning Levi Guthrey came over with some venison steaks for Letty and Joe and learned of the new baby. He slapped his leg with his hat and said she was the first of their bunch from Pennsylvania people to supply the population of Salina with one more person." "Ought to be an announcement," he said. That was a thought he liked.

The day after Christmas was Thursday morning, he was off to see Mitchell Hayes at the newspaper office. On his way back up the street Levi saw Carey Flinn staggering along with a huge board on his back. "Carey, what in tarnation you doing out in this snow at nine in the morning? "You don't usually see daylight before bar drinking time." "And what's that board you're lugging around. You look like an ijot all bent over like that. Here let me help you before you fall flat on your face."

Carey stopped and slid the board off his back down to the sidewalk. Levi walked around behind Carey to catch the board as it slid off Carey's back. What seemed to be a door stood there.

"Carey, what is this exactly? It must weigh thirty pounds and how did that broken glass get in it anyhow?" On closer observation Levi noticed there was a nice design in the glass. It had been put together to look like a daisy and seemed to be welded together at the petals. In fact, it was a great looking piece of work.

"You know, this is real pretty." "Where did it come from?" "And where you going with it?"

"Levi, you recall when everyone was helping to get Grady's house up?" I didn't mean to do it but I set down on what I thought was just a stack of something and not knowing what it was, I just sort of stumbled into it. Well, it was the glass winders for Grady's place. I thought he was gonna chop off my head with his axe he was holding and I vamoosed. But after dark I snuck back and gathered up the broken pieces. You see, when I was younger and not drinking I used to help my Uncle in his jewelry store. One of the things he did for extra money was to make colored glass lamp shades. I figured I'd see to making a window for his front door. It took a while 'cause I needed help from that blacksmith in town. You know he is as old as dirt and slow as a turtle, but we got it done last week. I'm taking it to Grady for a Christmas present if he will accept it."

Such a long speech nearly took Levi off his center. Did he believe Carey or figure him for a thief concerning the door. Finally he said, "Well, well, Carey. I didn't know you had a trade, but tipping a bottle at your mouth. This is fine work." "Come on, I'll take one side and you the other and we'll deliver this door to a very surprised Grady. I'm sure of that."

Usually Carey had a hard days work doing nothing. This put a new light on the subject. There was some real potential here; it just needed a brush up.

In the snow you can walk silent as dust, so the knock on Grady's door came as a surprise. He saw Carey and glowered, "Yes?" very rudely. Levi spoke up with "Morning, Grady. Santa Claus at your service. We brung you a gift from Carey. You better pay attention, too." "Just step out a minute and see it."

"What now?" Grady grudgingly pulled on his jacket and stepped out on the stoop. There against the wall stood a walnut door with a brass knob and a window in the top half that looked like a flower.

"Carey, how did you come by this nice piece?" Grady was suspicious.

"You know when I busted the window glass in October while you was building your house?" Well, this here is that glass. I cut it and Moose at the blacksmith barn put it together the way I wanted it. So now you got your window glass, it just ain't where you thought it would be. Now you got a good front door."

"You know, Carey, there may be hope for you yet. Thank you and it is a fine piece of work."

Christmas came and then New Years. There was a lot of excitement in town about several new businesses opening soon and the advent of the Easter pageant. That was a high on the expectations list. February was still very cold and possibly March. Millie had taught the girls to knit; Beulah had supplied the wool so Sybil and Sylvia Lee had made scarves for, it seemed half of Salina. The men working out of doors were grateful for them, too. Since Merry Christine was as near a New Year's baby as they had, the Sprow's received some item from each store and many from regular residents who wanted to be in on the celebration. It was a vast help to Joe and Letty as their money was getting low and the extra work Joe picked up was slow just now. They were happy for their own dear place, but times had been easier while living at Mason Philpot's. Joe kept finding reasons to need those big crates the coffins came in so he had a shed of sorts to ease the strain on the space in their house. It amazed him just how much space a baby and its equipment could take up.

By mid January Billy was on the prowl trying to decide what to get Sybil for her birthday which was on Valentines Day. February wasn't that far off. He adored his little red haired sister and especially wanted to get her something nice.

Consulting first with his Mother, he just didn't care about her suggestion of books. Manter had suggested a doll, but Sybil would now be eight and not so much interested in dolls. Next he asked Sylvia Lee who startled him with her suggestion of long white stockings. To the girls they were a sign of growing up.

"Not me!" Billy squawked. "I'm not going to buy any women clothes. Next he tried Daylene who thought she would have some fun with this and suggested a lovely hand bag.

With red face and fumbling fingers, Billy rejected that and asked didn't she know of anything?

"Well Billy Boy, you might try the dry good store and look at those new hair barrettes that came in before Christmas. I see other girls wearing them."

Now *there* was a plan, so off he went. He had fifty cents so he chose two yellow and two blue ones.

The lady said, "Billy, your sister's hair is red. I doubt she would like yellow ones. Why not settle on these silver ones?"

He hadn't thought of such things at all. In fact, he didn't see what that made any difference. *He* liked yellow. Oh well, he still had a nickel for pretty paper to wrap them in.

Ten cents for such a small thing seemed a lot, but for Sybil, he would have given the entire fifty cents for just one barrette. Once home he hid his small treasures for the day he could surprise her with them.

CHAPTER 6

It was Saturday, usually Billy helped at the mercantile store for his spending money and to bring home the items Millie needed. He was fourteen now and nearly as tall as his father. The past three years had gone by so swiftly he hardly realized how much had transpired in that short time.

The first Christmas in their new Kansas home had been as splendid as the ones in Pennsylvania and just about as cold. Among the presents he received was a red, hard cover journal from his mother. On the fly cover Millie had written: My loving son, this will be your fourteenth year and the start of your adult life. You are a special person and need to keep track of yourself in this world. Keep each day special and record your views. One day you will be able to see who you have become. We are who we have been. May our Lord Jesus be with you always, direct your path, and bless you richly. With a Mother's love, Armilla Good, 1877.

Billy started his journal that day and often looked back through it. His mother had kept a journal most of her life; he very much enjoyed looking through hers from time to time.

His first entry was:

Christmas Day- *Cold, snow and windy. Kittens into everything. Pig growing fast. Received scarf, socks, knit cap and mittens, a new sled and five dollars.*

December 26 – *Piece in newspaper; baby girl born to Joe and Letty Sprow named Merry Christine.*

December 27 – *Found homes for three kittens. Papa talking about butchering the pig in the fall.....*and so it read.

One day while helping Joe chop wood, Billy asked, "Joe, why does Letty call you Sam?" "You see, Billy, I have always been slow and given to poor health. When Letty agreed to marry me, I told her things wouldn't likely be easy as a lot of things I couldn't do. She said, "Well you are my Sampson to me." Of course Sampson was known for great strength; it just sort of stuck." If she says, "Sam", it's a nick name. If she says "Joe", you better pay attention. You listen to what a woman means, not what she says.

Billy wasn't really sure exactly what that meant, but agreed anyway. Sometimes grownups talked odd.

Billy had been working at the Mercantile for three years and no longer just uncrated merchandise and swept up. He was being a delivery boy as well and had many conversations with half the town. New people arrive weekly and he was about first to know who they were or where they hailed from, what trade they had, how many to a family or almost anything about them. Being an open, honest and pleasant boy, he had made many friends his own age as well as town folks in general.

The one person he tried to avoid more than anyone else was Carey Flinn. If Billy had a dime Carey seemed to know it like some sixth sense. Billy had a difficult time saying "no" to anyone. When Carey was sober, which was maybe once a month, he could be quite likeable. But if you befriended him on those rare days he would hound you near to death for weeks afterward. Another notice for Billy's journal, *"Learn to side step C. Flinn."*

"Has anyone seen old Buck?" Grady Miller asked nearly everyone he saw. Buck lived in a shack by the river and seldom came into town. No one knew exactly how he lived or where he came by the means to sustain himself. Yet he usually had what he called "his needs" and never asked for much. Grady liked the old rascal and would go get him on fishing jaunts. So far today his inquiries had fallen on deaf ears.

"I'll just mosey off his way and see if I can shake him loose." Grady started toward the river. He intended to go ice fishing and had his tackle box and ax, pole and sandwiches he had picked up at the restaurant from Daylene. The old mule from the stock barn seemed to like the cold weather and stomped around wanting out so Grady left his own horse and took the mule. About half a mile down river he saw Buck coming toward his small dwelling, so pulled up and waited.

"Buck, where ya been?" I been lookin' all over creation for ya this morning."

"Seems like you found me," Buck said without answering Grady's question. "Come on to the place and have a cup of java", Buck said as he kept right on going past where Grady and the mule stood.

"I'll be daggone glad to get that coffee. It's right nippy out today," this from Buck who is wearing long johns, a wool shirt, a mackinaw, and Sybil's red wool scarf.

"Nippy!" you old scally wag. It's five below zero!"

"But a pretty sunny day. I thought maybe if you weren't too busy going off down river somewhere," with a question in his tone of voice, "you might like to go ice fishing with me." Daylene made up a couple roast beef sandwiches and some cookies. If you can pour that coffee into that quart bucket you got there, we could keep it hot on the beach fire."

"Since you went to all that trouble, I guess we might go," said Buck with a hidden grin on his face. He knew everyone around wanted to know where he went down river, all alone, from time to time and he really enjoyed keeping it quiet. He just listened to the stories people invented, it was a real conundrum to them.

Buck had constructed a shanty, from parts unknown, that

set out on the ice. It held two boxes for stools, some blankets he kept in the boxes, a couple cans of peaches, a mackinaw, a fishing pole and a lantern. Once they left the house and the mule was inside the lean-to, Buck built on the south side of his shanty, the two men walked out to the ice house.

Grady said "This place is so small I need to go outside to change my mind."

Buck said, "If it was bigger we would freeze to death in an hour." Grady recalled Booth Gordon's sermons last Sunday when he told them: "Tough times never last, but tough people do. God has created us to be able to handle things. We need confidence and our faith will be challenged many times in life."

Sitting here with Buck now in his 80's, Grady wondered about old Buck's life. It was a mystery.

CHAPTER 7

By 1879 Salina had grown and prospered. Hard Knocks had come back from Indiana with a wife. He made any kind of promise he could dream up to convince Willa Bender to leave the serenity of her own territory, a job she loved and her family.

"I'd have promised her a pet buffalo if I thought that's what she wanted and tame the dern thing myself." Hard Knocks had a mighty fine imagination, that he did! After three months of his pestering, Willa agreed. She was so used to him after his coming and goings over six years she might as well just say yes and keep him for good. Knox loved that girl from her flat feet to her hair and was not about to leave without her if there was any chance at all.

Willa had two sisters and her best friend, Reva Thompson, for maid of honor and bridesmaids. She had chosen lavender and green as the colors for the dresses as it was spring and most blooming flowers were some shade of purple. Iris, hyacinth, violets, star flowers, pansies, heather, crocus and some primrose were all in shades of deep purple to lavender.

"I wonder if God had a favorite color." Reva remarked. Willa smiled at her dear friend and agreed it did seem so.

The day of the wedding was cool but pleasant, no need for

coats or heavy shoes. Willa looked lovely in her fitted gown with lace shawl and bouquet of lilacs, fern and white rose buds. Hard Knocks was such a mess of nerves he nearly bolted, but once he settled down he realized this vision in lavender was his and he would never more roam as the song said. He was so proud to take home a lovely wife and for once in his thirty years could start life like a normal person would. He surely did miss Rand not being there. Rand had been a trail hand on every trip Knox had scouted for. They had become close friends and depended on each other in good times and bad. He even entrusted his future bride to come back to Kansas with he and Willa. Willa's brother was the best man for Knox and the minister was her cousin. It was a small wedding for just close friends and relatives. Some snooty town folk thought it to be disgraceful for a girl from the saloons to have a fancy wedding. It suited Hard Knocks fine as he was a cow country man not used to fuss and feathers, even this wedding at the little town chapel had pretty well undone him. He just wished Willa could have sung a song at her own wedding. She sang like an angel and he adored her. She may not have had a saintly life, but she had no regrets either. Being from a poor family and out on her own at fifteen was not a criminal offence and nice people never seemed to take time to discover the fine points in others. They don't know but are quick to judge. They needed to read the book of Proverbs in their Bibles.

Willa and Hard Knocks remained at her small apartment for a week while she assembled the traveling things necessary for the trip back to Salina.

Although the transcontinental railroad was completed in May of 1869, it was north of Kansas but the Atchison, Topeka and Santa Fe line had been completed in August of 1859. That train trip back to Illinois was a miracle compared to the horse trail on his last venture east. Knox was so proud to take his new wife and pretty friend across country by rail.

It was really hard to realize the Civil War was taking place in the East while railroad history was made in the West. The war ended in 1865 – the same year the Suez Canal opened. So much construction in such a few years was difficult to grasp.

The Pullman cars were luxurious and had waiters with attentive care, fine food and sleeping quarters. For Reva and Willa, neither had ever seen such glorious accommodations and never ceased to talk about it for years.

When the train pulled into Salina it seemed to Hard Knocks that half of Salina was there. Of course it was mostly the families who had first come across with the wagons. Rand was nearly beside himself when Reva stepped down from the train.

Beulah Peabody came bellowing up to Knox and Willa with a sampler she had painstakingly labored over to give the newlyweds just in case Knox brought home a wife.

"You're a mighty pretty gal, Willa." All of us here are just so please you came back with this old hard headed cowboy." Beulah was so excited she stammered, "We can't tarry long because of evening chores but you will see Sylvia Lee and me around now and then." She waved goodbye as she took Sylvia Lee's hand and started for their wagon.

1879 had been a very eventful year for Salina and it inhabitants. Manter had set his mind to own the hardware store and Adam Insley had used his bank to back him. Millie was teaching elementary school full time.

A new attorney had moved to town and hung his shingle proudly: Claire C. Dent, Attorney at Law. Whitey Cobb had been reelected as Sheriff. Julie Johnson had opened a dress shop and millenary store. Mason Philpot had a stroke and turned more and more to Joe Sprow for help in his funeral home. Letty Sprow was pregnant again; Merry Christine, called Chrissie, was now three years old.

Grady Miller had taken over the livery stable and added a blacksmith shop to it. Levi Guthrey had organized a band from among the population and played for nearly all occasions. He had even purchased uniforms other than white shirts and dark trousers. They had become quite popular besides that Levi had met the love of his life. All was well in his world.

Billy's dog, Blue, had pups; Boots was on the fourth set of kittens. Booth Gordon had married Miss Nora Ellen; she made a wonderful parson's wife with her gentle ways and her unshakeable faith in God. Rand and Reva were married and purchased a clapboard house in town.

Matt and Daylene were setting a wedding date and hoped Daylene's brother, Nolan, would be in from the cattle drive coming north from Texas. Nolan Shank was a trail hand and loved the out-of-doors. He swore he would never marry and be "branded" as he chose to call a wedding certificate.

Starkey Blake and Boots McGuinnes were still the town's devilry, but close as brothers. Where you saw one the other wasn't far away. Carey Flinn was still a problem with his drinking, but on his good days he produced some remarkable good windows and glass lamp shades.

The summer months proved to be a grand time of year with nearly perfect weather. Manter and Billy had spent early spring in their work shed making shingles for sale for roofing. Millie had wanted to plant her garden closer to the house this year but this involved carrying water farther from the creek.

"Papa, why can't we dig little trenches up to the garden for Mama?" Billy had an idea to share with his father. In the evenings they worked out the details and, once the garden was planted, they tried out the new system.

"Millie, try to hill up your rows a little; it will leave a sort of trough between the rows." Manter took the hoe and showed her how to "hill" the seeds. Billy took a shovel to help pull the dirt up higher.

"Billy, do you know who invented the shovel?" Manter asked. "Well, it was a man by the name of Oliver Ames. He and his brother got rich off those shovels selling them to the railroad for their working crew's. In May of 1869, when you were four years old, the transcontinental tracks came together. There were five thousand people there to see it, if it hadn't been in Utah. I surely would have liked to have seen that!"

Manter brought out some stakes he had made and an arm full of heavy shingles.

"Come here, son, help me organize them into a flow stop." Manter handed Billy some baling twine, thin wire and two stakes. They suspended a shingle in the middle by using the twine and attached the wire to the bottom with the wire wrapped around the stake like a lever.

"Now, set the shingle down even with the bottom of the trough with the lever handle pointed up along side the shingle. Now, let's make a six inch deep trench from the outside of the shingle down to the water." Once this was finished it was noon and time to eat. Millie had gone to the house where Sylvia Lee and Sybil were busy slicing bread for sandwiches. There was potato soup left from the day before so it made a good meal.

"You girls please clean up," Millie said. "I need to go supervise a job I know nothing about." She laughed and gave a big hug to each child.

"All set," Manter called. Push the shingle down to the ground. Fine, now pull up on the lever attached to the wire. The shingles all rose in a row and the water slowly started up the trough. All three stood and watched with big grins on their faces as the trough slowly filled with two or three inches of water.

"Fine – fine. Now push the lever down, Billy." It shut the water off to just build up against the outside of the heavy shingle.

"And so," Manter clapped Billy on the shoulder, "see that son; we invented a way to get out of carrying water for your mother's garden."

"This calls for a trip to The Restaurant," Millie said. She washed her hands, fluffed up her red hair, collected the two girls and the three of them went to get ice cream.

While the girls and Millie were gone, Billy and Manter rode over to Starkey's to get another two bales of barb wire.

"You know, Billy, old Joe Glidden has made a fortune off this barb wire. It has been a blessing in many ways, but for the cattle that get cut up with it, it surely is a shame. I understand why the ranchers have found cut fences, too. I understand from the railroad agent they have had nearly a ton of that wire shipped on the trains and who knows where else. It will be a way of life before long.

Booth Gordon's congregation kept increasing each month, much to his pleasure. Having Miss Nora Ellen for a wonderful wife had helped with the increase. She was well respected and loved by all. Many of her friends and neighbors had started coming to church now, who before had seemed too busy.

She started a small choir with Millie's help at the piano. She and Booth decided to have prayer meetings on Wednesday evening like she had been used to in her church back in Pennsylvania. It was sparsely attended at first, but growing pains were to be expected.

"Booth, why don't we have a picnic basket lunch after church on Sundays now that the weather is so nice? We could ask for donations from the lumber yard for a few planks, some nails from Manter at the hardware. Maybe put the word out for a few strong men to build a couple trestle tables like we had on the trail coming west. By the way, what ever became of that table, do you know?"

After thinking about it a few minutes, Booth said, "Yes, yes, yes! I don't believe I know either." Miss Nora Ellen had been peeling potatoes when she asked her original question. Now she said, "I'm supposed to untangle that odd sentence or will you oblige me?"

Booth laughed as he patted her hand on his way out the door. "Well, my dear wife, yes we can have a basket lunch on the lawn. Yes, we can ask for materials for tables. Yes, we can ask for carpenters or whomever. And, I don't know what became of that trestle table, but I'm off to see who might."

The place to begin would be the bachelor quarters. They had scrounged up all they could and still remain in good grace with the neighbors.

"Yep", this from Levi who had given up his room at the boarding house to move in with Boots McGuiness after Matt and Daylene were married.

"Nolan had it in his shed and we were eating off a plank shelf Matt had nailed up." "You need it for something, Booth?"

"No, no, just tracking it down. We are looking for volunteers to build three like it for picnics after church, box lunch's, or hold loose item sales and the like." He didn't want to tell Levi they could have used it and saved making an extra table.

Levi grinned ear-to-ear, rubbed his hands together and then rubbed his belly.

"Really, you don't say. Picnic lunch ya say?" Hmmm. We bachelors could cotton to that pretty easy. Guess we could go to church, eh?"

"Well, for goodness sake, Levi, you could go to church without being fed, you know, but everyone is welcome for any reason."

"But bring your hammer Saturday and help build these tables, you hear?" Booth was just tickled with himself over the slippery way he had tricked Levi into volunteering. A bit shady, but it had been worth it to see the exasperation on Levi's face.

Once home from his rounds of the hardware and lumber yard, he told Miss Nora Ellen of his little chat with Levi and the outcome. Oh, he was so pleased with himself!

"You ought to be ashamed, Booth," she said all serious like but couldn't hold in her laughter any longer.

"Come here, you scamp," she said before she gave him a quick hug and sweet kiss.

"Boy, that mischief paid off," Booth said and ducked out of the way of a dish towel being snapped at his back side.

On Saturday morning a dozen men showed up at the parsonage laden with hammers, saws, levels, and other tools they might use including a big basket that Roscoe Peabody had brought.

Now, there was news! Roscoe Peabody at a church! No one said as much, but the faces on the other men was such a study in expressions that it made even Miss Nora Ellen laugh out loud.

"Hello, Roscoe, glad to see you. Nice that you come in from the farm to help," smiled Booth.

"Yeah, welllll, I didn't you see." "Beulah sent this here food for all of you's who is being God's people t'day." "Said you would need food by noon and she can't come, so she sent me."

Miss Nora Ellen came down the steps and reached for the big basket, "You give Beulah a love from us all, Roscoe." You have a wonderful wife and beautiful little girl. We are so happy to have you for neighbors here." "Why don't you stay a while if you can spare the time and help the men gets started on the trestle tables?"

Roscoe was so shocked to be invited he was tongue-tied. Everyone had made it very clear he was not acceptable without saying as much. He scuffed his foot on the ground, scratched his head, and allowed he might, for a little time.

Roscoe wandered over to look at the wood the lumber company had donated; he thought it looked like first class planks for anyone to just give away and muttered something to that effect to Jasper Hughes who had joined the group.

"Hello, Roscoe, what part you gonna do here?" Roscoe shook his head; he didn't know. So he stood aside to just watch for a time. There was quite a flurry of feet trampling about but not much organization. Finally he picked up a hatchet and started to plane off the ends to a one inch square piece of wood. After he had six finished, he asked no one in particular, "just how many tables you plan to build?"

"Three," came the answer from someplace. "Here are your

cross members; I pegged them out, just fit the legs to match."
Roscoe started toward his horse and buggy.

"Hold up there, Roscoe," called Matt Kimball. "What you talking about?" Roscoe turned back and held up the six, three foot lengths he had just pegged.

"These," he said. "They are ready to place in the table legs."

"I never say anything done like this. Starkey, come here and see what you make of these."

Levi sidled over to also study the situation. "Roscoe, maybe you better show us what to do here," said Booth. "You people were not on the wagon train so I guess you don't know what we are about here. We had a big trestle table that came apart and set up for meal time. We thought we could make three smaller ones to use for various things here at church. Now if you could give us a clue as to how you thought to construct this, I'd be very much obliged."

Roscoe was flattered, yet embarrassed, too. He took up several odd pieces of wood to make a model of sorts and explained.

"You set these pieces length ways between a leg on each end. Cut a hole the size of the end I pegged out to fit so the leg pieces look like the letter "H". Then you run one plank lengthwise from end to end of the table like a shelf down the middle between the legs the same length as the table."

"That is a sound idea, Roscoe, but how do you see to attach the table top then?" asked Matt.

"I'll tell you what, men. You go on and get that top made up, I'll be back in half an hour or there about and I'll finish the job." With that Roscoe walked to his buggy and road up toward town. True to his word he was back in about twenty minutes carrying a bag of clattering merchandise.

"Now, if a couple of you gents will tip that table on end sideways, I'll show you how to do this up tidy."

Four of the men did as he bid them and set it on the ground.

Roscoe took out four big barn door hinges and put them on the bottom side about six inches in from the outside plank. He handed the other three hinges to three other onlookers and then finished his own using a large screw driver. Once all four were in place he instructed them to lay the table over on its face, took the legs already assembled and placed them so the hinges could be screwed to the legs.

"Now that is complete," he said. "Turn it over and set it upright."

"See how the legs are held in place by the lengthwise plank? Now fold the table down the side of the legs on the left the way the hinges go. You can stack one on top of the other and save space."

"Now ain't that the cats meow!" was one of the many comments made.

"Roscoe, that was a fine idea and we are beholden to you," Booth offered, "and many thanks for your help. What a good idea."

Miss Nora Ellen came to inspect the new table and was so pleased. She said someone get that big basket Beulah sent in. Roscoe went to fetch it while the men washed up for their lunch. Miss Nora Ellen put papers on the table and unloaded the big basket.

"Oh my goodness, fellows," she gushed. "Just wait to see what your reward to this days work is." There was fried chicken, biscuits, pickles, potato salad, four sour crème pies and two crocks of buttermilk. Had there been a dog to clean up scraps, the dog would have gone hungry.

In all this time Roscoe had not had a temper fit, swore bloody murder, or kicked anything or anybody. Booth decided then and there that if a person is needed he will act like he is part of them. That was good fodder for Sunday's sermon.

Miss Nora Ellen agreed and watched lifes change in Roscoe Peabody. He, Beulah and Sylvia Lee started attending church that very Sunday and everyone prospered by it. Beulah could sing like an angel and did so quite often before services began. She also taught Sybil and Sylvia Lee to harmonize. They too did special music with the children's Sunday School.

Billy had grown too much this part year. His trousers were ankle high and an embarrassment. How Joe did like to rag him about it.

"Say there Billy, you want your Ma to sew ruffles on the bottom;" or, "Gotcha a new handle now; how about high pockets or something like that? Looks like you be treading high water now, Billy Boy." Joe was a good natured man. Such a pity he was poorly most of the time. He lived for Letty and Chrissy, did what he was able and made a modest living.

Billy loved to go to the Sprows' and usually found some excuse to chop extra wood or put down hay for the horse and cows, clean the chicken house or just run a hoe through the garden. Chrissy was three and loved Billy like family. He nearly wore that child in his hip pocket when he was at their place. He took her on rides in the wheel barrow, on his shoulders, his horse or whatever she enjoyed. His own beloved sister was too big for horse play now. He was saddened to see her grow up.

On Sunday Booth had planned a short sermon with the intent to let the congregation take part again. He had started this way and the people seemed eager to take part.

"Good Morning, Congregation," was answered by a unanimous, "Good Morning Reverend."

"Everyone take your hymnals and turn to page ten. We will sing 'How Great Thou Art' at the request of several of you. Beulah, will you please step up here and lead the music?"

It was her passion to sing and she did it so well. If you were timid about singing in public it didn't last long because you caught the gusto with which Beulah sang. As Matt Kimball had once said, "just let 'er rip!"

"We have several announcements this morning. First, there will be three weddings this week and Miss Nora Ellen could use a few extra hands with church decorations. There will be a pot luck after Friday evening's wedding – you can all kiss the bride. So if you're coming to feast, bring something to eat." Amen said with a knowing smile. There are always free loaders he recalled.

"If anyone wants to buy those geese of Adam's he needs to be rid of them. The town has grown past his place now and the racket they set up is being a problem. Besides, a coyote got in the pen but the geese ganged up on the coyote and killed it instead. Also, they are building a new depot and need help at the railroad station. We have witnessed tremendous growth in town since I, at least, have arrived and that goes for many of this congregation."

"It is surprising to realize that in 1867 there were only one hundred people here and by 1870 our population has grown to twelve hundred. The enormous herds of buffalo are roaming farther West the more people from the East are moving in here. We have much to be grateful for with such progress."

"Today's message will be short due to the weather. We are due for some storms and most of us would prefer to be home in case of any lightning strikes. We all have dreadful memories of the fires in 1871 and '74 when nearly all of downtown was destroyed and rebuilt of brick and stone. Our homes are for the most part still wooden structures which is a concern. Go to the grist mill for refuge if need be."

"Alright now, turn to the book of Ruth this morning. As we know, hard times seem to go on forever, but we are nearer to God in bad time. We call on Him for help but do we say thank you for the answer when it comes? God is not hard of hearing. He doesn't need to be reminded constantly of your troubles. He knew them before you were born. Like the song says, take your burden to the Lord and leave it there. If you keep talking about it, you're taking it back. If you want it back, God will let you keep it. Sometimes your problems seem to have no solutions but remember what He said. When one door closed, another one will open. If you allow time for God to work, things will be better than they were. We, as humans, don't care to wait it out, and then are tempted to step out of God's grace. But remember this, there is no such thing as a backslider. Once you are saved and have a Christian's spirit, you will always have just enough religion to be miserable and want back in the fold of Christ's arms. God will turn things around. The devil works the hardest on you when he sees you are near to having things better and tries to keep you upset.

"See how difficult times were for Ruth and Naomi. Along came Boaz who told his workers to leave grain in the field. God has set things in motion for your life as well. He gets people lined up in our life. The right people will be there at the right time. Another thing you should never forget is that God always gives you double for your trouble; hang in there – your time is coming. For any unfair things have occurred, He will be your vindicator."

"I heard a story I'll share with you. There was a man out fishing. The wind came up and blew him way off course. He finally drifted up on a small spit of land he didn't even know existed. He had no idea where he was and only what had survived the storm was left in his boat. After three days he was without any provisions and his only shelter was the battered boat. He started collecting limbs of trees, long grasses and most anything that would do for a shelter. This piece of land was not generous with food stuff and the man was getting desperate.

Then came another storm and with it mosquitoes in droves. He did have safety matches and had been able to keep a fire going. While out searching for something to eat, the shelter caught fire and burned down. He said, "Lord, what am I to do? I feel like you have forgotten me."

Within an hour a boat came by and the man thought he was delirious. "How did you ever find me?" he wept. "We saw the smoke from your signal fire," was the answer he heard. God's mysterious ways!

"God sets His plans in motion for us as well. In just these few years we have seen great strides in progress for which we have all prospered and continue to do so. We need each other for help, support, and friendship and to be able to depend on each other as well. Good works do not go unrewarded. "Manter, would you lead us in a closing prayer, then turn your hymn books to page twelve, 'Blessed Be the Tide That Binds."

After service Miss Nora Ellen hugged her husband and thanked him for a sermon that would fit all. "You know, Booth, it was only four years ago we started a church service in the restaurant for one hour on Sunday morning. Now we have a lovely brick building with nice pews, a donated organ, a piano, donated hymn books, talent among our flock that has grown to over two hundred in attendance. God surely has blessed us richly.

CHAPTER 8

Issac Foster had made a suggestion to the school board that they should split up the grades at school and hire two more teachers. The two new schools were full to capacity and too heavy a load for the three of them. After the next board meeting three more teachers were to be hired and the work load divided among the six.

This now called for another building also. Since Reva Thompson Blackwell had been a librarian in Indiana, she agreed to get a teaching certificate through correspondence classes or by going to Leavenworth for six months. She and Rand took the train over to Leavenworth to discuss the matter with the college there and learned she could study at home and take her final exams back in Leavenworth with the graduating class. Rand agreed to this proposal and plans were set in motion.

The two schools had a second story each added on to the building; the now closed grist mill was purchased and renovated into class rooms. The product of all these changes turned out to be a first class educational boon for Salina. The first and second grades were in one room with one teacher, third and fourth with another, fifth, sixth together with a third teacher. The second school had seventh, eighth and ninth grades, while the big grist mill school had tenth, eleventh and twelfth plus a gymnasium, an auditorium and a library. Celia Romic, hired from Dodge, had first and second. It was her first year to teach. She was so excited and fit right in. It didn't take Nolan Shank very long to see to her needs much to the amusement of his buddies. Sara Jane Fremont was to take the third and fourth grades, Reva Blackwell was assigned the fifth and sixth. Issac Foster had seventh, eighth and ninth mathematics and history while Ira Fletcher taught geography, science and English. A new principal was being selected when Millie asked Manter why he didn't apply. After some haggling he agreed to "put in for it." No one was surprised when he was selected.

There was still a need for the high school teachers, a gym teacher, music teacher, and custodians for all three buildings. Joe Sprow talked it over with Letty and asked about the custodial position at the elementary school, as in another year Chrissy would start school. Three more teachers were hired that summer so schools took on a new beginning.

Taxes went up and several more businesses opened. Where there are people, business follows. One of the new places in town, an Optometry office, was on Broad Street which also housed a drugstore and the local theater. The new eye doctor, as he was referred to, was Bertrum Nutt and wife, Nola who had relocated from Kansas City. Here there was not as much competition.

Mitchell Hayes' newspaper was now six sheets instead of one and came out daily instead of weekly. This year he had to hire help, also. One of the most controversial subjects had been when the city council passed into law that no more log cabins could be erected inside the city limits. This was a rough time for those who had log cabins. Most had been built out of the town proper, but the town grew up beyond them. Hayes said Salina was in the throws of growing pains.

The wagon train group was considered the town old timers. That sounded very odd to Billy. He spent his spare time as a paper boy, made grocery deliveries to several shut-in's, did the janitor work at their church and was interested in baseball. His best friend was Hollis Newberg whose family had come to town with the railroad. The boys liked to go fishing with Grady Miller and especially with Uncle Buck who never seemed to run dry of stories. Billy was quite curious about the stage coaches, the cattle drives, pony express and the stories about the Indians. Buck was eighty and had been active in the gold rush days. He knew first hand about the topics that Billy hungered for. Those two could sit for hours on a Sunday afternoon and go over Buck's remarkable life history. It was better than school. Buck decided one day he would take Billy along on his hike down river that everyone was so curious about. At his age he thought maybe he would let someone know where to find his treasures and money. They wouldn't mean much to most people, but Billy seemed to have a penchant for history and Buck had souvenirs from many places. He would study on that a while longer and take Billy into his plans. Buck's was a library of life. The year 1879 had been a happy one for Buck.

CHAPTER 9

It had been a very wet year which was a much different summer than Kansas was used to. Chickens had gotten cocksidiosis and died by the dozen. It seemed people had one common cold throughout the city. Schools started late due to the storms, fires had started from lightning, and pet rabbits died of moldy feed. In general the fall of the year was hot, humid, wet and uncomfortable. Getting wood in for fireplaces was a real chore. The ground was soggy, the wood was wet and hard to chop, and it was nearly impossible to saw - not to mention miserable to handle or stack.

By Halloween it had turned cold. People were still digging potatoes, carrots, parsnips and other garden produce. The women were attempting to collect flower seeds for the next spring season, but the damp seeds molded as did some bulb plants.

The retail stores were stocked with rain gear, gloves, heavy jackets, even a few canoes. Preparations were made in the individual homes for a hard winter. Billy had earned enough during the summer to buy things for school and was proud to do so. He was also able to put away a sum toward December with Christmas in mind.

"I believe this will pass in a few days," Matt told Daylene.

"Usually they have a week or so of nice weather here – they call it Indian summer." Daylene, Reva and Willa collected Millie and Letty on their way out of town with Reva driving the new buggy Rand had recently purchased.

"Daylene, what did you expect to buy in Junction City? You're making a mystery of this trip you realize." Willa was hoping for maybe a new wardrobe. She yearned for pretty clothes like the ones she had worn in Indiana, but there was seldom a need for them in Salina.

"Willa, I just *know* what you want," Reva chuckled. "New shoes, dresses and curtains, right?"

Millie added, "You girls better think toward cheaper things as Salina has truly taken on expensive ways lately. Even the yardage is up to fifty cents a yard!"

Letty wanted to get Joe a couple of shirts and Chrissy some long stockings for school this winter.

"I was speaking with Nola Nutt after church Sunday. She was telling us about the Harrison boy. He had been squinting to see things more often so his mother brought him to the office a week ago. Bert gave him an eye exam and realized the child was far sighted, he needed glasses. The boy picked out a frame and Bert made the lenses that same week. When they came in to the office yesterday, Bert asked the boy if he could see pretty well."

"Oh, sure. I just squint down to read is all." The child was very polite and sure of himself.

"Here, son, sit over here and lets try on these new spectacles." Bert indicated a chair across his desk. "Now let's see if these make a difference." He shouted "Oh" in such a surprised tone it made his mother jump and caused Bert to laugh.

"Here, see if you can read this better now." Bert handed him a story book from the magazine rack.

"Mother, it is so plain and up close!" he squeaked. "Can I see in the mirror, Sir?"

"Of course - here." Bert turned the shaving mirror around.

He had brought it from home for just such a purpose.

After looking at himself for a few minutes, the boy said, "Did you know I had freckles, Mother?" Now she said, "Oh, oh, oh, dear me. I never realized you couldn't see that." She hugged her son and they were all smiles as they left. "Wonderful thing spectacles are!" Millie remarked. "I am now wondering about my own family. Maybe I better get Billy and Sybil over to see Bert myself," she mused.

"Here we are, girls," Reva said as they pulled up in front of a fine looking building.

"This is my treat today," she climbed down to help Millie while Letty and Willa followed Daylene.

"*What* sort of a treat?" Letty wanted to know. Rand told me about this place when he came back from Ft. Riley so I decided we girls would take a day trip to see for ourselves. Reva pushed open the door to a soda fountain with an enormous mirror behind the bar.

"Did you ever see such a mirror?" Reva asked. Rand told me they sent this out on the train from back in Ohio some place, then had to pack it in hay sitting up on it's side because if it laid flat down it would split in two. They built a flat form on both sides and held it in place like a hangman's noose. The wagon was not long enough so they took part of a wrecked wagon and bolted it to the first one. What a story, eh?"

"So, have a seat and let's have a soda and sandwich before we go shopping." Reva was so pleased with her plan and the good time in store for herself and her friends. Each ordered their choices and relaxed from the several hours on the road.

"Should we stay together?" Willa had wanted to take her time looking at things, but she knew Letty would want to rush from place to place.

"It might be better if we each went to do our own shopping and meet later, don't you think." suggested Daylene the practical one.

'Yes, I agree," said Millie and started toward the dry goods store. She had in mind cloth for new dresses for Sybil and Sylvia Lee.

Willa was more interested in makeup and shoes while Daylene went to look at pretty sheets and pillows. Reva and Letty decided to go to the book store and ladies lingerie.

There was a park in the town square and that is where it had been decided to go as a meeting place in two hours. Letty was getting nervous about the time, so was the first one to arrive at the park. As the others came with bundles and packages it was a laughing good time. Letty said it would be late getting back home.

"Letty, we aren't going back tonight," Reva said. This caused a sudden quiet from all.

"Really, Reva, what are you up to?" Willa knew Reva well from their girlhood days. She knew when mischief was afoot.

Reva calmly told them she had made arrangements with a hotel for all of them. Their husbands had been told by Rand, when asked to verify their story that the ladies were off on a fling before winter grounded them.

Letty nearly fainted and sat down with a most unlady like gesture.

"Reva – oh dear Lord girl! You mean I have left Chrissy with Joe! And, overnight no less!" "He will be as wild as a creature captured in the woods not knowing which end is up concerning supper, bed times, baths, and – oh my goodness, Reva – you should have told me," Letty wrung her hands.

"Letty, Letty, I'm not feeble minded! It is taken care of. Beulah will take Sybil and Chrissy home with her and Sylvia Lee. The girls will have a party, bake cookies and, no doubt, be spoiled rotten. They couldn't be in better care. The men know this, too."

"I asked Beulah to come with us but she said she really didn't have the money but would gladly watch the girls. Billy is fifteen and busy with his father and odd jobs. So, I think we should pitch in and buy something special for Beulah, don't you agree?" This from thoughtful Millie.

The excited answers were a unanimous, "Yes!" Daylene, ever food conscious, thought they should start thinking about a restaurant and silently wondered how hers was doing and did the Murphy's also know of this trip. She then decided that of course they must.

"Shouldn't we get all these bags and parcels to that hotel, Reva? Also it is after five and my sandwich and soda are worn out,' she snickered. Daylene started gathering her things together as did the others.

"No restaurant, Daylene," Reva reached over to hug her friend. "You see that every day. We are going to *dine* in the *dining* room." She held up her hand with the little fingers crooked; strutted about a few steps to imitate some swanky lady laden down with jewels; then threw her head back and laughed. "This will be our last outing till Christmas holiday at school and I intend to have a jolly good time of it."

Once in the rooms at the hotel, bathed and dressed up again, Letty the worrier said, "now what about night gowns?" We aren't prepared for this, Reva, and no extra clothes."

"Surprise!" Reva plopped a package on her bed and said, "Who wants what?" She shook the bags and out tumbled five slim line gowns in different colors.

"You know, I'm just learning to sew and these only require side stitches and arm holes. Don't you dare inspect them, at least not while I'm looking!"

Each choose a gown and, as they had doubled up two to a room, Letty and Willa took off for their room leaving Daylene and Reva to go across the hall to their room. Millie had a single room to herself. However that did not last long once everyone was ready for bed. All four young women ended up in Millie's room until nearly midnight.

Millie laughed at them all piled on her bed and said, "I guess we are having a slumber party, too."

In the morning after a hearty breakfast it was time to think about the ones at home. Letty had shirts for Joe and ribbons for Chrissy besides her new long stockings. Reva had gotten cigars for Rand. Daylene bought Matt a heavy sweater; Millie had purchased a tie for Manter, western boots for 'Billy and a camisole for Sybil who was now eleven – going on twenty. Willa had been unusually quiet and wasn't much interest in her breakfast. Mille wandered about that but kept her counsel.

"Okay, Willa, what did you get for Knox?" "You're being secretive today." "Oh, not much really. A new belt buckle with turquoise sets in it and a new belt. Excuse, me." Then she bolted for the bathroom. In doing do she knocked over a package at the end of the bed. Out tumbled a few lovely baby cloths. Reva picked them up to return them to the bed just as Willa came back in the room. The ladies smiled and chuckled.

Reva said, "So, you have news maybe?" She ran over to the door and hugged her chum of many years. "Daylene was the one who wanted a baby when Chrissy was born," Letty said, "but it looks like Willa beat you to it."

"This calls for a celebration, girl," Millie clapped her hands together. This was delightful news.

"I'll bet old Knocks is about to bust his shirt buttons!" Daylene squealed.

"I haven't told him yet. I wanted to just put these baby clothes on our bed and let him find them." The news will sink in, she chuckled to herself.

"Now we better settle down and make up our minds about what to get Beulah. Millie, do you have any suggestions?"

Letty said how about yarn as Beulah loved to knit and did so beautifully.

"Good idea, Letty. Anyone else?" asked Willa.

"Yes, why not get something she wouldn't buy for herself," said Millie.

"Wonderful idea. I've noticed that old sweater she wears is about a thing of the past. Since we don't know sizes, how about a lovely soft wool shawl instead."

"Reva, that is just right; let's go shopping."

As soon as the five friends returned home they realized at once that something was amiss. A solemn atmosphere seemed to prevail as Reva pulled up in front of their home. Rand came out to meet them, he looked serious.

"What has happened, Honey?" Reva grabbed Rand's sleeve.

"There was a fire last night. That shanty Carey lived in went up like paper, as best as Whitey Cobb can figure. Carey must have had a candle lit and possibly fell asleep drunk. Anyway he was three-sheets-to-the-wind when he went by the hardware store. Manter called to him that he better get on home, if you want to call it that, and no one saw him again after that. Carey died in the fire; we guess the smoke got him."

"Joe found Carey lying in the alley beside his burned out place and ran for Whitey. Then he went to find Mason Philpot and Booth Gordon. It's been a rough go this morning."

Letty was so relieved Chrissy had been with Beulah. Joe would have been beside himself. The women went to their own homes and tried to not think of Carey. A drunk he was, but a human being never the less.

No one knew much about Carey except he had come from back east several years ago and supposedly had an Uncle with a jewelry store. Where the Uncle lived or whether or not he was still alive was not known.

The town council members figured the city would bury him in the pauper's grave lot and pay for a marker. Mason took charge of the body; Joe could not handle that. He would see that charred body for the rest of his life, no doubt.

It had been a pretty day as was predicted. A much appreciated Indian summer day was a welcome sight from the gloom and clouds of rain.

After the funeral Grady asked Billy if he wanted to go fishing.

"You bet" was the quick answer. How about go get Buck,

too?"

"Fine with me." Grady gathered up the fishing gear and headed for the creek. Billy was on a trot to get Uncle Buck. The three settled down on their log stump stools that Grady had fashioned. He took a two foot length of log and attached a leather strap handle so it could be carried like a bucket. I t had been a source of comfort compared to standing or sitting on the damp ground.

"Uncle Buck, did you ever ride in a stage coach?" Billy wanted to know. He also knew it usually only took one question to get Buck started on a story.

"You bet, young fella," came the reply. Billy grinned to Grady who winked back.

"That Butterfield Overland stage was a dozy, Billy. It started up August of 1857 and ran over three thousand miles before it ended in 1869. You was a tike about four years old then. Back and forth it went; near to kill the horses."

"The rail road was being built across the country. In May of 1869 the last section was run. The stage stopped four months later but alot of those stage stations still exist and the horses left there were traded off. The Bannock Indians were still at war, actually they just settled into three tribes down in Southeast Idaho about 1878, as I recall. It was in the paper a couple of years ago." Buck was going strong!

"I wish you had been here and big enough to go to the hullabaloo when they struck the gold spikes. Most nearly five thousand people showed and the story was in print for thirteen cents a program. Each end Captain had a contest to finish the last hundred miles and swore their crews could lay ten miles a day. It liked to near killed those workers, but they did it. Three thousand five hundred twenty rails - twenty eight thousand one hundred sixty spikes – fourteen thousand one hundred and eight nuts and bolts. I still got that paper, Billy. You can have it for history class if you like."

Uncle Buck reminisced for a while then started on tales

about the cattle trails. He had been on the Pecos Trail himself and had wondrous stories that Billy never tired of.

"Because I had been at stage stops, I got to knowing some fellers. A few had been with and made several trips up from south Texas into Pecos Valley so I had to go see. No family, no nothing stopped my curiosity. The one trip I was on I rode point and we had nine hundred head of cattle. We drove 'em to the troops for eating beef, five different forts."

"There was a gent by name of George Mendels came south from back east. He had some gentler breed of cows and, over a few years, cross bred his with the long horns and scrub cattle. They were better meat and could stand the rough trails as good as the tough long horns. Today we have red and white Hereford and mixed cows."

" had a ranch like you've never seen in a life time. He had forty acres, a four room house *but* run eighty thousand head of cattle." Buck shook his head and spit in the creek. I never seen such and never expect to again. Range land.

The idea of those cattle trails were a dream for Billy. He just ached to go out and join in this type of life, but no use to say it at home. Manter would frown and Millie would pat his shoulder and repeat the standard answer to any such talk.

"Why son, you're just a lad." "We need you here a few years and I was hoping you would consider college at Leavenworth. We will talk of it later, dear." That would be that.

On Monday Uncle Buck was waiting for Billy after school.

"You going to any of your jobs right now, boy?"

"Yes, I help at the grocery if they have deliveries. If not I check the post office to see if there is anything there to deliver. Then there is the flower shop and, most days they have pot plants or cut flowers for people in the hospital or to shut-in's. Why? You need something done, Uncle Buck?"

"Yes, boy, I do if you get time."

"Let me check on my scheduled things. They are all in a

three block radius. I'll be right back. Why don't you wait over there on the bench?"

Buck settled his bulk and watched the children leaving school. He thought they needed some manners and not be so loud. Then he laughed under his breath.

"Seems like I hear my father talking," he said to no one. "I suppose old folks don't like noise."

Billy was gone perhaps twenty minutes before he whistled along his way back to where Uncle Buck sat.

"So, okay, what's up?" Billy sat down with Buck "Are we going fishing?"

"No, I think we will take a hike if you're ready."

"Sure, let's go. I need to be home by five though. Mama will wonder what I'm doing. Usually my chores take half an hour or so besides."

"That ain't a problem, Billy. Let's get along then." Billy had an idea they were going *down river* as Buck always referred to his jaunts.

Weaving in and out of the alders and cottonwoods, they came to a trench like opening into a small cave behind a large boulder. It was obviously the home of some animal – coyote more than likely.

"You sure you want to go in there, Uncle Buck?"

"Its fine, Billy, I share this cave with a couple other varmints. We get on just fine," he chortled to himself.

"Over here, pry out that top rock. It looks like it won't move but it does." Once the rock was out of the earth wall, a box could be seen.

"Just hand it down to me." Billy did as Buck asked.

"Put the rock back, now, because we are leaving and you leave nature the way you find it. Always remember that, son. God put it there, you leave it there."

Buck carried his box up under his arm and steadied it with his left hand. Once back at his cabin, he opened it. Billy could only stare at the contents and wonder about this eighty-plus year old man.

"Uncle Buck, this is a gold mine of history in here." Billy was awed by the flyers, brochures and knick-knack souvenirs of Buck's life.

"I thought you would appreciate this old box." In the left hand corner was an oblong packet wrapped in brown oiled paper that evidently needed special care.

"Take the oil paper packet out, Billy, and hand it over." Billy did as instructed. While Buck unfolded the several layers of stiff paper, Billy eagerly fingered through the contents of the box. Buttons with slogans on them fascinated Billy. His imagination ran wild. There was a timetable for Southern Pacific train once the two lines had changed to one name, accounts of wars, gold strikes, the President being elected, etc.

"I want you to keep the box and contents except for this packet. You can have half and I'll keep the rest." Buck handed over the oil paper once he had removed some paper.

Billy accepted the gift and quickly opened to see, to his utter amazement, a stack of bills. There was money enough to go a long, long way, plus a deed to property in Texas, some bank statements and a marriage license.

"Uncle Buck?" asked Billy in the form of a question as he handed the license across the table.

"Yes, many years ago I had a sweet heart. Her name was Adell, but I called her Addy Bell" just for fun. We met in Texas. As soon as I saw her I said, "Buck, old chap, you will be wed to that raven haired vision." Three months later I was. Two of the happiest years a man ever deserved. We had a baby son; they both died in child birth. I never thought to remarry and never went back to Texas either. That deed is to a parcel of land in Concho. It's yours now, if you want it, along with everything else. This piece of land I'm on now will go to the hospital as an investment.

"I'd rather you kept all this to yourself, Billy; it is private. I have no kin and want to be sure things are in order in my last years."

Billy was a very sensitive young man and had a soft heart. It was all he could do to just listen and not choke up. Finally he reached across the table and offered to shake hands. It was enough; they were both satisfied.

"Now let me tell you about McPherson," Buck settled his girth into a rocker and prepared to start a new tale. "I had a pal by name of Wesley Bergan, a true Scotsman. We traveled the gold country, prairies, cattle trails and took a train trip to California. Best man I ever knew. On a trip back to Kansas, we stopped off at Cow Creek crossing for the night. It was good country. The next day it was on to Lyons and then McPherson. The government was looking for a new person to take over Crossing, Wes said.

"I'm it, Buck, here I'll stay."

"He died at that trading post where Buffalo Bill Mathewson had run. He had an inquisitive mind, too, much like yours. I learned a load along the way. He was full of things a body paid no attention to such as: watch for doves they follow water; in the fall caterpillars tell the winter – brown/black on their backs will be bad – tan/yellow means easy weather; that there's no place in the dessert you can go but within one hundred yards there is a plant useful for eating, medicine or to build a fire; grease wood burns hot, quick and with so little smoke it is next to impossible to detect."

"Uncle Buck, it is past five thirty and Mama will be getting worried. I need to get on home for now. Can we finish about Wesley later?"

Billy gathered the mementoes together and closed the box. "I'll leave it here until tomorrow. I need to figure out what to do with it." Billy frowned, scratched his back with his left hand as he opened the door with his right hand, gave a salute to Buck and left the yard at a trot.

"You O.K., son?" Manter called when he saw Billy on a lope.

"Sure, Pap. "I'm just later than usual and didn't want to worry Mama." Manter was proud of his kind hearted son.

After school on Tuesday, Billy hurried over to Uncle Buck's place to find him gone from home. He waited a while, and then walked across the empty lot to see if Letty needed anything. He carried in wood for her and naturally Chrissy jumped on his back. Billy had let her ride on his shoulders since she was two years old.

"Billy, what brings you over?" Lettie asked.

"Waiting for Uncle Buck. He was telling me about the cattle drives and part of his life."

"Thank you for helping with the wood. I enjoy a fire in the evenings." Letty was making tea, "you want a cup of tea with me? You can see Buck's place across the way."

"That's nice, Letty. Thank you." He took the cup and sipped at it. "Wow – that tea was so weak it needed help out of the cup."

"Do you have any honey, Letty? I like it sweet."

Of course, honey, I didn't think." She got up to fetch the honey jar and staggered. Billy flew out of his chair and grabbed Letty.

"What's wrong?" Billy wondered when Joe would be home.

"I've had such a head cold and it just won't leave. I'm about worn out with it. I just hope Joe and Chrissy don't catch it too," she said wistfully.

Billy thought he would mention it to Millie; she had all sorts of ideas about fixing everything from lice to ingrown toe nails. She would be sure to know a cure for a cold.

Buck had been down at the bank to have a private talk with Adam Insley. He wanted the papers in order. He had not felt well in some time but said not a word. Anything amiss would chalk up to old age and he had lived eighty-eight years. It was near time to leave he reasoned.

Billy saw him walking down the street so waved a quick

salute to Letty and met Buck at the door of his cabin.

"I'm too heavy, Billy, thought I'd better use my legs for transportation." Once inside Buck asked had Billy decided about the box.

"Yes, I have Uncle Buck. I don't have a clue how long this box has been in that cave and I'd have to mark a few trees to wind my way back, but it better stay where it has been. Buck was very pleased to hear that.

"I allowed that might be your wish and I'm satisfied your right in judgment. I had Clair Dent at the law office to get these deeds in order. Here is yours; put it back in the box."

Billy looked it over and noticed that Uncle Buck's name was Roland Buckland. I wonder if anyone in town ever knew that, he pondered.

Halloween was over and Thanksgiving the next week. That meant tests at school. Mr. Foster had loaned Billy books to study which he nearly devoured. One day he would get a chance at travel he hoped. He was not at all interested in the hardware business, newspapers or dry goods. He did like watching the masons build these big buildings that now dominated Salina, especially the new railroad depot.

Usually several families from the wagon train who had stayed close friends, tried to get together for Thanksgiving but held Christmas for their own families. This year there were several new faces; a few babies, a couple of newly wed couples, and the regular friends. Matt and Daylene were now married four years. Willa and Hard Knocks had a baby on the way. Rand and Reva who had recently purchased a new home just one block from Sunnyside Elementary, the school where she was teaching. Bert and Nola Nutt were asked to join in, as they had no family in Kansas; and so were Nolan Shank and his new girl friend.

Boots and Starkey were out of town on one of their excursions that no one ever seemed to know about, so Sally Blake was also invited. Even she did not know where brother

Starkey got off to for weeks at a time. Beulah, Roscoe and Sylvia Lee had stayed home as they all had colds and did no wish to infect others.

It was a hard winter that came along in 1880. Some things you can't anticipate and no amount of preparation gets you really prepared.

Christmas looked bleak. It seemed influenza had attacked half the population. Doctors' offices were standing room only, the hospital was full to capacity, the business's were not expected to reach there goals financially and Mason Philpot had ordered twenty extra coffins to be shipped in from St. Louis.

On the twelfth of December frail little Letty Sprow succumbed to the flu resulting in the total collapse of Joe. The funeral was on a day the worst blizzard in history struck the area. Section hands had to even dig the locomotives out. Mason had always depended on Joe to help with preparations when there was an overload of funerals, but this was out of the question.

Millie took little Chrissy home with her as Joe didn't seem to even know who she was. His mind sort of went with Letty's passing. On Letty's head stone, which arrived a month later, it read:

Letisha Susan Sprow
1844 - 1880
Wait my love, I'll soon be there
Loving wife of Joseph Hardin Sprow
Mother of daughter Merry Christine Sprow
Our angel has departed

No dry eye left the church and no one really knew what to do to help Joe. He was the walking dead. Chrissy seemed to realize one day and not the next. At seven, reality does not set in rapidly.

Manter and Billy were kept busy at Joe's place, the store, the school and chores for others ill with the flu. Boots and Starkey were pressed into service at the drug store and the post office because of help unable to work at the time. Matt worried about Daylene at school with so many runny noses and sneezing, coughing colds. Sally Blake closed her needle shop when she started feeling poorly, much to the relief of Starkey who was always overly protective of his sister.

Levi Guthrey's little band members were singled out for special funeral services. A violin solo here, trumpet there, Millie played the piano until she too realized she needed bed rest from caring for so many others.

Beulah took Chrissy and Sybil home when Millie did not rally from the flu. Roscoe for once was nearly stroke dumb at the thought of *his* family getting sick. He had always been such a bluster of a man and tried to make up with false pride what no self esteem seemed to fit. His attitude became quite different and offered to do chores for the other farmers near his place.

Billy hadn't seen Buck for nearly a week as he had his hands full at home. Manter told Billy it might be a good idea to go by the cabin and check on Buck. Buck died that night and Billy wept hard, hot tears for his friend and benefactor. He asked Booth Gordon to say a few words at Buck's service. Millie was too ill to attend but helped Billy with a short prayer and speech to convey his thoughts. It was the hardest thing he had ever had to do but he bit his lip and honored Uncle Buck in his own way.

Booth said, "Billy you should think on the ministry, son, you have a way to touch people's hearts."

"No way, Rev. Gordon, I could never deliver funerals. I loved Uncle Buck and it nearly tore me apart. I could maybe do for a stranger, but not people I know."

Christmas had been very grim indeed and by the fifteenth of January there had been over thirty funerals. Millie went into decline and passed away on the twentieth of January. Manter said his world had shut him out and showed no interest in his children. Sybil came home so she and Billy could look after Manter, but in February she too lost her battle with influenza. Billy was devastated. He felt like Papa – the world shut the door on life itself.

Mitchell Hayes said the obituaries took up half a page at least once a week as the influenza continued to run rampart. Claire Dent was run ragged with death certificates, last will and testaments, all other death related paperwork. He felt like the walking dead himself.

Willa Knox was due any time and Hard Knocks was in a state of anxiety beyond his own comprehension. This was a dreadful set of conditions for a vulnerable, pregnant wife and to bring a newborn into the world. He was tempted to take Willa to McPherson to the hospital; anywhere but in this infected city.

Daylene and Matt had no children and had taken Chrissy home with them. Joe didn't seem to realize Chrissy was even gone from the house. In fact, he never fully recovered his good mind. Chrissy remained with the Kimball's until she was legally adopted by the Nutt's.

Chapter 10

Disasters bring forth some wonderful things in people. By spring quite a few of the trail hands going up north had come east to Salina to have a look. It was now considered a metropolitan city and boosted quite an offering of cultural events, political interest and excessive sized modern buildings. Cole Fetters was a railroad tycoon who had settled in Salina and built a castle of a home compared to most people. He had married Juanita Westinghouse, daughter of the wealthy Westinghouse magnet. She soon introduced a higher principled and intellectual culture to the society minded. She founded many organizations, added another wing to the hospital, was the driving force to establish a college in Salina, and was loved by all.

There was a new nursing home in town for elderly or convalescing persons. Billy approached the lady in charge and explained the circumstances at home. He wanted to know if she would give Boots a home as the *resident cat*. She could help people with her love and patience, as well as keep out the mice. The woman was so impressed with the idea that she agreed. Boots was dually enthroned to be the ruler of the home. If there were kittens, Billy would not be the dispenser thereof. He hated to part with them anyway.

Blue had weaned her last set of four pups which meant four more homes *someplace*. She had supplied the town as it was. Most were cute but of very dubious ancestry to be sure.

One lady stopped him on the street to say how very sad she was about his family and added, "That pup Robert brought home may be man's best friend with a heart of gold, but the great lumux could wear a saddle and is kind to me. He seems over much interested in my welfare and trying to help me start a fertilizer business. His contributions to date are really quite impressively enormous. He is going to the pound as soon as I find one."

Billy nearly choked to keep from laughing as the indignant woman marched on down the sidewalk. His sides ached from holding his gut in.

Blue was now eight years old and a wonderful pet, pal, companion and mother. Such a happy old girl – patient and loyal. In these past months she had been a great comfort. Manter had taken Joe in to live with him and Billy. Joe sold his place and became a recluse. He led a solitary life, a bother to know one. Manter stayed busy and worked hard to interest Joe in things. Life was difficult just now for many people in town.

Blue followed Billy around now that both Sybil and Millie were gone. Neither Manter nor Joe really paid much attention to her. While helping in a grocery as part time clerk, handy man, deliver boy or what ever else, a trail hand who came in for some supplies, asked about a hardware store and wanted to know who that Blue Tic hound belonged to.

Her name is Blue, she is eight years old and I raised her from a pup. She came across on the wagon train and the best darn dog this side of Pennsylvania. Billy was so pleased someone was interested in his faithful dog.

"I have a Blue Tic myself," the drover said, "he is called *DOG* but he thinks it is spelled **G-O-D**. I'd part with a hand before I'd part with that dog. He is with me now, he walked all the way beside me and the horse – come up from Texas.

Matter of fact, that dog has walked or run close to 5000 miles with us on the cattle drives.

Cattle drive, ahhhh – there was a topic to prick up Billy's ears.

"You gonna be here long, that is, here in Salina?" Billy was excited to talk further with this man.

"Why?"

"Because I would surely like to hear about those trips you took, that the dog went on."

"Hadn't planned to really. Another buddy of mine is around town someplace. I guess it wouldn't matter much; we got us three weeks to wait on the herd coming up. Well, let me see."

"You live around here?" By the way, my name is Andy Jackson Cox – go by Ajax or A-Jax Whatever – it sounds the same. No one calls me Andy since Ma died; don't recall my Pa.

Sure, I'm Billy Good. My father owns the hardware store and is superintendent of schools. We live over on Maine St., *Maine* not *Main*. Our streets are named after states, cities or presidents."

"I guess you know we are just getting over a terrible flue epidemic. Once an outbreak took hold, we had been plagued with it for five months. Still some mighty sick folks yet. Joe Sprow lost his wife and his wits. Papa took him in and the Nutt family is going to adopt Chrissy if they can."

Rand and hard Knocks had just gotten back to town and were headed for the livery stable when they spotted Blue.

"Hey, Billy," Rand shouted into the store. Do you know yer dog done get her a boy friend." He he, ha, ha!"

Ajax poked his head out the door; he knew that voice but also wanted to see if it was his dog they were joking about.

"Well I'll just be damned! Rand Blackwell, you old son-of-a-gun, how the hell are you?" The two men slapped each other around a bit in good horse play.

"What brings you here to our neck of the woods?"

"A few weeks off and we heard Salina had really shaped up. Thought I'd have a look see."

"Well, I'll be dammed all over again. Is that 'ole Hard Knocks coming along? Well it sure as fire is him – how about that. You two still pullin' rope or settled in?"

Fritz Knox and Rand Blackwell had been trail hands together for a short time with Ajax when he was a trail boss. It was a good time for them even with dreadful sand storms, no water, cattle stampedes and all.

"Well sir, Ajax, I aim to hit the trail again if I get the go ahead," this from Rand.

"Who's go ahead I'd like to know?" Ajax said with surprise.

"You recall the cute black haired librarian in Indiana that I was fired up over. Her name is Reva *Blackwell* and she teaches school. We have a right nice home and I'll tell you it is a blessing to have a good wife – the bad ones are plentiful enough."

"I'm damned all over again," Ajax was just about speechless. He looked over at Knocks. "And?" he put a question into that one word.

"Oh yes, seems it slipped my mind to tell you. I went back to get Willa. It took three weeks of begging to persuade her, but I didn't know what else to do but plead my case. I knew I wouldn't leave without her. She is a fine woman, Ajax, and our baby is due in three weeks. No worry there, she is healthy as a horse and the most organized human I ever knew."

"Where you stayin' – hotel?" Fritz asked.

"Yep, I brought a youngster in with me. He is about somewhere – drug store no doubt. I can't fill that kid up on ice cream."

Hollis had stopped by to talk to Billy so Billy introduced him to Ajax. The men said Hollis was a good head and smart. If he wasn't, he would be on the trail with the rest of us old timers. Both Rand and Knocks were in their thirty's and had lived a life time.

Rand said he would go see if Reva had an extra spud for the pot and told Ajax to round up the sprout and come on over.

"Billy can direct you. I better run, she doesn't even know I'm back in town yet."

The "sprout" turned out to be seventeen year old Clement Gabriel, a Mexican boy whom Ajax had taken under his wing.

"C'mer, Gabby," he bellowed at Clem who was coming down the street. "Want ya to meet some real trail fellows. So where ya been?"

"Over to the drug store. You ought to know it by now."

"I reckoned as much. Ya got room left for a plate of spuds or maybe a steak or two or three" I never did see a sapling that could hold as much grub." Ajax grinned, slapped Clem on the shoulder and looked the boy up and down.

"You do seem a few pounds to the good," looking from Billy and his best friend, Hollis, to his ramrod pals. Ajax shook his head slowly.

"Not enough room at the table where he came from so I thought he better eat with us. There are always chores for earning a bed and grub. Besides that I never expect kids of my own so now I got me one." Ajax flung an arm over Clem's shoulder.

"C'mon, let's find that fine home Rand is so proud of."

With that Hollis said, "See you later, Bill," as he started home. The four others were off to Maine Street.

Billy hurried on home to help his father get their supper going. There were no more animals inside the city now; of course hadn't been for several years. Manter had their hog butchered; they ate the chickens and rabbits, but still maintained a good size garden. It was doubtful there would be one this year since Millie was gone. Manter, Joe or Billy knew very much except weeding and radishes.

"Papa, I met some people today I want to tell you about." Billy cleared off the table and sat down with his father.

"Did you know Rand and Knocks used to be on a cattle drive ten, twelve years ago?" He was so excited he ran his words together.

"Yes son, so were Nolan and Starkey. Not all on the same trail, but all came out of Texan down Pecos County. Who is in town that has your attention?" Manter asked quite interested in who Billy's associates were. Billy was a fine, decent lad and Manter intended to see to it that things stayed that way.

"A man by name of Andy Cox came in the grocery and asked about the hardware store. We were talking; he asked about Blue, said he had a dog named Dog." Billy stopped to laugh. "Said Dog was spelled God. Anyway, along come Rand and Knocks. Seems they all knew each other. You never saw grown men stomp about, slap each other, shake hands and hoot and holler like they did for five minutes or more. I t made me happy just to see how happy they were."

"Next thing I knew Hollis came along; then Rand said Blue had a boyfriend so I stepped out to see what that meant. By gosh, Papa, there was a Blue Tic setting along side Blue."

"Slow down, Billy, you're nearly stammering. We have the rest of forever to get your story out." Manter took out his pipe and Prince Albert tin, "O.K., now back to - - Ajax, was it?"

"Ajax has a Mexican boy with him, a couple years older than me, he claims for a son he never had. His name is Clem Gabriel; they are over at Rand and Reva's. You want to walk over and meet 'em, Papa?" Billy was already on his feet.

"Another time, son." Manter said. "I believe I'll just read a while." Billy knew that was not true. His father would sit there and grieve over this mother and sister.

"No, Papa, come on, it is pretty cool – you better get a coat or jacket." Billy said while handing the coat to his father.

"It looks like I'm going out, Joe. Be back soon." The two started down the porch steps when Joe came to the door.

"Believe I'll come along," he said. That was the first interest Joe had shown in anything since Letty passed away in December.

"Why Joe, we would surely like that." Manter stopped until Joe caught up. The three walked the four blocks to the west end of Maine where Rand had built his house. It was indeed a fine house as he had proudly told Ajax. It was red brick with colored glass window in the oak front door, white columns on each side and white shutters at the windows. "A home befitting a wife like his Reva," as he said with pride.

When Manter looked at that door it usually reminded him of Carey Flinn who died in the fire. Carey had taken the broken glass he was responsible for and fitted it together to make a window in the front door of Grady Miller's house. It made him laugh even now at the expression on Carey's face when he saw the hatchet in Grady's hand. Carey was nearly sober in a very few minutes. Then he told anyone who would listen that Daylene tried to drown him in coffee strong enough to follow him out the door.

It made Manter chuckle to himself as he walked up on Rand's porch. In answer to his knock, Rand said, "Well hello to all and come right in." Reva came from the kitchen all smiles.

"Manter," she extended her right hand, "and Joe." "Oh Joe, it is so good to see you, too." Joe shook hands and followed the others into the sitting room. Introductions were made, and then Billy sat over by Clem and started up his thousand or so questions. The men reminisced, Reva went to make coffee, and Joe just listened.

After a while Joe said, "I think I'll go take a walk. I'll see you later on." With that he took his cap and coat from the hall tree and said goodbye.

"Papa, it is nearly eleven o'clock. We better get on back don't you think?" Billy hadn't seen this much interest in any thing since Millie died. It was only two months ago, but it seemed like forever to Billy.

"Yes, son, I believe all of us need to let Rand and Reva have their home to themselves. We have rattled on for nearly three hours." Manter and Billy gathered their coats and caps and bid the others goodnight. Ajax, Clem and Knocks followed them out the door.

"It was nice meeting you," Manter said while he shook hands with Ajax and Clem. "See you around fellows," Billy called as they started home.

"Papa, do you think Joe is alright?" Billy was thinking of how abruptly Joe had left.

"I'm not sure, Billy, but I didn't want to ask him either. Joe has his private ways and we need to respect that. Joe is a very refined man, just quiet." Since each had their own rooms it was only a few minutes until lights were out at the Good house.

Next morning Manter tapped on Joe's door to come eat with them. He had made pancakes and eggs. Billy was in the washroom and called out.

"Papa, I'll get him up in just a minute – O.K.?"

"Come on, Joe; let's eat so Papa and I can get started today." There was no answer. Manter decided to go get him up.

"Joe? Joe?" Manter opened the door but Joe was gone. It didn't seem like he had been there at all. No dirty clothes on the chest from the day before, his towel was dry and the bed made up nice and neat.

Now what do you make of that Manter said to himself.

"Billy, did you hear Joe up ahead of us?"

"No, I didn't and Blue would have made a move off the bed if she heard the door."

"Well, eat up while it's hot and we will just wait for him to show up, he doesn't go much any place except to the cemetery or over to stare at his old house. He won't be gone long."

By noon no one had seen Joe although both Billy and Manter had asked several people.

Manter was sweeping the walk in front of the hardware store when he saw Mason Philpot hurrying toward him calling out.

"Manter! Manter! Hold up a bit." Mason was in a very agitated state and seemed very upset.

"What is it, Mason?" Manter walked down to meet Mason hustling along toward him.

"Oh, Manter, come get Whitey and find someone to get the hearse. I need to go get the coroner down to the court house.

"I needed to check the Hennessey's grave stone to see if it had been cut yet and found Joe dead lying on Letty's grave. Lord, man, what a thing to see. Thank God I was alone! Lets get him out of there before some one else comes along. Poor Joe – I guess his heart just gave out, but I'm sure he is much happier than here."

Manter was already on the way to get the hearse and Billy to go to the cemetery. They stopped by the Sheriff's office to tell Whitey Cobb what had happened. He too went with Manter, but told Billy to go back to the jail and grab a blanket.

Once everyone was collected, Whitey and Manter rolled Joe in the blanket, put his body in the hearse and waited for the coroner. Mason had gone back to the mortuary after getting the coroner on his way. This was a very sad day indeed. When Mason needed extra help, Joe was there. He and Letty had lived with him for a time while their small house was under construction. It seemed sorrow was all he ever saw.

Manter came with the hearse and helped Whitey with Joe's body. Mason directed where to put it and Billy just disappeared. He wondered who would leave his world next. In such a short time he had lost his mother, sister, Buck, Letty ad Joe. Carey wasn't a close friend, but Billy knew him never the less. Several older people he had made deliveries to, four of his school friends – most had succumbed to the flu.

Billy walked around awhile, and then went to find Grady.

"You home, Grady?" Billy knocked on the door.

"Yeh, that you, Billy? Come on in; I'm in the kitchen." Billy walked in and sat down at the table.

"Hey, buddy, why the forlorn face?" Grady pulled the other chair over and straddled it. Laying his arms on the back of the chair, he leaned forward and waited for some problem.

"Grady, Joe died. He was at Letty's grave when Mason found him." Billy told Grady about Ajax and the evening at Rand's; Joe not there in the morning and all the rest. It just poured out of him and so did the tears of grief for everyone gone.

"I'm so sorry, buddy. It has been a rough time. You're growing up too fast." In order to change the subject Grady tried some humor.

"You want a beer?" he asked with a sober face. After a stunned silence Billy's head snapped up.

"A beer?" "A beer?" Grady, Papa would have a stroke. Grady hid a broad smile when he lowered his head down on his folded arms.

"Guess that was a *no* for an answer." Grady stood and ruffed up Billy's hair.

"Get your cap on your pointed head; let's go fishing for a while." "What do you say, O.K.?"

Billy was glad enough to do most anything than go home. He hadn't even realized it was Friday, a school day.

Joe's funeral was Sunday, a windy spring day so a great many attended. Willa and Knocks were not among the mourners, but it wasn't expected of Willa at this stage of her pregnancy. As people separated to their own interest, Manter saw Fritz hailing him and the Kimball's.

Rand threw his hand up in the air in a greeting to his friend. "Yo. What's the hurry?" Rand had an idea he knew well enough but did not want to spoil it.

"I have a *son*! Willa had a boy, a *big* boy! Doc said ten pounds and perfect. My head just about didn't clear the door," he grinned. "Beulah was with Willa. She showed me out of the room, said she had to scrape me off the ceiling. She is big enough to pitch me out so here I am." Fritz couldn't stop laughing.

"A boy! How about that, eh?" Manter smacked Rand on the back and pumped his hand till Rand jerked it away.

"Where you guys been all dressed up?" realizing it as soon as spoken, he sobered his expressions and said, "I'd plum forgotten about the funeral." Fritz shook his head slowly like it was a thought he wished had not happened.

Rand asked, "O.K., so what's the new *master's* name?"

"Willa said 'Hamilton' after her father. I said not in my life time. No kid of mine was gonna be called HAM – sounds like part of a hog. We settled on 'Spencer' - that sounds manly, so the name is Spencer Leland Knox. How is that for a title to live with your life long?"

"Pretty uppity, don't you think?" this from Billy who wasn't used to fancy names. But I guess he will be called Spence – that's O.K." Billy was so serious the men exchanged wise glances and said, "You're probably right."

Boots and Starkey had attended the funeral, too. They were just catching up to the others when Fritz started his baby story all over again.

When Booth Gordon came along and learned of new *Master Spencer*, he remarked solemnly, "The Lord giveth and the Lord taketh away." One gone and a new one to start again. Yes, sir, it is a great process God set into motion. Congratulations, Fritz, give my best to Willa. I'm sure Miss Nora Ellen will be along yet today.

Reva remarked that those baby cloths Willa bought in August wouldn't last three weeks.

"That Spencer needs one year size right now. He surely had a start in this world," she said. "Now, can I hold him? Seems it is always someone else's baby I get to hold and I'll not be blessed."

The announcement of Joe's funeral was in Monday's paper along side the page that said a bouncing, ten pound son,

Spencer Leland Knox, was born to Willa Bender Knox and Fritz Knox - better known as Hard Knox to the general public. That was good for a laugh several weeks later even. Rand said even he hardly remembered Knocks given name.

After school Billy beat a path to the drug store hoping to see Clem. No, he wasn't there - maybe the hotel. Ajax and Clem were getting ready to start for the livery stable. Their bed rolls and supplies were stacked by the porch steps. Billy helped carry things down to the barn and get the horses ready. He hated to see them leave.

"Where do you think you'll be tonight?" he asked.

"We hope to be in Ellsworth area, or what is called Ft. Harker, day after tomorrow. It will take about twelve days to reach the trail going back to Texas. There is a herd going up into Montana and Nebraska now. We want to be on the next one going up. Or, we might join in one going up at the time we arrive there."

The last trip on the Trail was in 1875. It had been active from Texas to Abilene from 1867 and more than 100,000 cattle had come over that trail. Just imagine the stories that will be written about those days.

Billy was glued to the speakers. He was getting a notion to go along no matter what obstacles came into view, mainly from Manter. He had a good horse, health and was nearly finished with school. The itch to go was strong.

There was a long conversation in the Good home that night. Plans were set in motion and Manter went with Billy to talk to Ajax.

"No, Mr. Good, not at this time. We will be back through next spring and we can take Billy North with us, provided he still wants to go."

Billy was heart broken, but also saw the logic. He had talked Ajax into waiting one more day so he could convince his father. However, Ajax took that same time to think it through. He figured it was too quick a decision and it would be best to let it go a year.

School was out in May. Roscoe Peabody needed help on his farm, and since Manter was a fair hand at carpentry and had taught Billy, they volunteered to help him get his fences up. They went to Starkey who handled the barbed wire, bought what they hoped would be enough and tackled a mean job. It took all three of them a month to set the posts and string the fence, then put the barbed wire on the top like a separate row.

Cuts, scratches, infection in some places, rain and mud did not make for an easy job but it was finished. Billy swore he would not be volunteered for anymore such jobs. He did get over to see Chrissy quite often. He really missed Sybil and her ways. Sylvia Lee had been deathly ill also, but she came through it. The flu had left her weak for months. Billy wanted to leave this place and dreamed of the trail. It would be a long year!

The next big surprise in his life was Blue. About nine weeks after Clem and Ajax had headed West, Blue had six pups – *all* Blue Tic. He smiled at the little ones and told Blue, "So – you really did have a beau. Just you wait till Ajax gets back to see his grandpups." Billy laughed in glee at his own joke about grandpups. "Guess I am too and neither of us our married. That could be news for Hays," he said to nobody but the dog.

CHAPTER 11

Billy received a letter the next February telling him Ajax was in Texas. He would be in Dodge April 1st, and catch the train from Dodge to McPherson. He told Billy to meet him there on the 4th of April and to bring a horse.

From February to April seemed to drag on forever. The winter seemed endless and so dry the snow snapped when you walked on it. Construction continued regardless of the weather. The new music hall and theater were thriving thanks to the never ending push from Cole Fetter's wife, Juanita, a socialite from Philadelphia. They were wealthy, but invested heavily in the city's progress.

There were now four hotels and two newspapers. The railroad companies had advertizing on any available space and were thriving beyond anything ever considered. It was surprising how quickly things changed. Billy felt he had witnessed history already and was only sixteen. This letter from Ajax was like a birthday present to him.

On April 1st Manter and he were getting things together for Billy's trip down to McPherson. There a train *to* McPherson from Salina, so why the horse trip he didn't understand. It was a day and a half by horse and a half a day by rail. Nevertheless, on the morning of April 3, Billy left on his horse with another in tow. He rode directly to the railroad station to wait for Ajax to come through. To his surprise, Ajax was waiting for him. Beside him on the station floor was the best looking saddle he had ever seen – strong and with embossed leather and silver inlay.

"Howdy 'ole Billy, my lad," waved Ajax as Billy rode up to the station platform. "You been on the road all day?"

"No, I broke the trip down to about sixteen miles a day. Twenty miles is a decent ride, but why hurry. Actually, it was fun. Where you staying?"

"Got a room at the Overland. Come on and clean up. Take the horses to the horse barn on the way." They walked off with the saddle thrown over the spare horse.

"You keep those saddles in our room," Ajax instructed as he headed toward the horse barn.

"Why not leave them now so we don't need to carry them back?" Billy wondered.

"We can do that," Ajax winked at Billy, "smart kid." Saddles stashed, horses in the stalls, the two went back to the Overland to clean up.

"You ready for a plate?" Ajax thought all sixteen year olds must be starving. He related age to Clem who, he surmised, could out eat an elephant.

"I could surely do that, Ajax." "Riding makes you hungry when you didn't even know you were."

On the morning of the fifth of April, Ajax and Billy left McPherson for Salina. Billy had the new saddle that had been his birthday gift from Ajax. No matter the birthday was February. They each had a pack of food stuff and clean cloths. That was all. They would stay at a way station that night as Billy had done on the trip down. They had water canteens and that was enough.

April 6th, late evening, they arrived in Salina and went to the Good home. Seven yapping dogs saw them walking up from the livery stable and Ajax stumbled in his tracks.

"Who has all them yelping dogs?" "I'd put a stop to that if I lived nearby."

"Oh, you will see soon enough," Billy smiled to himself as they stepped up over the curb and Blue bounced into view. On the other side of the fence were six half grown pup's – nearly a year old already.

Ajax was absolutely shocked and pleased as if he had done the deed himself.

"Just looky there – oh, Ha, Ha, Ha, He, Hee, Hee, he screeched trying to pat all of them at once. "Why did you keep so many?"

"I thought you would want to pick one or two. They aren't any trouble except Papa said he would go to the poor house in another month," Billy chuckled.

"I'll be dang'd, just look at these guys! Boy, how we gonna get these dogs to Texas, you got any suggestions?"

"If we are going to ride, they can walk." Billy didn't really mean it, but he thought it sounded like grown-up talk.

"Well, yeh, I s'pose; be one rip roaring time through the buffalo territory though. Not so smart."

"I'm *not* leaving Blue here, Ajax. It is not going to happen, buffalo or not," he was firm on that point.

"Let's talk about it in the morning, Billy. I think some fried potatoes, bacon and eggs are due. I know its supper time, but it's easy to fix. My belly can't tell time, it just knows when it needs grub."

Manter wasn't home; that was odd. Billy went to clean up leaving Ajax with his *grandpups*. He laughed right out loud at his own idea of grandpups. They were just ready to eat when Manter walked in the back door.

"You're a sight for sore eyes, you two are. How was the trip, Billy?" his father asked.

"O.K., Papa – I guess I'm practicing for the trail. Wait until you see the new saddle Ajax bought for my birthday. Here, sit down and eat with us." Billy pulled out a chair with one hand

and reached for a plate with the other.

"No, no thanks, I been to Nola's to see Chrissy and stayed for supper – fried chicken and the works. Looks like you got just the egg," he grinned.

It was about nine when they called it a day, and glad for it. The next day the three of them hashed over the dog problem. Manter suggested leaving the dogs. He could find them homes. Billy wanted to ship them to Dodge on the train in a cattle car down to Clem, and they would collect them when they got there.

Ajax said, "Take Blue, leave the pup's except one; we could handle one – hopefully.'

"You know we can get more pups in Texas, Billy."

Billy was bewildered, "Where?"

"Why the same way you got these, don't be a dummy." Ajax looked exasperated. Billy wasn't slow, he just hadn't thought of DOG in Texas and Blue in Kansas. Once it dawned on him he remembered something Booth had said in church one Sunday: "God looks after fools and children." Right now he felt eligible for both categories.

"Yes, well I guess pups are born wherever there are dogs, right?" he grinned in embarrassment, shuffled his feet on the floor, pushed his chair back out of the way and started for the door. The pups had started up such a clamor you couldn't hear yourself think.

Manter decided today was a very good day to find homes for those dogs.

Ajax, Billy, Blue and *Here* got under way on the 10th of April, 1881.

"Billy you better get some tight pants – you will slip around on the saddle – be a mighty sore ride"

"Guess I'd better put on two pair then 'cause I don't have tight pants."

"We will fix that tomorrow when we get to Ellsworth." The day was nearly perfect, neither hot nor cold, just a cool breeze.

Billy sat silently going over his farewell to Manter. Leaving his father tugged at his heart with a sense of guilt; his mother had wanted him to go to Leavenworth to further his schooling. Then there was his best friend Hollis - but the excitement won out. He thought of the day ahead and was satisfied with his decision.

Blue and Here stayed pretty close with them. The old dog nipped at the pup when she had enough of the nonsense.

"Ajax, why did you name your pup Here? It sure is odd."

"Just easy; don't need to think of a name. Besides, every time I patted my leg to feed him or get his attention, I'd say *come here*. Once I said 'here' in a conversation with your Pa and here came the pup. He was used to hearing that. So I just say *HERE!*"

"That was easy." Billy thought it was short cut language; it made him laugh.

By noon Ajax figured they had covered about half of the thirteen miles, or half of the half of 30 miles. If they didn't press it, fifteen miles a day was not a bad pace. It was easy going because they could nearly follow the new Union Pacific tracks.

"You ready to stretch your legs some?" Ajax asked.

"I would dearly appreciate it and using *my* legs for transportation a while would be a relief from this *pants* business, too."

Ajax coughed over a smile he couldn't help and agreed, "It was possibly uncomfortable, but better than blisters."

After a sandwich and coffee Daylene had forced on them, they headed west.

"I'm beholden to Matt's wife for the thoughtfulness, the grub was fine. We need to send her back some trinket or favor of sorts." Ajax had no wife, no sister, no parents and was wed to DOG and the men on the trail, most of whom had been ranch hands with him for ten years. They were a close family of friends.

He missed Rand and Hard Knocks, to save his life he could not get it in his head to call Knocks, Fritz, like the Salina people did.

Both men had rather hinted they just might consider the tail north from Dodge on, if they could persuade Willa and Reva that it would be profitable. Willa said the profit would be him out from under foot as he was so clumsy with the baby. She wondered if he had been born inept and clumsy. On the other hand, it seemed a fine excuse to not do some things and could be a clever cover-up. Now *that* was quite possible!

"I never been to Ellsworth. Is it as big as Salina?"

"No, not yet, but growing. I was surprised at Salina; it was ten times the size I recalled. Nearly thought I'd got to the wrong place."

"Where we gonna be tonight?"

"A little place called Brookville. It started out like a fort or shelter because of the Indian wars. There was a big stir-up in 1867; then, like any place, it got down to business with the railroad and all. In 1876 they built a hotel, no where else for fifty miles for supplies and such."

"If they have tight pants there, I think it a good idea to invest in several." Billy was uncomfortable with the present arrangement.

"You do, huh?" Thought you would get the drift soon." There was a dry goods store next to the hotel and a restaurant next to that. Ajax suggested they eat in the restaurant as it was cheaper than the hotel and you didn't feel out of place if you had been riding a while.

"It seems good to see that town ahead," Billy remarked and stretched his back and arms.

"Be there in half an hour," Ajax said.

"Half an hour?" he couldn't believe *that*. "Why it's just a piece now, what you got in mind?"

"Billy, my boy, you got a lot to learn on a trail. When you see things at a distance, it's a lot farther than you think."

"Must be," Billy said with little enthusiasm."

"Once on a trail from El Paso on my first time out I thought we were in land God had forgotten was there. Finally we saw water reflections and I expected the cattle to bolt. Even they had better sense. It took us an entire day to get there. You see mirages."

"A mirage?"

Yes, it's an optical illusion. Some times it seems water is suspended in air. Sometimes its heat waves coming up off hot sand and you could swear it was shimmering water."

"You're right, I've got a lot to learn, but I enjoy learning, too. Mr. Foster always lent me books - especially history books."

"You are going to see history made in your life time, Billy. I hope you register it in your mind."

"I do better than that. Mama started me on a journal several years ago. I'm glad she did."

Coming into Brookville was a surprise to Billy. It was as modern as Salina, but about four blocks long. He had expected things to look prehistoric by comparison. He laughed to himself and was powerful glad he hadn't expressed his thoughts.

The horses were left by the water trough, dogs tied to the hitching post and the men dipped water out for the dogs into tin pans they brought for dog supplies. Once they secured lodging, the horses were taken to the horse barn, dogs and Billy went to their rooms in spite of glowering looks from the desk clerk. Ajax went to see about Levi pants for Billy and to check on the menu next door.

"Hey you," Ajax slapped Billy with his hat. "C'mon, we got to get you dressed proper."

Billy groaned a bit; he had not realized he had fallen asleep in the chair.

"Man, it's a long ride."

Ajax nearly doubled over laughing. He was used to the saddle – Billy better be soon.

"You wanted to go on the trail?" Man, oh man, are you

in for an awakening. By the time we reach Dodge you will either take the train home, be dead, or have aged ten years," he chortled and laughed till Billy felt like he was being made fun of.

"You think so, do you? Well, I have my own ideas even with sore legs and butt. Let's go get whatever you think I need."

At the dry goods, they picked out two flannel shirts, four pair of gloves; two leather, two heavy work gloves, three pair jeans once they had the right size and a regular cowboy hat, as Billy called it (one with wide brim for shelter from the sun and run off from the rain). He had his own hat but Ajax said it was a city hat, no good for prairie travel.

Ajax started to pay for it but Billy stepped up and shook his head as he reached for his own money. A startled look settled on Ajax's face, but he stepped aside.

On the walk over to the restaurant Ajax told him, "Billy, you better go easy on the money. Did Manter fit you out?"

"No, I have my own. I'm not beholden to anyone." He thought long and hard before he finally told Ajax about Buck and the box he carried in the bed roll. Billy had left much of its contents in Salina. If he never saw them again it would be a shame, yet things precious to old Buck in his time did not seem so important to a sixteen year old.

"Did you make arrangements for your life or things in Salina before you left, Billy?"

"Yes, Papa and I talked to Claire Dent one afternoon. He is a lawyer and Papa's friend. If anything happens to Papa and I'm gone, Claire will attend to it. He and Papa will fix things up."

Ajax was proud of this young man, he showed common sense. You needed that along with sharp wits on a trail. Often you didn't have much time to consider a situation or figure things out. You went by instinct.

After a good meal, bath, and rearranging his bed roll to accommodate the new purchases Billy was very willing to call it a day. By eight thirty he was out like a light. Ajax decided to go get a beer.

Morning came early. The dogs were taken out by dawn to run a little and tend to their needs. They collected the horses, which had already been fed, and were on their way. They reached Ellsworth before dark and the evening was a repeat of the day before. The dogs were worn out; they flopped down where they ate.

"You gonna make it, Bud?" Ajax kept an eye on his charge.

"O.K., so I'm green as new hay, but even a mustang has to be broken. The dog's feet are getting sore; they aren't used to this rough land." They had hardly been out of the yard except on hunting trips.

"Can we take them up now and then?"

"You bet. They will get used to it in a few days – so will you." Ajax reached over to pat Billy's shoulder.

In the morning after breakfast, Ajax explained the next forty miles would be rough. So far they had pretty much followed the Union Pacific tracks for guidance as well as distance. However, starting today they had a cross country trip of about three or more days of flat, undeveloped land with little of anything. They needed to fill up water containers and food for the dogs. They would go as far as Holyroad today, stay over and head for an area about five miles east of the Bend where they would pick up the old Santa Fe Trail and follow it on to Dodge City. About twenty miles west of Dodge they would meet up with the rest of the trail hands and herd.

"By the time we hit Dodge you will be broke-in or ready to throw in the rope. We will see! Billy, you have hung in there better than I ever expected," Ajax was favorable impressed.

The Santa Fe Trail was no longer in use on a steady schedule. It was just a normal route for whoever chooses to travel it now. It had been in use from 1867 to 1875 so was well defined and no trouble at all. You could make good distance in a day and ample stops for most anything along the route.

There were nine buildings beside the fort at Fort Larned. The Fort had been established in 1859 due to Indian raids and wars, to protect wagon trains and to escort mail coaches. In 1860 it had also been an agency of the Indian Bureau. All this Ajax explained as they rode along.

"What Mr. Foster wouldn't give to hear all this." Billy told Ajax. "I'll get you to go over it again so I can write it back to Salina. Mr. Foster was my favorite teacher," he explained.

When Billy arrived at Dodge he learned a great deal more than he wanted to know. The Fort was to be abandoned in another few months. It had been built on ground that at one time was a camping ground for wagon trains, now used for a supply depot. The first buildings were made of either sod or adobe and many remained.

The first day Billy and Ajax were at Fort Dodge Ajax was anxious to learn of his trail hands, where the cattle drive was located by now, and to get updated on events. It had been a month since he left Dodge for Salina and some two hundred and thirty miles on the horses. All, including the dogs, were tired.

He learned the cattle were about thirty miles south which gave them a good three days to reconnoiter, rest up, and see for sure what Billy was *going* to do, not just what he *wanted* to do. It would be a serious decision so he needed to be sure.

CHAPTER 12

Daylight came about 5AM, but when Ajax rousted Billy from his bed, Billy looked out through the window and in a surprised voice he called, "Hey, what is the matter, it looks like smoke everywhere?"

"No smoke, but I hope you do not need to get too use to this very long. It's a dust storm. Kansas is nearly famous for dust storms and it can get down to business once it starts. I've seen animals suffocate in their pens"

I'll take the dogs out", Billy said very soulfully.

"I already did, but when you do, be sure you stay with them, if they don't get blinded or lost, you probably will".

The windows rattled with the savage wind, the blowing gravel hitting the glass sounded like hail. He took another look and decided it was a no-go situation and glad they were not with the cattle.

"What about the cattle Ajax?" Billy loved all animals, he couldn't imagine any living thing out there in the stinging sand and whatever else was blowing around.

"You will learn soon enough that most animals have better sense then most humans. They turn their backs to the wind and tuck their heads down. In many cases they lie down during storms as their heads are protected by the heavy body of the animals next to them. You will see, I just hope not too soon". Billy thought Ajax was a walking book with a school room of information.

"You ask me once why I always wore a bandana around my neck" Ajax was tying his own on.

"Just for such as this. Pull it over your face to keep dust out, pull it tight against a sun burned neck, tie it on your head to keep sweat out of your eyes, use it for a tourniquet in case of injury or for signaling when you can't be heard." Ajax was pulling on his coat when Billy asked

"Where you going out in this?"

"To see about the horses, they should be OK and have been fed, I just went to make sure the stable man is there. I'll be right back then we will go eat, OK?"

Ajax didn't feel it necessary to explain the coat was protection from flying debris, as it was a summer day.

Fighting his way back from the barn in the wind and stomping his feet, he shook his coat out first, then Ajax said, "Whoo eee, that's a heller of a wind. They won't move the herd today. On second thought he added.... I hope".

"Who is ram rodding while your gone Ajax?" Billy hadn't given it any thought at all until just now.

"Lowell Pratt, best top hand I ever worked with, trust him with my life that I would"

Lowell worked the Chisolm, knows more about the land than any man I know". Has a Mexican wife Elaina, pettiest little gal I ever saw. Smart and savy to trail's. She used to go with him on the One Thousand Mile trails, but not this one, it's too rough. He is shrewd and silent, but you can depend on Lowell One Hundred per cent. Hard worker, saved his money, bought a hundred head of herefords and started out with three hundred acres but needed more as that wasn't enough to feed a hundred head. Now he has four thousand acres and runs a fine ranch. This is his last trip out.

Billy was anxious to meet this fellow.

"Do they have children?" Billy wanted to know.

"Yep – a son name of Tig about your age maybe, a year older, I'm not sure. Likable sort, quiet like his Pa, looks like his Ma".

"What sort of name is Tig ? Short for something or a Mex name?"

Ajax started to laugh and beckoned Billy to hurry up.

"When Tig was four years old he was playing in the patio area of their home when he started to yell. Elaina ran out to see what was the problem. The kid was trying to hide behind a rose bush and pointing to a place somewhere over his head and sputtering tiger tiger tiger in gulps of air while crying. What ? What ? Where? Then she saw a Bobcat staring down in their yard. She just had to laugh and pull the kid out of the rose bushes. Honey it's not a tiger it won't hurt you it is just passing by. He was learning words and to recognize things in his story books – the letters T I G to him, were Tig – it just stuck and the kid is Tig (like pig) and he doesn't like any jokes about it either. Ajax just laughed all the way to the door. 'C' mon sprout, time to get over to the herd", Ajax was prodding Billy along. It seemed like there was always one more thing that boy found interest in.

It was a good days ride to the arranged campsite, and nearly dark as they rode up. Lowell saw them coming and rode out to meet them.

"Been a hard trip," Lowell said, "we ran into some fierce weather, lost a few head and two horses, but the men did fine. We picked up a new old woman, name of Marcellino DeBeaseau, a sour Italian, but he can even cook rattlesnake so you wouldn't recognize it". Lowell smiled and shook his head.

"Told us it was sage hen and we ate it all, then Ira Ragsdel ask him where he got it from.

"Down a snake hole" Hmmm says Ira, must have been one hell of a big hole or dumb hen" he chuckled. "We could sure use some grub by now, ourselves", Ajax told him. "Sure, sure always some thing cooking no matter the time."

"I see your kid came along, how did he hold up Ajax. We don't have a full crew and no time for babysittin."

"He will be OK, a lot better than I expected and game too, don't complain much. Just wants to see everything and ask five hundred questions a day". Ajax just shook his head and chuckled. " I don't recall asking so many questions when I started in this business, but then no one had time to tell me anything much. When you work for John you work – silent as much as possible".

Billy had been tending the dogs but heard them talking. At the mention of Chisholm he ambled over to hear more.

Lowell and Ajax had both been on the two branches of the Trail and recounted several experiences, much of which they figured they would run into again during their time in the Utah and Wyoming Territories. The Bannocks were still at war in those same areas, the Blackfeet were also. It would do well to stay on the Old Western trail going into Montana, as far west as the trails went. This was called the Goodnight Loving trail as two civil war veterans Charles Goodnight and Oliver Loving had joined forces to make or blaze a new trail north. It was rough, ugly, mean territory that went from Denver to Cheyenne. This was a new trail used to bring cattle up into Montana and to the rail head sending the cattle east. Billy was sopping this up like a sponge; he soon started with the questions.

"How many men and horses did it take, it would wear out a horse a day I'd think", he pondered.

"Takes two men riding point out in front, two men to each side, four men riding swing to keep the herd strung out so the cattle would not bunch up, with usually two greenhorns riding drag. Now that's the worst job as the heat and dust is terrible."

"You ask about my bandana, you need it over your face". But that isn't all the job's by any means. It requires a wrangler and his crew 'cause a working cowboy will indeed need horses-two, maybe three a day per man. You can't wind a horse, he's no good for nothing anymore. Once your horse works up a lather you turn him over to the wrangler who cuts you out a remount. Then there is the cook! Usually a man yellin, hollerin, flapping his arms about and temperamental as all hell. Do **NOT** rile up the Old Woman if you intend to get grub fit to eat. He will cook up everything but the hoofs and the holler."

"Man there is a heap of learnin to do" Billy said, he wondered how much he could remember to write in his journal. "I imagine I'll learn a lot more by the seat of my pants if I live long enough" he said aloud.

"Either one of them still living?" Billy wanted to know about Goodnight and Loving.

"Well, Loving was killed in 1867 by Comanche, 1871 Goodnight joined up with Chisholm just outside Fort Sumner in New Mexico. They dug holes for shelter in the bluffs before winter but drove one hundred head to Santa Fe to pay for their supplies and to supply the Army post with beef. The next year Charlie opened a big ranch in Colorado, the biggest cattle ranch in Colorado really!"

"Charlie Goodnight had the first cattle ranch in the Texas panhandle in 1866 but moved on north."

"As to John Chisholm he was the first large scale cattle owner in the county. He had a string of cow camps near the Concho River in 1862-63 – but moved headquarters to New Mexico in 1873. That left ranching in Concho on a small scale and land sold easy. Fort Concho shut down and only forty-five or less people remained. Billy was mentally calculating time and years. This is where Uncle Buck had his land, Billy figured. When he got back to the hotel he would check out that deed. The Concho was going broke and the rail town of Salina was a cattle trail end – "So", Billy said to Ajax, "guess that's how I came by the 400 acres. Ajax looked surprised as all get out.

"By dern, Billy, I believe your right, it all fits in. The years are right, figures are correct and all areas mesh. Now you know how it all came to be." Ajax was as pleased as if it had been his doings.

"What you jawing about?" Lowell wanted to know. Briefly they clued him in on Uncle Buck, Concho, the acres and deed. : "The Lord works in mysterious ways", he said. Billy decided to learn as much about this territory as possible. He learned that at a place called Paint Rock, due east of San Angelo, the Goodnight Loving trail branched off from the Western trail into New Mexico. Most grazing land was sparse and the cattle were also. The things that survived in the Concho area were pecans, wool hides and mutton. The population was two thousand six-hundred fifteen at one time but now less than forty-five souls. I'd better keep this all in mind as that next trail north would be the last trip for him with the cattle drives. Billy was grateful for all this information.

"Well fellows, it's after ten and been a long day, I'm all talked out." Ajax stretched and headed for the hotel. Billy and Lowell said goodnight and followed each to his own bed.

Morning came at a six thirty dawn, the dogs were wanting out, and there was an almighty racket outside, Billy started to ask Ajax what was the hullabaloo only Ajax wasn't there. 'Man oh man, I must have really slept, I never even heard him leave'. Billy hurried into his jeans and boots, grabbed up a shirt and splashed water on his face, he called it good enough for now and rushed out the door. He found the noise alright, the herd had come in just before midnight and bedded down, but by dawn they were bawling their heads off, and milling around.

Billy located Lowell, Ajax and Tig. Tig and Billy were introduced to each other then given their orders, before Tig and Lowell left to tend the cattle.

"We need to push on tomorrow, so *lots* of work today, you can get acquainted as the days go along", he told the boys.

It was a nice day, not too hot and made work a little easier. It seem'd to Billy he did a lot of *staying out of the way to learn.*

But learn he did. He also met the *Cook* – He decided any questions would be reserved for later. Such a sour old man he never before had seen.

As the men came to the chuck wagon for grub Billy was introduced to each one. The boss wrangler was Ira Ragsdel known only as Rags. The two men riding point were old hands at twenty two and twenty four years of age. Paul Pulner known as Chick and Irvin Anderson or just Andy, both came from Kentucky. Both thin as a rail, whip post strong and skin like leather. A howdy was about as much talk as Billy heard there. When he approached the chuck wagon very quietly he was surprised by the cook who said – "You there, what you know of chuck wagons?" Billy politely said, "Not much."

"Let me tell you some – Charlie Goodnight bought a wagon off the army, stacked up cubby hole shelves to the rear, see?" – he pointed. "Put a place for water in a barrel over on this side and hinged a lid over the cupboard shelves and cubby holes – it drops down to a table or work surface. We put lanterns on top when dark, bed rolls are stashed in the wagon bed. This here one is made out of an old Army supply wagon. Then Lowell figured out a new plan – we strung hides along the inside of the wagon bed and nailed new planks over the hides. Lowell knows about every thing ya ever need to know and a mighty efficient cow hand too."

"Once, we were in Wyoming territory an old gent at a fort said the man didn't live who could bring cattle thru there, but Lowell, he was just born canny. We got through the Browns Hole and clean to Landusky, gatherin strays all along. You move 'em out but not fast, that runs the fat off cattle.

"We stop'd on the way back and the gent was nearly bambozaled – Said he'd not believed it.

"All this extra stuff makes the wagon heavy'r," he continued, "but in a storm the chuck wagon gets driven like a chariot out of hell and it better hold up.

"Now, I'm given ya a piece of advise. All these men been

121

over the land. If they tell ya something, you *listen*. They's plantin' seeds in your brain. You better keep it there cause none of them got much time to go over it very often. Ya don't dig up a seed to see if it is growin' so listen and learn. 'Round the camp fire you will pick up an education or while riding with a pard.

That's all the time I got for gabbin' so *git*."

CHAPTER 13

1882 – 1885
<u>Trail</u>

The sky was grey in the hours before dawn, with overhanging grey cottony shrouds of fog. It promised a day of cold wind and a dull trail. Billy had his own horse but the big dun he was riding was a much better cow pony as Rags had told him. Tig and Chick were riding swing one on each side of the herd, they had been out nearly ten hours and ready to call it finished. All three had a Winchester across his saddle, it was the finest gun on the market and all three were feeling a little better because of it.

Chick called softly across the herd.

"You keep your eyes open, those fellows at the Fort said there are rustlers about, we don't need company. All is fine so far" Ajax said we are about ten miles north of the river, let 'em drink as much as they want but try to keep 'em movin along. We need to make at least fifteen miles, if possible, today. Weathers good for the cattle, plenty of grass and water – not a hard trip – then he was gone on down the line to find food and a bed roll.

The drive was going well, Billy and Tig settled in fairly well too, being reasonably satisfied with progress and no immediate problems, Lowell rode and reminisced over the events of his life. Watching his son now seventeen, he could ask little more of life than what he had.

On a hot dusty day when he had been seventeen, he too was learning and working cattle. He had been on a ranch all his life, in fact he felt like he had been born on a horse. About the only time he ever knew any other life was when he met Elaina. At nineteen he thought he knew everything this side of the blue sky and had cut a pretty wide swath when he had the chance. Then on a drive headed north out of El Paso to Abilene with about one thousand head of cattle mostly under one brand, he had been chasing mixed stuff out of the ravines, washes, the brush and gathering strays, when the boss rode up and told him to go get a remount from the Wrangler. "You have nearly run this horse to the ground after an ornery old mossy horn", Art had told him. "That horse wont be no good once he is winded", he scolded Lowell.

Lowell went back for another horse and to his amazement the person who cut him out his relief mount was a lovely raven haired girl. Not just *a* girl but a beauty with large dark eyes and raven hair so black it looked dark blue in the sun light.

"Now this is enough to shock a man," he stuttered "Where in the world did *you* come from, how did you even get here? Or *why* are you here, this is a mighty dirty, dusty, hard working outfit."

She looked him over and finally said in a low smooth voice, "My father is the Wrangler over these six other men, even so they are short of riders so he is out on swing. I know this work well. You must have just hired on at Dodge."

Lowell was so surprised at her obvious refinement and manor of speech he couldn't seem to untangle his wits.

"You peg'd it right, I left home in Texas with one herd and going on north with this one. I have family and friends in Salina but for now – well, here I am."

He slap'd his hat across his pants and chaps swating dust

124

everywhere, combed his hair with his fingers and asked, "You going all the way?"

"Yes, father let me come this time but he surely isn't happy about it. He'd rather I was back east in school."

Chick who was riding point came back and said, "If you don't want to find yourself on drag duty, boy, you better pull your weight and no one will tell you again. No time on a drive for sweet talkin even if everything is quiet right now. That can change so fast you won't know what happened. You keep your eyes open all four directions and listen for *anything* that seems out of order."

He took that as sound advice and felt some down in the mouth that at nineteen he needed a dressing down.

"I hear you loud and clear, I was just so surprised to see a girl handling the Wranglers job." Chick smelled some interest on that subject and hid a grin as he scratched the side of his jaw.

"Does she always go on these drives?" Lowell asked.

"Some times, for several miles, this time she will be all the way, but her Pa is not likely to look kindly on a cow poke with interests in his lovely daughter. Just some advise!"

As Chick rode on after a bull that had his own ideas of where to roam, Lowell thought to himself he would find out about *that* subject himself.

By the end of that drive Lowell made up his mind he would see to it he had a few head of cattle, had saved his money and by all that was Holy he would marry Elaina and have a home and family. And that is just what he did. Now they had Tig and it was Tig's first time out just as it was for Billy.

Chick and Rags had worked with Lowell for ten years; they could look at each other across a herd and not say a word but know exactly what was to be done next. It was interesting to watch them.

It took eight days to arrive at Fort Sill driving the cattle into Oklahoma territory. The army needed beef and purchased three hundred head. This replenished the money to outfit of the rest of the drive. They also picked up a couple drifters fresh off a Wyoming drive that were headed for Salt Lake but had been side tracked by about eight hundred miles due to Indian attacks, wars and the need to join up with another drive. Herding cattle was their way of life and their money was getting scarce, they needed to join this drive.

Andy thought it better not to include drifters but soon saw they knew what they were about. He and Tig were riding point when they saw dust or smoke off in the distance.

"You notice that yesterday Tig?" Andy was a quiet type; he would tell you what he had to say and little else.

"Yes I did but it is only wind isn't it?"

"Don't know, don't think so, but it is better you ride back and tell Lowell to take a look up here."

Tig turned his dun and let the horse choose his own gait. He flag'd Lowell down with a wave of his hat, a motion he learned quickly. You do not unexpectedly shout, that starts a ruckus with the cows.

"You got a problem son?" Lowell was always alert.

"We are not sure. Andy said you come take a look over north east, we can see smoke or dust, one."

They trotted along up to the point. Lowell dug his binoculars out of his saddle bags to take a look and gave a grunt of surprise.

"Andy I think we better tighten up the herd, get all our hands ready for a scrap, just in case. They been following us two days now but not in this close, only about a mile or so off now. Edging in as time goes along. I'd say we are going to tangle with some rustlers; maybe tonight or tomorrow."

Then he turned back to pass the word along the line. Everything remained quiet however, even after sunset. The Cook had chow ready and as each stop'd by the chuck wagon, he filled his plate, drank coffee by the gallon and then went his own way. Relax by the camp fire, hit the bedroll or get a fresh horse for night duty. No one said much, but was not overly alert, just cautious.

Three more days passed without incident but as they approached the North Cimarron River they saw a gathering of men around a campfire. The obvious leader made himself known, and he said they had a small herd over this way, wherever that might be and wanted to buy up a hundred head.

"We don't have any to sell" Lowell told him, "These are headed for Fort Dodge and Fort Hays for the troops and to Abilene for market. We aren't of a mind to dicker either. I'd suggest you scatter out and round up the scrub's in the draw, ravines or loose range. There are quite a few with brands but evidently were left behind or bolted for one reason or another. Actually that's how we built up our herd. But ours are branded. Be easy for us to collect any that just happened to take a hike, if you get my point". The rustlers rode off.

"There is a small village not ten miles out and we should make it by tomorrow with no trouble." Lowell told us that night, so be ready for a scatter about midnight.

It wasn't even midnight and as dark a night as ever was, when a shot rang out and the cattle started getting up and maybe stampede.

Being as prepared as they could be, it didn't last long but it was hell to pay for about two hours. These men tried to hold the cattle down while two went on the chase for rustlers, six more were rounding up those that had bolted. By dawn a rough count showed over a hundred missing. It would take days to have a showdown over this. Fortunately many of the cattle had balked at the river and were easily influenced back to the main herd.

One drover had a broken arm, but other than exhaustion that was about the extent of damage. Chick said he could set the arm but the fellow replied "**NO**".

"You couldn't set a watch, you sure ain't gonna practice on me. The old woman is good with breaks, diseases or what ever ail's us, I'll just take my chances with him".

It made Tig and Billy smirk about the watch deal but also learned who to go to for health troubles. Of course they were not headed just for Dodge – but there was an Army Fort at Dodge and if they were expecting beef, then they may have sent out riders to join the drive. It was a good bluff that hadn't entirely worked on the rustlers. Once they were across the Cimarron River the drive was rougher for several days. Worries of Indian raids were on everyone's mind as well as rough country that did not lend itself to much comfort. It was fifteen days getting to Abilene and the rail head. Once the cattle were delivered, the hands had a couple of weeks to do as they pleased before starting south, east or west, what ever each had in mind. Since they were only three days out from Salina, Billy struck for home promising to join up in three weeks at Fort Sill if that's where the south bound men were going. Lowell, Tig and Chick decided to go to Salina also to rest up, visit old friends among older men and get outfitted for the trail south. Marcellino (cook) needed to refill all his supply on the chuck wagon and wanted a fling with a bottle of Red Eye, so he fell in with the others. As they rode into town Billy was flabbergasted at the changes in the two years he was gone. He went directly to see his father and catch up on everybody. Manter could hardly contain his emotions when Billy rode into the yard. After all the back slapping and hand shakes they settled down to talk away for a few hours.

"Where is the drive now?" Manter asks.

"We sold the cattle in Abilene, Lowell and his son Tig are here with me, Chick came in with us too".

"Well go find them son, they can bunk down here as long as you intend to be here".

Billy was off and *walking* – that seemed strange after miles on horseback and it felt good too. He found Lowell at Rand and Reva's just where he expected to find him, and offered his fathers invitation. It was readily accepted at once.

Lowell continued his conversation, "Rand you have a great place here".

"Yes, I'm doing well, but selling out my business next year. We have a few plans made and no children to concern over".

"Any place in particular?" Lowell asked.

"Not just yet, been chewing it over some! "

"Well Rand tell him," this from Reva who usually spoke her mind.

"You got another herd in mind Lowell?"

"As a matter of fact there is a gather going on right now. Next trip up we'll be into Montana territory, we are going to take the Goodnight trail for a way then switch over to the New Western. They had one hell of a terrible time on the north end of the Goodnight trail, lost twenty-seven thousand head in the two trips up. *Just unbelievable.*"

"Matt and I plan to be on that drive if you can use a couple more hands." It took some doing to convince Daylene, she was not happy, not with the restaurant and all.

"By God, that is the best news we have heard in a few years. You plan to leave with us? We will be here a couple weeks yet."

"That was the plan as soon as we knew you were coming in."

"Billy lets go collect Chick and head to your place. Everyone had any supper yet?"

"No, OK – lets all head for the Restaurant, oh – does Daylene still run it?" Matt and Rand both laughed at that.

"Run it? She works there but yes, I'd say she runs it alright. Everyone else too. If you doubt it ask Matt."

Billy went to get his father, the others went to find Chick or head for the restaurant. Rags was there to everyone's surprise and Daylene already knew the rest were in town. She took one look at Billy and started to sniffle.

"Boy, are you a sight to see. You must have grown four inches and you look more like Millie than I could ever have expected. Must have been a shock to Manter, to see you," Billy was embarrassed but happy; he hugged Daylene and shook hands with Matt.

"I understand we are going to have some extra help this next trip," he grinned a big smile from ear to ear. Chick was down at the bar just laughing and glad to see the others. As they gathered together Starkey was driving down the street and nearly twisted his neck off.

"Hay, ho – you hold up there now," he bellowed.

"Man oh man what a time we gonna have tonight. Matt and Rand told you any news?" he couldn't stand it, he had to cut loose. "And I'm going too. If we can convince Nolan and Blaine we will all make one last trip together."

Blaine being the only Veterinarian in town might take a bit of persuasion but Lowell decided he would make it his life's intention to do just that. It was a good plan and he was just tickled pink.

The next two weeks were a wonder of good times and a rehash of stories told and retold. Billy told his father of so much that Manter had to slow him down.

"Papa, cattle can live on the darnest food, you would even think anything could eat. They do not eat sage or thistle but some cactus they do. Just walk along and chew off stubble, weeds, berries, most anything. They weather well and seem to do better where they have to go hunt for food."

"Another thing I wonder if even you know – Did you know that the Trail was named after a man named Jesse Chisum. His father was Scottish and mother was a Cherokee Indian. He started laying out the trail with mounds or hills of earth and headed up to Abilene but never made it. He died after eating food cooked with spoiled bear grease."

"Billy you're a story book, you better plan to see Isaac Foster before you leave town, he will be so interested." Manter was impressed with Billy's knowledge of history.

"Where did the man named Chisum come from then, how

did it happen people think him as the founder of the famous trail?"

"His name is Chisum not Chisholm but the names are pronounced CHIZUM. Lowell said, "Records show by 1868 there were seventy-five thousand head bound for Abilene and by 1871 there had been roughly seven hundred thousand cows up that trail. Hard to imagine isn't it? But settlers and farmers moved west, the drives pretty well petered out and ours may be the last one to use it for cattle."

The third day Billy was home he took Tig along to visit the teachers, Booth and Miss Nora Ellen, went to see Beulah and Roscoe and there he met his Water Lou. Sylvia Lee was now 15 and looked like an angel. Tig was a goner at first sight. Billy thought to himself, 'this will not be the last time Salina see's Tig Pratt'. Indeed all the way to Texas, Tig was plumb moonstruck and all he had on his mind was Sylvia Lee Peabody.

CHAPTER 14

1885 - 1895

Once the gather was made, the plans were filled in and all arraignments in order, the entire crew of 16 men, fifty horses, and the chuck wagon now restocked, orders handed last out and things were ready to move. Everyone got their gear together and settled in for the last easy sleep they would have for the next six months.

Several of the hands had ridden into El Paso for one last fling and rousted up some trouble. Ajax made them return next morning and pay for the damages they caused.

"If you have a bad head, it better get cleared up, we start at noon, hoping to get his bunch trail broke by sundown."

That was the last he said as he scowled a farewell look at the men and went to lead point. Four of them went to ride swing, the rest fell into place. Over the last drive Billy had started helping with the chuck wagon, only helping where it was necessary. The flank riders were in the rear closest to the chuck wagon as it followed at the end of the herd. The swing riders are out on both sides of the herd to keep them in line and to gather them close in at the end of the day. Some of the cattle would be strung out well over a mile. There were six thousand head in this drive and many hardships anticipated up

132

the trail. Going from Texas to New Mexico, Colorado, Idaho, and into Montana was a big order to stick with.

Ajax was trail boss, Gus and Rags would be riding point, Tig and Blaine would ride swing, other crew members were Boots and Starkey who had come down by train to join the drive along with Matt and Rand. The group figured it would be their last drive and wanted to be together on this one. These men had become Billy's extended family by now. He was twenty years old and a seasoned cow man to hear him tell it. But the older men remembered when Billy was twelve years old and never let him forget it. A lot of good sport was made of this along the way.

Back in Salina, Daylene and Reva had each other to rely on; to keep in close touch with Nola and Bert since they had adopted Chrissy, also were helping Willa with her little boy. The women were too busy to think much about their men folks off kicking up their heels as Booth Gordon said. The church had been remodeled; the congregation was filled with remorse about the final demise of the trestle table. Booth ordered new hymnals and developed a passion for Revival meetings. Ira Fletcher had passed away, Sara had taken over for the first four grades at school, she and Nolan had gotten married the first of June 1882, had settled down to raise a family and **NO**, he was not going on that trail.

Billy's father Manter Good had turned over management of his hardware business to Hollis, who mostly taken care of the place anyway. Manter fished and tried to keep track of where Billy was. The Peabody's had added another one hundred acres and were raising sheep, Sylvia Lee was back east at boarding school, Merry Christine (Chrissy) was now eight years old going on twenty according to Nola. Grant and Ella McMurphy had opened a second restaurant. Hard Knocks would join the drive in Colorado. Most of the businesses were run by the same men who had started them while Billy was home. And such were the letters from Manter as Billy picked up his mail at various points along the route. Tig always wanted to know if the letters held any news of Sylvia Lee.

"Well couldn't you ask him once?" Tig was annoyed with Billy's joking about his love life.

"One day you will see how it goes," he snapped.

The weather was cooler as they headed north which was better for all concerned. In New Mexico they were blasted with a freak hail storm that scattered the herd. That took a few days to get back lost time but so far no Indian trouble afoot.

Lowell kept looking north east, he didn't like the sky so he rode along the line informing each man as he approached, "That sky looks like snow. April it may be, but we are in Rocky Mountain country and the mountains are not free with their information. One at a time collect your heavy gear and bring an extra horse back with you."

He rode on to the chuck wagon to tell the cook and Billy to get prepared for snow. Billy lit out scouring the area for extra wood. He wondered about forage for the animals in the storm, he would ask about that. Before noon one hellatious northern came swooping down, the snow nearly blinding the men. Cattle hung their heads against the blast and men were thankful for slickers over their mackinaws, even though their fingers inside wool gloves were stiff.

Billy asked the cook, "How can it be fifty degrees at ten and freezing at noon?"

"You never been in a blizzard before?"

"Sure we had them in Kansas but we were in town or our homes not out in land that looked like it was unfinished," said Billy, while Marcilleno chuckled to himself.

"You get those dogs up here on the wagon and keep them back by the bed rolls, out of our way. We are in for one wicked night of it; I feel it in my bones."

Blue, Dog & Here were trying to stay under the wagon as it was, so after the first sharp whistle they were not hard to find. Blue was with pups again and Billy hoped it would be her last litter; she was nine years old and had possibly covered ten thousand miles in her life.

"All good here?" Lowell shouted over the noise of the wind.

"Good as we can make it," he was told.

"Come on Billy if you have the wood in and the other stuff done, I need every hand. There is nothing out there to stop the cattle if they take a notion to run out of this. They see ghosts or goblins in every shadow, even a sudden movement by one old steer can start a stampede. A long horn can run as fast as an antelope."

Lowell went to the Wranglers next, told them he was going to set the men on two hour watch so keep the horses ready. That blizzard raged on for nearly another eight hours. By ten that night no one had eaten or had time to even think. It would be a night to remember around the camp fire.

Marcellino, referred to as the *Old Woman*, had started four kettles of stew and kept adding everything to the pots as the men thawed out by the fire and shoveled in their grub. Large size Dutch ovens were filled with biscuits and those disappeared like melting snow. Billy kept coffee going and cleaning up plates and cups. The dogs wanted down but wet feet and fur was not a good thing among blankets and bed rolls. They ate up on the wagon bed. By midnight all the men were fed, horses had grain and cattle were milling about moaning to themselves. The wind died, sky cleared and by morning light a warm wind came over the ridge. A Chinook cleared most of the snow off, "How amazing to see this happen," Billy thought.

Ajax told Lowell, "One new years in Montana we were at a Grange Hall for the festivities, the lot of us having been ask out of the goodness of the community. It was eight below and about four to five inches of snow and ice. The bells and whistles, sirens and all were one hell of a racket when one of our crew threw open the door to shout 'Happy New Year' and stop'd mid sentence.

"Hey every body he bellowed, come looky here – its rainin'." Everyone laughed at him; he never had experienced a Chinook before. Those Santa Ana winds come through and melt the ice right off the trees – water was running six inches deep down the street. Ajax started to laugh.

"I bet that poor sod thought he had hit the bottle pretty deep," it made him laugh again and shake his head.

The crew and cattle holed up for a day setting things to right, trying to rest a while and repair any damage done to equipment. The following sun up Lowell called the familiar *move 'em out*, he hoped to reach Santa Fe by the end of the following week.

"Hey Tig, you going to Kansas at the end of this drive?" Billy wanted to know.

"I planned on it; yep I hope it will be decent weather. I thought I'd ride through as I wanted to see that country, but not by train."

"I wanted to go back home for a month, so I'll fall in with you then."

"What about Matt and Rand, you think they will finish the drive?"

"I'm sure of it; they would never let Lowell down, not for a minute."

Andy was yelling. "You guys get going up the line. Ride swing for three hours each."

"Chick has a rip roar of a toothache and Blaine is making up his mind if he thinks he can pull it."

Billy did not speak his thoughts for fear it would get back to Chick and someone would be bound to have fun at his expense. Billy thought 'If it was *my* tooth I'd sooner have Blaine poking about in my mouth than the cook, *he* would whack your jaw with a frying pan, no doubt'.

Instead Billy said, "Who is riding point?"

"Ajax is," and he sent Andy and Rags on ahead to scout

as he is in a lather concerning the Indians. "Claims the Good Lord himself could not make peace with the Sioux and he sure didn't want a tangle."

"Yeah, right, OK – I'll go back and ride drag, it sure ain't dusty!"

The Boss wrangler had a crew of six men who kept the horses and gear ready at all times. They sort of stuck together except for eating arrangements when they took shifts. Billy got to know a couple fellows reasonably well, that's when he learned Gus was related to one of the men and that man had come from Concho area.

There were questions Billy wanted to ask, so he hung around with the wranglers when he could. There was a good deal of maverick stock and unbranded scrub stuff that was loose on the range. Sometimes the wrangler helped in the gather and branding. These cattle were left over from abandoned ranches, Indian and cattle wars, those left behind on wagon trails and other reasons. That's how a lot of big cattle ranches were started.

Ajax was always on the lookout for places of briars, scrub, brush and low tangles of berry vines, ravines or any place they might collect a few more head. Often there would be forty to fifty head in a bunch, not always too well mannered.

Evenings were usually the best part of the day. The Cook had his *rules* and made them stick. There was a little ditty often repeated.

> Bacon in the pan
> Coffee in the pot
> Get over after' it
> While its hot.

Cook's Rules
> No one eats until the Cook calls
> Then come run'in
> Eat first. Talk later
> Hungry cowboys wait for no man

OK to use your fingers
Food left on your plate is an insult
If you come across fire wood, gather it.

Andy seemed to be the best shot among them, so was sent looking for game. Fresh meat of any sort was a treat and sweetened up the disposition of the cook to just above the tolerable stage.

By the end of June they had reached Salida, Colorado area traveling over some places with some pretty sparse pickings for the cattle. However water was not scarce, they had crossed the Timpar, Trinchera, Huerfano and into the valley between the Sangree De Christo mountain west and Rockies to the east. The Grape River branched north east but it was only about one long days travel to the Arkansas River then another day into Poncha Springs and Salida, Colorado.

Another hundred miles to Denver, if all went well they could be there by mid July, sell off half the herd and lay over for a week's time and still be in Wyoming and Montana before snow fall or foul weather. It had been a good drive without too many stressful weeks.

The next leg of the drive would be into Wyoming territory which reeked of Indian troubles and not looked forward too with much joy. Denver was a mile high so they had not suffered with heat; the cattle were fat and would have no trouble but some mountainous terrain. They would be deep in the grasslands before Ft. Lorraine.

Again – *if* all went well, they could sell off another hundred or so beef to the Fort and see the Wyoming line a week behind them.

The one thing neither Billy nor Tig could hardly bear and refused to witness or be a part of was the killing of new calves. They could not keep up, so must be destroyed.

It was a source of veal but the boys had no appetite for it. They would have chili, until they learned what *that* meat was too. Veal. They would soon be in Bighorn sheep country and there were also pheasant, quail, sage hen, salmon fishing and an abundance of deer, elk, antelope and buffalo coming up soon.

Lowell was listening to the young ones talking about the problems with a few hard core hands, finally he told them, "You two need to remember something I'm going to tell you now. When you come into this world you're like raw material, what you make of it is up to you. You get an education when you leave the trail and go out and earn respect, its *character* that counts".

He told them of one time on his first drive with Chisholm, about a particularly hard, dry week, no water, not much grass, no river in fifty, sixty miles, hardly enough to get by. When a man with two teams and two wagons came by their camp one evening late and asked to light a spell and for coffee – They said of course, no one was turned out, especially in this God forsaken country. They ask him what he was pedaling, he said he had two huge wagon loads of water melons and he was headed for the Fort about forty miles east. He offered melons to each man and ask about their conditions. He was told no hay, no grain, little feed, low on water and fifty miles to the river. That fellow got up and started throwing water melons to the horses and took one wagon out to the cattle and dumped nearly five hundred melons for the cattle to eat. It possibly saved the drive but he wouldn't take a cent. Now that is character!

At Dandy crossing Ajax and Lowell bought five hundred rounds of ammo before crossing the Colorado River, extra colt revolvers, canteens and ropes – The merchant ask if they intended to start a war.

"No, just to have it on hand as north of the Colorado River is Indian country. If you aren't prepared it would be like going to a hanging but forgot the ropes." At that, the store keeper's imagination blew a fuse.

A couple fellows in their twenties introduced themselves

and asked if they could join the drive. Lowell said they surely could use some extra hands.

One drover spoke up, "I see your carrying that Sharps rifle – Can you use it? We can use a good hand with a gun".

"I'm still alive ain't I?" he grinned.

"We just got hooked up with a cow outfit being plagued by rustlers when one come out of the brush with a shotgun. Made a terrible roar and buckshot everywhere. Cattle plum crazy, near run me in the ground. I caught up with one of them, shot his hat off, told him he best light a shuck out of there and rattle his hocks. Told him in uncharted territory we were self appointed sheriffs and I was in a mood to hang his pelt from the nearest tree.

"It took us four days and fifty horses to round up that scatter and some how two of those rustlers needed a bed six by three, if you get my meaning."

There were now fifteen men plus the Wrangler and crew of six, the cook, three dogs and three thousand head of cattle. It was nearly noon and a *hot,* **hot** August 4th when they hit the stock pens at Cheyenne. There would be a five day lay over after the sorting of the cattle, the count made and our twelve hundred head bedded down, these were going on into Montana territory.

The town was young and had weather beaten false front buildings, buck boards and spring wagons dotted the dirt streets here and there along with women in calico dress's, bonnets sheltering their faces and children tethered along side. It made the men homesick.

Some houses had trees in the front yards with birds darting about, chattering their gossip from limb to limb. Some withered looking dogs lay on door steps or in shady spots.

"Billy, you want to sell your pups?" Ajax asked.

"I will if *I* can see who gets them."

"Andy you want to go help Billy get those pups from the wrangler's tent?"

"Guess it's too hot to argue, but I taken a liking to those dogs, Ajax, I'm not to keen on parting with them."

Andy sat down at a water trough and thought back to the night Blue had her pups. It was fixin' to rain and no place for birthing pups. Tig and Billy shoveled out a wash tub size hole in the ground under the chuck wagon and filled it up with old news papers they saved from everywhere they could get any. Reading matter was scarce as hen's teeth on the trail.

Blue showed sign's of labor so the men kept an eye on her. It had started to sprinkle when they shoved her in the "bed" they had provided. She had seven within half an hour. It was pouring rain and starting to spill into her "<u>bed</u>". Rain or not, three men got under the wagon and carried those pups and Blue, up in the chuck wagon bed. The cook nearly had apoplexy and yelled his head off to no avail when they used clean blankets for Blue and family. They stayed in the wagon a week much to the sorrow of Marcellino De Beaso. That was one furious Italian. Everyone ate mush for a week.

By now, Blue's pup's were ten weeks old and eating anything loose. Game was plentiful and much needed, it helped feed the pups. Supplies were restocked and six of the pups found a new family. Andy balked at letting go of the little runt female. He kept her and named her Iris.

"Now what in hell kind of a name is that for a trail dog, Andy?" It sounds like the name of a movie star or something." Chick was just vexed at the thought.

That's the pretty'st flower I ever did see and I never hope to have no flower beds, women or kids. So she is Iris and that's that." Andy called his pup and walked off down the street to find a mercantile store, he badly needed socks. He never told any of them but that pup had chewed up near all his socks and even a pair of gloves.

There had been a church social in town with ice cream, home made pies, cakes and salads of various kinds. The men were asked to join if they pleased. They pleased -- also devoured every thing in arms length. The ladies took a dim view of such lack of manners and commented on the destiny of such a group as they were. Little did they ever know of a trail drive!

After their time off the drive, it was *head 'em out*. This stretch would be from Cheyenne to the Lodgepole River for an over night stop.

Five more days to the old Fort at Chugwater, or what was left of it. It would be another day of rest as in such hot weather horses, men and cattle felt the weariness that the heat brought on. So far no Indian problem although they were set for it. Another 400 miles to the end of the drive, at least it was in sight. Most of the men had earlier on made up their mind it was the *last* drive for them. Most cattle were shipped by train now if there were spur lines in to cattle pen area's, or near enough for less than a days drive.

Baring any unforeseen catastrophes they should get the cows to Billings by the first week of October. It would be nip and tuck weather wise, but hopefully they would catch Montana's Indian Summer season.

About seven to ten miles north of Chugwater their world exploded. Starky and Grady were sharing Point this day; Ajax insisted no one be out front alone. They had since dawn noticed a dust or smoke off east but it did not let up.

"Should one of us go see to that?" Grady asked.

"Not by a damn sight, not me nor you neither. Ajax said not be fifty feet apart. You know he has been up trail three times since he was seventeen and him and Lowell they both are wise to things we never heard of and I hope never to see."

Starky and Boots had been on a drive eight years before with Ajax and Lowell, Nolan and Blaine had too. Blaine had gone to Veterinary school after the last drive on the Chisolm and settled at the rail head town of Salina, so, in time had five other of the hands who had become close friends or pal's. There were Boots, Starky, Blaine, Nolan, Rand and Matt. All were here with Lowell and Ajax on their last drive. Lowell had his home in Texas with Tig and Elaina, Nolan remained in Salina with his wife.

Fritz Knox had married Willa, they had a son, but he joined the outfit in Dodge on the trip into Texas south, to pick up the herd and start north. He left at Dodge going east to return to Salina – He had a business to run.

About now everyone was on edge when they saw Ajax unloading all the ammunition they had deposited in the bed of the chuck wagon. The cook thought Ajax to be deranged but was thinking better of it as they continued to see the air to the east.

"There is no land to kick up that much dust over that direction less it would be a cyclone, I'm reasonable sure that's not the case."

"Then what?" asked a wrangler who had just exchanged horses for Ajax.

"But cut me out a good runner, I'll take him along with me, OK."

"You really expect trouble?" the man was worried.

"Yep – any time now, I have feeling that's a wagon train on the Oregon Trail's north spur. Not used as much now and possibly the last ones out. The rail road is branching off its original line, you know."

"Well who needs to be afraid of a wagon train?"

"Just be prepared. There are renegade Indians up here, ones who won't go to the designated reservations or accept the acres given them by the Government. Also there are scraps between rival small Indian bands and small groups who can't get it through their thick heads that Indian attacks, scalps for coup, gold diggings etc. are nearly a thing of the past."

"You got me a good running horse there?"

"Good as they come."

"Keep your eyes open – Indians still steal horses as well as beef," and he was away to alert the swing riders as to his concerns. Since Indians do not fight at night, the drovers felt a bit easier, never the less Lowell posted nine men out on two hours off and two on, for the night.

At dawn the smoke was worse and just as they were grabbing bacon and biscuits, drinking coffee and set to go to each job assigned, about twenty Indians come whooping up with rifles waving above their heads, jawing up an unholy racket to make up for loss of man power. The cattle were off about four hundred yards north so the Indians made a circle around the chuck wagon and wrangler's camp, including what men were not out on the range minding cattle.

They were in full war paint and desperate looking. Lowell stepped out toward them with his hand raised in a general sign of peace among most tribes. One *warrior,* evidently the leader of this rag tag group, rode up to within six feet of Lowell and demanded ten cows. Since they like to dicker Lowell shook his head and held up eight fingers. One of the Indians came forward with a bundle and offered it in exchange for ten beef.

Lowell said, "What you got there worth two extra beef?"

He took the bundle and it started to scream. He nearly dropped it because he was so absolutely shocked. All the men came charging up to see what the hell was going on.

"We keep papoose – trade for food."

"You can have the cows but I don't want the child"

With that, the Indian reached down from his horse and snatched up the crying baby planning to swing it toward the wagon wheel to dash its head in.

Billy screamed like he was on fire and dove over the four or five feet, grabbing the baby away from the Indian. It all happened so quickly no one had said a word or even moved. Billy held the baby up to his chest and was so angry he couldn't even speak. Ten beef were cut out of the drive for the Indians.

Finally Andy said, "Now what? This is a fine kettle of trouble we don't need."

All who were milling around looking from one to the other

not knowing what to do or say.

"You gonna *KEEP it?*" asked the cook in astonishment.

"You can't kill babies for God's sake." Billy *never* swore but he was so incensed over the whole thing he was ready to fight anyone over anything.

"Lets all go on about our business here, I need to take a ride. I'll be gone about two hours I think." Billy you better come up with some answers before I get back."

Lowell started east, the Indians and their beef had gone south east, he took two .44's and his Winchester, stopped to tell Matt where he was headed and started on. Chick came off swing and followed.

"I sent Tig to ride swing, I know what you're doing and I think you better have some company."

He swung along side with an extra horse and the two started forward toward the smoke.

They had covered about twelve miles or less when they found what was left of six covered wagons and their owners. It made Chick wretch and Lowell nearly wept at the sight of all the children that had been so badly burned. There was nothing to salvage, even the mules and three sheep had been killed, some chickens were pecking away at the ground, all three dogs were dead and most of the wagons burned as well.

It took them a couple of hours to bury what they could, collect hand tools such as spades, shovels, hoe and rake, some buckets, one cage for the chickens they scrambled after and two lanterns. These items were bundled into a blanket they found and strapped it to the extra horse they had brought along.

He had said a couple hours, but it was nearly four in the afternoon before they returned. No one said much, it was pretty clear what had take place.

Blaine had looked over the baby and told Billy she was seemingly in good health and possibly two months old.

"Now what on earth are you going to do with her?"

Billy was very solemn and looked sick at heart.

"I'll manage," he said.

"You men here never met my family except the one's from Kansas, that is, but I had a little red headed sister who was the sweetest little kid who ever lived. She and my Mother both died of the flu one January. They both had red hair just like this tiny thing does, too.

I don't **know** how I'm going to manage – I may have to drop out of the drive but I **will** keep her and I **will** manage. I'm up for any help or advice." With that he started for the wagon to get a bucket. There had been a couple calves born a few days before and milk was plentiful. Just how to feed the baby was not figured out yet. But he would!

"Oh Lord, oh Lordy, Lord, we need to think, any of you fellers got kids to home?"

Andy was running his hands through his hair and shaking his head. The wrangler boss was a quiet little Mexican from Laredo, Texas who spoke up.

"Si senior Chick, we had eight, I know plenty, bout keeds! He smiled.

"So where do we start, we can't let the sprout down, he made me right ashamed of myself."

There were nods of agreement among the others who were still standing around.

"First we need bottles, then neeples, den you gotta to have diapers. You gotta feex a place to sleep.

"Also need clothes and most you need the patients of God."

"Next you need pray preety goot for times of belly ache and the teeth coming in. Else you feel like you gonna keel the keed for crying and no stop."

Some of the fellows gathered together to exchange ideas, which was a blessing to Billy. Twenty years old he was and felt helpless as the baby.

"Ella Mae McMurphy raised some pet lambs one year, she

used a beer bottle and rubber hog nipples."

"There are beer bottles o' plenty but no nipples," Billy said.

"I have an idea" the cook offered, speaking slowly.

"Fire away Marcie what do you have in mind?"

"You men who have leather gloves, anyone have a pair or even one glove that wore throw the palm from ropes?"

Starky spoke up "I do, as a matter of fact I have a pair, what you want with them?"

If you cut the fingers off we can poke a hole in the tip, soak the leather fingers in salt water and line them bottles up with a finger on the top, let them dry, they will shrink down tight as iron" "But how to get the milk in the bottle then?"

"Now there is a notion" Andy was scratching he head.

"How about if we cut the hole in the end of the finger, filled the bottle and let the hole shrink."

"No, the milk would sour waiting that long."

Tig rode up and was listening to them when he said.

"I guess we could use the cooks funnel."

"Small end of the funnel is to big, it would slip down over the finger" Marcellino was listening too.

"How about that long needle thing with a bulb on it that Blaine uses?"

Blaine spoke up "Yes, that would go in the nipple hole and we could fill the bottle, it would be slow but it can be done. The bulb holds one cup of liquid, it is a syringe I use for the stock."

Everyone had a grin on his face, it seemed like a good plan.

"Where *is* Billy?" –

Trying to spoon milk into the baby's mouth. He is wearing most of it.

"That out to be fun to watch, joked Ajax.

That takes care of the bottle, so next comes clothes, diapers and a bed."

Lowell had just rejoined the group and ask what was the big pow wow. They told him about the beer bottle and glove nipples. He had to laugh at their excitement, and ask, "You fellows have any shirts ready for the rag box?" Several said yes –

"So lets tear up the backs and sleeves for diapers."

Billy ask "Anyone know how to sew?" all eyes turned toward the cook –

"I aint got time for no such thing" he said.

"Well *could* you sew?"

"Done some in my time."

"OK then, what about flour sacks and sugar sacks and the like?"

"Yes, got some, been using them for dish rags."

"Well could you spare some?" Billy ask in a sarcastic tone –

"I'll think on it" just as sarcastic came back the answer.

"Good" Billy snapped.

"Now that mountain is crossed does anyone want to eat?" The cook was not happy.

The cattle were quiet, the meal time was uneventful, so Billy brought up the subject of a bed for *his* baby girl.

"Where is she now?" someone ask –

"Wrapped up in a blanket between some bed rolls and I need an extra five gallon bucket."

"What for?" Starky wanted to know.

"Washing diapers and all."

"Oh, sure, here are those gloves, by the way."

"Those I was talking about" he added.

It was amazing to see the interest this baby girl stir'd up. Men arguing about who was going to make finger nipples – who would nip holes in the end, who rounded up empty bottles and stuck them in the cooks dish water.

The next day two drovers rode out to the massacre scene to find any thing useful, if it had been left behind. Under a partly burned out wagon there was a box of apples, also some scattered cloths, a few cooking utensils and burlap bag of potatoes.

"Not much else here that hasn't been mashed or burned up, but we can take this back to camp. Maybe the apple box could do for a baby bed until she gets to big, what do you say?"

"Worth a try and I know the spuds and apples will be et up."

They came into camp with their trophies, to be met with the news that a horse had died.

"Blaine said it looked like poisoning."

"Now where could that have come from?" Chick was shocked.

"Who had that horse out last?"

"I think one of the men riding swing why?"

"Which side of the herd?"

Andy said, "It was me – we were on the west side."

"Did you let him graze any?"

"Yes, as a matter of fact I did, I had a natural call to the brush and let him pick around while I was at it.

"There is burdock growing along the rim, its poison to animals if eaten when it is wet. I never thought about it. We better keep the herd east of the rim even if they get off in the draw's. It's better to chase cows than have them dead".

Starky was taking this all in and asked if anyone had seen strays in the bottom land? "I took a hike among about fifty head to have a look for brands. There were some and all out of a drive several years ago over on the old western trail. I wonder if they had been rustles or some wandered off and never found. Could be they are there do to a rustlers gather even now. Curious about those cows and that brand, where did they come from, I wonder?"

I heard that man Ayers went broke so these may be abandoned and just multiplied naturally."

Lowell told Starky to take a wrangler with him and go back and have a look the next day. "Be sure you are not alone, you don't need any surprises off by yourselves. If they are just loose, herd them back this way."

There were eighty six head rounded up and added to this drive. That brought them up to around eighteen hundred head of mix'd stuff. But it all sell's to ranchers or for eats, in town or to the Fort's. They were glad enough to include the stray cattle with their own drive.

"You going to give this baby a name Billy or make a contest so we can all have a hand in it?"

Several had asked him and he was thinking about that. At chow time that evening he announced that he thought it best to let who ever took her for their own should be entitled to name her too. All agreed that was fair.

By the time they were in Yellowstone country there were miles of grass just waiting to be eaten. It was good country and easy going. Weather was turning to fall and so far they had had a very successful trip in spite of snow, hail, wind, stampede, Indian raids, rustlers, a few broken bones and teeth pullings. The wind storms had been vicious, heavy rains churned up mud a foot deep with a few thousand head of cattle plodding along. That made for frayed tempers and stubborn animals too. But all in all no tragic things occurred.

The last week of September they figured they were about ten days out from Billings, Montana. Spirits were high, yet each knew they would part with the baby at Billings. She had been a hand full for Billy but each helped in their own way. At stops along the way, cloths were purchased and baby shoes collected, real diapers had appeared but no one claimed to know of that!

Once in town Billy, Lowell and Rand went to the Sheriff Office and told of the Indian raid, the baby and how it all came about. They ask if he knew of any family who would take her in.

"I know exactly who to see" he smiled and said.

"Come on, bring her and lets go see the Governor, his office just down the block and I know he is in."

"He and his wife are personal friends of my wife and

myself. They had a little girl who died last year. She was four years old, it nearly killed them. Marcia just never has gotten over little Cartha's passing. This just may be the best thing that could have happened."

They found the Governor in his office with several other men and they had to wait a while, but when they were told to go in he met them warmly.

"Hello Lionel, I brought you several pieces of news. First off however", he turned to Lowell, "meet the Governor of Montana, Lionel Longworth." They shook hands, then Lowell introduced Rand Blackwell. "And this string bean is Billy Good, they are both out of Salina, Kansas. They have the cattle drive that just came in today."

He then related the story of how they came to have this child.

"We need to find her a home. Billy has been in charge of her welfare for over two months now and we think she is between four and five months. She can sit up and eat pretty well, being raised on cow poke grub, mashed up of course, not a one of us can keep her and after the cattle are sold we will split up. Some will go to their homes in Illinois or Kansas some of us back to Texas," Lowell esplained. "Four of my men are headed for Salina while the chuck wagon and forty horses will return to Abilene. I'll be headed to San Antone by train day after tomorrow myself. Just wanted to see to this situation first."

Lionel Longworth was a man in his early forties with a lovely wife. He had married Marcia Mellon the daughter of a wealthy Pennsylvania industrialist. They had only one child who they lost at four years of age. Lionel sent a page to fetch his wife.

"Marcia, see what you can do about this baby will you please?" he ask his wife.

"Why darling, where did this little child come from? Oh dear, she needs a bath and clean clothes, oh, see here, her ears are dirty." Here, give her to me, where ever is her mother, my goodness me."

The men all smiled at each other and Billy handed over the little girl who he had saved from the Indians then retold the story to Marcia Longworth who was juggling the baby up and down between hugging her and kissing her sweet little face.

Billy said, "I did my best, I had a little sister who died, she was 6 years younger than me so I used to help watch her for Mama. But I can't keep her of course. I was hoping to find her a home before I leave here."

Marcia threw her one arm around Billys waist while holding the baby in her other arm. "God bless your precious heart honey – God does work in mysterious ways. Lionel, we shall keep this precious bundle and thank our Lord Jesus for His grace." She took the baby's blanket, kissed her husband before heading for door.

Then she turned around and asked Billy, "What's her name for goodness sake, I must be without thought to anything," she smiled an apology.

"We never named her mam, we thought it best to let the adopting family name her themselves, after all it should be their right."

"How wonderful, oh thank you men."

"Lionel dearest, shall we call her after your mother?"

"If you wish sweet heart, it would be fine with me."

"That's settled then her name is Nelia Adelade Longworth we shall tend to legal matters later on. Bless all of you – goodbye for now, Nelia and I are going home."

Billy felt hot tears in his eyes – some for gratitude, some for a little sorrow but mostly from happiness. "All's well that ends well, that's what Mama use to say."

Lowell turned to the Governor, "How do you spell that name your wife picked, I never heard it before."

"It is N-E-L-I-A pronounced Nay-lee-ah– it is an Island

name, Marcia's mother was from Tahiti, a beautiful woman of grace and education. In their native tongue the letter "E" is a long ā, the "I" is a long ē as the Hawaiian words are also pronounced.

"I think it is a pretty name" Billy remarked, then started to laugh and couldn't stop.

"What got you going?" Rand asked in surprise.

"Just think on it man. Here is a red headed baby, possibly Irish in the background somewhere – she came by way of an Indian raid, to a bunch of cowboys mostly from Texas, who saved her in Wyoming but she lives in Montana with an English father and a Half Tahitian mother. So what nationality is she?"

Lowell said, "I think that is 100% American." Everyone had a good laugh about that and agreed it certainly was. The USA was a melting pot of all nationalities that had arrived from someplace else.

After the cattle were sold and the men paid off, each was making plans of their own. The four Kansas bound men were together in a restaurant when who should come in but Mrs. Longworth carrying Nelia.

"Would you ever recognize that baby?" Billy was floored.

"Well, I'll be darn'd" Chick spoke up –

"Hard to believe" said Lowell and Tig –

"Hello gentlemen, we came to see you before you leave town."

She sat the baby down on a stool and held her against falling off.

"Nelia has lovely red hair; I *adore* red hair, and such pretty blue eyes.

"We went shopping this morning, how do you think she presents herself now?" Marcia was just ecstatic over it all.

"Pretty little doll" said the waitress –

"Look at that beautiful dress and tiny shoes to match, just a doll" then she went on to her tables. Billy was writing something on a napkin.

"This is my name and address, if you will please, keep in touch with me, I'd like some pictures when you can, as well."

He immediately got up and walked outside. This was hard for him, as he had grown very attached to the baby girl, who he felt had rather taken his sisters place. Sybil Good would always live on in Billy's heart.

By Friday, it had turned really hot and indeed Indian summer had come to Montana. Those who were taking the train south had already departed. Rand, Tig, Billy, Hard Knocks and Matt were waiting for their train tickets going to Salina. Andy with his pup "Iris" would be leaving by horseback the following Monday, he was riding over to the Fort at Benton on the Missouri river as he had heard there was work there and a spritly community for action.

The ones headed south to their Texas homes or New Mexico bound by horseback, took the dogs back with them to the chuck wagon and Wranglers crew of horses.

The rest of the friends were discussing their views.

"This is the end of the drive and I am headed to Alaska to try my hand at the gold mines. There'll be no more dust, cows or threat of Indians for this old lad." So the conversations went around the chuck wagon the last night out.

Gus thought it over and decided he would stay. "You know, fellows, there is work a plenty right here in Montana. Me and Boots are striking out to the copper mine for a spell- maybe even drift on up to Flathead country, too."

Grady added, "there is logging and coal mining and, God knows, there are the river boats needing hands."

"Hey Doc," Boots hailed him as Blaine sauntered up. "You going to your business in Kansas or hit the trail for new stuff?"

"Don't know yet, Boots, I got no ties so where I set my saddle down is home at the time maybe Alaska gold fields. I know Rand and Matt will be out of here by dawn headed for the depot. They have family in Kansas. Bless'em. Billy and Tig will be headed east Salina way also.

"What about you, Hard Knocks?"

"Yep, me too. I gotta sweet lady waiting for me and a son who will be walking by now."

Grady spoke up then, " Fellas, I'm gonna hang around Montana for while then head for Californ'y. I've had my fill of cold, cows and trail grub about now. Think I'll try my hand at fishing trawlers later on, it's about as far west as I can get. Besides, fish and ocean water is a long way from desert and cattle", he said with a broad smile.

Levi said, "Maybe I'll hang my hat in Utah a spell. Twenty one years with cows, cussing, storms, dirt and hard earth for a bed as about worn out my bones. House, bed, bath and regular grub sounds just fine. I may even enter into business or the like. Restaurant maybe!"

It was quiet for a while; the dogs flopped here and there, coffee tins rattled and talk faded away into the velvet skies of an October night.

In the early morning hours, the Kansas bound men finished their packing, and then looked for breakfast and places to shop for their wives, before heading to the train depot.

"Since we have over four hours until train time, I'm going to shop around to find something nice for Reva." Rand was a good cowhand and a business man when at home, but not to much at what he called *woman things*. He would be satisfied to buy a box of handkerchiefs, like the ones with lace and pretty flowers sewn into the corners. He knew most women carried them about. When the waitress came with coffee he asked her what might be a nice gift from Montana to take home to his wife.

"It depends on your wife, you know. Does she like perfume, jewelry, clothes or what ever?"

He had to think on that a bit. "Well, Reva is a school teacher and pretty down-to-earth and practical," he offered.

"Where are you from?" the waitress asked.

"Kansas."

"I never was to Kansas. What weather do you have there?" she asked.

"Decent, I guess, hard wind, pretty cold winters, lots of prairie flowers."

She thought about it as she went on to another table, then came back over to Rand, Matt and Hard Knocks.

"You might consider some books on Montana or one of those big maps over at the newspaper office. They mark out the interesting places for folks to go see".

Rand said, "That's a fine idea, appreciate it, she could use it at school, too, I'll bet," he thought.

"Another thing," she offered, "there is a town northwest of here name of Dupuyer. It nearly faded out but some fellow turned his store into a kind of museum. I hear it has all sorts of odd things, mounted heads, and Indian jewelry. You might think on that if you have time."

Why thank you, Miss, it's a fine idea but we are homeward bound today."

Hard Knocks spoke up, "You know that jewelry sounds like an idea for me. Willa just loves gee jaws; she has some quite expensive pieces she enjoys wearing. Mostly came from back east jewelers who had some specially made."

Matt wondered what would really be nice for Daylene and asked the others, either of you got a notion as to Daylene? She nearly lives at the restaurant or over to Bert and Nola's, she is mighty fond of Chrissy. Too bad we don't have any sprouts- she'd be a wonderful mother." He sighed and finished his coffee. Maybe it was just as well they didn't have children as he was gone lot of the time.

They paid their bill and started browsing through the stores on the way back to the hotel. At the jewelry store Hard Knocks picked out a broach with Montana agate surrounded by small sapphires set in gold filigree. It had a clasp that could be worn as a locket or it could be used as a pin for lapel or blouse. He decided he had done very well and Willa would be pleased.

"You know Knocks, it might be nice to get a bottle of scent to go along with that fine pin." Matt was thinking about what to buy Daylene and decided he would settle for a pair of sapphire earrings. She can wear those anytime or anyplace he reasoned. Plus she wouldn't spend this money on herself.

After looking over the selection of fragrances, Hard Knocks said everything smelled the same to him. "Too much trail dust up my nose, but I sure do like that blue bottle with a tassel on it." He picked it up and read, 'Evening in Paris.'

"This is the one!" he said, very pleased with his choice. "I'm done, fellas. Where you going to next?" Knocks asked.

"I'm headed for the newspaper office to look at books and that map the girl spoke of," Rand replied.

Knocks gathered together his purchases and, as he walked out the door called back, "See you two at the hotel by eleven."

"You gonna get anything else but those ear 'bobs', Matt?" Rand was still in a quandary about the choice of books.

"Well, yes, Daylene likes different things in the house. Why don't you come with me to look at those Indian blankets or the Hudson Bay blankets? Or maybe one of those fur muffs from Alaska – that's different than anything in Kansas."

"Sounds like a fine idea – let's go," Rand agreed. Off they went in search of their individual treasures. About a block along the boardwalk they saw Billy with Blue and Dog.

"Hold up there, Billy," Rand called, "where you been this morning?"

"Out hunting down some trinket or whatever to take back to Chrissy and Sylvia Lee."

"I'd think twice about getting something for Sylvia Lee, Billy. Might better let Tig take care of that, eh?"

Rand knew which way the wind blew where Sylvia Lee was concerned in Tig's interest.

"Well, golly sake, she is like my sister," Billy objected.

"Do as you please, Billy, but I'd concentrate on little Chrissy was it me," Rand advised.

Billy took the dogs and started to the train station to pick up his ticket. He hated to leave the dogs with Starkey and Lowell – he would miss them. He and Tig had decided to return to Kansas before heading back to Texas. Tig had Sylvia Lee on his mind and Billy wanted to visit his father a few days. They could pick up their horses in San Angelo when they returned to Texas. At the depot there was an Indian family selling a collection of things that tourists buy. Billy looked them over before settling on a locket of ivory embossed with a black flower in it. These were from Alaska and called scrimshaw. It would be good for now or when she was grown; besides no one else would have one. He was satisfied with his choice.

Back at the mercantile, Matt brought a beautiful seal muff for Daylene, a little something more to go with her earrings, while Rand purchased the wall map and a Hudson Bay wool blanket for Reva.

At the hotel Boots was showing off his hair cut and shaving kit he bought at the barber shop.

"Now see here, boys – I'm all gussied up and ready to howl," he said as he swaggered about with an evil grin. "Y'all just go back to mama. This ole boy is out for fun. Then I'll think about other territory."

"Oh yeah, we know your type of pestering fun, if you don't end up in the hoosegow it will be a wonder," laughed Matt.

"What is all this stuff you boys are packing?" Boots wondered.

"Things to take back home," Billy offered.

"Ha! Peace makers for you married ones no doubt."

"Couldn't hurt," grinned Rand.

"What did you get for the son?" Billy asked Hard Knocks.

"Some chaps and a few reading books. Willa would have him at university by age eight if she could. Beats all I ever saw;

she is teaching him out of the newspaper. Ain't that sum'thin'?" he laughed.

"We better get our gear down to the depot. I hear the whistle coming at the river crossing."

Billy, Tig, Matt, Rand and Hard Knocks began hauling their gear and purchases down the block to the depot. Billy had a lump in his throat about the size of a watermelon trying to get on the train with Blue staring that bewildered look at him. Where he went the dog went, but this time Blue would need to stay with the drovers and chuck wagon along with Starkey, Lowell and the cook.

Once the train pulled out, the others met at the local watering hole by the hotel to hash over who was going where. Gus elected to stay in Montana as he had a niece there.

"I'll go to Choteau to see Ruthie first," he said, "Sister passed on but Rex, the brother-in-law, lives there with the girl. She was just a sapling then, cute as a bug's ear. Right fond of that youngin', I am that. All growed up and all now, might get to know her better later on."

"What's up with you Grady?" Gus wanted to know.

"Think I'll go up to Bozeman and have a look see. I'm not ready for any one place for a few months."

"You curious about that copper mine up at Butte?" Gus asked.

"Yes, Joe heard tell it is so deep you can look near a quarter of a mile down into it. Largest open pit copper mine in the world, they say."

"I'd like to go see it myself," Grady agreed.

"Might be I'll ask for work there." Gus was thinking about winter and wondered if outside work was such a good idea.

"On t'other hand, I might think a bit more about the Crow Reservation and set up at the Fort to tend the stock and horses They have good bunk houses and God knows I surely do know the trade." Gus shook his head and wondered if he would live to see the day he would be without a horse.

"Levi, you got plans yet?" Grady was still speculating about his own.

"I been pondering that for the last two hundred miles. Blaine's taking off for the Alaska gold fields, but I'm forty three and trail worn, I don't cotton to the cold. Believe I'll head for Utah or parts warmer." Levi was a Kentucky man who hit the trail west by age fourteen, had no family and loved music more than anything. He never failed to find a group where he could join in with his harmonica. In the cattle drives you could hear him long before you saw him and it was pleasant.

"I thought I'd like to own a restaurant with a corner for some music. You know – a fiddle or two, guitar, maybe a squeezebox, a piano, a banjo, my harmonica, too" he mused. "Some living quarters overhead so I could hear it if I cut out early. Be warmer, a place to eat, sleep and with entertainment there would be no need to leave home"

"My, that did take two hundred miles of brain searching I reckon." Gus was grinning but impressed, his remark was in sarcastic fun. Blaine was young and adventurous, he too laughed and nodded his head.

"I'm for a bit of travel before I settle and that may take a lifetime," he laughed loud and long at his own wisdom. He of the itchy feet had adventures in mind.

"You know, I'm a veterinarian, so I have a good trade regardless of where I go."

CHAPTER 15

On the train east out of Cheyenne the scenery had changed over the past five years. In some places it was difficult to realize what the area was. Building the railroads had left some new town sprouting up and way stations looked like ghost towns.

By Wednesday the Salina bound passengers were home. What an uproar that was among the friends and relatives. Willa and little Spencer were on hand to greet everyone, she explained Fritz would be along later.

Manter pounded Billy on the back and started him for the house. Reva collected Rand, while Tig borrowed a horse and headed out to the Peabody's farm. He carried a Cameo broach for Sylvia Lee, if she would have him, he intended they would marry the next spring. They had kept in touch these last eleven months by mail and phone, so it was no surprise when Beulah learned of Tig's intentions. Roscoe had no objections and it would have done him little good if he had. Roscoe had settled down, mellowed out and become a more accepted part of the Salina people. Once his place started to prosper he quit fighting the world he felt had dealt him a poor hand to play. He set up a wood shop in one corner of his barn and was turning out some mighty respectable pieces of furniture, as well as raising sheep and even belonged to the church where

Buela now led the choir.

Billy noted many changes in the town's growth and population.

He commented about this to his father who took about an hour to catch him up on time, places and people. The phone rang; it was Willa hunting for Billy.

"Billy go collect your friend Tig, get your father and all of you come over to our place by five o'clock. We are calling all of you in. Clem is here, Fritz is making a huge BBQ for all of us. That's what he was about and not at the depot."

Billy was as excited as a child. This was a *real* home coming.

"Did you know of this Papa?"

"Yes yes son. It's all been talked out twenty times" he laughed.

For the next few hours Billy was kept busy with talking of the Indians, the baby, Blue's pups in the mud and every detail of his life it seemed to him. He felt like a celebrity of sorts. Tig brought Sylvia Lee back into town with him, she drove her buggy and he returned the horse to the livery stable.

Reva noticed the Cameo and poked Willa.

"Did you notice the lovely Cameo broach that Sylvia Lee is wearing?"

"No but I will." Willa still sometimes missed the way of life she had before marrying. Her dance hall clothing was a memory from her past. *Way past* she thought, and smiled.

"Sylvia Lee that is a lovely piece of jewelry you're wearing. I have never seen anything like it around here."

"I doubt you shall" she dimpled up and hugged Tig's arm."

"Ah ha – so that's the way it is" Reva clapped her hands.

That got everyone's attention, she said, "Tig you have any news to share while all of us are telling stories?"

Tig looked at Billy who knew nothing of this, he scuffed his feet around a bit, cleared his throat to say

"In May of next year my folks and a few *friends*" – he shot a look at Billy – "will be back for Sylvia Lee and my wedding," he hugged her to him.

Billy sat down and stared at Tig like he never knew him.

"Well I'll just be darn'd" he said.

"How did all this happen and me know nothing?"

"Because you poked fun at me so long after we were here last time," he bragged and laughed loud and long at the look on Billy's face.

"You could not have done better Tig, I'm really proud for you. Sylvia Lee was Sybil's best friend, she has been like a second sister to me ever since she was seven years old." Billy slapped Tig on the back, wrung his hand nearly blue and kissed Sylvia Lee on the cheek.

"By all that's Holy, I'm sure proud of you both" he preened.

There was much to do, things to settle and plans to make before Billy and Tig took the train back to San Angelo. They would leave just after Thanksgiving. Tig had stayed with Manter and Billy, he learned about Uncle Buck and the box, the Sprow's and the life Chrissy had now. So much more that he was wondering by the time they left for Texas – "Am I going to live in Texas or Kansas?" He had known only ranching all his life, could he leave it and come here where he was so well received or take his new wife back to Texas. Now here is a new thing to consider, he said to himself. "Once married, we can decide that." The next two weeks passed way too fast.

The trip back to Texas was relatively uneventful. Billy was glad to see Lowell and Elaina *and Blue*. They met Tig at the depot and there was his dog in the buggy. Blue jumped out and ran to Billy yapping her head off.

"Hello old girl." Billy gave the dog a hug and a scratch behind the ears, a pat on her head several times, but she jumped around and licked his hand till he said, "OK enough now, let's head for Concho, we have our own home."

He untied his horse from the back of Lowell's buggy and thanked Elaina for all her help and care of his animals then he and Blue started east. It was roughly thirty five to thirty eight miles from San Angelo to Concho with a few way stations that were leftovers after Fort Concho closed. It would take him two days or three to ride into Concho. The railroad had gotten into San Angelo in 1888, he wished there was a spur line going his way – just dream on he thought to himself.

There was much to do at the place left to him by Uncle Buck. Over the years the Army had pulled out, the population had melted away from over two thousand in 1880 to about sixty people now in 1889.

He had four hundred acres and it boarded the Colorado river for over half the length of his land. Wild cattle were mostly gone except a scatter here and there over several hundred miles of territory, grain was not popular to this soil but sheep did well. Once he settled in, tore down the one room cabin that had seen it's time and cleared out for a foundation, he contacted the Army head quarters to see about buying an empty barracks. He needed to find some abandoned buildings to establish a home and outbuildings.

CHAPTER 16

1895 – 1945

When Christmas came he had a house, a herd of sheep, an abandoned Army building to be used for a barn and one for shelter. There was a hospital the Army had built in 1872, being used for a clinic as well as a town gathering place. When the 19th Infantry Company "K" pulled out in June of 1889, there were a lot of tables, chairs, kitchen equipment and many other useful items that were left behind. Billy nearly outfitted his *new house* from the leftovers. For the time being, he was well situated and satisfied. With the clinic close by he needed little else.

For now, Concho depended on Paint Rock for supplies and other needs. It was amazing how places failed once the Army pulled stakes, a trip to San Angelo took too much time and Billy stay'd busy with his place, he was grateful for Paint Rock. Lowell, Elaina and Tig came to visit the following spring and collect Billy for the trip to Kansas for Sylvia Lee's wedding. Billy had two boys helping him with the ranch who lived there in the bunk house. It had been a forage house built by the Army in 1876 and was in good condition and moved easily. They even had their own kitchen.

He explained his absence of a couple weeks and collected

his things giving them their orders until he returned and then he left. The wedding was officiated by Booth Gordon, Beulah sang the wedding "Here comes the Bride" as well as the popular song "Sweethearts". Sylvia Lee was radiant; it was a very lovely wedding. Tig was a good looking *very nervous* groom, Billy was best man and Chrissy was the Maid of Honor, a very lovely wedding. Miss Nora Ellen held the reception in the church parlor, it seemed to her most of the people she knew were in attendance, all of the wagon train people who could be located had been invited.

"So Tig – what did you decide to do?"

Billy had been discussing his best friends living arrangements.

"For now, we will remain here in Kansas, I'll help Roscoe with the farm and his shop. He was hurt last winter and has a game leg now. He can use the help for a time."

"When you decide for sure, you contact me Tig" Billy said seriously.

"I need help myself. The herd is now two thousand head and let me tell you at shearing time it's hell to pay with only my permanent help."

Tig was taken aback in surprise –

"Well I'll be darn'd Billy, you never mentioned it before."

"No, I was waiting to see which way you were gonna move. I doubt you will remain in Kansas."

The first of June Billy was back on the sheep ranch. He had planted trees around the house for shade but also for extra income. Pecans were a good business. He needed to go to San Angelo to see about the trees and get seed for a garden, he recalled what his mother had planted. After a day of running here and there, he was more than ready for a steak, some apple pie and a clean bed.

At the hotel dining room he ordered his food and a drink, settled back to relax and think over his purchases. He bought a second wagon for his supplies and was considering a buck board as well. When he looked up as the main door opened, he saw, what to him, was the finest looking woman he had ever seen. His food arrived but he doddled over it as long as possible. She was sitting at another table with a man whom he took to be her father.

Before I leave town I need to know who that *Lady* is, he made a decision there on the spot.

"I need a wife he muttered." When the waitress came to collect his plate he ask her.

"Who is that woman across over there at the second table?"

"That's Katie Harmon, she plays the organ at Church, also the violin, very talented and a dear kind person. She takes care of her father. He had a stroke and no longer able to speak. It must be hard but she is an angel, that one is."

Now I wonder how to go about meeting her? I haven't had time for women, didn't really want one, his mind was running on ahead of common sense and he knew it. She stood to help her father up from his chair, but he stumbled over the leg of the table and nearly fell. Billy hurried to assist, so once those two were upright, he took that for an opening.

"I'm Billy Good from over Concho way, glad to help here" he offered.

"I do thank you so much" she smiled. I am Katie Harmon and this is my father Jake. He can no longer speak due to a stroke but I will thank you for him also. She reached over to hold her father's arm and started across the room toward the door. Billy hurried to open it for them then returned to his table. He felt happy all of a sudden and ordered another beer.

In September Tig and Sylvia Lee joined him on his spread. The two men formed a partnership with Lowell supplying the funds to back Tig. They prospered and did very well. Sylvia Lee took over the book work, the hiring of needed help and ran the business end of things.

Billy made unnecessary trips to San Angelo but he managed to find a reason to stop by the Harmon home as often as he was in town. In 1902 Jake Harmon passed away in his sleep and in June of 1903 Katie married Billy Good. He moved to San Angelo, leaving his house to Tig for now.

In 1902 Teddy Roosevelt had been elected President and in 1903 the Ford Motor Company had put their first automobile on the market. Billy was mesmerized by the auto industry. Since Jake Harmon had owned an implement store selling farm machinery, and since his death Billy had taken over the management, it took some persuasion but he added Ford vehicles to the inventory. They contacted the Michigan office and formed a dealership. In time this caused some touchy situations at home. As if it had wheels Billy wanted it.

In 1903 he sold autos and purchased the first one, but in 1905 the REO Motor company came up with the Runabout. That temptation finally won out in 1906 when Billy bought the REO and came home to Katie with the news that he had purchased stock in that company while selling Fords.

"I've always trusted your judgment in business matters, but this is a cause for some big problems," Katie said.

"This REO is a good seller but won't last long," Billy explained. "I'll stick with it a while, make some money and step out", he was sure he was on the right track. By 1907 the REO had gross sales of four million dollars and was one of the top automobile manufacturers. Besides there were REO, Olds, Chevrolet and Ford.

In early June he was thinking Montana.

"Katie, you know Nelia and Woody chose our wedding date for their wedding too. She is just twenty-three and well educated, I believe that they will be successful whatever they tackle. We need to leave for their wedding my dear wife." Billy adored Katie and hugged her to him.

"It's three years already but only seems like yesterday that we were married." Billy had been thirty eight years old.

"I'll see about train tickets" she said.

"Well, I hoped to drive" he pleaded.

"Where will you find gasoline?" That would require some research, so in the end the train won out.

Nelia's wedding to Elwood Barton was a big fancy todo which Billy thought unnecessary with all that splendor but secretly he was so very proud. *His* little baby girl was now a lovely young woman.

At the end of his term as Governor, Lionel and Marcia had relocated to Great Falls , Montana several years before when Nelia was only four years old. Since the state had provided a new Governor's mansion, Lionell purchased the first governors house where they lived their entire long life.

Back home in Texas, Billy sold his REO and bought an Olds, two years later a Model T Ford then back to General Motors for a Cadillac which was replaced with a LaSalle. The Studebaker Company produced a car he could not resist and in 1937 he brought home a black beauty with grey mohair upholstery. It was to be the last of his car purchases. There were war rumblings across the ocean that did not sound good.

By fall of 1905 Concho had a post office which was a blessing for both Billy and Tig. Although Sylvia Lee took care of the accounts, hiring and ninety percent of the paperwork, there were many envelopes of importance passed through that Post Office instead of running to Paint Rock twice a week.

Captain McKenzie had driven the Comanche out of the area by 1874 and later after the Fort was abandoned the population fluctuated. Concho remained a shipping point for hides, wool, pecans and sheep. However by 1939 the population was less than fifty people. No one here was concerned about the war overseas.

But 1941 was a horrible year for Billy. Lowell had died of pneumonia in March, Tig and Sylvia Lee had moved to San Angelo to be with Elaina. Robert Yates, who had helped him with the ranch, had joined the Army in April. Katie passed away in August and the Second World War began in December. Billy sold out his business in San Angelo and returned to Concho, he was seventy-seven years old and not sure what to do with himself.

He had no responsibility, not even a dog. After Blue was gone he couldn't bring himself to get another dog. He suffered over that loss as much as if Blue had been a person.

Gus had been after him to come to Montana where he lived in a Senior home for men run by his niece Ruth. Billy would be closer to the Longworth's and Barton's but...? Maybe he *would* call Gus; while he was thinking this over the phone rang.

"You comin' Billy?" Gus asked.

CHAPTER 17

1945---1959

"Well I don't know Gus, I'll give it a good think over and let you know. Yeah sure I promise! I'm not so sure I'll know in a week, what's the hurry? Of course I know I'm eighty you idiot, so are you, what's that to do with my whereabouts? Yes, yes, I'll get back to you. What say? No, don't have your niece call me Gus. I'm not feeble or feeble minded, I just need some time to collect the life I've lived and see if it will fit into another frame of mind.

"We'll talk again Gus and thank you old friend for your concern."

Billy hung up his telephone and rubbed the side of his face in thought. He disliked change more and more with each advancing year. Disorder was like a tooth ache.

"Now there is a thought" he said to himself out loud.

"I don't even have teeth except these store bought kind" he laughed to himself.

Gus was a friend of fifty years, who knew him well, too well. Gus seemed to know things by instinct. Maybe I should consider the move to Montana but what a change that would be. Scenery and fishing would be better, people his age that

171

were friends would be an improvement over the present, that was for sure. The weather was cold, be down right wretched come winter but he wouldn't be alone day in and day out.

Lately there had been more aches and pains to deal with and the doctors were forty miles away. He hated that drive on the highway in his 1937 Studebaker and maybe the move to Montana wasn't such a bad idea. It still needed studying over.

It was four years since Katie passed over to be with the Lord; Billy had accepted the aloneness but not the loneliness. Thirty eight years can not be eased by a grave. How he wished Booth Gordon, his minister friend of his youth, could have been here, but Booth too was gone.

"I believe I'll go have a talk with Katie" he said to himself, and reached for his *cowboy hat* from the rack by the kitchen door. In June you seldom need a sweater but he took down the grey well worn plaid shirt, so often a part of his everyday apparel. He caught the screen before it slammed, smiling to himself he said "Don't slam the door Billy" an admonishment he had heard her say five thousand times.

So many wonderful memories; the happy days out weighed any troublesome ones. He had been a very fortunate man nearly all his life. The only improvement would have been for Manter and Millie to have been part of Katie's life as well. He missed his family, now all of them gone.

Walking slowly but directly to the cemetery, Billy stooped to pick up a few wild flowers along the path as he went to visit with Katie.

"Sweetheart, I'm here, we need to talk out my quandary. It will soon be scorching hot again which my old bones don't seem to tolerate much anymore. And I didn't put out no garden a'tall. Not much use of my staying on really.

"Gus is pestering to go up to Montana with him and of course Nelia and Woody are after me, too. Winters are a caution but no need to be out less I want to. Fishing is good; I sold the guns, no need for hunting.

"The Yates boy is getting married in July and his folks have asked me a dozed times if I'd thought to sell, I always said no but we need to hash this over. Might be the time honey, what do you think?"

Billy sat on the head stone until evening and watched the sun sizzle its way across the valley. Now and then he patted the stone like it was a baby's back, shook his head and said,

Katie dear I think I'll be leaving now".

It was less than a half mile from the grave yard to the home they shared but right now it seemed like a hundred miles.

In the morning he called the Yates' and asked Tom to bring young Robert and came out soon, they needed to talk it over. Yes, he would go to Montana.

By the end of the week arrangements were made to go to San Angelo to get the deed and paper work done while he still had the plan in his mind.

"Mr. Good," Robert spoke gently, "You are not going to regret this move? Amy and I will be happy there and I promise we will take care of the place to make you proud." He shook Billy's right hand and clasped his shoulder with the left hand. Robert wasn't exactly sure just how much affection the old gentleman was accustomed to.

"Just right" Billy shook hard and too long. It was emotional for him but he knew in his heart he had done the right thing. He had a conversation with his Lord about it, too. Billy's faith never wavered in his life. Millie would have been so proud of her son.

"This will be a red letter day for my journal" he remarked, which stirred up thoughts of his mothers gift of a journal when he was twelve years old.

The Yates dropped Billy off at his home then Robert went to pick up Amy. It was three weeks until their wedding and things were falling into place. Gods guiding hand, Robert thought.

Now what to do about all this household stuff? Maybe a sale, no he couldn't stand it to see strangers pouring through thirty eight years of his life. Maybe, just maybe, he had a thought.

Robert answered the shrill ring of the phone.

"Yates house…"

"Robert, this is Billy Good, I'd like you and Amy to drop by tomorrow evening or next day being Saturday, if you can."

"Why sure, Mr. Good, that is no problem at all. We can come Saturday morning. Amy has a wedding shower in the evening."

"Fine boy, I'll be here all day."

Billy hung up the ear piece in its cradle on the box. "I reckon the young ones will get a new phone that sets on the table," he thought. Lots of changes he would never see. That's fine he *had* seen lots of changes in his eighty years, goodness yes! Sixteen presidents, four wars and twenty thousand miles of travel.

He never had another dog after Blue died; his sheep were sold several years before. Except for the milk cow and a few chickens and they were more for the company than eggs, was about all the stock left. His tools and Katie's garden hoes and all such, needed to be rid of. Well, he'd see what Robert wanted.

Saturday was hot and no rain in days when the young couple drove in they were driving Amy's '38 Ford coupe. Now what am I to do about the Studebaker, he was thinking. Robert didn't have a car. He had only been home from the war about a month. Maybe, just maybe, he thought again.

"Hello Mr. Good, we have a couple hours to stay, so what can we do for you?"

"I'm having a time to decide what to do with a lot of these things. Since you're just getting married I thought maybe you could use a few things before I give it away."

"We have about all we really need. Amy has her own place and things, but what do you have in mind?"

"There is this furniture, some is old enough to be antiques and the newer things are just out of date for your age but not yet antique. Then there is all the kitchen and linen; you know a house of items I live with."

This made Amy clap her hands and do a little jig in her kitchen chair.

"Oh Robert, isn't this grand?" she squealed. "Most of what I have is what Mama, Gram, and the aunts gave me to start with; out of the back room, attic and garage. Mr. Good just leave it be. We will sort it out. What we can't use we will see that our young friends also getting married get a chance to use the rest. None of us have much and most anything is welcome."

"What about the towels and the sheets, they are well worn? " He disliked giving away shabby things he had used just for himself.

"You know, Mr. Good, when you first start out you don't have rags; those seem to just accumulate. There are floors to mop, windows to wash, cleaning furniture and all sorts of reasons for rags, inside and out. Worn items make good rags."

Robert hugged Amy and said, "See what a practical wife I'm getting?"

"Much like my Katie", Billy nodded his head and smiled a loving smile filled with happy memories.

"Now one other thing, Robert, do you know any one interested in the Studebaker? It runs fine and new cars are not being built yet. I'd be much obliged if you could give me a hand with this car."

"I'll need to get back to you on that, but I have an idea." Robert asked if there was anything else.

"Yes, there is if you could come another time. I see you're anxious to get on your way."

They shook hands before Amy gave Billy a hug. He had a tear in his eye as he patted her back. It was several years since any form of endearment had taken Katie's place.

"God bless you lass, we will talk again."

Once the young couple departed, Billy sat on the back porch in the shade, he just wanted to think a while but his mind took him back through thirty years of time. He chuckled to himself over the amusing things in his life. One of which was his compadre, the Blue Tic hound who was like a brother, not a dog. Laughed out loud at the thought of his mother's cat Boots and the litters of kittens she supplied the town with. Or like the time he and his little red haired sister took his father's shaving mirror out in the back yard to put shelled corn on it, to watch the rooster try to eat it. Of course it looked like two kernels and the poor old rooster pecked away until he got dizzy and fell over. Naturally their father caught them and that game was over for good. It made him laugh even now to think of that dizzy rooster.

"I guess I better send Hollis my latest whim, he will repeat for the thousandth time. 'Billy Billy you can't stay put.' Oh I can hear it now. Ha Ha Ha Ha". Hollis has lived and will die in the same house all his life. I wonder what Salina is like by now.

It was a cooler evening than it had been for days. Billy took advantage of it to start packing the things for his trip north. That leather trunk of Katie's, there now, he could use that and keep her with him in thought. She had used it for a hope chest.

"I wonder what all is still in it?" he muttered to the empty room. Pulling it out from the back of the bedroom closet gave him a sharp pain in his back. It *was* time to set a spell and not work or have chores. "Yes, this move was right" Billy acknowledged.

He was getting excited about it now and stepped up the pace of sorting things.

"Well looky here, I haven't seen these in years, actually forgot about 'em" he mused.

"The buckles from the rodeo, those were wild days whooeee, he whistled through his teeth.

Also, there was a book of poems he had given Katie one year. She had pressed some flowers in it.

"It smells like lilacs, but we don't have any lilacs. I'm getting old, talking to myself, I been alone long enough. Soon I'll be senile" Ha Ha Ha.

Thumbing through the book he noticed little notations along the edge of a few pages, it made him smile as he read the neatly written notes. So lovely had been his Katie. What's that tucked under the folded newspaper, about the end of the war? He tugged it out to see.

"Of all things, I didn't know what ever became of this" he said as he straightened his back. "This gives me a fine idea" he took the box out to the kitchen table to further explore its contents.

"When Robert gets over here I'll sure have a fine surprise for him." Billy was pleased with himself.

The next item was his old sheriff badge. My, my, that was thirty years ago. Billy started to laugh and rocked back on the legs of his chair. The more he thought about that day in town with Katie the funnier it became.

Katie had a beau when she met Billy, but that ended soon enough. The beau became a saloon keeper and Billy became the sheriff. This day as they were walking along the street they passed by as Tim was sweeping up his place. Tim waved and Katie waved back. Billy said, "Now see how things turned out, if you would have married him you'd be the wife of a bar man." Katie squeezed Billy's arm and looked up at his six foot four frame, and she smiled sweetly.

"If I'd have married him, he would be the sheriff." It took him back a bit before he realized that indeed it had been Katie's *push* that installed him as sheriff.

"Oh Katie, Katie, my girl, the good times we share even yet." It made him shake his head remembering her laughter. So what else is in the box, a few pictures, and his pocket knife his father, Manter had given him for his ninth birthday, their marriage license and a lace handkerchief." He closed the lid and went out to feed his three old hens he had kept. Bessie, the cow, had gone to live with a neighbor a few days earlier.

"It has been a good day girls," he told his chickens. The hens pecked away at their meal and set about to dust themselves in the loose sandy soil.

"You look like feather dusters," how timely a remark he chuckled to himself and returned to the porch.

Robert Yates had been a sergeant in the Army during WWII, recently discharged. He came home to Concho to marry his high school sweetie and settle down.

He and Amy stopped by Billy's on Wednesday evening bringing ice cream with them. That was one treat Billy never had his fill of.

"Come on in, come in." he greeted the couple as Billy accepted the offered package. He knew its contents from the bag it was in. A quick smile and a "Thank you, thanks" accompanied some bowls and spoons. Once they were seated and *licked the bowls clean*, so to speak, Billy said, "I have something to share with you two. See this shoe box; it has been part of my life since I was fifteen years old." He told them the whole odd story of Uncle Buck, the winding way through deep cotton woods to the cave and his being given the box, its contents or most of them, which included the deed to this land. That had been sixty five years ago.

"It held momentums of his life, the deed to this land and his marriage license. It also held ours; Katie's and mine. I'd be much obliged to give you the box and hope you will carry on the tradition."

Tomorrow we are going to the attorney and the recording office in San Angelo, to transfer the deed to your names, however I have a stipulation. You see this place was given to me, I've sold off three hundred of the four hundred acres and your father has agreed to buy this one hundred that the buildings are on. It is my wish to give you the five acres which includes the house, as it was given to me. The price for the remaining ninety five acres will be worked out, I've already talked at over with your father. How you pay him is your concern."

"Now about the Studebaker, have you had any luck with

that job, Robert?'

"Yes sir, I'll buy it. I have a lead on a job up at Leaday, but that would leave Amy no way to get back and forth to her job."

Amy had sat quietly until now when she burst into tears. "God is so good. All these blessings are pouring out on us and **no** way could it all have come together otherwise. I'm just so happy and so *blessed.* She kissed Billy on the cheek, put her arm around Robert's shoulder and tipped his head back against her, as she had walked over to stand behind him. She hugged his head against her and kissed the top of his head.

Billy was full of contentment. He knew he had done the right thing. He would go tell Katie in the morning. The sun rise was yellow, pink and orange, perhaps some rain today, he pondered that on his walk to the cemetery. "Katie, it's all figured out, I'll sit with you a while now and be back on Monday morning."

The wedding was Sunday; he had stayed over to attend it, so on Monday he called Gus with the time schedule of the train to Great Falls. Next he called Nelia and Woody what time to pick him up, then called Tom Yates to come take him to San Angelo to the depot. He had given the car keys to Robert on Saturday so the young couple could pack what they were taking on their honeymoon.

Tom picked him up three hours early, giving them time for a quick lunch after the drive across to San Angelo.

"Now Tom, here are the house keys, the hen's feeders are full. Things are just as I lived and I'm beholden to you for your help over the past four years and before."

When the train came, Billy took his ticket and the old leather trunk to see it was stowed away. He shook hands with Tom Yates and climbed aboard to his next faze of life; however long that might be. He was a happy man of eighty years, good health and anxious to be off.

CHAPTER 18

September 1945 State of Montana

Finding the Pullman car a relief for his back, Billy settled in to enjoy this trip to Montana. What a total difference from the first trip up by horse back. It hardly seemed possible it was even in the same century. Texas was over run with people, buildings, factory, and cars. The people had planted trees everywhere. Such a sight he had never expected to see. Being naturally curious it was his nature to try to see everything at once and ask questions of everybody.

This trip is worth just getting to see things, he thought. He vividly recalled the building of the Atchism, Topeka, and Santa Fe. Now he has riding on it. The next stop would be Denver in two days then a transfer over to the Union Pacific for two more days, taking that train through to Butte, Montana then change for Great Falls, on the Great Northern Line.

"No one could believe it." Billy told his travelers in the seat nearest him.

"I've relived in six days, fifty five years of my life."

"How's that sir?" the young man asked. For the next part of an hour Billy told of his childhood in a covered wagon to Kansas, the cattle drives; both Chisholm and the fateful

180

Goodnight Loving trail, life in Texas near the Louisiana line and this last trip across country he intended to make.

"This trip to Montana will be about all the excitement I'll need I reckon." He chuckled to himself remembering the wild cattle trail years, the hell raising days before he married Katie and the trials of being a sheriff in a fairly lawless country.

The splendid luxury of these coaches was nearly beyond comprehension for Billy; his life had consisted of *just enough and to be comfortable*, not superfluous in any way. The changes had already been set into motion. So far Billy was impressed.

As the locomotive chugged its way to a stop at the Great Falls depot, Billy arose, limbered up his legs and stretched his back. At fix feet four he could touch the roof easily, so he flexed his arms to reach up and further stretch his back.

"May I help you sir?" asked the young man who had been his traveling companion and listener these past miles.

"No, no think you son, I have my satchel and sweater, the trunk is in baggage, I'll do just fine. Been a pleasure visiting with you" he said as he started for the steps. Nelia and Woody were in view , as he started their direction she ran across the platform nearly knocking him over with her enthusiasm.

"Uncle Billy, oh bless you, bless you. We are **so** happy to have you here. What a world of things to talk about and...."

"Whoa up lass, your running words together getting them all out at once. We have plenty of time."

He hugged this lovely woman he had diapered as a baby. It's nearly impossible he thought as he looked at this little slip of a woman in her sixty's. Red hair fading to rust color, blue eyes just as snappy as always freckles still there under the powder that was supposed to hide them. If *his* life had been a story, imagine telling hers.

Briefly his mind wandered back to the Banneck Indians and her rescue from being bashed to death. The subsequent scant rations at hand to sustain a baby, the inventions the drovers had come up with; yes, yes what a story. "Maybe I should get her to write it out," he thought.

"Are you tired out Uncle Billy?" Nelia was concerned over his absent mindedness.

"Oh, yes, somewhat but it's age, not inconvenience, you see. I was just thinking back a few minutes that was all. I'm fine Nellie, just fine." He had reverted to his old nickname which she disliked. She said it likened her to a cow or brood sow, she was happy with her name, so use it, she said. Woody offered his greetings and went to bring their car around, it was easier to load that leather trunk of Billy's than carry it.

"I am certainly glad to see you have your own car; I was afraid you'd have that hearse of your father's." Billy referred to the limousine the Governor had always used.

"When exactly was it you and Aunt Katie were here?"

"It was 1935; honey, you and Woody were married twenty nine years then. You was fifty two years old and I couldn't believe it. I hadn't seen you since your wedding day. Time just runs on without us, doesn't it?" He pondered that.

Once at the *house* which really was a mansion, Billy was installed in a bedroom. He decided a bath would surely be in order to tidy up a bit. There seemed to be an unlimited amount of hot water which felt wonderful. He relaxed his old bones and nearly fell asleep in the tub so when Nelia called up the stairs he needed to rouse himself and dress.

"You look wonderful Uncle Billy; it is *so* good to see you. Had you made plans for a stay with us?"

"Not now honey, I need to call Gus and let him know I'm here all safe and sound. He is expecting me there in two days. His land lady is expecting me too, so I better stick with the plans already in motion."

"We can take you up when you're ready, besides we want to see where you are going."

It was an idol statement but Nelia and Woody really wanted to be satisfied about his lodging.

"I need to go up on Wednesday." Billy just marveled at the

time involved. One week ago he had sold the ranch and been in Texas. Here he was seven days later in Montana and ready to start over. His head never got the message he was eighty years old.

"Looks like August is headed our way," Billy commented. "The leaves are wearing their funeral clothes of red, brown, orange and wine, soon be a carpet on the ground. Nelia I see you're wearing your Topaz ring; it will soon be another birthday coming up. That one you're wearing was Katie's idea when we were here last."

"Since we could only guess your age, we figured it was about three months, so we used November first as a birthday." he chuckled, "You will always be a little younger than you are, how's that for not telling your age?" He seemed pleased with his own mirth!

"We will be having my birthday on the first of November as always, so plan to be here, we will come and get you. Don't forget, will you?"

"Nelia, my mind is as sharp as yours. Like a rat trap, once something is in my head, it don't leak out."

This was a lovely July day, he had missed all the hub bub of July 4th except the favors given out on the train, but it was good to think ahead to any festivity, there hadn't been much in the past four years. A person needed goals to keep their mind busy.

"Are you hungry yet Woody?" Nelia asked. "I thought we might go down to the Ivy House for dinner."

Billy spoke up, "We had dinner at noon on the train, you must eat mighty late. That's alright, you have your dinner and I'll eat my supper," he said kindly.

"Uncle Billy, it is fashionable now days to have the meals called *breakfast, brunch* if it's a ten o'clock breakfast, *lunch* at noon until one p.m. and *dinner* after six p.m. I'm not correcting you, mind, I just don't want you confused while looking at menus." Nelia was such a dear, kind hearted woman always alert to things that might offend or embarrass another. She reached over to pat Billy's hand.

"Well don't that beat all? At home it was just meal time, on the trail it was chow, in our house it was breakfast, dinner, supper. That did the job alright; I wonder why it got changed? If it don't need fixin' you don't fix it; don't that just beat all?"

Nelia hid her face in her handkerchief to hide a smile. How she loved this old man.

"Yes, well I guess it is just the sign of the times. Lots of new things since the war; people from east marry people from west, south or over seas and pick up new traits and habits. Other country's influence on our's also tend to earn a place in our life style. Much of it is an improvement and an upgrade from our sedentary life styles. I find it quite refreshing to learn new ways and style." Nelia was not a snob but was member of the elite society. She had a college education and was a poet in good standing. Billy marveled at her mannerisms and deportment. He was proud of her achievements and graces.

Nelia had met Elwood Barton at a political rally while her adopted father was Governor. They knew each other only six months when they were married at the mansion. The Longworth's had a daughter, Cartha Ruth, who died of scarlet fever at age four, so when they were approached to raise this baby the drovers had saved from the Indian raid, she was welcome as the sunshine.

Marcia Mellon was the daughter of a wealthy Pennsylvanian industrialist; she set her cap for Lionel Longworth who was in politics. He later became Governor of Montana which moved them from Miles City to Helena the capital. Upon his retirement they, with Nelia had moved to Great Falls. Nelia lived in their huge home left to her at their demise. Such a life story, Billy thought yet once more. She should write in down!

"If you're ready?" Nelia said to her men folks.

"I can do justice to a good steak." Woody loved his beef.

"I don't eat much in the evening," Billy wasn't really hungry, "but I'd be ready for pie and ice cream no matter what the time is called." He was wondering if dessert had a name now, too. He might better ask about that. He didn't want people to think he was deranged just because he was long in the tooth.

Breakfast consisted of *Bangers,* that was sausage he discovered and hotcakes, which are flap jacks, applesauce, coffee and then *hurry up* which he deduced from the maid removing the plates and utensils. "New revelations abound," he muttered.

His clean clothes were now placed in the new valise he had been given to use, the old satchel stayed behind, he stepped into the car and headed to Choteau. Once they crossed over the Sun River this land was yellow with wheat stubble or fields not yet harvested. It was hot and dry in July and August but a blessed relief from the scorching sun and wind of Texas. The fields looked like a good yield and he remarked about that.

Next came Freezeout Lake and then seventeen miles more to arrive at his new *"digs".* That was present day living quarters talk, "I wonder how that came to be?" he mused. "Digs, well I'll swear"

Woody pulled his big LaSalle car up in front of the address where Gus lived and Billy would be living along with three other elderly men. The car wheels had hardly came to a full stop when Gus came to the porch steps as fast as his bowed legs could manage.

"Yee ha," he bellowed. "Ya ol' varmint, I knowed ye'd git here." Gus nearly drug Billy out of the front seat.

The two old partners shook hands, slapped each other on the back and tried to look away as they had tears in their eyes. Gus reached over to pound Billy on the back one more time.

"You old fool, I got a bum back, don't be wackin' me."

"How am I supposed to know you hurt some "ers? I don't' see no blood runnin'." Gus laughed and started to slap Billy's shoulder but Billy ducked out of his line of fire. With arm's across each others shoulders the chums each reached for a railing and started up the steps.

Elwood had pulled the leather trunk from his car while Nelia gathered Billy's hat, jacket and valise from the back seat. She too had tears of joy just to see the happy faces of those two up on the porch. As they took the items from the car on up to the steps, Woody leaned closer to Nelia and softly said, "I'm certainly glad we did not attempt to coax Billy to remain with us."

Nelia nodded, "Yes, or worse, try to find a nursing home. He would have absolutely taken the next train back to Texas. It amazes me how spry and sharp he is at eighty. If only we can attain such status, I'll be pleased with my life."

Ruth Romic was holding the front screen open for everyone as they entered the hallway of her home. She was delighted to see everyone and was introduced to Billy by Gus as they passed right on through to the living room. They hardly gave Ruth time to even nod her head.

Nelia shook her head, smiled a lovely greeting to Ruth and introduced herself, then her husband Woody.

"I'm pleased you delivered Mr. Good, he seems right at home," she chuckled.

"Hardly even said hello," Woody remarked.

"I'm sure he will just take over soon," Nelia laughed her tinkling little sound. Her laughter resembled ice clicking in a glass of water; it was contagious and everyone else laughed with her.

"Billy Good is a self made man and doesn't stand still long, always doing something, mostly for other people. He will settle in, I don't think he ever met a stranger in his life."

"Would you like to stay for lunch with us?" Ruth asked.

"That would be lovely, yes I believe we shall, is it alright dear?" She thought she should ask Woody, not knowing if he had any plans for the rest of the day.

"Fine, just fine," he agreed and sat down.

"May I help you in the kitchen?" Nelia wasn't so sure what

good she would be, but would offer never the less. She had been raised with a nanny and servants so she wasn't too frequently on speaking terms with cooking utensils.

"No, no my dear, we have a wonderful cook here, a cleaning woman, gardener and laundry lady. Everyone knows each other, all have lived in or near here most of their lives. We are nearly family."

Ruth was proud of her staff, the home she had created for the aged, but mostly she was happy to be useful.

"Come with me to the garden," Ruth invited. Our flower beds are a thing of beauty and my pride and joy. This is one place I shine. Oliver tends to the shrubs, trees, weeds and what ever but the plants are my children."

Indeed it *was* a lovely flower garden, roses in bloom, snapdragons, asters, zinnias, marigolds, nasturtiums, all in bright colors arranged to show off their best. It would be a wonderful place for Billy; Nelia had not a doubt left.

After lunch, it was goodbyes for now, we will be up once a week or if you call. There would be no *end* of talking on that front porch the rest of this day. That was a foregone conclusion. Nelia told Woody, "We may as well start back home."

Billy's room faced the street from the second floor where he could see over several blocks and acquaint himself with the area. "Best thing I could've done," he said aloud.

In the morning he smelled coffee and ham among the other tempting odors floating up the stairwell. He normally didn't eat a great deal anymore but all at once he was ravenous. Billy dressed quickly, stood straight to ease his back. "My posture needs attention," he decided, and hustled down to greet that coffee pot. As he was the first to arrive he met the cook who was an amply built woman of Norwegian ancestry; name of Marta.

"Morning Mr. Good," she greeted, "Sit you down, 'tis good to have you aboard. Now what would you like, a cup of coffee, maybe?"

"Sounds fine, just fine," he reached out his hand for a mug being offered. "Ahhh, good coffee, starts up your day in a good mood," he chuckled.

"So here you are already after our cook are you, you old rascal." Gus came over to pull out a chair across the table.

"Well old sock, how did the night go?"

"I wouldn't know Gus, I slept through it."

"Bright eyed and bushy tailed already at seven in the morning. I guess we are in for a days worth of blarney, eh? Good to see you Billy."

Billy thought he might try out his newly learned vocabulary.

"Marta, what do we eat here in this house? I've learned several new fangled ideas about food this past week. Do we have lunch at dinner time and dinner at supper time and I haven't yet figured out exactly what it is that's called *brunch* unless it means a snack or piecing before a meal." He poked his coffee mug her direction while asking. She refilled it for him and explained.

"Mr. Good...." He interrupted her.

"Name's Billy."

"Yes, well I'm fifty years old and was brought up by the hair of my head, suppose I'm old fashioned with some of my notions, too. But I cook breakfast, dinner and supper. You can name it as you please, just clean up your plate, I don't waste food and I hate leftovers. I ate leftovers for the first sixteen years of my life or go hungry."

"I'm rich now by the good Lords standards. I don't need for anything, but NEVER waste food. If you're a picky eater, you better learn to cook. I'll allow as I don't fix two meals for each different person."

"Anything else you need to know before I get my apron on? No, then you two get out of the kitchen or go set the table."

Gus nearly collapsed in a front room chair; he laughed until he had hiccups.

"Want to go back to the kitchen, Billy?" he whooped another snort of mirth, then said, "Come on, best we set the table and get ready to eat. Be sure to clean your plate." He mimicked Marta and snickered at the look on Billy's face.

"Am I to judge from that haranguing it is best to stay out of the kitchen?"

"No, no, no, she loves to be boss and usually is. Good soul and a wonderful cook, she seems to delight in mothering everyone. To tell the truth, we look forward to her attention."

Billy pulled at his left ear and frowned at Gus. "You mean we hear this *every* day?"

"One way or another," Gus was having a high old time of it at Billy's expense. "Just wait till she gets on about the Bible. Last week she told us Moses climbed Mount Everest and told about Simon Peter had to go jump in the lake to get his eye sight back. Don't dare contradict her; she wages war with her wooden spoon."

"I'm beholden to ya Gus, I'll manage to be absent from the kitchen, however I do like my morning coffee, that I do."

"Then just walk in, pick up a mug and help yourself, then keep your trap shut. She gets started on to deep thinking; you won't eat till nine or worse."

Billy wasn't sure this had been the best part of his later life.

"I'll do, Gus," he sighed.

The four men gathered on the front porch after a monstrous meal of oatmeal, biscuits and gravy, pork chops, fried potatoes, peaches and coffee. Gus said, "Just don't take more than you can eat."

Billy started to laugh and wheeze at the same time. "She's gonna make me sit to the table till I clean my plate?" He choked on his own laughing. "Mama use to do that if we had something we didn't like. "Puts a whole new picture on this business of *entering our second childhood* after we make eighty years." He slapped his leg and he-hawed some more.

"Anything important to do today?" Billy wanted to be up moving around.

"Not usually," this from Harry Reese.

Harry was from Oklahoma originally, he had a niece who lived here in town. She had made arrangements for Harry to live with her but he begged off as she had teen age boys who nearly drove Harry crazy. "They just can't be quiet," he protested.

The other tenant was Sam Graham from west Texas, Billy enjoyed his company. The morning was a pleasant sixty eight degrees, no need for sweaters. Each found a chair or picked the porch swing, this soon became a pattern. Each had his own private choice and the others respected that choice. Gus Romic was Ruth's great uncle and had been born in Illinois, ran off from home at fourteen and at seventeen had ended up on the same cattle drive as Billy. They formed a friendship for life. They had spent many, many hours together on horse back, out on drag, around the camp fire or chuck wagon. Mainly discussing *once the drive is over*, talk. Gus had gone to Montana to work on a cattle ranch and stayed there. Billy had the property Uncle Buck left him, but he never spoke of it. Ajax was his only confidant. Once the drive was over Billy went to find the Concho land.

Uncle Buck had staked it out during the craze for gold that was a most elusive item, Fort Concho had been erected in 1867 and remained a busy part of history until 1889, and many buildings were deserted when the last troops left. 19th Infantry Company K had been stationed there from May 1888 until June of 1889. That year Billy took over his property, moved a barracks onto his land and became the owner of the general store that was closing up. Paint Rock City was the county seat, seven miles away, so it was not a problem for supplies. Billy was twenty four years old, had saved his money religiously, and wanted some roots and a family.

Concho had a Post Office from 1905 until 1937 then a

school opened 1906 with one teacher. Also there was a cotton gin, a grange hall, the grocery and a black smith shop. There were two other businesses, a few houses scattered about, then school was expanded to accommodate thirty one students. It went from first to seventh, so another teacher was added. The population was now fifty people above ground and twenty below, at the cemetery.

All this Billy explained to his three listeners on the front porch his first day in Choteau. Over The next few years about everything in their lives was hashed over and retold countless times. They knew each other well.

Winter was bitter cold from November until January when a Chinook came through. This was a complete surprise to Billy a Texas man. You go to bed at twenty below zero and wake up to green grass and rivers of water in the gutters, the trees dripping water off their naked limbs and it is now thirty eight to forty degrees. The hot Santa Ana winds come down out of Canada across Montana, Utah and into California. Nearly unbelievable. Everyone was ready for spring way before it arrived.

One late April morning the four men had taken up their usual places on the porch to watch the world go by and wonder about the after life. A topic much discussed among them.

A young woman perhaps in her thirties came up the sidewalk, waved to them in passing by and went on up the block.

"You know who that is?" Harry seemed to know everyone still breathing.

"Never saw her before," seemed to be a universal reply.

"Wonder where she is going," spoke up Sam, "she's pretty good lookin'."

"Now Sam, I got sweaters older than her," Billy said in jest. Sam gave him a lame excuse for a smile.

Along about four in the afternoon the woman returned. The men called a greeting, she smiled and waved back.

The following morning she came swinging by with a five gallon bucket full of something, a mop and broom over her left shoulder and a lilt in her walk. With a "Hi, fellows," she strolled on down the sidewalk.

"Don't that beat all", Harry looked distressed, he thought he knew everyone in town plus their dogs and cats.

"Guess you could ask her," Sam speculated.

"May do just that," said Harry.

The next morning, Harry, true to his word, had stepped down to the end of the sidewalk and said to her, "I see you're off to your chores."

"Oh yes sir, I have a project to tackle and it will take awhile."

"I'm Harry Reese, these old goats are my cronies. Gus Romic, Billy Good, and Sam Graham. We been wondering what you're about."

"Nothing backward about old Harry," Sam said.

"That's okay, I'm Julie Johnson and what I'm *about* is cleaning out the old John Deere tractor building."

"Why you want to do that?" Gus wanted to know.

"Because I'm going to open a dress making shop in there once I *ever* get the grease cleaned up. I could certainly use some help, it's too bad you guys are all used up. Well, I better get going or I'll never get finished." Off she went swinging up the walk.

"*All used up*, did you hear that?" Billy was indignant, put his arms akimbo and stared down the block watching her trim slender body hurrying along, her long dark hair swaying from side to side.

"Gus, you feel all used up, do you?" Billy asked in a voice that was filled with outrage.

"Well do you?" he demanded.

"Never gave it much thought, Billy." Gus too was looking down the sidewalk, watching Julie until she turned the corner and was no longer in sight.

"Sam, you feel old and feeble and all used up?" Billy couldn't let it go.

"Guess I hadn't considered much, Billy, we don't naturally have much to do so I just didn't think on it." Sam got up out of his chair to walk down the steps and join the others.

Harry came out of the house to join the men but saw they were down the steps out on the said walk.

"Anything exciting going on?" he called.

"Not now" Billy snapped, "but you need to consider if you feel useless, do you?" he was in a sour mood about the *used up* remark.

"Don't know Billy, I haven't done much of late to know if I'm useless or not, reckon I'd need to ponder that a spell."

"What's got you riled up anyway?"

"That young woman that passes by here told me that we old guys were all *used up*, now ain't that a caution!"

"I've done more in my life time than she could even know about or try to do. There aren't anymore wagon trains or cattle drives or to set on a horse eighteen hours straight in all sorts of weather." She wouldn't know about sech a way of life.

"No used to get all worked up over it, she never knew us. For all she knows we might be homeless tramps with no where else to go."

Sam decided to go for a walk; it was a warm spring morning. This conversation had stirred up the realization that maybe he really was on his last legs.

"What you gonna do Sam, foller or something?" Billy couldn't let go.

"Come to think of it, I just might. You want to come along?"

"I guess not but it is tempting." Billy sat down on the porch steps to think about it. He was still feeding chickens, doing his own house work and caring for the place by himself nine months ago, he wondered if he really had grown soft and useless.

"Well fellows, I'm going to be ready in the morning to go help Julie, I am not going to seed so long as I can be *useful*." It had really needled him to think he wasn't fifty anymore. But eighty wasn't that bad if you kept busy.

"Now there is a good idea," this from Harry who had joined Billy on the steps.

"Why don't we see what's out in the shed and ask Ruthie if we can use it, then go give that young lady a hand.

"Good idea, shake a leg Harry, let's go do that."

Julie had no knowledge of the hornets nest she'd stirred up this spring morning. Setting her bucket down, she propped the broom and mop up along the wall to unlock the door. Once inside things looked a bit grim.

"It's cold in here." She took her jacket off but left her sweater on. Thank goodness there was the old cement utility sink in the back room; at least there would be hot water to clean with as she had lit the gas hot water tank the day before.

In the bucket she had rags, paper towels, SOS pads, Dutch cleanser, rubbing alcohol, turpentine and two kinds of soap. Once those items were set up on the shelf over the sink she realized she had forgotten scrub brushes.

"I'll sweep up first then go buy a big sturdy brush, better get a dust pan too while I'm at it; some window cleaner and newspapers, some vinegar and see if I can round up another bucket." Talking to herself she realized how big and empty this shop was. After an hour of prodding dirt out of corners, brooming down cob webs and spider nests, she took a break. She turned the bucket upside down for a stool and opened her thermos of coffee she had tucked in with the cleaning supplies.

She thought back over the past months that had brought her to this area. Her occupation was in electronics working on a Government job. They were putting in the Interbelistic missal silos along the American Canadian border; her part of the project had been installing the alarm system around the opening to the underground silos. There were twelve on her team; each assigned an area of forty miles. These areas overlapped so they could be checked twice before sealing off the trigger systems set for any disturbances. This would alert the headquarters if tampering was being done.

The job completed, Julie had three weeks vacation time and had accumulated six weeks sick leave. Two months she could squeeze out to do as she pleased. This gave her a break from twelve hour days on the job regardless of the weather; it had been a hard winter so extra time sounded just fine. "Maybe I'll take a couple extra months off and travel this area of the country," she had thought. But having made several close friends over the past nine months she was reluctant to leave also.

"If I stay here, I'd need income or live up my years work or wear it down pretty thin." After her lunch one day she had a talk with herself. "Now let's see what I could do in this lovely little town of perhaps nine hundred people, plus or minus?"

"I won't count the skunks that walk down the street or wander into open business doors; the dogs who seem to know everyone in town and the deer who eat out of everyone's garden or chew up the trees. It is an interesting life here, I love it." She thought out loud. "So let's see, I'm an excellent cook, but no one needs that. The two restaurants here have cooks. I can sing, I have belonged to a band for several years but no one pays for that either. I can hang wall paper but not much call for that either. What else: Ah ha-I know, I can sew and I do it well. How about a sewing shop? I wonder-maybe it would work."

In the morning Julie started down the block to the far west end of the main street; stopping in at the business that *maybe* could use some help.

"Good morning Keith, I'm on a pilgrimage for myself. Do you ever have need of any sewing or patch work on these cars that come in to your shop?"

"What you got in mind, Julie?" Keith Miles owned the Ford garage and new car sales business.

"I'm thinking of opening a sewing shop and want to see if anyone needs enough to keep me in business."

"From time to time we do have loose head liners or ripped upholstery, now and then a split seat cushion, with the vehicles mostly ten years old and new ones just being built, they have seen some pretty hard use. Yes, I think I'd have some work for you now and then." Keith was busy, "Thank you Keith, I appreciate your time." So Julie went on down the way to her next stop at the cleaners.

"Do you have a few minutes? Roy, I won't keep you. I'm thinking of starting a sewing shop, who does the mending, sewing on buttons, replacing zippers, etc. for you? Repairing linings or tacking up hems that come loose in the cleaning process, for instance?"

"Mrs. Wright, when we can find her. This is a pretty good idea Julie, have you asked around other places?"

"I'm starting this morning Roy, what do you say, would you hire me?"

"Of course I would. If you have a shop I'd know when and where to find you and that alone would be a blessing."

"Okay then, it's a deal" Julie shook hands with a grateful smile, to hurry on down the way to the JC Penney store.

"Jim, I have a proposition to put to you, is there time to talk a few minutes?

"Of course Julie, what's on your mind?"

"I have this notion to open a shop. It will be a sewing shop here on main street, I already have a few others lines up so I thought I'd explain myself and see what you think."

"Who does the alterations for you when sizes aren't just right or puts cuffs on suit pants? What about draperies if not just the correct lengths after they were ordered? You know this sort of thing."

"Mrs. Wright does when she is available, which isn't too

regular but she does a nice job."

"Would you hire me if I had a shop?"

"I'd give you a fair try, you bet I would, be right handy. You do it girl, I'll bet you would pick up some individuals too, I know my wife isn't even acquainted with a spool of thread? Could show you my socks as proof," he laughed.

"Thank you Jim, I'll do it."

Next was the church concerning choir robes, then the restaurants to see about uniforms. Would it be more economical to make them than for them to order the manufactured ones? What about the nursing home? Who tended to the mending and needs of the patients? She found a favorable answer at each stop.

Back at the little one bed room house she had rented from the high school principal, she called to her nearest neighbor, Vera Potts, next door.

"Vera, do you have time for a cup of coffee when you're finished weeding?"

"Goodness yes dear," said the sixty year old friend.

"I have a plan in mind, I need to bounce it off someone, can you help?"

Vera pulled off her gardening gloves as she walked across the lawn to her younger neighbor she had grown quite fond of.

"Now honey, what's up?" Vera smiled.

So Julie told of her days rounds with satisfaction.

"It is a grand plan, Julie, just what we don't have here. It might start slow, but it would catch on. Word of mouth is the best advertisement there is and small towns LOVE to talk. She squeezed Julie's hand and gave her a hug.

Once she felt comfortable with the idea of the sewing shop, the next step was to locate an open building. So back down the street first one side then the other. The only empty store available was one half of the John Deere tractor dealer. Looking in the big plate glass windows didn't inspire anyone.

It was filthy beyond belief. What potential was there, if any? May as well go take a look, she thought.

"Hello, I'm Julie Johnson; I was interested in the other half of this building if it is available."

"Don't belong to me lady, but I need to call the owner today anyway, now is as good a time as any. She lives down at the Falls and usually home."

After several rings he said hello to the invisible person on the other end. He discussed his business and that there was a woman who wanted to speak with her.

"Her name's Doris Webster, near deaf so speak plain."

"Hello, my name is Julie Johnson; I live here in Choteau and want to open a new business. I wonder if the empty side of this building is available, ma'am?"

"What you going to do with it?" came the skeptical reply.

"I plan to open a sewing shop as soon as I have a sight available."

"I see, when did you want it?"

"Today if it is possible, ma'am."

"Let me think about it, I'll call up there later today."

True to her word, she called the John Deere shop by three that afternoon, and then the negotiations were settled. I could rent it for twenty five dollars a month, clean it myself and don't dare even think of using it for a flop house for those drunks in the bar next door. Talk about shock, yet it was really funny.

"No, no, I want a place large enough for a cutting table and sewing machine."

"Give Ralph a call, tell him give you the keys."

With that she hung up. Since it was early yet, Julie walked back down to the John Deere store, got the keys and discovered a mess. Stop thinking and go buy the stuff you need, she thought.

"Here I sit in all my glory or gore-y whatever."

It was noon, "I better go get a sandwich and tackle this floor once I buy the scrub brush" I said to the unresponsive walls. Go get the bag of items I need, no more excuses, just get on with it.

By four o'clock, she had seen all of the place she wanted to for this day, then started home.

Next morning as Julie turned the corner she saw the elderly men standing on the walk at the end of the porch steps. What on earth are they doing? She could see what looked like rakes, a shovel and what all else she couldn't make out.

As she approached Billy spoke up. "Miss Julie I reckon we are **NOT** a useless bunch so we are going to help you today."

"Well, oh my, I see-it is three blocks from here and what are you doing with all these, these, these….." she pointed at their gear.

"Sam knows that building, said it needed mucked out. We have all the stuff Marta would part with and the pickle bucket from the shed."

"I see, this is a surprise and you're on." Julie waved her hand down the side of the street, with a salute and a giggle to herself.   As they approached the building she stopped and laughed a jolly laugh from the pit of her stomach. She saw the "crew" in a passing window reflection. She looked like a mother with kids tethered to each side. The wash day band marching down the sidewalk. Maybe it really was a sight to see and many were *seeing*.

Harry said, "Gimme the key, Julie."

"I'll get it" said Sam.

"Never mind, I'll get it" Julie unlocked the door and stood aside to let her flock take a good look at what they had bargained for.

"Lord o' mercy, Julie, did you even *look* at this place afore you took it on?" Gus was not impressed.

"I certainly did, it will be just fine once the grime is out. They fixed tractor parts in here and sharpened plow shears, the sink back there is worse, they soaked parts in gasoline or kerosene, turpentine and what all else is left up to your imagination."

"Who want to tackle the floor?" Billy asked.

"I think we better divide that up Billy, it must be forty feet long and thirty feet wide. It would break a man's back to do it all alone." Gus knew Billy had been having back troubles and so did Harry.

"Let's make a list as long as you're all still of a mind to be involved here." Julie got out the pad and pencil she carried. "Let's see what all needs to be down first," she said.

"The oil and grease needs to be out first," Sam offered. "Least ways we will only trample through it and never get it out of the way."

"We can mark off sections and work two at a time" Harry said, "That way we wont back up against each other."

"Yes, I can start on that sink and back wall," Gus offered his idea.

They all started preparing their duties for the day. Harry and Sam took the floor on the left side of the wall, leaving the right side free for walking. Gus started on the sink, Julie took the bathroom and Billy started sweeping down the walls, Julie had swept out the floor the day before.

"The noise level sure quieted down," Julie had to wonder how long this would last.

"Yep, it takes all our breath to work; we aren't useless, but surely out of practice. Good for us, too." Billy was still pretty brittle over that *useless* remark. "I'm use to working on my ranch and I don't cotton much to idleness. You can thank Harry for this, Julie, his curiosity went to work over time and we fell right into your trap."

"Oh, you figured that out did you?" Julie just hooted.

"I figured you would. Everyone needs something to do. Besides I'd already spoken to Ruthie to see if she thought it *really* would be too much. She said, not at all, you men needed a job."

"Well you **all** have a job if you will stick it out."

She hugged each one and them and offered them coffee she had brought along.

The first day was slow and discouraging but no one gave up. The next morning her flock was ready at nine when she came by.

"Do you think we can finish the floors today?" It wasn't a prod, she just didn't want to go buy paint and have one more thing to step around.

"Maybe so, it's been a sight worse than it looked." Harry's back was bothering him,

"Billy, you want to start on the wall over there where I have that floor section done?"

"I'm most finished here on the back wall. Harry, grab a bucket and have a siesta.

Billy dragged his job out to give Harry a rest. Harry was not about to renege on his share of the work day. A few times he figured they bit off more than they could chew, but no one complained. By Friday, the walls were ready for paint that needed to be next; otherwise wall paint might drip on the floor paint. Saturday and Sunday were to use for themselves.

Julie went to church then home to change into work pants. She was helping Vera put in her vegetable garden.

"I'd love to have a garden, but I'm not sure how long I'll remain, so I'll help you with yours, okay?"

Julie loved flowers and had put petunias at her front door.

The first Monday of May the floors were finished in a soft gray, wall were an apple green, the bathroom was a light blue and they were ready to consider the shelves, table and window seat. Everyone was surprised at the carpentry Sam could manage. He built six shelves three feet long and four inches wide, placing three on each side wall at a height anyone but children could reach.

Gus and Billy put together saw horses to hold the four by eight sheet of masonite used for a cutting table, while Harry put the finishing touches on the window trim. Once it was clean and painted, the men took a few days off, which left Julie to her next project.

"Vera, do you have any odd kitchen chairs in the garage or somewhere?"

"I have a wooden one on the back porch you can have. It's sound but weathered. Will that do?"

"Just perfect" Julie was tickled with her plan. "Do you know anyone else I can go bum from?"

"I believe the Allen's had some old chairs on their back porch last fall, you might go ask."

"Thank you, I will. Now where shall I start on this garden?" she was looking at the seeds packets and started on a row of green beans.

Monday Julie went to the Allen's to ask about old chairs. "Yes, I do have a couple of old chairs on the back porch; I had hoped John would haul them off, well that didn't happen. You want John to bring them over?"

"If you could ask him to drop them off down at my shop I would appreciate it very much."

"No problem, I'm sure he won't mind and it saves him a trip to the dump."

Julie started to giggle, "One day when I have time I'll tell you a story about a rocking chair and the city dump." She snickered, "Thanks again, Mrs. Allen."

"How are you coming along with your shop, Julie? Everyone is anxious to see what you're doing. Several have been down to see but your *army* won't let them in. It is a good joke for all of us. Those men think you can walk on water."

"Thanks again, Mrs. Allen, I need to get down there before they descend on me."

Julie hurried on to the shop. Now she had three chairs. I still need one more straight chair and a rocker, she figured. Maybe a small table, too, if I can scrounge one up from some place.

Mr. Allen, with the chairs, arrived at just a few minutes

before Billy and Gus. She went to the pick up truck to accept them with thank you just as the guys stepped up.

"What is this for?" Billy picked up one of the chairs to carry it inside.

"They need to be sanded down and refinished or painted; I have another one at home I'll bring down tomorrow. Where are the other two of you?"

"Harry is down in his back and Sam has a doctor's appointment. You got sand paper or brushes? Can't use rollers like on them wall, sis!"

"I thought one of you could go get that while I set up my machine and start filling up my shelves."

"Sure be glad to, what paint you got in mind?"

"I thought an ivory or white maybe with a red for trim; a quart of red and a gallon of white. You decided about and paper and steel wool."

"I'll go," Billy offered.

"Gus, help her with those machines, will you?"

Julie had her own sewing machine that went where she went and had borrowed one from the Home Ec class at school until September so that fit her purpose to a T.

"Billy you surely have been busy this past month" Lucille said as she handed him his items.

"Oh yes, yes indeed, Julie put us old fellows to work. Ruthie said it was the best medicine on earth and we were eating her out of house and Money."

"What's she up to now?" Lucille was the manager of the Coast to Coast and knew everything everyone was doing. That store was the gossip center of the entire area. They had nearly everything anyone could want and Lucille was a gem.

"I'm not real sure, she came dragging in some derelict old chairs for some reason, now wants them made new again. Well thank you Lucille for your help and drop in, we will show you around." Billy took his purchases and started his lanky frame in motion.

"I think it would be better to work on those out back rather than have all that paint scraping and dust in here. We just got it all clean and tidy." Julie hoped they would agree.

"Here Gus you take one chair, I'll take the other one, bring your bucket to set on and grab a couple rags. I'll wet a couple more to wipe our hands on, too," Billy was already on his way outside.

Once they were settled at their new project, Julie went down to the used furniture store looking for a stand or table with at least one drawer. There was a small chest of drawers, but it would do just as well.

"You're getting right along down there are you, Julie?" the proprietor remarked.

"Yes, I'm delighted to say it's above what I thought at first. Mercy, it was a mess."

It was a beautiful day and much warmer than usual. On Wednesday it started to rain, then hail, wind and sleet. It seemed nature had no sense of justice. In two days time it was back to normal. Work resumed at the shop.

Two ladies from the quilting club stopped by to see the new shop and asked, "Is there anything we can do? We see you have some help from the *men's house*; maybe we could offer a hand from the *hen house!*"

"What did you say?" asked Julie in a startled tone.

The ladies repeated their statement going on to explain that among the older generation's Ruth Romic's home for elderly men with no family, was referred to as the Men's House while the old folks home ninety five per cent women was called the Hen House.

"That is so funny," Julie had a good chuckle over that. "Why yes, there is something you can do if you like. I need five cushions, four for straight chairs and one for a rocker.'

"That won't be a challenge," spoke up one while "When do you need them?" came from another.

"Next week if you can; do you need supplies?"

"I don't think so; we have boxes of scrap material and yardage that people always give us. Really it would be a good way to use up some of it."

"|That's wonderful ladies, I'm looking forward to what ever you decide. You can use your imagination." Julie walked them to the door.

By the time she returned Julie found her crew still working, slowly but busy on the chairs.

"Did you think to get paint stripper?"

"Yep, some rubber gloves, too. Our skin is so thin it would strip us, too." Billy grinned.

"I see you two are having fun at this. I had hoped it would be an easy job and I don't have time for it."

"We are so used to being here everyday our legs get out of bed and head south."

Gus laughed at his own joke while Billy thought he needed a root beer. Lately he had taken a liking to root beer; he liked it almost as much as the ice cream. "Fancy that," he said "I'm getting like a kid again!"

Things had come together slowly but in time to open before Mother's Day. The four odd chairs and an old rocker had all been stripped down, repainted and sporting brightly colored seat cushions.

"Julie this little table doesn't fit here, why not move it over on the far wall with two chairs flanking it?" Billy realized one could see much more from a side wall advantage.

"Okay Billy, where ever you wish. I'll be back in about an hour, does anyone want something to eat or do we need anything more? We will open in the morning."

She had made arrangements to meet the pastor of the church to ask about the old coffee urn in the basement. It was agreed Julie could have it as it had been replaced two years before. The next stop was down at Brownies Café to pick up some coffee mugs no longer in use and a sugar dispenser.

"Anyone free to lend a hand?" Julie called as she opened

the front door.

"In a minute, I'll be right there." She heard this from out back.

Gus if you can take these cups; I'll bring the pot. Now where did I put that piece of oil cloth?" It seemed everything was tidy in one place and scattered in another. Once the pot was put in place, cups washed and turned upside down to keep the dust out of them, the sugar dispenser a safe distance from the table edge, things looked down right homey.

"Wouldn't it be better to have those mugs up on hooks above the pot?" Sam always looked for the easiest way to avoid leaning or stretching. Lately his shoulders had been a problem with bursitis.

"That's a great idea Sam, you want to walk over to Coast to Coast and buy some large hooks? Lucille will help you."

She gave him a few dollars and saw him out the door.

"You three come back here and sit down quickly. Next week is Sam's birthday. Ruth has a little surprise worked up but wanted the rest of you to know. You decide among yourselves if you want to do anything special or just share in the activity at your house. When you make up your minds, let me know if I can help, okay?" Julie said hurriedly. She saw Sam returning.

On Wednesday, the fifteenth of May, the Needle shop opened its door for business. There was coffee and cookies for all comers. Billy had jokingly remarked the *comers* would come back, so he would dispense the cookies. Billy, Gus, Sam and Harry were like cleaned up children perched on their chairs having been told not to get dirty. All had on their Sunday best and proud as any grandfather would have been. Julie had become **theirs**.

Very little business was done that Wednesday but a few orders were made along with a hundred or more questions.

"Are you going to sew from patterns?" one lady wanted to know. "Do you have a price list somewhere?"

"Will you do regular mending?"

"Make baby clothes?"

"Sew men's shirts?"

"What about repairing dolls with cloth bodies?"

"What time do you open and close?"

On it went until four p.m. She closed early to straighten up. Her guardians in the back row had taken naps off and on most of the afternoon, since she had the car, they road home in high spirits. It had been a success and Julie was proud of her shop, her elderly companions who had more than proved they weren't *all used up*. Even the thought made her snicker to herself.

A very talented girl in the senior art class had painted the sign on the front window in gold letters outlined in black. Julie stood on the side walk to admire it again. The eye of the needle held thread, it read, "The Needle Shop" with the thread spelling out the words flowing behind the needle. It looked grand.

The first customers wanted fancy aprons, some curtains, a basket of mending, some children's dresses, a maternity smock and so forth. The second week the shop was open a woman came in with a long fur coat wanting to know if Julie could cut it off to a three quarter length with a full back. Fortunately Julie's aunt had been a furrier; and you did not *cut off* a fur. You turned it inside out, skin up, chalked in a pattern and cut it with a razor blade.

"Yes ma'am, it will take a week or more as I have a back log but it can be done. Also realize it will cost you more than a regular job."

"That's okay, when and how much?" came the next question.

They settled on a price and a date, the lady left and Julie grinned. A big challenge plus the word would get around. That will be good advertisement, she told the empty room.

About three o'clock Gus and Billy came strolling in to have a seat and get the daily news. You would think she worked for them. It was amusing and so sweet.

"I had a big job offered this morning," she told them, then explained about the fur coat.

"Who was it?" Gus wanted to know.

"Her name was Margie Stralton, I don't know anything further."

"Oh **I** do" Gus perked up, "She runs the bar next door, got money, don't do it for nothing, Julie. She's a tight wad, too," he added.

"That's all settled Gus, before I agree to do it."

"Good girl, you're smart Julie. You will make a go of this place," he clapped his hands together and both men nodded their heads in agreement.

"I think we three will eat out tomorrow morning. How does that sound?" Billy asked.

"We better call Marta then," Gus was headed toward the phone.

"Billy, did she catch you this morning?"

"No, I didn't see her; she wasn't in the kitchen when I sneaked out my coffee, why?"

"Oh Lordy, she's on about the scriptures today; collared me right off about being grateful I had my eyesight. Told me the dad gummest story you ever heard of. Said Jesus was on a fishing trip with some fellers and a storm put them out to sea but they *walked* back to the bank and ate the kid's picnic lunch and had leftovers. On the way back to town they passed a sick man laying by a water puddle waiting for someone to dunk him in, for some reason, and Jesus up and tells him he ain't sick, pick up yer bed and go home. Now don't that beat anything you ever heard? How can anyone get that tangled up on a Bible story I don't know, but it didn't run that way in my Bible."

Gus just said, "That's as wild as the day she preached us a sermon on a fire in a bush on Mount Shasta, which caused the big fire in Kellytown when the train derailed."

Billy was plumb stupefied. "You don't say" was about all he could manage.

Margie stopped by to survey the progress in her coat and Julie explained that by taking the eleven inches off the bottom, splitting them in four inch wide lengths, splicing those together with tough or course, heavy duty thread and inserting those strips every six inches around the newly exposed coat tail, it made a lovely flare to the *new* coat.

"Julie, can I try it on yet?"

"Of course, but it has pins still in it so don't run your hands along the bottom."

Margie was tickled pink with the results, she even knew where she would wear it the first time. Evenings were still cool during May and there was a dance at the Grange Hall this coming Saturday night.

Julie pecked on the window of the saloon or bar next door, crooking her index finger she made a wiggling motion for Margie to come over to the shop.

"Your coat is ready and it's already been steamed at the cleaners."

When she came over to get her coat she said, "it is beautiful, I love it, *I love it*. I'll get another ten years for my money." Margie whirled around to watch the back sway out. "Just right," she was elated.

The men stayed home for a few days helping Ruth get the garden planted. The potatoes needed to be in the ground Gus said, by the dark of the moon; otherwise it would be leaves only and no spuds. He was full of that sort of advice. A walking almanac was Gus.

On a Friday of the following week, Billy, Sam and Harry had walked to the shop with her. After everyone was settled in, coffee made, and her sewing items out of there various living quarters, Julie started sewing on a wedding dress to be worn in June. It was slipper satin and slithery to control. One needed their full attention here as even pin marks make minute holes.

The door flew open with a bang. Julie grabbed the fabric in her lap to avoid it slipping to the floor.

Harry had drifted off momentarily and jerked up with a start. Billy roused up at the same time. Before anyone could say hello, this character plopped a box about two feet square, down on the cutting table and announced he would be back after it the following Friday.

"Whoa up here, Bud," Billy was on the defensive immediately.

"You got something to say, you ask; don't order. 'Smatter with your manners?

Julie gathered the beautiful fabric from her lap to lay it in her chair.

"Let's start over, okay? I'm Julie Johnson. And you are?"

"Name's Duffy, Aaron Duffy, I'm called Duf, I'm Irish, a sheep man, them's dirty washin' and I'll collect 'em next week; Friday. Never talked so much in six years," while shaking his head.

"I see, so what is it you want of me, Mr. Duffy?" Julie was more curious than rankled.

"Matter with you women, I jest *told* you it was washing."

"This is a dress shop, I believe you have been guided to the wrong place sir," she stood her ground as it looked like he might throw the box at her.

"Now see here, that Margie gal from the bar told me you could do anything, and this is something. It's called washin'-dirty clothes, you see."

With that, one disgusted Mr. Aaron Duffy departed like he came in, he banged back out again.

"I swear Julie girl, that feller is so ugly he'd make a freight train take a dirt road." Billy was just put out with such actions.

"His *washin'*, can't imagine the gall of such a person."

Harry had come in as Mr. Aaron Duffy banged out.

"What's got that smelly gent in an uproar? Did you *smell*

him? I wonder if he is acquainted with soap and water."

"Not as you would notice," chimed in Harry.

We still have the five gallon pickle bucket and scrub brushes Gus, next Friday be sure we are here. Somebody gonna' get a bath."

"No Billy," Harry interrupted, "You'd need a curry comb."

"Hey guys, it's okay. We won't start that too, seems it's a laundry as well as sewing shop but I don't want it out that it is also a bath house."

Julie laughed with glee, the whole incident was so outrageous from the beginning she could hardly believe it.

"Okay fellows, now what do I do?"

"You want we should go next door and get him?" Harry was headed for the door.

"No Harry, don't make waves, I'll figure out something."

Things settled down, the three guarding angels as Julie privately called her brood were nodding off in their chairs and quiet reigned supreme.....for now. Once they huffed and puffed, yawned, stretched and started reminiscing, she would get her pad and pen to start taking notes. It was wonderful history these three were revealing. One day she would write a book.

As the days grew warmer, the men came down later in the day. Each had a part of the garden to tend at home and each tried to out do the other. Mrs. Allen offered to pay them to tend her garden, too, since it was right next door.

"Nothing doing," was her answer.

After some time dedicated to the subject of dirty *washin'*, Julie walked across the street to speak with Bob Bayer who had the appliance store.

"Bob, do you have a free minute?"

"You bet Julie, how's it doing with your shop?" he asked as he wiped his dirty hands on a shop cloth.

"Really quite well I'm happy to report, except I have a small problem," she began to laugh. "Do you know a rank smelling man, name of Duff?"

"Who doesn't; been in your place?"

"You could say so," Julie related the dirty clothes story, just shaking her head.

"My *men folks* threatened to take a curry brush and five gallons of soapy water after him. It would be a sight worth seeing, but I've never been in a jail and it doesn't strike me as too appealing."

"So what do you have in mind that I can help with?"

"By chance, do you have a used washing machine I can just lease and not buy?"

"Never thought of it," Bob scratched his head. "Matter of fact that is what I'm working on now, that's why my hands are greasy. A customer turned in a square tub Maytag on a new round Speed Queen that just came in. We can work something out; just give me a time to think. Do you need it today?"

"No but as Mr. Duffy so abruptly announced, 'he would be back to collect it on Friday', period, end of topic." It made her laugh all over again to think of the indignation on Gus and Billy's faces. Julie went back across the street. She better get cracking on her orders and let the dirty clothes problem rest with Bob for the time being.

On Monday Bob called across the street. "Yeh Julie, step over a minute, okay?"

"Am I getting a washer? Pray tell, kind sir."

Bob ran a hand over his head and told her, "Yes, I figure it's better to let you have it for ten dollars a month as long as you need it. For now it is taking up space here, not sold, it will pay its own rent that way. Is that okay with you?

Great, just great. Help me roll it across the street, will you Bob?"

You can believe every business within eye sight was looking out their windows. Bob and Julie grinned at each other and started pushing the washer out the door.

Once the washer was in place beside the big cement

tub previously used to soak tractor parts, rubber hoses were installed and laundry soap purchased, it was time to bring the odorous box back inside. Gus had deposited it outside near the back fences. He swore even the dogs didn't bother it.

"Here Gus, just dump the contents in the sink, I have it half full of soapy bleach water." Julie stirred the contents with a blue broom handle.

"You honestly believe it will come clean?" This came from Sam who had just wandered in.

"Where you been?" Gus demanded, "Seems like you get up later everyday."

"Recon so," he said with a sly smile twitching along his compressed lips.

"Nothing to say for yourself?" Harry prodded.

"Recon not."

"You're just plumb full of information, ain't you now!" Gus began to smell a joke coming up; he had lived with Sam nearly three years already and recognized the sign.

"You keepin' company with one of the hens maybe, that would be news." Gus guffawed to his heart's content over that picture.

"Just tending to my own business, seems I'm the *only* one guilty of that."

"Don't go all huffy now, the boys are just teasing." Julie always the peaceable one said with a straight face; but in jest she added, "So what are you up to?" and laughed her tinkling laugh that made everyone listening, laugh along with her.

She stopped stirring the clothes to let the water out and fill the tub with rinse water.

"About three more times will finish the job," she muttered as a mouse went zooming across the floor.

"Ho ho, looky here, we are invaded with varmints." Gus grabbed the broom Julie had just set down and went banging about after the mouse.

"Don't scare him to death Gus, he will find slim pickin's in here. Leave that back door ajar, he will find his way back out, no doubt." Billy was forming a plan in the back of his mind.

"Those things washed up pretty good Julie. Where you gonna hang 'em up?"

"How about just throw them over the back fence for now, okay?"

"Looks like I better use the mop 'afor one of us takes a skid in this water slopped out." Harry returned with the mop from the bathroom. "Now I'm a swab jockey," he chortled.

When the fellows got home for their supper, Billy was surprised to learn there was a message waiting from Nelia and Woody. So that's what Sam was so smug about. He called them right away to learn they had planned to drive up Saturday and stay over; going back on Sunday.

"Could you call the hotel and secure us a room?"

"Good as done, by a Good," he laughed. "And I'd like a favor if you don't mind."

"Of course, Uncle Billy, what is it?"

"You see this Sunday is Sam's birthday and Ruthie has plans afoot, don't know what exactly but anyway I would like to get him a new sweater. It needs to be a size to fit a hundred and ninety five pounds or so and he likes blue. Could you pick up one for me, please? It needs pockets on the front for his snuff box and chewing gum. I have not figured out how he chews gum with store bought teeth!" Billy shook his head and finished up the conversation with, "What time do you plan to arrive and should I tell Marta there will be two extra for dinner?"

"I don't believe so dear, we are bringing our friends along so that makes too many for your seating arrangement there, Uncle Billy, and I will purchase a sweater."

"I'll be obliged to you honey girl and I am looking forward to Saturday." He hung up the phone and got ready for supper when he thought about that mouse. Instead of going to the bathroom to clean up, he went down the back steps, over to the fence and called Mrs. Allen.

"Hello there Mr. Good, how are you?" Mrs. Allen was all smiles.

"I need a favor if you can."

"What is it and we will see."

"Does that old tom cat still prowl about at night? Have you seen him of late?

"I haven't heard him yowling about recently, but then he may have found better pickin's in another territory. I don't think Ruthie would take kindly to pets in the house, she has her hands full as it is Mr. Good."

"Yes, yes, yes I know that; don't want it for me anyway. Julie has a mouse at the shop. I thought I'd get her a mouse trap on legs." He grinned at his own joke.

"My daughters' cat has kittens big enough to leave home, they are about teenager size. Would you be interested in that for an answer?"

"Just might be, can we go see the cats?"

"After supper, if you like. Will that work?"

"Suits me, I'll see you about seven then." Billy was pleased with that outcome and hurried in to eat.

"Gus, come with me after supper," he said quietly as he passed Gus's chair at the table.

Marta had made scalloped potatoes, meat loaf, green beans with bacon seasoning, peach pie and ice cream. Billy felt he was in food heaven. This move was the best *ever* that he could have done for himself.

Tuesday Julie was sewing up torn seams, replacing missing buttons, patching pants, darning socks and ironing shirts. It took three washings but the clothes were presentable. The four men were dozing in their chosen chair assignments except for Harry in the rocker, his back had gotten worse.

Every time they roused up awake, the stories would once again begin. "Do you mind the time Blue had pups in the mud hole," was all it took and the four of them were off on another part of memory lane. Julie's business increased enough to hire a part-time seamstress so she could continue to write while they were busy talking stories.

Friday about noon, true to his statement, Mr. Duffy made his appearance, not too rambunctious or quite so smelly.

"Here are your clothes but in a better size box. I don't do laundry Mr. Duffy, you better make other arrangements."

"Too bad, I got about six other pals lined up; they will be in later today. How much?" he asked quite without thought or courtesy or any sign of good breeding.

"That's five dollars and I don't like your attitude. Stop your friends from coming in please," She said as they tramped in, stomped in would better express it, she thought. They looked like five miles of bad road.

"Aaron Duffy, this is too much," Julie was troubled, she didn't like these rough ways.

He looked in the box at his clothing and slowly said, "How much did you say for this?"

"Five dollars and it's worth twice that, if you have objections I can burn them," she stormed.

"Aaron bent double laughing and flipped open his wallet, he dropped a twenty dollar bill on the cutting table. "You're a peach, little lady and *you* are worth ten times what you ask for."

She was taken aback for a few seconds then reached for the purse to make change.

"No way, you keep it and I'm so pleased, I don't know how to tell you."

By now her men folks were silently taking this all in. One with a broom, another with a hammer, and Billy puffed up to his six feet four with fists clenched behind his back.

The other sheep herders introduced themselves and said they too would gladly pay twenty a week for clean clothes if Aaron hadn't botched it up with his smart mouth talk.

"It isn't that big a deal," Julie said, "but I'll make you a proposition. You can come in here on Friday's if you clean up first and wash your own laundry. I'll mend and iron; I have the iron here anyway to press seams on finished garments. You will still pay me twenty just the same or no deal."

It took about twenty seconds for a rousing "Okay, you bet, hot dog and a wow!"

"Done deal," said Aaron.

"The Lord works in mysterious ways," Gus muttered as they relaxed, poured fresh coffee and resumed the old stories.

"Julie, you won't need to worry about your rent if you ever were." This from Harry as he slid back down in the rocker and soon nodded off.

Saturday morning dawned cloudy but cleared by ten o'clock. Billy was on the front porch by seven thirty watching for the big eight cylinder LaSalle. How he wished he had one like that. He had a hard time to remember he was **OLD**.

At nine o'clock Nelia and Woody pulled up at the curb. Billy hurried down the steps to greet them and be introduced to the new comers.

"Uncle Billy, I'd like you to meet Mindy Sue and John Chouteau, you possibly recognize the name. John is the grandson of Pierre Chouteau who established the fur trading post on the Missouri River.

Billy shook hand and invited them in.

"Mindy Sue," Billy rolled that name around in his mouth a bit and offered his opinion. "Mighty pretty name, never heard of it before," he muttered.

"Mr. Good, my name is only half there," she giggled at the astonished look on Billy's face.

"Half a name; now that is odd indeed."

"How so?" he asked.

"The entire thing is Minerva Susan Watson Chouteau. Cut it short and it became Mindy Sue."

"Mighty perty name," he said again.

John Chouteau was a handsome man with steel grey hair

not tall but well put together.

He put his arm around his young wife and said, "And she's all mine. Everyone laughed.

When Billy had a chance to speak to Nelia, he asked about such age difference in the Chouteau's.

"His first wife was Davidean Westinghouse who passed away in child birth; he only remarried three years ago. Uncle Billy, they are happy and she is delightful."

"That's a good thing, I was tolerably older than my Katie too, loved her with my whole heart.....still do," he spoke softly.

After all introductions were made and people settled in places to sit, Billy spoke up.

"Mindy Sue, I'm not a nosey old codger but I'm curious about your family back ground. Nelia tells me you're a newlywed. That is grand. How did you come to be in our neck of the woods? She says you're from Pennsylvania; well, so was I....Pine Grove. Went by covered wagon to Kansas, settled in Texas and I'm *sure* you know the story of Nelia's childhood." He felt like he was rambling, He had found new territory to unload his memories on. "Not fair, Billy boy," he thought to himself.

"Why yes, Uncle Billy, if I may?" he nodded.

"John's first wife was a Westinghouse. I am her sister's daughter who came to visit." She held up her left hand and said, "and I stayed." Big smiles showed up on every face in the room.

"There is a peculiar thing," Billy said. "There was a Westinghouse family came to Salina when I was thirteen. Juanita opened up society to our growing town."

Mindy Sue nearly jumped out of her chair.

"My goodness, oh my goodness, those were our family, they too were from Pennsylvania, were they not?" she asked excitedly.

"Yes, they were as I recall. Very influential people; good

people. Built the first hospital, dedicated the library and helped start the theater group. Good people they were."

This proved to be a wonderful weekend for all.

Sunday afternoon Ruth had arranged ice cream and cake for the birthday surprise. Billy was pleased with the blue sweater and asked Ruth to *box it up* pretty. It was a happy occasion; no one knew at the time that Harry wouldn't be there next year.

As for now, once everyone was gone, the four cronies gathered on the porch.

Gus said, "Alright Harry, where you been gallivanting off to here of late? I got an inkling to believe it's familiarity with the Hen House. No one is spying, you understand, but you don't play pool or drink. No car; you use shanks mare, so?"

"Curiosity killed the cat," Harry grinned.

Billy jumped up, "Lordy, I plumb forgot, Gus. Come on, we got to go to the Allen's right now."

They hurried through the back yard, through two gates to the Allen's. Mr. Allen was sitting on the porch swing when they hurried up the walk.

"Evening John, is the Mrs. home?" Billy felt reticent, but better explain himself.

"We were supposed to look at those kittens yesterday, but I got company from the Falls and forgot about it."

"We know Billy, they are in the house, I'll get Mother to bring them out."

"No you won't," she called "they'll scatter and who is going to track them down? You men come on in, now."

Gus and Billy made an odd looking pair. Gus was bald, short and bow legged. Billy was over six feet and thin as a corn stock and a full head of hair. They bent over the box of six kittens; this was not going to be easy.

"I favor that yellow one." Gus picked it up out of the box and looked it over. "Here, take it," he picked up a three colored and set it back. "I like it, too," Billy agreed.

"We agree on the yellow one," they said in unison. "Pick it

up in the morning, be alright?"

"One of us will be here; don't need to set a time."

"Thank you for this Mrs. Allen," Billy patted the cat on the head one more time before they left.

On Monday Billy went to claim the cat but as he came in the back door Marta spotted it.

"What you got there, mister?" she squinted her eyes down like an owl and walked over to see what it was.

"Oh Mr. Billy, where did you get that kitten? You going to show it to Miss Ruth" She don't take to animals in the house, you know. Purty little fellow ain't he?" Marta reached for the kitten.

"It isn't for me or us here. Julie has a mouse." That was explanation enough.

"Ha, I'd give a pretty penny to see her face. That girl loves every living thing; make a pet out of a skunk if she could."

"Did you see the skunks walking down the sidewalk yesterday, Marta? Right proper and friendly like, don't leave your door open back here, you may get a visitor not expected," Billy warned.

He and the cat went through to the front door.

"Got it, did you?" Gus reached for the kitten. "So soft and not a bit sassy," he said.

"Better get on with it Gus," Billy started down the steps.

"Where is Harry, gone again?"

"I didn't see him past breakfast, did you?"

"Sam is over to the church, said he was going to mow the grass early."

They continued their conversation all the way to the shop.

"Morning you two," Julie greeted in her happy go lucky voice. "Seems like you grew a pouch overnight Billy or your hiding something inside your shirt." Julie walked over to pat his "*tummy*" only Billy was thin as a rail, so then what!

He opened the top button on his sweater and out poked a little yellow face wearing twitchy whiskers and startled blue eyes.

"*Where* did this little darling come from?" Julie squealed as she made a sudden grab for the kitten.

"You darling little doll," she squeezed the little fellow up to her nose. "Is it a stray, does it need a home, can I keep it," she asked all in one breath.

Gus said, "Billy and me picked it out, thought you needed a mouse trap. Got you one with four legs, like him, do ya?" Gus grinned.

Julie was delighted with her mouse trap.

"We need a couple bowls for water and food, a box to sleep in. Hmmm yes, I suppose another box better be prepared in the bathroom."

"We will get to it after our coffee. Well see here Gus, there are donuts. Where did the donuts come from?" Billy asked as helped himself to one, no two, then had a seat.

"Odd thing you know, a couple of ladies from the Hen House brought them by and asked after Harry. Have you seen him yet today?"

Gus slapped his thigh and snorted a laugh.

I knowed it, I just *knowed* it, that old dog is out sniffin' about for new territory. Even if he was to find a female woman interested in his ways, he likely wouldn't know what to do about it. Now ain't this somethin' ho ho ho, I'll just be dogged."

Billy started to laugh, too.

"Let's get this cat business taken care of then we may just *happen* to take a stroll down the avenue. What do you think?"

Both men were having a good time with this; the two old chums forgot Julie was even there as they headed out the door.

"So, little cat, you and I are going to get acquainted." Julie put the little fellow down to go explore.

"Guess you need a name, too," she thought. "Here kitty, kitty, kitty," she called as she followed it along. "Let's see what your name should be."

"Uh huh, now there are two girls in here with four men. I can imagine you will soon be as spoiled as I am." Julie petted the cat and cuddled the little ball of fur, up under her chin.

"You're a dandy little girl," she told the cat, "and that should be your name, I believe. Let's try it on for size. Dandy, hmm, yes, it sounds very appropriate."

There were items of sewing here and there, and all needed to be finished up. She sat down at the sewing machine and time passed swiftly, it was past noon when she realized she hadn't seen a thing of her men folks. She was humming a song as she worked, but stopped to look for Dandy.

"There you are; oh how sweet," the kitten was asleep on the rocking chair cushion.

"We better find you a bed, little one, that's Harry's chair."

Julie walked to the end of the block for a sandwich at the restaurant. The Kettle had been there for time out of mind and for good reason, too; they had excellent food.

"Myrtle, have you seen Billy, Gus or Harry?"

"Not Harry but the other two been up and down several times, it is just plain comical to watch. Look like Mutt and Jeff. One tall and thin as a blade and the other bandy legged, looks like a cork screw. Those two acting like they're up to something."

"Out looking for Harry would be my first guess." Julie ordered a BLT.

By the time she returned to the shop she found a grocery bag at the door; condensed milk, cat food and litter for the cat's bathroom. No sign of the delivery *boys*.

"Come on puss," she called, "time for lunch."

Her own curiosity was getting the better of her concerning Harry.

Friday came with stormy clouds; it would not be a favorable forth of July. The men elected to stay in; the sheep herders arrived with their boxes or baskets, no matter that is was a holiday. Julie had anticipated this and opened the shop. There were the school's choir robes to finish inspecting as well as new aprons for the waitresses at The Kettle and Brownies. Not much work but it was time consuming.

Dandy was into everything and making a racket with rolling empty wooden spools that thread had been on. It made a startling noise in an empty room with a cement floor. If there was any trace of a mouse, she hadn't seen one, so it had not provided a meal for Dandy or maybe it left of its own free will. Either way, it was gone. Julie did not like mice.

Saturday was always a busy day in town, the ranchers came in for supplies, small out lying villagers came shopping and people had left their sewing items with Julie at the shop, to be picked up at the end of the week. Saturdays were like a small fair, with children running everywhere, people gathered in little knots visiting or those seeing each other for the first time in weeks.

Harry rocked back and forth while telling of his experience at the Hen House. Yes, that's where he had been.

"Built that fence in three weeks,' He looked pleased with himself. "Maude stopped me one day to see if I could put up a picket fence in the back yard you see, and it liked to have puffed up my head. So this old fool says, you bet, be glad to."

This fence business had been news to the others. They didn't know Harry had a gift with a hammer and nails. He usually begged off at much work at all.

"We were really curious Harry, how you managed to be out of sight so much. It took awhile before we figured out that you must be at the Hen House as you wasn't no where else."

"Didn't want you to see things if I botched it up and them women wouldn't know no better if I did." He had to cackle over that for a few minutes.

Dandy jumped up in his lap for the ear scratching she expected.

"I'll tell you boys, for sure and certain, do not offer your services. Sidewalk superintendents all and if I heard, *if man was living he could have done this, that or t'other*, one more time, I'd have wrung someone's neck."

Julie started to laugh. "But we profited by your efforts Harry, nearly every day there was a batch of cookies, a pie now and then, donuts or candy. All arrived via the hens at the Hen House. They appreciated you and we appreciated them."

He cleared his throat a few times and said, "At least you didn't have to listen to a rousing conversation between grandmas who related such wonders as how joyously they embraced toilet training. Like it was life's effervescence to uphold the duty of teaching a kid to pee."

Everyone went into a fit of laughter. Poor Harry was a character but his descriptions were a caution. He went on to tell of one woman who had nothing but grief to speak of.

"I'll swear to you boys, I think she sharpened her views on the whetstone of personal tragedy and saw to it we knew of it day in and day out. I'm so happy I'm single that I feel young again."

That brought on more leg thumping and hoots.

"You need help to even change your mind, you old dog. What would you do if you was really alone?"

August, true to its usual schedule was mostly hot and dry. Now and then an electrical storm or heat lightening came. Julie's company had notified her she needed to be back in California by September fifteenth or lose her job. She knew it was coming, but it seemed so soon. Where did time disappear to since April? She knew she would keep in touch with Ruth concerning the men.

Julie was walking to her shop when she saw the men were seated in the shade of the porch. She came up the steps and stopped at the edge of the porch. "I have something to tell you," she said. No, she could not *set a spell*, "but thank you. I haven't the time just now."

"I'll be selling the shop. I've been called back to my work in California. We will have a talk about it in the next few days, okay? Gotta run now." She felt tears well up in her eyes and hurried on.

The silence on the front porch was deafening.

"What do you think?" Gus questioned.

"Not good," Billy shook his head.

"Be mighty lonesome," ventured Sam.

Harry sort of chocked up, "Won't never be the same."

"We ought to tell Ruthie, maybe she can fix a party or give a dinner. What do you think?"

"Fine idea, let's go tell her."

They trooped in with their news for Ruthie; they were sort of feeling let down.

"Julie sold her shop with the understanding the sheep herders could do laundry. Dandy became a resident at that address and the name was to remain The Needle Shop.

The last Saturday there Julie was going to the Falls and asked Billy if he wanted to ride along. She recalled he had friends there.

They took care of her business first, had lunch next and then went to visit Billy's *people*, as he referred to them.

"Do you know the way, Billy?"

"Yes, I do, just follow how I tell you, Julie."

At the out skirts of town was a hill to the east where they started to drive up. Julie had a 1955 Ford and she kept in up nicely. It rode comfortably for Billy's back but he swore by his old 1937 Studebaker.

"Now, turn here to the left and go up this long drive way."

She did, but it seemed wrong.

"Are you sure? It doesn't look like anyone's home, Billy."

"Well it is. Just go on," he directed.

Soon a mansion came in to view through the trees. Julie hesitated.

"It's alright, go on," Billy urged.

They drew up to the home on a lovely circular driveway flanked by a manicured lawn and beautiful rose beds. Billy gathered his long lanky self up and out off the front seat, then started for the door. Julie felt they surely were trespassing, but the door opened with the first bang of the knocker.

"Land sakes, Nelia come see who is here. Woody pumped Billy's hand saying, "Tell your young friend to come on in."

Woody beckoned to Julie to come on and join them. A scurry of feet arriving at the entrance could be heard as Julie joined them on the threshold. A tiny woman possibly in her sixties popped up in sight; she hugged Billy and was nearly screeching.

"Uncle Billy, Uncle Billy, oh my dear, it is *so* good to see you. Come in, come in, you too," she said to Julie as she pulled her along the hall way. Nelia was a lovely gracious lady; full of excitement and absolutely beaming at Billy.

Julie was amazed at their décor; it truly *was* a mansion. The Bartons escorted her though their wonderful museum of a home, while explaining that it had at one time been the first governor's home and purchased by her family when the present governor's mansion was built. Julie said what a joy it was to see all this.

Within the hour Julie explained that she and Billy would need to leave as she had to finish packing, also she had other odds and ends to take care of. By four thirty they started back to Choteau. As she pulled up in front of the home, there seemed to be a party going on. When she opened the door for Billy to enter, she was met with a shouted '*welcome*', one that she would never forget.

It seemed to Julie that half the town had stopped by Ruth Romic's home for elderly men. This was a day to cherish for the rest of her life. The last things she packed were the huge collection of notes and two work books of accumulated stories she had written down while listening to the tales being remembered by her four friends and helpers. Billy, Gus, Harry and Sam had nearly become like an extended family to her.

She nearly regretted she had not been privileged to have

known them from the time Billy moved there at age eighty. These twelve years must have been a wonderful time for those companions. Billy was now ninety two, Sam had reached eighty eight, Gus was ninety and Harry turned eighty one. Julie corresponded with Ruth until each of the men had left this world, but she never returned to see them again. The pleasure of her time spent in those six months would last her a life time.

She smiled and closed the book of notes.

Later the company she worked for sent her to the Honolulu, Hawaii offices. There she met and married a Texas oil man. Her story with Jessie goes forward in part II of this book entitled "Jessie and Me". Follow their wonderful life as they traveled where *the wind blows*.

Epilogue

This story is comprised of those people mentioned on these pages. It is as near accurate as I can recall after sifting through my notes.

There really was a Billy Good, his story is true, and his wife Katie, Concho, Texas and the baby on the trail are also true facts.

I've done my best by them all; you see I am the Julie Johnson of The Needle Shop. There really was a yellow cat named Dandy who lived to be twenty, a man named Gus who was Billy's closest friend. Gus was over ninety when he passed away; Billy was ninety four. Harry was eighty nine and Sam left us at age eighty eight.

Nelia lived to see her seventy sixth birthday and Elwood "Woody" passed away peacefully in his sleep at age eighty four. They had lived at the mansion all their married life. Billy is asleep in Concho beside his beloved Katie. It was his last trip to Texas. He saw much history in his life just as his mother Millie had predicted when she gave him his first journal at age 14.

Choteau is a real town in Montana where I lived briefly just after the Second World War. I hope you have enjoyed this saga as much as I enjoyed living my part in it.

The Author

Jesse and Me

Part II

PRELUDE

1972 had died and I'm sure of its final destination, since it had no wings. I'm sure you know where it went. To say I was happy for its demise is a masterpiece of understatement to say the very least. The vast amount of misery doled out during its time on earth, would fill volumes. Suffice it to say, gone but not forgotten.

To begin with, I was keeping company with the menopause and any prudent adult knows, those can be sad, mad, glad, singing, arguing, teary, laughing days all in the course of twenty minutes. With little provocation and a minimum of understanding, we of the female gender, endure the torment of wrath from exasperated spouses, family and friends, to sympathetic understanding from elders and a pathetic desire to straighten up and grin threw it all. Especially on the days you're looking, with blood in your eyes, for someone on whom to take out your frustrations.

Of course, working two jobs and trying to get along with a hubby who is interested in a younger woman, a hypochondriac mother-in-law, a sassy mouthed sister-in-law, who's husband had just found religion (in time to excuse his errant ways), a thirty-three pound tom cat who ruled everyone, two Pomeranian dogs who thought they were people, and a three month old billy goat who thought *he* was a rooster, who lived with a calf named Rufus in the tool shed, that also had pigeons for tenants. All this seemed to work toward my downfall. Well, I really didn't fall down, actually, just came unzipped at the seams. Do I not sound like it?

It did seem an interesting subject to consider, this running away from home idea. I would have too, but I couldn't find the check book, so I didn't think about it too long, you see. When I finally did leave I wasn't entirely broke, but I was badly bent. Nothing can perk you up quite as quickly as a good big thrift store to plod around in, especially as it's cheap, when you are "badly bent" that is, so I did one store justice. A suit case for seventy-five cents and a plane ticket to Hawaii on a Friday, *thank God it's Friday*. I left on a 7 AM United Airlines flight and never looked back, for five years.

1973 was considerably *different*, but not all infamous either, but I can tell you the experiences were on a grand scale. Since I'd worked for *Kenny's Shoes* and in a *JC Penney* shoe department, I was acquainted with feet well enough to tell fortunes by the feel of them so I went looking for a job. At Roberts, the manager handed me an application blank that I filled in just fine until I came to the line that say, "Why do you want this job?" It took about a millisecond to jot in that space, "'Cause I like to eat". I was hired forth with and remained there five years. The incidents there are another book. You just haven't lived if you never sold shoes. That is sold – not 'souled'– and for that you need a good soul; believe it. Fact.

Although the Hawaiian language is archaic, that is the only thing behind the times. I had located Shangri-La. Wonderful people, climate, a non hurry, hurry, lift style, located a twenty foot by twenty foot apartment I adored and would gladly resume as a residence even today. Mr. Chin, who owned the building, ran the VW dealership. He helped me secure some wheels that I could manage to pay for and let me manage the apartment complex for my rent, plus a small salary and I had it made. Life in the apartments is yet another story in itself and a hilarious one at that.

School teaching was my primary occupation and in time I returned to it, but for now I was pretty well burned out on kids, noise and husbands, so fit myself into the swing of things at the Ilikai Hotel. The top of the "I" was, at that time, the gathering place for the 25 to 45 year old business people type crowd, single or couples, good band, quiet fun and because of the traveling business people, the military and tourists, dancing was a dream come true. I must have left about 1000 miles of shoe leather on that dance floor over the next few years.

Enters into my life, two good friends I shall cherish until death do us part. Helen K. is Japanese Okinawan, small of stature, big of heart. A beautician by trade, rearing a daughter alone and friend who has made my life better off because she was in it. We could nearly read each other's minds. I could start a sentence and she would finish it. One such instance took place on a Sunday morning while driving my car, a Plymouth station wagon named Flossy, to the Kam drive-in theater lot (transformed into a flea market on Sundays). We had our own little clan of associates and one was Bob R., who has been on another island visiting. The conversation began with me asking, "Do you know if?"

"Yes he is back," her reply.

I followed with, "Did he bring?"

"Sure, both twins."

"Oh", says I. "Where are?"

"With Fran, of course."

She nodded her head, so I said, "Blue or yellow?"

"Blue."

"Where is the yellow?"

"Broken." End of conversation. Kathy, Helen's daughter sitting in the back seat was quiet about three minutes and then said, "Well, what kind of conversation that?" The habit of reverting to pigeon talk I find highly amusing.

One evening as I was walking the boulevard, I saw this beautiful, Spanish girl, rather confused looking, and asked (projecting the Aloha Spirit), if I could help. She answered me in Spanish, which I speak, then learned such a fantastic story as you would never believe. Another book? Perhaps! As she is the second good friend I mentioned. But, to come to the point, I was on my way to a political rally, as one of the six hostesses' for the evening. And that is where this book begins.

CHAPTER 1

The Palladium floor was swarming with dignitary of every size, shape and description, garbed in as many flavors of wearing apparel as Baskin Robins and just as luscious looking, I might add.

If you could total up all the Jade, Diamonds, Pearls, Emeralds, Sapphires plus paste jewelry, you could start an emporium. Pay handsomely on the National Debt.

Evie Y steps over by the hors d'oeuvres and asks had I seen the fellow by the door. "No," I reply, as I turn to look, I utter, "Oh dear". There was a most outstandingly dressed man I had seen in many a year. About five feet six inches, perhaps 175 pounds, sandy hair, brown eyes, rather small features for man, delicate hands, rather effeminate in shape; how deceiving that was. I had much to learn.

After ten minutes or so, I noticed he was still rather lounging there so I glided over, in my heels and full length gown, to see if I could learn why. After all, snake skin boots, blue jeans, stiffly starched cotton shirt with the tail out, was hardly evening attire acceptable for a tux and tails affair. The non-interested, casual look wasn't appropriate either. "Good evening. Are you here for the promotion or perhaps to inquire of someone or lost perhaps? You seem a bit lost."

234

"Nope."

"Oh, excuse me," I could see he was a great accomplished conversationalist. I asked, "Would you care for a punch, coffee or a drink perhaps?"

"Sure." But, he did not move.

"So which will it be?"

"Coffee," he said quite matter-of-factly.

After arriving back with the asked for coffee, I thought I would try again. "So, have you been to other Democratic Party functions?"

"Nope," swallowing the coffee in two gulps.

"I see. What brings you to this one?"

"Saw it." He sat down his cup and wiped his hands on his pants!

"And do you live here then?" I'm prying, of course, again. "Family?" I ask with a dazzling smile and gritted teeth.

"Yep."

Since I'm a most tenacious character myself, I was not just about to let this galoot make a fool of me and decided I'd kill him with kindness if that's what it took.

"That's nice. What family do you have here?"

"None," still stretching his neck.

"You don't appear to have lived here long. So are you visiting or come over with a company position?"

"Yep."

By now I'm getting a little weary of smiling politely! "I'm a teacher here. Who do you work for?"

"Hood," he smiles briefly.

"Hood?" says I, with raised eye brows. I thought a hood was a welder's hat, so I ask, "What's a hood?"

Now, I get a response, with a look of incredulity and mixture of disgust and disbelief. I'm quite impatiently told that "Hood" is a huge pipeline company, which leads me back to square one.

"Which housing tract are you working on," I ask in all

innocent sincerity, as to me, a pipeline must be what they call the water and sewer lines being installed.

After the eyebrows are raised so high they nearly pushed his hairline out of place, he says, in a soft southern drawl, "Pipelines carry oil, lady."

Then I realized what I had said must have been a rank insult from the look on his face and that his face was growing more agitated by the minute.

"Sorry, I have no idea what it is you are describing. But, I am happy to see you can put four words together without a strain." This got an even more sour reaction.

By now I felt pretty sure this guy had come in on the last load of pumpkins. As I started to move away, my friend Dee came by to say most of us (we hostesses) were going to the dance at 10 o'clock and seeing this character, she felt the polite thing to do was invite him along.

"Nooooo," drawled my bumpkin, "I don't... ah, thanks soooo, uh, well, sure, why not?" Oh dear Lord, I thought. Now we are in for it. Here am I wearing seventy-five dollar sandals, a hundred and fifty dollar gown, a diamond and jade necklace, one carrot diamond earrings and diamond rings, a diamond encrusted watch and now comes this scarecrow in our midst to an elegant night spot. So, what's next? We might as well make the best of it. As we stepped into the elevator, I nudge Evie and whisper, "Let's grab him and poke his shirt tail in. Come ON! 1, 2, 3." The poor guy nearly climbed the wall to rid himself of our shenanigans. I did not learn until long after we were married, that he didn't have any shorts on and he was mortally terrified we *would* poke his shirt tail in.

Once seated and greetings were gushed to all, came the business of introductions.

"By the way, my name is Julie, this is Evie and Dee, ... and you are?"

"Je.... Blam..," mumbles our guest.

"Beg your pardon sir, I didn't understand that?"

236

"Je...... Blammnn." A repeat performance.

"I see, well, no, I don't see, or hear either, for that matter. Try it again?"

"Jes..... Blaaammnn." A bit louder.

"Well, sir," I said, "I speak five languages, four of them fluently, but what ever it is that your speaking, it is NOT one of them."

"Jesse, as in James, Black, as in, one negro." He takes a swallow of his drink while the rest of us remain quite uncomfortable.

"I shall remember that," I said.

As we all wondered off to our various cronies, I stayed as close to Bob and Otto as I could without being in their hip pockets. Bob was a divorced friend who owned a plumbing business and the one whom Helen and I were discussing when Kathy could not make head nor tails of our conversation. Otto was, at that time, my steady beau of some two and a half years, and the head psychologist at the veteran's hospital. These two were a part of the ten of us who pretty much chummed together with out much interruption. I felt considerably more comfortable the rest of that Friday night.

I worked weekends at Robert's Shoe Store and as Saturday dawned, I yawned and arose around seven AM. Ah, shoe store day! Very eventful really. We had a Chinese man by the name of Clint, who was quite a ladies man and always made a dive for the good lookers as they came in. This particular morning he was in high form as he was taking the Dale Carnegies course and anxious to put his knowledge to the test. Wrong decision. These two twenty plus ladies sat down in their skimpy tennis skirts and nearly non existent tops. With boobs half out, they leaned way over to unlace their shoes (which he would gladly have done), when they look *up* and see he is looking *down* in. They proclaim horror and are highly incensed at his familiar behavior and go on and on and on, about how vulgar and rude, how ungentlemanly and what a fool he is etc., etc., until I took pity on Clint. I moseyed by just at I mentioned to my customer I had in tow, that I guessed the two twenty plus teeny boppers were getting the attention their lack of taste was trying to accomplish. This just loud enough to be overhear. All grew quiet on the western front. Clint bought my lunch!

Next, a phone call came in. The stock boy took the call because we were with customers. So what do I hear coming at 9000 decibels from the phone?

"Julie, the lady you sold the white oxfords to, died during the night and her daughter wants to know if she can get a refund?" I'm sure his throat was raw from screaming that fine information for the people in Saskatchewan to hear. And so went our day.

A man, all irate and pushed out of shape, stormed in to demand a refund on a pair of kid's shoes because, "the dam things ain't no good and are fallin' apart." I asked to see what was wrong. After a quick look, I see new clothes on the boy, and a pocket knife. Looking at the shoes, I saw "u" shaped indentations on the shoe leathers and the toes torn loose from the sole.

"Um hum, so did you just have a birthday kiddo?" I ask.

"You bet lady. We had twenty kids!" I learned what all they ate and that the boy got a new basketball hoop, too.

"Did you learn to skate?" I asked the boy.

"Well, I fell down a lot", he admitted.

"Oh, that's OK," I said. "I did too, when I learned, but getting stopped is the hardest part isn't it?" I remarked, quite sympathetically to his cause.

"Sure is, but I drug my feet." I handed the shoes back to the father who had a very red face and his only comment was, "By dam, you'd make a hell of a detective."

Finally, the time came to go home and soak my own feet. Now *that* required a half mile walk. If you ever lived in Honolulu, you know a car is nearly useless. No where to park and it's bumper to bumper, twenty hours a day. So, you live as close to work as possible, or take a bus and its name is "the bus" its real name, honest -- or commute, and "that ain't easy".

Hardly had I stepped through the door, when my phone rang.

"Hello."

"Yeah, you want to go out to eat?"

"Excuse me?" *Now who is this??*

"I thought you might like to go to a dance and eat out," said the faceless voice.

"I just stepped through the door, plus I do not know with whom I am speaking." I replied.

"I saw you come in. Look across the street and up." I detest phone games as much as I hate people who hurt animals.

"To whom am I speaking, please?"

"It's Jess."

Oh mercy, I think to myself. *Jess? Jess? Jess? Jess who?* I do not know a Jess, so pulling back the drape I looked up and across the street. Oh yes, I see the bumpkin waving down.

"What on earth are you doing in the towers?" I wanted to know.

"I live here." *Dear God! That's an expensive place to live for Pete's sake and this character neither acts, nor looks (or dresses like) he has sense enough to pound sand in a rat hole.*

"Well, I don't really know. What and where did you have in mind?" I feel reasonably safe now, as there are no dives or road house type places, but no one I know goes to any.

"I thought, maybe, the Sand Box," he offered.

Good Lord! I might have known, the one and only undesirable, of course. Pure curiosity set in and I heard a voice familiar to me saying, "Why, I guess so, well OK, when did you wish to go?"

"Now," said my long winded buddy here. "But you will need to drive as I don't have the company truck tonight." Fifteen words! Believe it! And all in one sentence. A miracle has been wrought. So the place to pick him up, what one is expected to wear and all those finer points, were discussed by me, answered by him and forty-five minutes later we were on the road to the infamous "Sand Box".

Wearing the first pair of jeans I ever owned in my life and a freshly ironed white blouse with handkerchief scarf at my throat, I felt like I was out playing hooky from decent society and loving it. Until we arrived, then, oh boy, he opened the club door and who is coming out but two of my male clan members, none other than Bob and Otto, from the Ilikai. After their chins settle back in place, Otto said "Turn around and I'll take you home. What ARE you doing here in the first place?" *Jesus, Joseph and Mary, I can't believe this.* It's enough to give me a migraine.

So I stood there, feeling like an escaped lunatic and muttering that I'm NOT alone for Pete's Sake, when Jess softly said, "She is with me." He was promptly ignored, while Otto and Bob proceed to propel me about like a child's top, and start for the door.

"That is enough," comes a bark from the back, with enough authority to stop us in our tracks. Then this soft gentle voice says, "I said, she is with me." Now I'm lead back in again and nearly in tears of mortification.

Once we are shown to our table and ordered he says, "Your keepers I take it?"

"No, just close caring friends of long standing."

"Who are stuffed shirts."

"Why no, not at all. One is a psychiatrist, and the other is the owner of a plumbing contracting business."

"Hmmmmm, ya like Mexican?" So I guess the subject was closed. Just as well because too many questions are worse than acne.

After a very tasty and silent dinner, the band started playing western music, much to my delight. We don't hear it often in Hawaii. Did I want to dance? *Does the Pope come from Rome!* I'd let food grow cold, to dance, and I can really eat. I can really dance too!

Once on the dance floor, it was bad news. He can't dance, just stomps around and not even in time with the music. I'm considered an excellent dancer, so I could see we were hitting it off like salt and strawberries. But, his attitude reached for grandeur and failed, I said I better get home.

On the way out of the restaurant, we were met by two ambulances, one stretcher with a big Samoan man on it, his entrails trailing to the ground and a dead stabbed victim at our feet. A lovely time was had by all.

"Now you have been here and seen the place. Don't ever come back no more," he said. What an amazing statement. I hadn't asked to go in the first place. On the drive back into town from the club called the "Sand Box" as it sits out on a spit of land, nearly an island, in fact, it is called Sand Island Road, we drove mostly in silence.

Then I hear, "Y'all took up termarrer?" *Now what does that mean?*

"Decipher that please."

"What?"

"Repeat your remark."

"I said, I s'pose y'all's took up for Saturday?" After a fast trip through my mental calculations I decided that must be an inquiry as to my Saturday plans. I thought I'd take a chance that was correct and ventured a reply I hoped would fit his remark.

"Saturdays are quite busy, as I have to accomplish all in one day what most house wives do in a week. Clean, laundry, shop, cook, hair, nails, etc. etc., you know."

"Yeah, well, ya could rest settin' in a show couldn't ya?"

"Delightful idea, what did you have in mind?"

"I don't know yet." He ponders the question and comes up with a brilliant idea.

"You decide, OK?" Oh my, this is quite a deep thinking guy. But pleasant company and so completely different from any of my friends and associates that it is a bit of a challenge.

During the next few months, I had quite an eye opener. When one is traveling so far out of their own element, you pay close attention to conversations and details or you look illiterate in their world. The higher echelon of the blue collar people is little different from the white collar ones, really. Just a different set of people and vocabulary, as the intensity of planning, cohesiveness of structure, integrity and personal set of values, remain the same. They just walk the walk, and talk the talk, on levels that apply to their own occupations. A lawyer may catch a plane in a business suit and brief case going to a required place, while one of the men in jeans, western shirt, boots and an old Stetson that looks like it needs an oil change, may be in the next seat, on the same plane, taking care of his business, which is just as important.

At company picnics, gatherings, at dances (his was not improving) banquets or other social functions that I was asked to, I began to meet his people and had no problem fitting in. A very congenial group and they had a way of accepting you at face value, until they learned they couldn't, "if some one screwed up", as I kept hearing.

My attire took a definite turn around from hose, heals, jewelry, up to the last minute coiffure and evening gowns, silk pants suits or other acceptable wearing apparel, to sweats, jeans, shirts and knock abouts, I found to be quite comfortable as a matter of fact. But the boots, not a chance, there I drew the line. To this day, I abhor the thought. Even for square dancing, they look ridiculous on women but they would sooner be dead than out of style.

After a few months with Jess's working companions and his closest friends, I began to realize how I'd neglected my own. But face it, I must, he would be most uncomfortable as he just wouldn't fit in with the professors, business executives, doctors, lawyers, merchants, chiefs, or my relationships and didn't seem at all interested to even attempt it. In fact, he resented even my correcting his speech or pronunciations.

To me, it was inconceivable anyone would *not* wish to advance his status in life or acquire a better vocabulary or inform ones self of current events, social graces and the like. The laid back life was certainly a new experience and not altogether easily accepted. Many times I felt like I was falling into the 19th century, not abreast of things in the 20th century. But, I had fallen in love with a very dear, kindly, hard, hard working, gentle, sweet guy. When you're in Rome, you do as the Romans do, right?

One day, after we were married, I asked to go to the job site. Wrong choice! But, I went. Thank God I'd followed his truck with my Monte Carlo, because I stayed only two and a half hours. When I returned to our apartment, in that "expensive place" where he lived, by the way, the mirror showed me bad news. I looked like five miles of dirt road and I was exhausted. Then and there I figured out how HARD and DIRTY his work was and I believe I'd rather have been butchering hogs than attempt going back out on the line ever again. One learns respect the hard way!

CHAPTER 2

After the Sunday morning trip to the Kam Drive-in Flea Market, our group of twelve took our grass mats, food and gear and headed for the beach. It was a lovely day and after swimming, surfing, eating and sitting around talking stories, we departed, heading each to his own destination and evening plans. Jess wanted to go out to the Sand Box again, as some of his cronies and their wives were celebrating some ones' anniversary.

About seven-thirty we arrived to find a hilarious bunch enjoying the music and seemingly indefatigable dancing. After some hors d'oeuvres, we too joined the dancers. A beautiful song I'd never heard before was being sung and I was trying to listen to the pretty vocalist, all at once Jess says, "I don't suppose you would do that, huh?" I hadn't heard one word he said, so I didn't know what to answer to. It is safe to just smile, so I did. After a few minutes again I hear, "Well, whaddo think, will you?" Again, I hadn't heard him say a thing and had no idea how to reply, so again, I just smiled and returned to listening to the music.

When the chorus began, he abruptly stepped in the near center of the floor and said, "Well?" I ask, would he please hush, I was trying to hear the words to that song. "So take my hand and walk through this world with me", ended the refrain, such a lovely song, I said.

"Now, what did you ask?"

"You hear that song?"

"Yes, it's beautiful."

"Well, will ya?" *Will I WHAT? Oh, Oh... Oh my!* Finally I saw the dawn.

"You mean ME marry YOU?" I squealed in astonishment.

"For God's sake, shut up!" He exclaims while pulling me over to the wall. "Yes, that was the idea", he grinned, and I nearly fell over. Since he was so nonchalant about it I said.

"Sure, OK, I have nothing better to do," and in his quiet way, with wet eyes, just hugged me tight and went right on dancing, his type of dancing. I wondered if I'd ever get used to him and his way of life. Showing so little emotion and having adolescent innocents.

When we walked back with our group, he held up his hand for silence. With that done, Jess announced that we were getting married in three weeks which was also news to ME. The ensuing commotion would run a close second to a win at the Indy Five Hundred. To overcome my insecurities was indeed pretty uphill work for a few days, but then things began to fall into place.

Being a repeat performance, as both of us had been wed before, lent little to the confidences either of us was feeling here. Love is a marvelous healing ointment, I can attest to that.

First came the fiasco of living arrangements. It would be far more economical to have remained in my studio apartment since both our working hours left little time at home. He was on call twenty-four hours a day, if not on steady shift that was approximately fourteen hours at a time. I was teaching at the University, involved in curricular activities and still with the shoe store some evenings, weekends and most holidays. But, that idea did not set to well with my mister. He had come from near poverty circumstances in childhood, three broken marriages of his own, due mostly to his occupation and its unsettling hours and effects on family life. (What family life?) So, he was quite impressed with his high cost of living apartment in the high rise. It was an ego trip he earned and deserved. Besides, his roommate was a married man who was pleased to move into my small place so he could save money and a minimum of work required. Once this was sorted out, next came the plans and people involved. What started to be a simple church wedding ended up with everyone we knew. Picture the Hawaiian Wedding Song, with luau, music, food and to coin the expression, "the whole nine yards."

I had selected, after 40 choices, a coral colored floor length, cling knit with matching jacket. He had trousers, not jeans, and a lovely silk Filipino shirt, with attendants clothed accordingly. Gib's wife, Mary and Henry's wife, Gwen, were bridesmaids. Helen was matron of honor and Gib was best man. Henry and Bob (My foster son) were groomsmen. It was altogether a very lovely wedding. So where do you suppose all of them wanted to go afterward? Right, the "Sand Box" for dinner and dancing. I couldn't believe it. With all the gorgeous places in Honolulu, he wanted to go to that place, club, dive?? It was insulting to me, but they seemed quite happy. Once out there, about twenty miles, I saw why. The dinner reception and dance were all reserved for us, by his company. They played "Take my hand and walk through this world with me", first and he said, "She DID!"

And thus began my new life and what a life it was to be. Jess couldn't have chosen a better mate for the type of life he led and I loved it. Every day of it. Such a challenge for a newcomer to the trade. One could never realize what all goes on when you pump gasoline into your vehicle. I've experienced it all the way from oil exploration to the end product, life in foreign countries, places in this country I'm sure even God has forgotten about, the wonders of which would fill a library if I could even begin to do them justice with pen and paper. Amazing!

Right from the start I ran into trouble. We kept my phone number, as after all, it had been my home most of my life and I had retained the same phone number through three marriages. (One divorce and two widowhoods. Widowhoods? Is that a real word, I wonder?) But somehow, two ex-wives discovered this phone number. One in Wyoming, and one in Texas. As so often happens, things go in threes and this one day was no exception.

About 1PM, while still cleaning house, the phone rang and after turning off the vacuum, I answered its insistent ringing.

"Hello, Black."

"This is Mary."

"Oh hi, are you and Gib going with us tonight?"

"I am Mary Black. Is Jesse there?"

"Why no, he isn't, would you care to leave a message?"

"Would I care t leave a message?" in a nasty, mimicking tone, "Hell, no, I don't. I just want to tell the SOB what I think." Now here is a news item I could live without.

"Sorry, you have the wrong number, *my husband* has a lovely mother, try else where to locate a bitch, OK?" As I hung up, I wondered what that was all about. Within the hour another phone call for Jess.

"Hello, Black."

"Is that so – well this is Mary and I want to speak with Jesse."

"I just told you he isn't home, he is working."

"Lady, you damn well didn't tell me nothin' and I need to talk to Jesse."

"Excuse me, I do not know to whom you think you're speaking, but I do not appreciate your choice of words. He is not here and I don't believe it necessary for a return call."

"I'll be damned, ain't you just too good for words? Now you tell him, miss high and mighty, that Mary Frances called and my papa died." Bang went the phone.

So, wife number 2, called Mary, as well as number 3, also knew our phone number. Hmmmm – I'll do something about that. But I hadn't gotten out of the room when the phone rang again.

"Yes," – not so sweet a tone –

"Julie?" – says this inquiring voice—

"Now what?" I ask, not politely I'm afraid.

"Gee, you're crabby. What's wrong, this is Mary." *Dear God, not again.*

"Which one," I asked, a bit more ladylike.

"Why, Gib's wife. How many Mary's do you know?"

"You would be surprised!" I said, with relief in my voice. I proceeded to relate the events of the past hour. She was sympathetic, but just howled anyway.

"I'm going down at Happy Hour", she said – did I want to go along, the men could meet us there. You can rest assured there was a record breaking change of clothes and the door hit my shirt tail on the way out. Three Marys in forty-five minutes was quite enough. I was unnerved some what, but Gib and Jess thought it quite amusing. Some sense of humor there.

Plans were made for an Island hop the following weekend, only I grew gravely ill on Tuesday and was in the hospital three days. To this day, no one knows what was the matter and it has happened many times since.

The first experience with the instability of (his line of work) schedule came two months later and I began to realize my paradise had berry vines as well as roses for companions. At 4:30 he comes in announcing they will finish the project in two days – be ready to move. Period.

"To where?" I'm rather alarmed.

"Texas." – just like that!

"What am I to do about our things?" For a reply I received this whoa begone look like a stupid child would receive and get…

"Box it, store it, and pack two cases." End of subject. In two days we were on the plane to Texas.

CHAPTER 3

We were met at Dallas by Jess's brother Roy and his wife Ann, who had Jess's car. After all the introductions, greetings and bag gathering, we arrived two hours later at his mother's home. Several family members had gathered there and I was a natural curiosity and interest, of course. They were all very down to earth, practical people and easily adaptable.

Grandma Black's house was quite interesting. She and Grandpa (now deceased) had built it, every nail, by themselves, from an old school they had torn down or dismantled. It had a farm kitchen, dining room, now used for a this and that room, three bedrooms and a generous sized living room, a front porch and rear veranda, one bath that was very accommodating and all of it really old and much neglected.

Irene Black was one of the dearest, sweetest "proper" people I've ever had the privilege of knowing and I simply adored and cherished that tiny lady. When she passed away, there was no one of her own blood who could have missed her more than I.

Over the next few years, Jess and I rebuilt the front porch, painted the house, caulked the 100 plus windows of 8 X 10 glass squares, bought a deep freeze, new carpeting, papered four of the rooms and remodeled the bathroom. Jess's pretty red-headed daughter, Lindy and her hubby Paul, had the septic cleaned, and his sister, Esther had the driveway re-graveled. To the best of my knowledge, that is all his family had ever done for her. Thank God I was in that family now and things got done. If I'd had a mother I'd have turned every stone to help her.

One day we drove to the cemetery to clean the graves of Grandpa Black, Irene's Father and Mother and the Great Grans., Uncles, Aunts and Cousins. That was a long day and should have been a routine job – well, just dream on.

When we were finished, we drove to Waco, to brother Keith's for dinner (supper there) and to spend the weekend as we were headed back in a few days to a job starting in Montana. During dinner/supper, I started to squirm, constantly. Finally I was asked if I were uncomfortable or what?

"Yes, I must have gotten into something", I complained and scratched. Betty said to go to the bathroom and let's see *what on earth is the matter*. The *matter* turned out to be *chiggers* of which I'd never been acquainted with or even heard of. My entire body looked like raw ground hamburger, I was so chewed up with bites. Betty, my sister-in-law, was Keith's wife.

"Oh my Lord, get in the tub and I'll fix soda water", which she proceeded to do and darn near drowned me, to no relief of bites. I ended up in the hospital for three days, with eyes swollen shut, fingers and toes so swollen they would have passed for Vienna sausages, and a body plastered with every contrivance know to man, which accomplished little to ease the itching. I've since learned that chiggers are a tiny red insect, nearly naked to the human eye. If they were the size of a fly, I'd be dead at the rate they gnawed on me. Also, I've learned to my sorrow that if it flies, wiggles, squirms, crawls or bites, it lives in Texas, along with poison ivy, oak, nettles and an assortment of other miseries Texas generously hands out to us strangers to the area.

Whenever my wonder lust gives me a sharp poke in the ribs, I do not aim it toward Texas. Many years later, after I was alone, I returned to Texas for three years to teach at Midland

College, but my adventure took me little elsewhere but the Abilene zoo or yard sales.

Back to the story. Once I was ready for travel, we collected our little Pomeranian dog, Half Hitch, (Hitchy Boy for everyday use) the sixteen year old cat who could tell fortunes – that I shall explain later, and headed for Montana.

Texas is full of Mexicans that are now days called Hispanics, which I do not comprehend in the least, and by and large are very practical and generous people. I have found my dearest and closest friends are of Spanish decent, living in California City, California. Their life and mine will be found in a later chapter.

We started north via El Paso. Never having been in Texas before, the distance from place to place I was sure, lead to another country altogether out of the continental United States. That strip from Van Horn into El Paso, confirmed my suspicions so far as I was concerned. I was pretty sure there were powers afoot that were stretching out that road on the western end so it would reach to Hawaii without the ocean being involved. Not even a self respecting pack rat would be caught in that God forsaken desert without a knapsack and thermos of water. The only thing I saw was a cemetery and I could jolly well understand *that*. I did get Jess to stop there so I could prowl about a bit and stretch my legs. I have an absolute fetish about old cemeteries and can spend hours in them reading the old beautiful poetry for inscriptions, the old names that were once prevalent, Rueben, Flora, Charity, Lemual, Uriah, Amrita, Bethany, Rawson, Rufus and Abner to recount a few. So I wandered around and found to my delight, a grave from the Spanish American war with the pictures of a wagon full of ammunition engraved on it with the information that Liam Perkins had been a Wagoner for the army in 1812. I took a picture of that, and then wandered on to see a virtual sidewalk of grave stones, rows of them, flat to the earth, over in some wild rose briars. Curiosity killed the cat (me), and got my feet and legs scratched up quite properly, only to find each said exactly the same thing, "Unknown". Served me right.

It was time for us to go, but the Lincoln wasn't going -- not at all. Such a time to get it going.

We finally got on the road and into a motel by 9 PM – oh great fun. The people over us in that room had an all night party. By 5:30 AM we gave up and looked for breakfast first and tried starting the car, however, it wouldn't start. So, across the street to the gas station we go – changed something under the hood and off we went. By now my kind, patient, quiet husband is gnashing his teeth over delays and problems. First chiggers, now car troubles and growling at every Mexican we see.

"Get out of the way bean eaters", "Don't sit there till you die on the vine", "Come on, come on", "Move it Spic", "Well damn", (from him who doesn't swear) "What's the hold up?" When it's a millisecond after the light turns green. Then I spot a sign telling of a cave and I want to stop.

"OK, but don't drag yer feet." He is not too enthused over the idea, you see. When we are ready to leave – the car isn't ready, again, and we grind away the battery. A nice Mexican man comes over and kindly offers to jump start the car – All at once now I hear "That was one good Mexican, eh?" I laughed out loud.

Since I am somewhat of an author and write children's stories mostly, I had found a bonanza in material while in Texas. While we were on the way back to LA International for a return trip to Hawaii, I had plenty of time to start notes for several stories later on.

The trip kept getting interrupted by my sighting things dropped, or blown off vehicles or what the wind had tumbled along the road, with my explosion of "Stop, stop, wait, let me out to see what it is" and popping my treasure into the trunk of the car – so far so good. He hasn't complained about my haul. Coming through Arizona on the way to California, there are many things to see. One could take a month to just poke along from one interesting spot to the next. For me, one of the most interesting is Gila Bend, Arizona, (pronounced He-lah Bend from the Spanish influence of the "G" having an "h" sound but so does the "J" as in Jose – (Hozay) – the "ll" is as a "y", etc. One needs to master Spanish if you choose to be in the south west, or otherwise speak like your illiterate.

Gila Bend has some very odd history. It once was a ranch that blossomed into a town, but moved to the present location in the 1800's, along the Southern Pacific railroad tracks. If you have a four-wheel drive vehicle and get permission from the Papago Indian's, you can go see the village which dates back to about 1200 A.D. It is up on the plateau over looking the Gila River.

Next to know about is the Butterfield Stage with its mail route which began October 3rd, 1858. The town still celebrates the Stage Fiesta Days in October. When the railroad came through in 1879, the town simply picked itself up and moved over.

These people were of hardy stock and didn't rattle easily. When a cyclone struck in 1898, once again, they gathered together to rebuild. The word is that once they were started and sent for supplies, the first was for eight barrels of beer. That ended with some wild carnal building days also hoodlums, drunks and other varieties of scoundrels. Since the jail was blown down, they simply dug a circular pit twelve feet deep, covered with crossties and earth, which soon was know as the Snake Pit. They put the offender down a ladder and pulled the ladder back up. If there was too much hell going on, they threw a snake down with the drunk or whomever. It had a very sobering affect.

There are petroglyphs from prehistoric days, the remains of an old adobe trading post, the Oatman Stage Station and sight of the Oatman massacre. The family graves are a few hundred feet below the massacre sight. One son survived after being thrown over the cliff into the river below. Although cut with a hatchet, the cold water saved him to we found by the next wagon coming through two days later. The town of Oatman stands today. A virtual ghost town, but people are coming back. It is a most interesting story in itself.

After our drive through the ghost towns, we arrived late at my son's home in San Berdo, where we stayed overnight and talked half of it away. I hadn't seen him in four years. His wife's name is Sharon and that's all I have to say about *that* subject. We left our car there when we returned to Honolulu. Now time to consider stories again.

For some strange reason, I had another one of those ghastly sick spells on the plane and straight to the hospital upon arrival. Still no diagnosis except - maybe 24 hour flu or indigestion. Well, we soon had a post mortem on that idea, as it reoccurred within a month when we learned I had Crohns Desease, of which little is known to this day. This will be covered later on down the line of "incredible statistics".

After the plane trip home to Hawaii, we settled in at the high rise apartment on the 17th floor and as Jess related "We took up housekeepin' for awhile". Henry and Gwen lived three floors up and the men usually stopped off at our place first, coming home from work. One evening, while they were enjoying a drink and I was baking bread, Henry wondered into the odors wafting from the oven to grin at me and said, "It sure is good to see Jesse so happy. We all get a charge out of him at break times." Naturally I found that a curious statement and asked, "why"?

"Well, he looks sad and heaves a sigh and announces to anyone within earshot that he sure is homesick" – which causes the speaker to slap his leg and a, ha, ha, ha, laugh that goes clear to his eyes. Some people are easily entertained. As they had been sitting on the floor leaning against the couch, their 7-UPs were on the floor as well, but I thought nothing of it until the next morning, while vacuuming. That's when I noticed a wet spot. So, I took a soiled towel and stepped on it after placing it over the wet spot. All was well, or so it seemed. But I had things to do, places to go and people to see and left within fifteen minutes of replacing the vacuum in the closet.

Both Jess and I arrived home about the same time that evening and during a hurried meal preparation I said, "Why didn't you wipe up the floor after you spilled your soda last evening?" He looked pretty perplexed, so I said, "Or tell me, I could have done it."

"Now where was this supposed to have happened?" he asked.

"Where you were sitting on the floor last evening. I took a towel and dried the carpet." So he walks over to inspect the area. I heard a grunt which one can often interpret for words with this new husband of mine.

"Wahll, if I done spilt it, I must've done it from the bottom of the rug up," he says.

I ask, "What does that mean, exactly?" You see I still had years to go to interpret the slow drawn out and sometimes pretty odd (to my way of thinking) expressions this Texan used.

"See here, how it is spread out two feet wide?" – which I hadn't – "it's comin up from underneath". Now we do have a dilemma as it is a concrete floor under wall to wall carpeting. I called the complex security who called maintenance, who called the owner's who called a plumber. The plumber discovered the air conditioner plastic drain hose was plugged with lint, ie. – "stuff", and repaired it. By now, the carpet was 65% wet, as the overflow had leaked through a crack in the concrete. There was nothing to do but take wet carpet up and drape it over the furniture to dry out. This took four days and it smelled like very dirty socks. We dispensed with company you can bet. This was the first of many water calamities in our married life.

In this apartment where we lived on the 17th floor, the kitchen door was the only entry. Passing through to the living room, the hall to the left took you into the bathroom at the end of the hall. On the left was a big walk-in closet across from the bathroom door which was on the right. Several of my women friends got together on two afternoons a week for what Jess called our Hen Parties. This one particular day, we were listening to the music on the beach and time slipped away. All at once, I realized I had 25 minutes to get home, bathe and prepare dinner. Once upstairs, I put some food on to cook, stripped off and had just gotten in the bathroom door when I heard his key in the lock. I turned around and dove into the closet instead. I could hear him muttering around out there. "Food is on, she can't be gone too far – oh, well, I'll get a beer, shower and she'll be back soon." He took his shower and grabbed a towel, with that over his shoulder he opened the closet door to get clean clothes and I said, "Surprise! What you see is what you get!" You never saw such an unbalanced look. He backed up about four steps and grabbed his head.

"You know woman, one day you're gonna' do me in. I never know what to expect when I get home." The dinner was a little late that evening.

During dinner I saw water on the kitchen floor. We got up to investigate only to see water pouring down the wall under the sink, but our water wasn't running – so we called the maintenance man again. He could not locate a break, leak or valve which would cause this flood. After a trip upstairs, he discovered the lady above us was asleep in her chair with the dish water running.

Another water disaster. Carpets up again, drying out again – stinky poo again and with hope in our hearts, all was replaced again.

I gravitate more and more toward his world and enjoyed freedoms from social pressures quite gratefully. Both of us loved music, the beach, dining out, company in, poking around through old historical things and came to grips with married life as we both had been single for some time. But, this ideological episode ended with the company sending us to Kauai, Island (where I was from) to work on a project there.

We settled into a two bedroom apartment across from

the beach and four other couples found residence in the same condominium. That first night, all congregated at our place and we had a fine time. The couple that lived up in the penthouse were the oldest of us all and Edith was a saint, everyone loved her. She and Ron had seven or eight grown children, one married son (Harry) worked with our crew. He had been in Australia and brought his wife back from there where they had met. They lived next door to us on the ground floor. Needless to say, the stair's got a workout. Harry wife, Phyliss, could sing quite well and used to sing impromptu at gatherings. I never told anyone I had sung with a band for seven years and had cut twenty some records – she needed the attention. I was content as things were.

We purchased an old car from some kids who were broke and everyone used it until it blew a fuse or whatever an engine blows when it dies, and that was that. Next came a company truck. One day, while crossing the parking lot, a car passing by threw out four little kittens on the roadway. I dearly love animals and gathered them up, but unfortunately, two died. (As a matter of fact, the older I get, the better I like animals over people.) One kitten was silver in color and I named her that. Silver!

Jess said, "You can NOT keep that cat!" So I fed the tiny thing by the front door outside. Each night when he came home he growled and frowned, but did not have much to say about this cat. Until in a pouring rain, I brought it in and fed it on a newspaper in the kitchen.

"Where's that dam cat? It isn't on the porch."

"Well, no, it's pouring, so I brought it in and it's eating in the kitchen."

"And just where is it going after it eats?" He says with a thunderous expression and hands on his hips.

"Guess you will need to ask Silver," I ventured trying not an answer.

"Silver? Silver! – so now it has a name and is in the house

and eats in the kitchen?" That's OK I know by now that the bark is worse than the bite.

"You want to put the tiny thing out in the rain?" I ask as pitiful as I could summons up. "Would you like to stay out in it?" By now I'm all puffed up on the topic.

"I guess you can keep it till you find it a home", he mutters on the way to change clothes. So Silver now lived with us and grew rapidly. She was smart and quick and did such funny things. If I was standing by the stove, she would reach up and pat my leg until I would hold the stirring spoon down for her to smell. She never once touched it, just wanted to see and to smell. She would sleep under the furniture as soon as Jess came in, but slip on the bed at night. We couldn't let her out the front door, as she would get run over in the parking lot, like the other's had, but we would take her out in the park behind our patio and watch her play. He eventually acknowledged the cat had a good home.

One day, the wives and I had gone to town, getting home after the men's shift was over. When I went in the apartment, there was no sign of "my man". I looked out the back and there he was having a most intelligent conversation with Silver. Something to the effect that, "The dam cat now had found a good home." Now I know longer needed to search for a good home, which I hadn't anyway, to tell the truth. After that, she learned that he left tidbits of food in his lunch pail. She would meet him at the door, standing on her hind legs, so to pat his legs when he came in. The endearing and adorable trait cemented the bond. Next came a velvet pillow, via Jess, "Because I don't want no cat fur on my good pants when I set down" – *oh, sure*, that's why he held her too, no doubt. And a collar and toys that just appeared in the lunch pail.

At Christmas, I wanted a tree, but of course there are no trees of the fir or pine species. So, Jesse climbed an Ironwood tree and cut the top six feet off, I decorated it with silver balls tied on with pink ribbons and silver foil cut in this strips for ice sickles. All went well until the cat decided to climb the tree. The next day, the tree was wired to the door frame in its corner of the room. So Silver sat underneath the tree and batted the foil off except for what she ate.

And guess who came home with gifts for Silver! Not me! A toy mouse, cat nip ring and a sneaky look. When we left Hawaii, she remained with a Filipino family and we never heard of her again. That was the first of a LONG string of pets over the years.

CHAPTER 4

The next few months took us back to California and to stay at Lake Shasta, working on the turbine under the dam. Not having anything in particular to occupy myself, I suggested a small dog as a companion. "Well, you go get what you want," was the usual reply to any request and this was no different. Earlier I had seen a Pomeranian Kennel along the highway, so I decided to see what it had to offer. After three hours of elimination, I had a beautiful three year old male Pom, champaign colored, and an absolutely delightful little gentleman. He had been the stud dog for his occupation and sent to retirement. Such a love as he became, also spoiled beyond description. He was my constant companion for the next 12 years.

Jesse immediately decided that Hitchy looked like a "sissy" and he had utter disregard for the beautiful golden coat with gorgeous tail that came back over the hind quarters, skimming along the ground. The silky rear pant legs left no impression of high esteem, either. Just a gorgeous knot of fur, which led me to choose his name, Half Hitch. Of course, this became Hitchy Boy and pet number 2 was enthroned.

So, Hitchy came to live with us. We were in the higher grounds of Lake Shasta, California, in a beautiful setting, with lovely accommodations, at the job sight provided by the company. A living/bedroom combination, with kitchen and dining area, a very ample bath just to the right of the entry door, which was wisely thought out by someone, as it was easily accessed by muddy feet, wet clothing or what ever else nature provided one with.

As soon as I put Hitchy down, he initiated the carpet and base board and received a good sound scolding for his efforts. This began the little dog's life with us. He had many trials learning to put up with us too, if we could see life from his view. On the whole, things went well and life adapted. I used to take him for long walks in the woods and down to the pier for the fishing boats. The wooden steps were steep for his little three inch long legs, and after the second time, he went tumbling heels over head, following me down the stairs. He decided to just run alongside the steps through the colorful carpet of fallen leaves. Then one beautiful fall day, he ran down the slope ahead of me and jumped off the leaves into what must have appeared to be just another pile of leaves. However, it was the leaves floating on the surface of the lake that had funneled up under the platform and looked solid to the dog. He jumped in and disappeared. I started screaming at him to come back as he continued on his way swimming away from the pier. The water is ice cold coming off Shasta Mountain. I don't swim, but I grabbed a stick and beat the water until he turned and saw me still yelling at him to come to me. He finally turned and swam back. By now the tiny fellow was shaking so severely, it seemed you could hear his bones clicking (his teeth of course). I snatched him up, wrapped him in my coat and ran for the cabin. Once there, I stood in the hot shower with him until he was nearly hot with water, then dried him with my hair dryer and fixed him a nest of bath robes and blanket.

When Jess came home, I told him, at length, of our disaster of the day, while preparing our dinner. Each day, Jess took his fishing pole along to work and each evening he brought me at least one large German Brown Salmon that are plentiful in the lake. I love fish and never tire of them. I possibly ate 30 during our stay there. Although he never once said so, I can well imagine Jess would have drooled at the sight of a hamburger and wept over a T-bone.

The following morning after the impromptu swim, Hitchy didn't seem very perky. Instead, he just sat when his usual self jumped, ran and wanted out of doors. He didn't eat and seemed unable to drink water. This was too alarming to endure; it was time to locate a vet. Once one was located, I gathered up my furry bundle and asked for help. Doc Wright said his tonsils were nearly swollen shut and needed to be removed. THEN! I hardly believed it. A dog has tonsils??? If that was needed, then do it! An hour of waiting did not do much for my nerves.

Once we were back home, he went directly under the bed and there he remained the rest of the afternoon. When Jess and his daily catch came in at five, he looked around and said, "Well, where is that fuzzy little feller?"

"Under the bed, but don't bother him yet. He is still a little drowsy or dopey."

"Dopey? Why, what does that mean?" So we had a conversation concerning tonsils. Jess just looked at me absolutely blank.

"The dog had his tonsils out? TONSILS OUT? Well dam – I ain't never even had MY tonsils out! Tonsils out – now how much did that set you back?"

"Sixty-five dollars," I said.

"Sixty-five dollars for DOG TONSILS???" He had such an incredulous look on his face, I had to laugh in spite of myself.

"We will eat more fish instead of meat," I said. Like that would save sixty-five dollars. I felt sure he was elated.

"Oh Lordy, Sooky, I can nearly grow fins now, don't worry over the sixty-five dollars," he said while heading toward the shower. The last I heard before the door closed was, "Dog tonsils, well I'll be." For Jess, I'm sure that started a new dimension of possibilities when it came to that dog.

One day, while at the thrift store, I happened to find an old fashioned, fold up car seat. I purchased the seat, padded it with a large tan colored Turkish towel, wrapping it so that the leg openings were solid and Hitchy couldn't slip out. At 3 ½ pounds, he could fall through the cracks. Once completed and hooked over the back of the seat, he could see out the windows and was a very happy little fellow. Then Jess came in from the job – "What in the world is that contraption?"

"I fixed a car seat so Hitchy can see out!"

"Well, I am NOT riding in no car with no darn dog settin' up in that thing lookin' like a danged ijit." And he banged off in the house. That car seat stayed in the vehicle for eight years, he never gave in and road along, but followed in the pick up. So who looked like a "danged ijit?" The dog, however, seemed clothed in respect and dignity at all times.

Next came the war of chairs. No matter which chair Jess choose to reline in, Hitch sat along side and stared at him until he would move to another chair. Then the game began all over again.

Once day, a neighbor observing this amusing set of circumstances, said to me in jest, "Would you say that dog is spoiled?" I replied that "no, he smells that way all the time." After a few seconds, the dawn came with an explosion of mirth enough to startle poor Hitch from his concentrated efforts to dislodge Jess from his third chair of the evening.

We left California to start the next job in Montana. We had settled into a small Montana hamlet with the work office 50 miles northeast. This distance meant up at 5 AM, to be ready for a 6 AM departure. A 12 hour work day and one hour return trip. This left me to my own devices for a 16 hour schedule in a strange area and a town of maybe 500 souls. After covering the small museum, art gallery, city park, cemetery, school, three churches, (also eight bars, I do not frequent) the plant nursery, historic hotel and the thrift store, I was at a stand still for any diversion after three days.

"What did you find new to do today?" I was asked at 9 PM on the third day.

"I went to the library, took a trip to the dump, which was interesting as I learned everyone goes there Sunday afternoon, to see what's been discarded. I understand some items make as many as three or more trips on Sunday in pick ups, or what ever, as people take stuff back".

"Hmmmm – and so what do you *want* to do?"

"I thought I'd like to build a house." I commented rather

nonchalantly – I guess it goes without saying, that that comment met with a look that deemed me a certified bonafide idiot. "Well, that's what I want to do," my determined tone of voice left little doubt.

"Go ahead; just don't bother me with it until after September." Since this was May, I was safe. First came the real estate man to locate. I found him to also be an apartment house owner, the local insurance man, real estate agent and president of the Lions, Kawanis and had a lousy, trigger happy temper. His garage windows had been replaced on an average of once a week, since glass does not prevent hammers, wrenches and rocks from going through them on a regular basis.

We started looking at available property. I had inquired as to the most costly, least costly, and started in the middle. The fifth place I saw, I wanted. Perfect roof line, foundation excellent, house was stucco, old fashioned in keeping with the 100 plus year old town. I loved it.

"I'll take it." I was thrilled to pieces.

After his jaw came back in line, he said, "Well, would you like to see *inside*?"

"No, not necessarily." I said.

Another dropped jaw – Your husband hasn't even *seen* it." Poor Mr. Appleton, he simply does not know me. I was born in overdrive and want things done yesterday.

"Never mind, what's the price?" Another odd look, and then a quote. I pulled out my check book and wrote it out, using my knee for a desk and never saw such a dumbfounded man in my life. Thus began our life in Montana. It became our home base from this time on. Our next job was in Utah.

CHAPTER 5

While in Utah, Jess purchased a new 33 foot Terry fifthwheel RV unit, the first arrival at the lot in Murry, Utah. We pulled our 26 foot travel trailer up along side, put a plank from door to door and proceeded to "move house" as the Texans say.

After arriving back in Bountiful, Utah, and getting set up, we went out to dinner and called it a good day. However, after Jess left for work the next morning, I got down the saws, hammer, nails, and all the other paraphernalia I thought I'd need and started to dismantle the cupboard doors.

As my Grandfather had been a superb carpenter, he taught me carpentry from the earliest time I could remember. By age five, I could sort screws and nails by there proper size and names. So, like anyone with a natural talent added to instruction, I would rather build, then knit, remodel, than do embroidery. First came off the bottom small doors, placing the side hinges on the bottom's and side latch to the top. With what lumber and wood I could scavenge or cannibalize from the maintenance area, I built a trough to screw to the back side of the doors, thus, making a vegetable bin on the back of all five doors. This was a half day project, as once a pattern was established; it fell into place and went smoothly. With a drill,

266

saber saw and sander at work, it didn't take long before I had an audience of neighbor ladies – not just wanting to see the new RV but what was I *doing* to it. A few turned pale and one nearly choked, finally Lucy said, "I hope to God you know what you're doing."

"Oh, yes indeed, I built our house." This got some odd expressions on some startled faces. Under the closet, in the rear bath room, was an entire wall three feet high, from the floor – behind it was a storage compartment that opened from the outside. "Me thinks that should open inside." I said to no one in particular. I started measuring and ended up sawing a two and a half by two foot hole through the wall, screwed and glued a waste basket of similar size to the piece I had removed. I then hinged the bottom and then made a trip to the hardware store for a patterned trim to glue half way around the piece I'd cut out. Add a handle and now I had a clothes hamper that looked like a wall opening with a pretty wooden border. It only took up about ten inches of space inside so, plenty of room was left for the storage area.

With time off to start dinner, nearly all was complete by five thirty. I had saw dust, bits of glue, wood scraps, nails, screws and whatever else was required, all over the floor. Naturally, this was a short – ten hour day for Jess, who came whirling in early with a working buddy, to see the new fifth wheel, of course.

The door was open, extension cords all over and there stands a man white and trembling, can hardly speak and sputtering his head off, while I, all smiles, say, "Well, hi, your in early today."

The shock had not yet worn off; Jess seemed utterly devoid of humor and finally said, "Where this woman is, pandemonium reigns. What in God's name are you doing?"

"Making use of empty spaces. Do you want to see what I've done?" He was as silent as an oyster. A most reluctant and weak "yes" now escaped the trembling lips. So, very proudly I showed those two that all was well.

"I'll be damned – Black, you gotta' gold mine in this woman." Said the admiring buddy, who I soon learned was named Fritz.

"Get yourselves a beer and steady your nerves while I clean up here, OK?" I said.

The first words I heard wafting from outside were, "I paid $14,000 yesterday to get her what she wanted. Today she saws it to pieces, but it is better and I love her. If I didn't, I'd kill her on the spot." Fritz then said right out loud, two words I'd hardly even think to myself inside a dark closet. It was suppose to be admiration, I hope!

The job they were on, was to run a natural gas line over the top of the Wasatch Mountains into a town on the backside of Bountiful (Leadville by name). Although it was summer, each day the men came down off that mountain with snow packed inside their pant legs tight to their boots. Some areas were so steep, only a helicopter could drop them off at the machinery. The road, if it was one, was so steep and winding, with cutbacks, like the letter "N", which were cut out of the hills. Long tractors came around the first half of the bend, but a crane on the other side would swing the trailer over the cliff edge and set it back on the other side of the road while the tractor was still driving along. This takes exact precision work. One gets a new insight into the enormous skill required to work on any pipeline jobs.

The saga of the fifth wheel continued for many days, with the addition of a few shelves, some turned poles, new drapes and spread for the bedroom, all materials gleaned from thrift stores and the parks scrap pile. It really took shape and we were proud of it. Quite a lot of dinner guests followed the completion of the renovation and many, many, good times were enjoyed.

The day I decided to saw up the new fifthwheel, had more than one repercussion. Our next door neighbors were the

Jensens, Bob and Lucy. He worked in a copper plant and she was the head cook in an elementary cafeteria. Bob was not tall of stature, but had a broad chest about the size of the US map and a heart that fit therein. A radiant face, marred only by thimble size dimples, a few freckles and topped by a thatch of dirty blond, (ash blond) curly hair, pretty well describes the appearance of Bob's sweet little five foot tall, petite wife, Lucy. Big things come in little packages and you can believe it. That little mite of a woman raised four sons, who in time, brought home four wives, each from a different country. She held a full time job at home and at work. She baked anything that would fit in her oven, loved animals, with three cats and a poodle dog, who thought he was a Saint Bernard, that all lived in a 36 foot travel trailer.

Bob and Jess could get on with about anything for an hour at a time, especially a fishing story. The two families of us would play dominos until the sun rose and often had dinner together in our trailer, as it had the larger of the two kitchens.

If you think my husband turned pale at the sight of electric cords and saw dust, it did not hold a candle to the expression on Bob's face when he came over to see our new fifthwheel. He nearly strangled and choked out "What ARE you DOING?"

"Fixing it to suit me," I said.

"When does Jess get in today?" Bob asked wearily.

"I'm not too sure, possibly in an hour."

"Wh – huh_," says he. "I believe Lucy and I will leave now to go out to dinner."

"That's really nice," I said, while still gathering up staples, paper, pencils, tape measure, finishing nails, screw drivers, chisel, etc. He just faded away into thin air when I turned to ask where they were going. At that time, it had not yet occurred to me that Bob was pretty well convinced Jess would murder me on the spot. Indeed, we did not see either of our neighbors for two days. Seeing our roof was still attached, not even an ambulance in view, they sauntered over on Friday to see if the dominos were on for the evening. Neither one of them glanced about at anything, and very tactfully avoided any mention of recent carpentry. However, my dear mate up and says, "By the way, did Sooky show you the additions she created?" You could hear a pin drop on a feather bed. Was this a compliment, or sarcasm, so who dared speak first??? The solemn expression nearly through Jess into a spasm of glee.

Their day would come much sooner than could ever have been expected. Tables were turned. The fall weather had turned cool, with an ill wind shaking the trees, leaving a rust colored carpet of leaves where they were piling up in whirly gig fashion. The early morning tooly fog causes Oh's to sound like O's – oooo, as if you had Dublin fog in your throat. Our uniform of jeans, T-shirts, and tennis, was quickly turning to sweats and socks.

By now the trees and grass had lost most of their green, but not yet put on their funeral robes of red and gold, just a rusty, musty mess now invaded the air. The sun sets farther south in fall and winter, and it gets dark sooner, as the months go by. Early shadows reach greedy fingers along your view each evening. But, the harvest moon comes along with night skies being studded with diamonds. It is the close of another lovely sunset that looks like satin ribbons, as do the rainbows we see so often. There was so much beauty around us that we sometimes don't even see it or appreciate it. Also, our fellow man.

We four, had been out to dinner, and everyone was ready for a nice relaxing early evening. Jess hardly had his paper open, when a thunder clap, of giant proportions, was followed by one thunder after another. That could get your attention in a hurry. The cat flew under the bed. Lucy's little poodle set up a howl at a volume not know before to humans. Jess beat me out the door and met Lucy screaming his name as she flailed her arms about and her eyes as big as silver dollars. Jess grabbed her, as Lucy was blubbering some wild tale concerning a bath tub.

He marched her back to their trailer to try making sense of all this racket. Once inside, their Holiday Rumbler, he knew exactly where the trouble was. There was a cloud of blue smoke accompanied by cuss words even my Jess was unacquainted with, pouring like thick syrup from the bathroom down the hall. Upon inspection of the disaster, all Jess could say was "Well, I'll be." His usual comment about most anything. This brought forth another explosion of venom for the occupant of the bath tub. One Mr. Robert Jensen sat bare naked, with the plumbing bent over his head, feet scrubbing the far wall, hands and arms slipping every which way in the water, which continued to flow over his head. "Turn the water OFF!" he bellowed. For some unknown reason, the floor had given away under the tub. It had sunk straight through to the framework, which tipped it at a most precarious angle, suspended from its plumbing.

A lizard could sprout a mustache sooner than you could have shut off the flow of fury in that bathroom; it had reached colossal proportions by now. Bob could not get any footing at such an angle, and being wet didn't help the skidding about. Jess said, since the lower end of the tub was now even with the floor, why not just scoot down and roll over onto the flooring. Two hundred plus pounds of a slithering body with nowhere to get traction did not make for a happy camper. Try as he could, Jess could not dislodge this 245 plus man who out-weighed him by a good ninety pounds and keep his own footing. By now, I too had gone inside to see what had happened. When I saw this beached whale in the tub, I started to laugh. Bob looked up and nearly had apoplexy. "Damnation, get her OUT of here!" he yelled. Jess surveyed the contents of the tub and calmly said,

"There ain't nothin' here to see, we don't have at our place," and almost stangled on his own brand of humor. "Not unless there is just more of ya'." That propelled Bob up only to bang his head on the bent down plumbing.

I retreated to the lawn along with Lucy and repeated the conversation, which sent us both into doubled over laughter. She was standing cross-legged and announced she was going to pee her pants at the same moment another neighbor walked up to see what the commotion was about. Marge said, "I'll go get you some," which was so out of context to the problem that we both asked at the same time – "Go get *what?*"

"Why, the pins for your pants Lucy, isn't that what you just said?" – That brought on such a fit of laughter that Marge was embarrassed. We explained the situation as best we could, while still trying not to laugh, along with our hickups. Marge said she would go over and get Rex, as he was strong enough to pull Bob out, or maybe he had a rope. That brought on another stomache wrenching fit of laughter.

Lucy said, "Oh NO – not a rope, Bob will hang some one of us with it. Rex Price is not a refined man, but a "good guy" and built like a prize fighter. Marge returned with Rex in tow, who climbed under the trailer to see "what in the hell went on," as he said, then went inside to view the product of all the bellowing commotion.

He took one look and with an intense study of the situation, said "Well Bob it's a good thing your ass is at that end of the tub, else wise, you could of lost your crown jewels on that busted off drain pipe poking out. Here, gimme' yer arm and brace yer feet on the tother end of the wall and I'll heave you up on ter the floor. Take note not tah scrape up your personal equipment, that floor edge is jagged as a porkypine." This said in all sincerity, just about was the undoing of my poor husband, who by now was gripping the edge of the sink to be able to stand erect any longer. The laugh lines in his face were approaching the furrowed look and he was getting weak from myrth and pulling on Bob. Once on his feet, Bob wanted whisky, him who does not drink.

Jess said, "Now, Bob, that was quite a frolic you put on here, so what's next?" Had he not been so exhausted, he just might have flattened one Jess Black, who handed him a robe and seriously asked, "Say buddy, do you want Sooky to redo your bathroom?" That did not meet with approval at all. However, my mind is well enough furnished to think on that a great long while.

Bob sat down as though waiting for something or some other time better than the one in which he lived just now. Partly dressed, he studied his shoe tops a while and declared that a fish could stay out of water longer than he could ever stop talking about this ordeal.

Rex went home, Lucy and I decided they better stay with us a couple of days. Marge, in her kind way, recited something she picked up along her life and quoted that it was days end, dark and that "The lights go out from east to west, and God puts the day to bed and rest", possibly a good idea for us all. As she walked away, we heard her saying, "oh dear, oh dear, oh dear, me!"

For the next few days, Lucy, Marge and I were busy clearing out everything in that bathroom, so the carpenters could repair the damage. We unearthed stuff in those cupboards that had been there since before the time of Jesus and in the smashed storage space beneath the bath tub we rescued tools, fishing gear, old rags and assorted other of Bob's prize relics, over which he would rejoice no doubt. As for Lucy, she declared Bob must have a high threshold for filth to have hung on to all this assortment. Everything from fish hooks to the odd nail, screw and battered looking cotter keys. Not to exclude the old flash light batteries or pieces of wire and twine. Trying to understand why these things were even there, made one wonder. We haven't a clue about the inner regions of someone else's thinking.

After all the alterations to our fifth wheel, I continued to make changes within our home to fit our needs. I decided the mattress was just too soft to rest comfortably, so my neighbor Helen and I started going through the stores who sell mattresses. It was an all day task. We would lay on one and another and another. Each time we slid off, my hair would stand up. A customer watching us commented on our hair as we were leaving the store and without loosing a step, Helen said, "You see, they are nylon and we have been trying on mattresses all day. It's static electricity."

The poor lady said, "Trying on mattresses?" And hurried off away from us. I'm sure she had an interesting afternoon to discuss at home that night!

We took a lunch break and that turned into a complete fiasco. Have you ever seen the coupons for Arby's that advertize "two for the price of one"? We had coupons, as Helen lives by coupons. She could paper the house with them. We, like so many, went to the end of the line at Arby's in time reaching the counter, side by side. Each to order what one of us could easily have done, only to "mess up" royally. I said I'd have my sandwich, coleslaw, coffee and then went to find us a table, leaving my money with Helen. So far so good! Only, I waited and waited and then waited some more. As she was ordering when I left, it seemed a long wait for items ordered.

After a good ten or more minutes, she came with a tray full of food and a very long face. Once she sat down, she held her head in her hand with her elbow on the table and said absolutely nothing. Not knowing what seemed to be an obvious problem, I unwrapped the sandwiches, took the tape off the coffee and shoved hers under her nose. Still no response at all. Finally I said, "What is the matter, Helen?" No response. Now I'm getting a little alarmed.

Half way through my sandwich she muttered, "Was anyone looking at her?"

"No, not that I see, why?"

"Oh, I just made a complete fool of myself up there."

"What did you do?" Now, I'm serious.

"Remember the coupon was two for one?"

"Yes, but you had the coupons, I saw them!"

274

"And I ordered two Arby's, two slaw, coffee and coke."

"So, OK, that's what you brought here. I don't follow."

"The man asked for $6.42 and I said, 'But, I have the coupon.' He said, 'Yes, I know $6.42,' so I repeated, 'I have the coupon.' Again he said, 'Yes, I know. That will be $6.42.' By now I'm getting mad and said, 'But I have the coupon – one is free.' He said 'Yes Ma'am, I know that, $6.42 please. I stared him down, so he finally said, 'But the rest of the order is NOT free.' I never felt so foolish in my life." Poor Helen took a ribbing over that a long time.

We ate in silence until a waitress asked if we needed our catsup. We said no, we didn't, so she took it. Pretty soon she was back, do we need our sauces, no, we didn't, but in a few minutes, after taking those she was back, did we need our salt and pepper, no, we didn't, as she lifted those as well and I'm watching them go, I noticed a woman at another table struggling not to laugh. I smiled at her and she chokingly asked, why the waitress removed all from our table, I said I didn't know except to supply someone else's table. She couldn't stop laughing at the expression on my face as I watched each item leaving.

Once we had eaten and resumed our search for the right mattress again, we found that it was nearly past time for our exercise class, so I paid for the "right" mattress, told them where to deliver it and we scurried on our way. But, now what to do with the three week old, new mattress in the fifthwheel. This was cause for a search through the trailer park knocking on doors to peddle the mattress. Once again, Jess came home early, of course, and said "Hi, Sooky, what's up?" I told of our day, only to be met with exasperation. Now why the face I'm thinking.

He asked, "Did you find a taker yet?"

"No, not yet."

"Well, I'll take it to work tomorrow for one of the guys campers and don't be like the gal with the bicycle."

"Where did *that* come from?" I thought, "I never learn." This quiet, dry droll humor of his is a trap and I get caught every time.

"I don't want my wife peddling her ass all over town or the mattress either." Off he went so pleased he caught stupid me again.

Just a few days later, it snowed. Now I detest snow for myself and surly hated to see the men struggle with the stuff both on the ground as well as on the mountain. After coffee, kisses, lunchbox and breakfast at 5 AM, I followed him out to the truck. The snow had fallen some ten inches deep and covered the open bottom of the truck so it looked like it was floating with no wheels. I could hear an animal crying so pitifully and said don't you hear that cat? Jess knows me and the animals and just shut the truck door he had opened. Very quiet and patiently he said, "Well, come on, let's find it, I've got time." By taking a few steps at a time, we could listen at each halt. It soon became evident; the crying was coming from under the car. Jess took a shovel from his truck bed and punched a hole in the snow, under the car door. Swish – out came a flurry of fur and hissing that shot past us like a poltergeist. But, it landed in a heap in the depth of the snow. He slowly retrieved the kitten and handed it over to me. Poor little thing had sought shelter under the car and gotten snowed in.

Ten hours later, when he returned from the mountain, he took a hot shower, when in warm clothes, he got his beer, and his first words were, "So where is the dam thing?" I laughed so hard. "Oh yes," he says, "I know the cat got a good home." We named her Snowflake, for obvious reasons, but she was jet black. Not a white hair in view.

Since this job we were on would take over a year, it was decided I should fly back to Hawaii to straighten out left over business, retrieve our stored things and visit my friends Helen and Dee for a week. I called Utah, to let Jess know of my progress and flight time arriving at Salt Lake, only to be informed little Snowflake had died in her sleep. She had feline Leukemia, but who would know. So there was the third pet.

Another pet that "just found a good home," was Matillda, a fist sized, white bunny someone had just turned loose in the city park after Easter. Why people do such things is beyond my comprehension, I'd like to abandon them also. I put up a fuss about it and of course it came home with us. She grew to 12 pounds and had not a clue what a rabbit was. Dandy, the cat, seemed to think it belonged to her and Hitchy, the dog, thought it must be a toy since it hopped about, she possibly thought she looked like either of them. She was potty trained to the cat box and could jump up on your lap like the dog. She expected to be brushed, have her own eating area and became a family member. Matillda had full run of the house or fifth wheel, whichever we were in at the time and never left the yard while outside.

I admit it did get a little hectic while on the road. At road side rest's, we would occasionally stop for a rest and let the dog out, that meant all of us were out. Times to get started again meant enlisting the help of the other travelers who just had to see the puppy, kitty and RABBIT??? All got passed around and rounded up much to the disgust of one tolerant husband.

After a dog killed Matillda, we rescued three little raccoon babies. They did not yet have their eyes open. Did you ever see a new baby raccoon? Only a mother could admit it belonged to her. They are nearly transparent; the head is out of kilter in size, the mouth looks cavernous compared to the rest of the body, little to no fur and claws for feet. But, oh my, how fast they grow. These little fellow were approximately three days old when there mother was run over on the road. I can NOT stand to see animals run over and over, so stopped to pull her lifeless body over to the side of the road. I heard a baby's cry and looked around in alarm. The raccoon babies sound nearly human. They were in a nest down the bank of the ditch. A decent person does not leave anything to die or starve, you just

277

can't. I gathered them up and put them in one of Jess's caps that was in the trunk. Back at the house, I located an eye dropper and sweetened some powdered milk. Those precious little tykes were about the size of my index finger so no problem to hold and feed them. I was sitting on the patio with a bundle of rags and my little ones when my mister came in. He took one look and said, "NO – you can't keep 'em." I handed him one and an eye dropper. After a few seconds, he decided that was no doubt the ugliest thing God ever made and looked somewhat like a terd.

"Well you just can't kill them." I said.

"So how do you expect to manage this now?" He asked.

"Why, just like I am!"

"Here, take this thing." While pushing it back at me. "Now I suppose this means every hour feeding like that dam Rosita (skunk). Don't you never learn?"

I solemnly advise anyone to not try raising baby raccoons. If you don't end up in jail, it isn't their fault. Those busy little hands can be shredding up things while the innocent little bandit faces and angelic expressions are winning your heart.

In time, I gave two away and the smallest one became a child. Her name was Tomasa; we thought she was a he when we named her Tom Cooney. She ate at the table in high chair, had a real doll bed, knew her blanket, stole everything loose and got into more trouble than six children could even conceive of. One pet project of hers was to sneak up on the kitchen table to stick her head in the sugar bowl. The first bowl was round at the neck and smaller than the body of the bowl. Once the head was in, she couldn't get back out because her ears were inside. The insistent hammering on the table brought me on the run. No more sugar bowl. Another of her tricks, was to stand her two hind feet on the floor, over the garbage can. When the lid flew up those two front paws went to work on the contents. Eggshells, coffee grounds, potato peelings, banana skins – whatever she did NOT want, landed on the floor.

278

She had a harness and leash that worked quite well, until she figured out how to unbuckle the harness. She went for a stroll only to get chased up a telephone pole by a dog. She wasn't afraid of dogs as Hitchy never bothered her. When this monster took off, so did she. She set up on that pole three days. When she came down, we don't know, but she came home a week later – pregnant – an so became Tomasa.

I was excited, but Jess said, "No, you cannot keep them." So she moved to the zoo. Years later, I wondered how many times Jess wondered what four legged critter had taken up residence during his absences. The only time he meant NO, not just said it out of habit, was when we first came to Texas, after we were married. On a back country road, we saw a little white calf with enormous brown eyes and ears located in the wrong place for any cow I'd ever seen. It was alone and standing by the road. I said, "Can we keep it? I'll care for it."

"Oh Lord, Lord, Sooky, that's cattle rustling, and NO, we are not even going to stop for you to look at it." I later learned it was a charolais – pronounced, Shar lay, and its' ears were right where they belonged. They come from France, the white ones do, and Australia has a smoky red to pink skin. They are beef cattle for use and such a pretty breed. Their faces are shaped like a doe. It is a wonder Jess didn't have heart failure in the end.

Once back home at the fifth wheel, we learned the crew were encountering a dreadful time on the job. The mountain can be unforgiving and the weather was impossible. To this day, I know it had to be Gods grace that kept them alive. One particular day, we heard the insistent blowing of the danger (accident) horn, which just pounds dread in your heart. A huge piece of machinery working on a slope so steep that another huge machine anchored above it had cables attached to the lower one, so it could stay in place to work. Something broke or came loose and the lower machine, operator and all, came catapulting down the mountain side, went airborne for 1000 feet, ejecting the operator in mid air (hospital time for him) and landed in the play ground of the elementary school only 20 minutes or so after recess ended. Another accident could have killed seven more, when the van they were in could not turn sharp enough on a hairpin curve to fully negotiate, and tumbled end over end down into a steep ravine. They were packed in so tightly, they cushioned one another and survived with dreadful bruises and some broken bones. When you light your gas stove, think of how the gas got there! Many other close calls, but more good times then bad.

We made friends there that were with us long after the job was complete and we had moved on. Besides Helen and Rex, were a couple several years older than most of us in the 40-50's range. Keith and Mattie Jerukes were both very gifted people. She played the pipe orange as well as conventional organs and had a remarkable resume- of accomplishments in the field of music.

Keith and his elder brother had been in the motion picture industry most of their adult lives and he too had a most enviable background. One was his being the voice of God, in the movie Que Vadis, in the 50's, and other religious films as well. However, his most admirable accomplishment was his wood crafting ability. He made the most beautiful violins on earth. The prices were unearthly as well! You were afraid to handle one at all, scared silly you might soil it or worse.

He did carvings as well, those being just as magnificent as the violins. Hitchy used to wonder over to Keith's workshop and just lay down by him and could be content for hours. One day, Keith asked me how Hitchy got his very odd name. I told him it as because he resembled a knot of fur and a half hitch was a "knot", it just seemed to fit. At Christmas, Keith came by during the day with a small gift wrapped box for us. It was a carving of Hitchy in such detail you could see the fold in his lip and the depression down the center of his little tongue; the beautiful curve of his tail plumage, fur of "pant legs", toenails and even the small whiskers. It had been carved out of a knot of wood. What a treasure. It has been with me these nearly 40 years and one of my most precious memories.

Today we are the last of our group that worked that job. Paul and Shirley, Marge and Phil, Bob and Lucy, Rex and Helen are all in a very "quiet" place. They left us a more valuable life and precious memories.

From there, we sold the fifthwheel and went to Texas to await orders for Equador. We had three weeks with mama and her little Chihuahua dog, Honey, during which time the temperature dropped so low, ice formed on her goldfish bowl in the kitchen window. Not a flake of snow, but six below. As Luther would say, "Waall – who would huv thunk it?" He was the company character.

Since it is not too far to Hope, Arkansas, where Jess's foster son Mike, wife Lindy and son, Mick lived, we took advantage of the time to visit them over Christmas. The day we arrived, their church's children's Christmas party was being held and, of course, we were delighted to attend. Once the singing was over, the Santa Claus arrived to sit his ample self down to produce a lap for the kiddies who told of their hearts desires. When the line was down to Mick, he hopped up on Santa's knees and at the usual, "Ho, Ho, Ho, my lad and what would you like for Christmas?"

The answer that spewed forth from this seven year old was, "Well, what the hell is the matter with you? I done wrote you a letter." After the deafening silence, I turned to speak to my loving spouse, to find any empty seat, with his Stetson on it. Lindy was in tears, Mike was howling and dear Jesse? Out in the lobby doubled over in fits of laughter. We left. Mick ran to his Dad. Santa's wife deposited herself on his lap and said all she wanted for Christmas was him. Another deadly silence for a second or so before everyone left for a spaghetti dinner. Out of the mouths of babes. The Equador trip was cancelled for that time, due to rescheduling.

Once we were back in Texas from Arkansas, we collected the Lincoln and started north for Montana. On the way, Jess spotted a little 18 foot travel trailer along the curb of a house we were passing. "What do you think, how about I go look at it?" I thought that sounded like a new adventure, which I very much enjoy. We learned the elderly gentleman had purchased it for his grandson to live in at college, but the grandson had his own ideas of shelter and that wasn't it. The owner's wife had passed away the year before, so he decided to sell it. That was one of the best cross country trips we made. We stopped in each town with a yard sale along the way. One stop netted us a couple of pans, the next, set us up with some linen and pillows, the next came utensils, blanket, etc., etc. And by California, we were fairly comfortable in our "little home". The main office was in California and business came first. We then headed back through Utah to Montana and our little grey house. However, we had a favorite restaurant we always stopped at on that northern jaunt we had taken many times, the Black Angus at San Luis Obispo. Now remember, I had mentioned back a few pages that I had a penchant for gathering stuff along the roadway. Every so many miles, I'd shout "stop, stop!" I saw a scarf, pillow, rug, blanket, box or whatever. My quiet patient Jess, would pullover and let me go after my next treasure. Usually, by the time we are home, the trunk is full and more. Once, I found a purse, another time it was a suit case full of sheets, a box of books, we once had 13 blankets and 22 towels, etc. This time, instead of stopping at the Angus, he drove to a drugstore, which was odd. When re-entering the car, he threw a skinny package in the back seat and then proceeded to the restaurant. Once on the road again, I saw a head scarf caught in the weeds along a fence. The usual "stop, stop!" sang out and the usual, pull over, followed. After a scramble for the item, I opened my door to see Jess assembling some stick thing. It turned out to be a snap together fishing pole. I said "Oh, that's so cute, who's it for?"

"You." My talkative mate announced.

"Really? Why, I already have a great rod and real."

"Uh, huh. Well, you just put that window down and snag your crap from now on, 'cause I ain't stoppin' NO MORE." After the surprise wore off, I got so tickled, I just leaned over and kissed him. I received a sideways smile and a squeezed hand for an answer. My dearest Jesse – my love.

When we neared Lebec, California, we turned into the park at the top of the hill. We had learned, through the pipeline, of many interesting and out of the way places little known of, so we hunted out those we could find along the way.

Lebec was, at one time, a fort and housed, of all things, camels, to be used in war time. Eventually, they were turned out of their stables to just drift where ever. But off to the right of the fee station is a huge old tree with a cement slab patching up a large hole. Written with a stick, I would guess, is this message. "P. LeBec Kilt by a X-bar." Nowhere to bury him, his companions placed him in the tree trunk and cemented it shut. Further on, we hunted for Colingo diamonds at the old camp site. Many points of interest, including route 33, which isn't a route. The oil camp built it for their use years ago, but opened it to the public as a short cut across the desert plains.

Heading on home to Montana, we stopped at various friends. In Utah again, we learned, Phil, Marge and Helen had all passed away. The little grey house was a welcome sight, as we had been gone over a year. That house also had a history, as does the town where it is situated.

Earlier, I spoke of this house and said it would come along later. Once the purchase was made, Jess said to do as I pleased, but not to bother him with it. He had to drive nearly 100 miles each day to the job site and back, seven day s a week, 12 to 14 hour shifts to get the requirements met. Oh, I was in hog heaven to be sure. Carpentry was my hobby and I was turned loose to do as I saw fit.

After planning out the basics, I tore out the front bedroom

wall, to learn the 2 X 4's were solid oak, lath and plaster had been made of oatmeal and had mice in it. I uncovered a chimney and found a ladder to the attic, too. The front door opened into a mud room – or dirt floor and place to leave wet or snowy boots, etc. then step up to the living room floor. This odd arraignment, in time, became a sunny library room, with three walls of windows under which roses went to live. The once bedroom/living room, now became a combination living, dining room, and the old large dining room became a downstairs bedroom, after a seven foot hall came into existence, via part of two rooms. A divider arrangement across from the kitchen doorway, to the door of the new bedroom, became the end of a walk-in closet. The doors were scrounged up from a thrift store. Many trips for wall paper, paint, drywall, nails, glue, bathroom fixtures, water tank, cabinets, counter tops, stove, refrigerator, free standing fireplace, curtains, etc., etc., etc., and three months later, we had a darling little home.

I did not "bother him with it" as he asked, not because I was being a good wife, you see, there is nothing on earth Jess can't run or repair on machinery, but if I ask him to hang a picture, he would knock the wall down and never hit a nail. Bless his little pointed head.

However, when I started on the dreadful kitchen, I ran into some pretty odd happenings. I used the old dining room, now bedroom, to build the cabinets and counter area in the kitchen, which was straight across that four foot wide hall. One day, the toilet flushed itself several times. Since the dog and I were the only inhabitants, that got my attention. The next day, the back door refused to stay latched, in fact, I saw the knob turn with no one out there. Hmmmm – the dog now hiding under the new stairwell going up to the new bedrooms that emerged from a spacious attic.

Two days later, I needed to do quite a bit of measuring while building drawers. But, no matter where I set the measuring tape down, it was not there when I went to use it again. Once up in the window sill, once along the opposite wall, once out in the hall. After about the sixth time it seemed to be no where and I jokingly said, "come out, come out, where ever you are," and it scooted out of the closet. This is a true story and also spooky.

Six years later, my friend of forty years arrived to visit for a month. We had not seen each other since the Texas trip three years earlier. After the first night, I found her asleep in Jess's big chair, although there were two beds upstairs. "So what's up?" She didn't reply right away, but just sat there. Finally, she ran her hands through her abundance of jet black hair and looked at the ceiling.

"Have you ever slept up there?" She pointed to the ceiling.

"No, our room is here across from the kitchen, why?"

"There are people up there, and in the back yard." She said.

I laughed out loud. Jess wondered in with his coffee and said "So, tell me too." We did – he scratched his head and said, "Is that a fact and who would they be?"

"Indians!" Marie supplied.

In unison we said, "Indians?"

"Oh, yes! One sat on the bed. So, I am down *here*, forever!" Who will ever explain that? Later that year, while watching TV in our living room, a picture on the wall above the TV, simply lifted off the hook and came floating through the air to land on the floor about 12 feet away. After nearly five minutes of silence, Jess got up, picked up the picture and said he really needed a beer.

Another mind boggling event was in August when the house smelled strongly of cigarette smoke – neither of us smoked. Soon, we saw a cloud of smoke about the size of a pillow, come floating up by the ceiling through the hall around the living room, up the stairs and into the upstairs rear bedroom. There it ceased and stopped in front of the closet. The only thing hanging there was George's old California

Highway Patrol coat, given to Jess after George, a dear friend, was killed directing traffic. We sat on the bed, contemplating this strange event. Not a clue – however, the next day, George's widow called to say their house burned down the night before because the oldest boy left a cigarette burning when he fell asleep. Go figure. Another true story.

CHAPTER 6

Our next job took us back to Hawaii. Dee Yokum and I were at lunch watching people coming in and out of an employment agency. While watching the faces, you could nearly tell of their success or failure, disappointment or disillusionment.

"Julie, have you tried to get a job in the past three or four years?"

"No, not really, I have substitute teaching if I want it, but with Jess's job so erratic, it would really be hard to keep any sort of schedule. Why do you ask?" I wondered if perhaps Dee was interested in working again.

"For those of us who have worked our entire adult life, it is hard on us to NOT work."

"Yes Dee, I know it well, how does one learn how to do nothing? Are you considering?"

"One of these days, when each of us has time, I have an idea I'd like to explore a little. You willing to let me bounce it off you?"

"Of course, anytime." I wondered what this scatterbrained idea would be. The last time it had been to go to a used car dealership and "try out" a car. This was in order to run errands on their gas and then decide not to buy it today, just think it over. It was never dull where ever Dee was. We decided to meet the following Wednesday, and we parted each to their own destination.

Once at the benches along the goldfish pond, we each took pen and pad to make suggestions if any came up. "OK, fire away my friend. Let's see what's on your mind." I settled on to the bench to wait for what I expected to be nonsense.

Dee asked, "You're what now, 44?" I replied that I was. "OK, so I am 47. I've been talking to several people I know who are interested in getting back into the work force. Kids married, off to college, on their own or for what ever reason, they have an empty nest and a lot of *go power* to invest someplace. I thought it might be neat to start an employment agency for people 55 and over. What do you think?"

Off guard, an answer was slow in coming. "You know, Dee, it is needed and might work. Do you have a plan yet or is that why we are sitting here?" I smiled to myself over that one.

"You know that place on Kapiolani Boulevard where the over seas agency is? Well, I know the wife and I thought if we worked at it together, maybe Bob would let us use one empty room and we could set up a business in there. It *is* an agency already, so sooner or later the word would be out. Word of mouth advertizing is the most profitable anyway."

"Good idea." I said, "Let's go over there now and see. He can't do worse than veto the plan and might even help, who knows?"

We greeted Wilma at the desk and could see Bob wasn't occupied, so sauntered back to his desk. "Well, to what do I suspect this is about?" Laughed Bob. He *very well* knew Dee.

Dee began, "Bob, Julie Johnson Black, my teacher pal here, we have an idea and need your opinion, OK?"

"Sure, what's up?"

We explained our idea, or rather Dee explained. I'm just taking it in.

"Now *there* is a thought," Bob agreed. He scooted his chair away from his desk, ran his right hand through his thick grey hair, while swinging his glass's back and forth with his left hand. Every now and then he tapped his teeth with the ear piece of his glasses.

Bob and Wilma started their business when he retired from the Army as a Master Sargent; he, like many of us, needed to be busy. Some of his buddies were hunting second careers or a part time employment while they were in transition.

"I'll give this a lot of thought, discuss it with Wilma and get back to you, how's that?"

We agreed, "Just don't still be thinking till next year. We *do* grow old, you know." We laughed on our way out the door.

"Dee, what do you think, you know them, I don't?"

"Pretty good chance I believe. He is usually abrupt and he *didn't* say no."

Jess and I left for Kauai Island the next day to spend some time with friends there, returning home on Sunday evening. Messages on the phone revealed that "Yes – we had the room. Hooray!"

The next several days were helter skelter as we scrounged up a file cabinet, a few odd chairs, some shelves, a desk and odds and ends of needed items; pens, pencils, writing paper, desk lights, paper clips, etc. It was really fun, like setting up house keeping. Also fun to go to Goodwill, thrift stores and yard sales to save money.

Jess stayed conspicuously absent, he and Gib had fishing on their minds. Gib had been Jess's best man and a friend who lived in Hawaii.

It seemed like a year later, when three weeks had passed, but between us we had made over 200 calls to businesses in town. The conversations went something like, "Hello, if you have a few minutes to spare, I need some help, (people love to help)." The pat reply was usually "OK" or "Oh sure." I continued with, "I'm Julie Black, along with a business partner, we are opening a new business, it is an employment agency for those over 55. Do you have any need or opening for people in this age range?"

It was surprising how many places actually did, mostly on a part time basis, which was excellent. "What did you get today?" I asked Dee on our third day open.

"A lot of question." She said.

"Really." I wondered what.

"Like, why do I need them? No, older folks think they know everything and I want things done my way. Are they bright or crippled or what're you doing this for? What kind of pay do they expect?"

"Now there are some things that are food for thought." I said. "Maybe we should compile a pamphlet of information, expectations, rules and regulations." Bob helped out with that, things went well.

"You know Dee – if we kept track of all the people and stories we hear, it would make a movie."

"I agree." Dee said. "But who has time." Each day I would report to Jess what progress was made and every detail of conversations with clients. I'm sure he learned to have selective hearing. I could tell by the volume of the grunt I heard for an answer to a remark I'd made.

One day, when I came up through the parking lot I noticed Dandy peeking out of the bottom two jolicy window slats. She had to be standing up on the stove top as that is where the window is. When I opened the door she jumped over to my arms and I called to Jess.

"Hey – did you see Dandy peeking out the window?"

"Sure." Came the reply, "She knows your walk and starts for the door as soon as your heals hit the sidewalk."

Dandy was yellow and white angora mix. We called her the Aristacat – her mother surely had a back ally romance as evident from the long legs of an alley tom cat – but the aristocracy was plain in her glorious, long fur. She had been stuffed in a trash can with the lid weighted down to smother her, when a close friend passing by, heard her wailing and let her out, Dee told me and I went on a cat rescue mission. After a week, I found her perched up in the rafters of the parking barn where she had been abandon. Once I got her in the car, she proceeded to tear into the head liner. Wearing my sweater over her head, I rushed her into the apartment where she disappeared for 4 days. She was there but not to be seen. The fourth day, as I opened a drawer in the dresser I saw her tail disappearing up into the next drawer above. Evidently, she had made the trip through the drawers every time we opened them. It took a while to tame her, but she lived to be 20 years old and the scourge of Jess's life.

Jess said, "When Dandy jumps up into the window it alerts me that I'd better look alive and worth my keep – Ha, Ha, Ha, Ha, Ha."

"Speaking of which," says I, "how about you getting dinner once in a while?" That remark got a short reply.

"ME?"

"Yes, you! You're goofing off and I'm working."

"Oh, I *see* how you're working. You're having a blast, but I'm glad for you girls."

In the morning, Jess says, "So, what you want for dinner?"

I know for a fact, he would burn water, so I said, "Why not Jambalaya or a Curry, plenty of rice on hand." Not a smile on my face as I kissed him on my way out. I smirked to myself all day just imagining him exasperated with even locating the rice, let alone knowing what to do with it. I had told Dee at work about this cooking venture, she made me promise to tell her how it went, provided I was still alive the next day.

I parked the car and started across the lot. No cat in the window or at the door. Now what? But the aroma emanating was mouth watering. That I could not believe. Mama Black was a wonderful cook, but I doubted she had anything to do with this. Jess's grandmother, as I'd been told, could make a meal from scraps and have left over's – now I wondered do people reach out from the grave to meddle in the affairs of their favorite people, how could this marvelous odor come about?

Once I opened the door, I nearly jumped back out. The table was all set with flowers, even if only from my flower beds, napkins that had started life as paper towels, my Jess in the most godawfull riggin' you could imagine.

"Good evenin', Sooky." Says this apparition, "Welcome home to this humble domicile." *Who taught him that word?* "The Chef at your service!"

Talk about aphonia – that was a master piece of understatement altogether. Aphasias is a better word. I careened over toward a chair to catch my balance. Jess continued to bustle about with elaborate gestures of imitating copious amounts of manners. That attitude reached for grandeur and failed. "He was the most amazing sight you could imagine." I told Dee.

Wearing a paper grocery sack folded down to make a chefs hat, my nylon slip folded over at bust line and tied with the jump rope at his waist, he was wearing his jockey shorts and knee socks, no shoes and my out doors work gloves with gauntlets to the elbows so rose thorns would not jag me. There he stands, brandishing a spatula like a firearm and announces, "Madam, yer dinnah is sarved." I laughed so hard, I needed the bathroom. "We have shrimp curry, bakin' powder biscuits, Dego Red wine and that bowl of rabbit food, but you have to pour on your own type of dressin – by the way, why is that bottle of stuff called *dressing*? You always say you *dress* the ckicken too, but y'all really are *undressing* the dang chicken."

"You know honey, I really do appreciate all this fuss you have gone to, if I could stop laughing long enough, I'd give you a hug and kiss. That spatula you're wielding about isn't too comforting either. Just why are you wielding that spatula about anyway?"

"I'm gonna git that curry out of the oven."

"With a spatula?" I asked.

"Mrs. Young said I was to turn the curry out of the pan with a spatula."

"Mrs. Young?" I think I'm beginning to see the light at the end of the tunnel.

"Well sure, you didn't really 'spect ME to cook did you? I got smart and asked her, so she made it, but you got here before I turned it out."

By now I had a dreadful stomach ache from laughing. "Oh dear Mercy Jess – give me the spatula and the pot holders."

"What pot holders?"

"Those on the hook beside the stove."

"Oh *those*, I thought those was what you put under your

293

flower pots."

"I'll finish this up if you want to get clothes on, by the way, what's with the under drawers, socks and my slip?"

"Uh, huh – you see, I spilt that curry stuff on my pants and boots, so I shed those, you don't have an apron, a towel won't go all the way around and nothin' else long enough in case I messed up again. The grocery bag started out as a joke to look like a chef's hat and if you're satisfied now, can we eat?"

"I need to get this shrimp dish recipe from Dora, Jess, this is delicious." I said as I helped myself to the rabbit food. He had cut up carrots and radishes in the lettuce. It was colorful.

Dee weighs 200 pounds, *all* of her was laughing so hard she coughed. "You having Jess *cook* tonight?" She asked.

"Yes, he can warm up a pizza." I laughed.

"You sure of that?"

"No, not really."

The next day when I came in the back door, I saw we had company. It was a fellow worker and his wife. The wife had been crying, so I really didn't want to hear about any of this.

"Hi, you two, where you headed?" I asked, hoping it was a nice way for them to exit.

"Oh, we stopped by on our way to the park." Kelly said.

"Have a good evening then, nice of you to stop in. Jess can you help me with the rose bushes please?" I stood my ground till they were on their way out the door.

"What rose bushes, we don't have rosebushes." Jess said with a side grin on his handsome face. "I'll swear, Sooky, you can tell someone to go to hell so kindly, they say thank you. Come here and give this ole boy a smooch. We went out for a crab legs dinner and to the piano bar, where our friend was singing.

The employment agency did pretty well. Dee left with Galen for Germany, and Jess and I were headed back to Kauai for a six month job. Bob absorbed ours with his agency and paid us off. It was a fun eleven weeks for us all.

The strangest thing to happen during our marriage was a cat – the fourth pet, Dandy, that we acquired while in Hawaii. Jess claimed he did NOT like cats – BUT, it was Jess who watched over Silver (our first cat), in the park on Kauai during our third year of marriage; who brought her toys and nibbles and found her a home before we left; who buried little Snowflake in Utah, during the snow and when we left Hawaii to return to Montana, United Airlines sent Dandy to Seattle, when her ticket read Great Falls – poor Dandy was lost three days and Jess made the 50 mile trip four times to see if she came in on the next plane. He put her next to him on the seat where he could pet her on the way home. This mean ole guy, who didn't like cats! When he got home early enough, he would go to the river to catch her a fish while I cooked dinner, who shot a stray that had chased Dandy in the back yard. But, that cat repaided the kindness in her own peculiar way. No matter where he sat, she sat too, staring at him until he would move, then she too would move, chasing him from place to place, when really what she wanted was to be held. No peace with the newspaper or even in bed, as she crammed herself between us.

However, the thing he nearly had apoplexy over, was her ability to tell fortunes. It nearly drove him to distraction. A typical example would be as follows:

"Sooky, we will be moving location's tomorrow, so get things from the shoe repair, cleaners, bank, cancel any appointments and take the jacks down under the fifth wheel before I get home." However, Dandy did not start moving house. She had the uncanny sense of knowing when we would change locations.

She would pry open drawers and cupboards, snake a paw in and pull out socks, bra's, shorts or what she could reach and crawl in among the pans and push some things out. Once, we awoke and saw it, I knew we would move that day, no matter what he told me and I would get started. Jess would *swear* we were NOT moving, but by noon, he would be home to announce our new location. He had such a disgusted look of a defeated man and shout, "You and that Dam Cat!" Oh so often, she would "move house" and we learned to recognize it and plan accordingly.

One night in December while in Utah, she woke me up just staring at me. I said, "What is it?" She batted her eyes and continued to stare. I started through our friends names after family and close associates. I said, "Is it Helen?" She leaped off the bed and ran to the door. Helen lives in Honolulu and we resided in Utah on that dreadful job. It was 2 AM and snow on the ground. We had no phone and the nearest one was a pay phone at the 7-11 store a block away. Bathrobe, slippers and all, Jess got up and went with me to the phone. I called Helen with no answer, so I tried Dee. She answered the phone with, "Yes Julie, Helen is here, Kathy is OK – Grandma's in the hospital." I asked what HAPPENED! I was told the oven on the gas range blew up and blew Grandma through the wall from the second floor and received third degree burns. She asked how I knew and I told her the cat told me – from Jess – "That Dam Cat!" But, he spoiled her and not the dog. I do believe he was jealous of Hitchy Boy's attention. Oh, well.

CHAPTER 7

The summer we were home in Montana was such a joy. We worked together in the yard, painting, tree trimming and so forth. Jess painted the house, it was a great job, but then he could fix any big thing. It was just a pretty soft grey and we trimmed it with white woodwork and shutters with a red brick planter around both sides of the front door. The door was the original with glass door knobs and long thin glass that curved on both ends. The molding was missing in a few places, but tender care with putty soon took on the correct forms to look good as new – or old, as you see fit.

My garden was a sight to behold from the beginning. Not having had a garden for many years, I was delighted with the prospects in view. At the rear of this corner property was an alley seldom in use and a garage of sorts at the left of the sidewalk, from back door to the alley. This "garage" was not a work of art and required help in the first degree. To the right of the walk had from all indications, been a wood pile in existence for half a century at least. Rot, decay and pulverized tree bark was about ten inches deep. A gardener's treasure of soil, when spaded in a foot deep or nearly that. It was mid April, balmy weather, trees showing signs of awakening with tiny yellow-green growth, the coragana hedge and row of lilac's also had a bit of color, so I decided to have a lovely flower bed back there when I could see it every day from the utility porch or lawn furniture.

With meticulous care, the ground was prepared with newly purchased rake, hoe, spade, trowel and 75 feet of bright green water hose. Since Jess was from Texas, it seemed quite appropriate to make a star in the center and plant Texas Blue Bonnet seeds. This done, I was in my glory with various other varieties of flower seeds. Starting with the back row, next to the alley was a fine place for zinnias, next in height came giant marigolds, then dwarf snapdragons, which still left room for petunias, alyssum and lobelia. All were graduated by height, so that the final row was grass level. Inside the star, which was six feet by six feet at the farthest points, I had planted stocks and coral bells in the points leaving room for the petunias in the center.

Once all was lovingly planted, we watered and watered and watered for three weeks until there was a three quarter inch crust on top of the topsoil. That wonderful, rich soil was not raising even a disturbance, let alone a spear of green to be seen. In disgust, I went to the only nursery, purchased tomato plants, cabbage, bell peppers, onion sets and parsnip seeds. Next chore was to rake the entire plot to a new surface and plant my new vegetables. Oh dear, within a week *all* the flower seeds sprouted. It seems the soil must warm-up to a temperature where the seeds will germinate. In Hawaii, things grow in three weeks. This was *not* Hawaii. What a garden that was. The tomatoes had zinnias, the cabbage had asters and snapdragons, the peppers were cozy with the alyssum and other assorted items raked about during my tizzy. Hollyhocks sprung up behind the semblance of a garage, which camouflaged it somewhat. The flower gardens turned out to be the towns Sunday afternoon jaunts to see that weird lady's amazing garden.

Jess trimmed all the plum trees in the back yard, put up some clothes lines that he continued to shake his head over. "I spend $800.00 for a washer and dryer, crawling around under the house, fixing plumbing and she wants a clothes line." This remark being emphasized by a slap on the leg with that dreadful filthy old hat he was practically wed to. He would have slept with it on were it possible. He wore it to annoy me I'm sure, but he got *such* fun out of it. Like his derelict old slippers I threw away no less than four times, I couldn't get that hat. No matter where I stuffed those slippers, he would resurrect them, finally declaring the next time they were thrown out, he would be in them.

But then, I kept moving furniture about and he kept skinning his shins, this drove him bugs. One day, he announced he knew his way around under the house via the water pipe fiasco and one more move of the furniture and he would nail the legs to the floor from underneath. I doubt it, but I didn't try him either.

In Benton, the fourth of July is a big thing, as in any small village, just about anything is a reason to have or celebrate is a big thing. This year was little different, except for the participants. The older one gets, the less important trivia becomes and it is left to the coming up generations to fill the gaps. Also, as nature provides, each generation has its own idea of what is acceptable as entertainment, fun, way of dress, vocabulary, etc. Such as the progression from mamas day of saying "twenty three scadoo" – what ever that meant, on up the line to "jazzy", "neat", "cool", and "rad", short for radical I suppose and "spaz", etc. There are times I feel as old as dirt, I'm so out of date with today's "vocab", way of dress and lack of manners.

Anyway, Violet and Max Tomlinson were coming in from their farm east of town to attend the street dance with us after the fireworks and socializing. Jess had made a freezer of home made ice cream and Vi was bringing a cake for our time together. It sounded just wonderful to me who has little to no social life any longer. I would get so hungry for educated conversations, the night life I had enjoyed for a number of years and my dress up days. Well that was not part of the present day program and what I had was more than enough on its own value. The men retired to the living room and started a conversation on how to build a wood splitter. Six o'clock became nine or ten and eleven. So much for the street dance. Vi was asleep in the rocker, I was trying to find any interest in the TV and we were still in the building stages at midnight when Vi awoke and said, "This is IT!" She is a dear precious lady and a wonderful friend, but enough was enough.

I put the last of the ice cream in our deep freeze – wrapped the cake in foil, did up the dishes from that chore, while Jess prepared for a shower and bed. It had been decided since the next day was Saturday, and my son's birthday, that the men folk would start on that splitter. It had been hashed over for flaws until they were positive it would be a work of genius.

At 4:30 AM the kitchen phone awakened me, and I was on it by the 3rd ring. Nobody calls that time unless there's a powerful reason. I was awake immediately, but the news on the other end just would not compute. I kept saying what? What? What? WHAT? By now Jess was taking the phone away from me. Max was dead! A nightmare at 4:30 or a nightmare period! How could this be? Jess nearly collapsed. Max was his dearest pal and buddy in everything. I took the phone back and tried as hard as I could to be calm. That took a will of gigantic proportions I can tell you.

"Vi, where are you?" I asked.

"At the hospital." She whispered.

"We will be right there!" I replied.

Jess was just blank – I handed him his clothes and boots, while he was trying to delete this horror from his mind. In four hours, one hardly accepts the demise of your best friend. We drove over to the hospital, but found Vi across the street at the Archibalds, who had a few years before been Vi and Max's nearest neighbors, before selling out their farm.

It took some time before the facts settled into place and

reality arrived. They had gone home and to bed, but it was still nearly 90 degrees and the bedroom fan just was not cooling things down. Max said he would take a quilt and pillow to the living room and lay down on the floor in front of the open door. There was some relief in the night air. Vi said she heard a thump and know he had layed down. Max was six feet tall and just over 200 pounds. That large a body does not lie down gracefully nor without a "plop". At about three AM, Vi got up to use the bathroom and peaked in on Max, he seemed quiet enough and still, so she did not bother him. At four, the alarm went off as it was milking time and other chores to get started on before the heat of the day set in. She went to see why his nibs had not rallied to the shreak of the clock and noticed he was still in the same position she saw him at three AM. When she went to shake him, he was blue, tongue protruding and silent. She went screaming to call the hospital to send an ambulance, got dressed and followed it into town, where she called us. By 4:30 it is daylight in July and things began to take on some semblance of normalcy.

I called her family, mother and sister, 50 miles south, her two sons, 40 miles east. Just exactly how everything else was arranged, I still don't know. The next three days were made up of headaches, tears, sleepless nights, sorrow and laughter of "do you remember when?" – Jess came and went, things got done, I stayed with Vi as much as I could, but she had her family there, too.

Jess just fell apart at the funeral home and Vi ended up comforting him. I stayed at their house, answering the phone, greeting people, accepting food donations and condolences from others, addressing thank you envelopes, keeping a log of those who came to the house, baby sitting grandchildren and anything else I could locate to stay busy and be useful. I guess Jess did the chores or helped, he was in and out - he just functioned and wept.

The day of the funeral dawned hot and bright. We had,

just a month before, gone suit shopping for Jess, as he had a business function to attend that jeans and a stetston (again) was not suitable attire. He selected a medium, tan to brown, light weight wool that was quite well chosen and looked great on him despite his grumblings of looking like a sissy – which he did not.

He wore the new suit for the funeral. The pants were a bit loose at the waist, which allowed them to be a bit too long in the legs. There were boards on either side of the grave opening, that the pall bearers needed to trod in order to set the casket down on the lowering strips. Just as Jess (who was in the middle of three to a side) turned right to use both hands on the coffin handle, he stepped on his trouser leg, which nearly pulled his pants down. With his left hand holding his pants at the waist and using his right and to balance the casket, he was heard to mutter, "Hold up a bit Max, I'll be in there with you in a minute if I can't hang on to these pants." This was heard by both the pall bearers on either side of him. The casket started to rock slightly, as it set down on the strips. It is truly hard NOT to laugh, especially at a most inopportune time.

Things proceeded well during and after the internment and back out to the farm. People came and went, there was a steady stream of dirty dishes, which kept me busy, along with many phone messages to take.

Then the unthinkable happened. On the first of July, Max had cut the long grass along the highway, as it also contained red clover, timothy and alfalfa. Since it also cleared the area, there was a two fold reason to bale the cut grasses. That became extra hay for his cattle. While the funeral had been taking place, so was mischief. Someone had stolen Max's hay he had baled the day before he died. We need this?

I month later, while my six year old grandson was still visiting, we went to the farm to help butcher chickens for the freezer, pull vegetables for canning and freezer and teach Vi how to start the mower and use the weed whacker among other things. She had scarcely needed to even write a check. Max did those things. It was their way. Vi is a dear, sweet, kind-hearted woman, who bore her future struggles. I must be at the bottom of the heap for strength of character by comparison. They say everything comes out in the wash. Well, it did for her too, in time, by God's grace I feel sure of that.

In September, we put up storm windows, put electric tape on the water pipes, turned off the water, loaded the fifthwheel; that which Jess did at his peril. Every load I brought out, he would proclaim, "Mother, it's not an 18 wheeler! I have to pull this over three mountain passes!" He began to resemble a peccary. That is, time to stop. We could purchase anything else we needed. Of course, what I always *needed* might stretch ones imagination now and then.

This next job was in Cut Bank, Montana, and the last outpost of Montana's civilization. Situated on the US, Canadian line, Cut Bank is primarily an Indian town. Not a great deal to offer, but quality never the less. The best hair do I've ever had was in a tiny shop, down a long hallway, with two operators. The girl was Indian, possibly 250 pounds, beautiful face and hands that just flew. In and out in 25 minutes. I couldn't believe it. Many times over the years I've thought of that girl.

Jess lost his wedding ring in the tall grass under our fifthwheel one night, while leveling the chassis. Until midnight, we were on hands and knees, with flashlights, crawling through that wet grass. The ring had three diamonds and finally a beam of light detected their presence. Why it took two, cold, wet hours to locate, we never figured out.

We made a brief stop back by the house on the way south, to next location, in Decatur, Texas. The fortune telling cat rode in the trailer, while Hitchy Boy rode up with me. Jess located a space by way of the CB unit and a pal already on site. Once ensconced on our pad, we started to locate a Mexican restaurant. The morning brought a big surprise. We were under an overpass and being told the wind had several times picked up 18 wheelers and hurled them over into the road and campground below. Fine morning with fresh air, coffee and knotted up stomachs. Jess was crew boss on this project, it wasn't especially eventful until they found a horse in the five foot wide ditch they had trenched out the two days before. A law suit of course. One wonders why the horse was in the area? The company had to pay for the horse.

We met a family there, by the name of Spathe. Actually, it was another hair dresser contact. They had just built a beautiful big home and Anna was telling me the progress. We became such close friends, that to this day; we travel cross country to visit.

Since we were so close to Mama Black, we stopped over a week after the job ended in Decatur, to visit with family before we started cross country to Montana.

Stopping off in Bountiful, Utah again, to see Bob, Lucy and other friends, I happened to see a 63 Buick for sale. I think the lines of that car are still the greatest. We bought it and after some time with the Jensons, we headed North in tandem. Bob Jenson is a bull of a man with broad chest and hams for biceps. Lucy was a tiny, full of fun, lady, who worked in the cafeteria of the local elementary school. The good times will never be erased. In fact, the following year they came to Montana for a week and stayed with us. That summer, Jess decided to take a leave from his usual work and stay home. It didn't last. Within a month his itchy feet were a source of irritation. Since the neighbor across the street was working at Zortman, Montana, in an old gold mine, Jess had to see what that had to offer. Another entire chapter to our lives came into being.

He took the fifthwheel and off to Zortman. The next weekend, I followed him up the Little Rocky Mountains, to visit, cook, do laundry and explore. What a treasure for the likes of me, who loves history. The town consisted of three houses, five log cabins, a bar/pool hall/gathering spot, all in one and an enormous quansit hut. One you could store a freight train in. Its use was for overhauling big machinery, but it also had the only washer and dryer in this tiny camp-like town. The weather was good and I could explore for hours. Many abandoned cabins from gold mine days, old cemetery, with wooden markers, wild fruit trees and bushes just loaded for the picking. There I was, introduced to June Berries. Wonderfully sweet, little purple berries the size of a currant. You could eat them as you walked along. Wild onions, asparagus and other edible things were plentiful. I was in heaven, as I like to cook and am quite a good cook. As Jess said, "Mother, you're the best cook in the world."

305

What they were doing on that mountain was reworking the old tailing piles from 50 years before and using an acid bath and monstrous rubber tub about three feet deep and thirty feet across. It performed some procedure way beyond my comprehension. Try as he might, Jess never could get me to figure out the function of this contraption. Every time there was an accident or cave-in, the whistle blew three short blasts, then three more repeatedly, the God awful dread of any wife or human not involved. This one afternoon, a week later, I heard the whistle and just froze. One prays a great deal in this profession, I can tell you! Within an hour, I heard the Dodge truck on the dirt road and knew at least my man was safe.

He came tearing up and yelled "Get in, get in!" I did. What happened, I ask in near panic. We had friends on the job. It seems the big bulldozers were on top a "heap;" or mound, pushing the contents of the tailings over into this acid bath thing, when the surface below the dozer let go and the machine, operator and all, plummeted down some fifty feet into, what at one time, had been a tunnel. The operator had a broken back and was hauled up to safety, but the dozer had a new home. However, with head lamps and gear, the place was explored to find two skeletons, several coal cars laden with gold ore and a number of other paraphernalia related to that time in history. This had been part of a tunnel buried by a cave-in years before. We drove over rocks large enough to give me a stroke, tipping this way and that, until I never expected to see the trailer again. I was profoundly impressed by that Dodge pick-up that I mortally hated.

It was time for me to go back home, school was out for the day and since at the end of the road there was a one room school house, still in use, I thought I'd take time to investigate it. Fortunately, the teacher was on the premises and so glad to have someone new to speak with. Lola Adams was a thirty seven year old, most attractive woman, with auburn hear, green eyes and a generous smattering of freckles. At five feet two

306

inches tall, she looked quite able to care for most anything and I soon learned I was not mistaken in my judgment. One of seven children, she had been reared on a North Dakota farm, a harsh life of work and strict rules at home. She vowed to never see poverty again, no matter how menial the job and accepted this very rural, one room school no one else wanted. She was right at home in her scant accommodations and free time in the mountains. She taught all twelve grades and had seventeen students. They lacked for nothing in education, local sports or otherwise. What a treasure she was. On my trips up, I used to take her things she did not have access to, such as, make-up, perfume, books and magazines, or such things she would request occasionally.

Back to the grey house, I was pleasantly surprised to find word from my son, Jake, in Marysville, Washington, wanting to know if Eddie, there six year old son, could come up for the summer. Jake was finishing his degree and his wife worked six days a week at Boeing Corporation. I called immediately, said that it was very OK and send him on. A few days later, I picked up a very independent six year old, at Great Falls airport. What a summer that was.

First off, he wanted to put in a garden, so Mr. Decker next door, rotatilled up the large area beside the Corrigana hedge, as the original garden/flower bed was now a strawberry patch. We worked the ground down one day, collected seeds and items needed for a fine vegetable garden.

First, we put string on two sticks the width of the rectangular garden, to place at each side, thus a straight line to hoe a trough for the seeds. Then began the questions. Why did I mix radish and lettuce seeds together? So as the lettuce was pulled the radishes could grow and not waste a row left empty. Why did the carrot seeds go in with the parsley, the same as radishes? What to do with beans? Poke a stick beside the string, put your foot down and poke the next hole at the end of your toe, drop a bean in the hole and do like wise to the end of the row. Three rows later we went though the same process with onion sets. So far so good.

Next came parsnips, rutabagas and then the turnips. When he was ready, I handed him the seed packet, as it was his job to plant, mine to make trench rows and cover them behind his planting. All went fine up to the turnips. There he balked. He handed the packet back and I ask, "Now what is the holdup?" With arms akimbo and serious face I was informed he did NOT care for that wedgetable and would prefer to plant pork chops. "Oh, I see. Well I'm fresh out of them now so let's do the squash." No, that wouldn't do either, as he was tired and thirsty and it was break time. Now where did that come from? Break time, no less.

Since we had purchased a used bicycle the day before, it was far more interesting to learn to ride than plant potatoes and *yours truly* could carry on. Now was my turn to flub up. I had never heard of zucchini squash until Jess took me to Texas to meet his family (fine people). There I became acquainted with zucchini and it could be fixed in fifty different ways; steamed, boiled, fried, pickled; in casseroles, mixed with onion and tomatoes, baked, sliced with cheese and sausage covered with crumbs for an oven dish, on and on. What a wonderful 'wedgetable'. Also, I was on a first name basis with okra, the likes I'd never before seen. I love it still. I thought I would grow some of each, but you see, Jess was in Zortman, so I went about the planting with abandon not knowing how prolific both are. I put in fourteen hills of zucchini, four seeds to a hill. One plant will feed a family of four. Oh, yes it will.

That crop yielded about 30 a day and they grew overnight. Since I'd been most generous with the fertilizer, the plants were knee high. Each morning I honestly hesitated to go to the squash patch and peer down among the vines. It was like a forest with things lurking to jump at me. I must have had 30 packages of zucchini in various dishes in the freezer, canned or frozen, so I began giving them away by the grocery bag full at night, on peoples' porches, so I wasn't seen. I gave them to the hospital, restaurants, nursing homes, the old age center, even the grocery stores, and yet they came to ten to twenty a night. One vine climbed the coragana hedge and up a cottonwood tree where it bore a squash in the crotch of a tree limb, growing half to a side, looking somewhat like a drunken horse shoe. Since it was twelve feet above ground, it remained there. One day the neighbor boy across the street wanted to know if he could have that squash. I got a ladder and he retrieved the squash. Several days later, he came running up the street from the fair grounds waving a blue ribbon and shouting my name. "What have you there?" I ask.

"Oh man, I won a blue ribbon with the squash!"

I was abashed. All I could say was "How? How wonderful; let me see it." It said 1st place-the most unusual entry.

The event of the okra took second place after I'd torn out all the zucchini and took them, plants and all, out to Vivian's farm for the hogs. That was another record-breaking day. She had put some Bosco in a cup and milked the cow straight into the cup. She handed it to Eddie, who at that time was called Little Bear. He drank it down. But back home that fall in school, there were many squabbles over his insistence that Vivian's cow made chocolate milk and he stuck to his story even when he got a lickin'. I was not popular once he knew the truth.

After the garden was in, we went back up to Zortman. We mowed the grass first and watered well. The garden could do its own thing in its own time. I never saw such a happy child as he was in those woods with so much to see. We would watch the deer out the trailer window, eating just out side or see the little cinnamon bears eating berries along the dirt road.

Jess made him a rope swing and I showed him how to make box birdhouses. What a happy, busy little boy. Exhausted by 7 P.M., we made homemade ice cream, took hikes and discovered a hill out side of the town with a steep path. It led to a tiny church at the top. It had log seats in a row and a pump organ for music and all were in use each Sunday. What a wonderful surprise.

We met a raccoon family coming down to water and the little ones walked on our shoes, as we stood dead still in fascination.

Eddie did not want to return with me and cried. Said would I talk to his dad to see if he would get a job up there. I couldn't leave him with Jess because of the working hours being 6 A.M to 6 P.M. So we headed back down the mountain with a blood letting of promises to go back next week.

But soon it was time to get school clothes, new shoes and plane tickets back to California. The new shoes part was a fight to the finish. His old tenny's were on their last breath of life, tattered, holes in the sole, strings in knots and totally gone, but no, he did not want to part with them. We went to Great Falls for plane tickets and Sears for new shoes. Once home, I said give me the old shoes and the box from the new ones. I wrapped each shoe in new tissue and went to get a shovel from the garage, dug a hole behind the shed and buried the shoes with marigolds for funeral flowers. He just stood there a long time, turned around and lit for the house on a run. I followed in time to hear the conversation on this end of the phone.

"Mom, when can I come home?" OK! Well Gram has gone crazy. She just buried my shoes and Grandpa is up the hill and I don't know where to go." I laughed so hard, I cried. I imagine he remembers that to this day.

After Eddie went home in September, the job shut down a few days and another couple we chummed with, the Bonners and ourselves went on a scavenger hunt of sorts to see what we could find in the old cabins. Not much, but a small treasure here and there. Then, one day Jess came back off the job quite unexpectedly with surprising news. He had been out on the dozer going across country, so to speak, to a short cut when the front of the machine all at once started to tip down. After he threw it in reverse, he jumped off. Once on his feet, he chased the machine down and shut it off and very cautiously walked forward to where the land seemed about to drop into oblivion. As he approached further, he realized there must be a hole or cave or worse, ahead, so took forty or fifty steps to the left and holding to a small tree trunk could look back to the right where he had been. Amazing! There was a drop off of approximately a hundred feet or more. This was really a curiosity and needed some more exploration as 500 feet or so across the gaping place the land continued on at its present level.

Once a few more yards of ground were gained with very cautions steps, he could see what looked like a house roof or part of a building. Traversing the perimeter nearly a quarter of the way around to the left was a far better view and astonishingly, there sat five small cabins, what appeared to be a field stone chicken coop or shed, a two story building, partly intact and various parts of a wagon, which consisted of rotting canvas, broken wheels and scraps of iron and leather, odds and ends of whatever.

After locating a way down the open side and searching for roots as hand holds, protruding rocks for foot holds and other conveyances, slipping, sliding and a few jumps, Jess descended to the floor level of this hollow. This days work was at a climax as in no way was this discovery to be ignored. Such an amazing sight left one with as wild an imagination as there are stars in the universe.

After looking for a better route back to the top and another scramble up and out, he retraced his track with a wider way back, much safer than near the rim. What the haunting dilemma was, how did they get there as NO way in or out was visible anywhere. Who were "they"; where did they go? No vestige of existence anyplace. It was like a campsite had suddenly hovered itself to the depth it now sat in as all surrounding earth was many feet above.

As soon as he came home I was told all about this adventure and nearly frothed at the mouth with hyper adrenalin surging through my veins. I could scarcely think for the shear joy of getting to see this. Another couple on the job with us was Tony and Shelby Bonner, so on Sunday we packed up picnic baskets, ropes, tarps and a curiosity gone wild as we started across the fields to this find. At the time, we four were the only ones who knew of this. Once there, the use of ropes tied to a sturdy tree let us lower ourselves down into this bonanza of mystery. Each of us took a different route to explore with small yelps of excitement over the most trivial of things. One cabin had an iron bedstead with sheet springs, those being a metal mesh type threading and intertwined like lace; however, it is of metal and strong enough to hold a mattress. A beauty to behold and

I wanted it. Another cabin in remarkable condition held a highboy chest of drawers that animals had chewed away the bottom drawers. The top two drawers still slid open to display empty mouse nests. Another cabin had a homemade table and chairs. The table had been nailed to the floor (I thought of my house). This was another curiosity until Jess found the reason. Under the table was a trap door that led to a tunnel that connected to the next cabin. We pondered that for some time and Tony decided it was a place to hide in case of Indians. The table being immobile might deter progress to enter the opening if it was noticed.

For fear of snakes, spiders or rodents, we could not enter the space but by opening it from both ends, we could see daylight through it. The end cabin had a large iron cook stove completely intact. The warming closet on top had a big stainless steel letter B that hinged down to act as small shelves. One could place a dish, pot, pan or other related type cookware up there to keep warm or be off the stove surface to save space. It even had a big water reservoir on the end. Shelby decided she would like the B shelves and make use of them in some manner as their name was Bonner. Of course, ours was Black, but I'd already confiscated the bed. The men went to explore the barn or what was left of it. It had leather equipment, odds and ends of broken tools and about 20 leather straps hanging on square nails. Those appeared to be harnesses or traces for horses. Shelby and I picked our way through what possibly had been a garden area, over to the stone building, which, in fact, was a chicken coop. Tree limbs with bark still on, had been roosts for the chickens comfort at night and to our surprise, we also found two wooden boxes that obviously had been nests for eggs.

No graves, no bones, no sign of human life were visible anyplace in the entire hollow; also, no road or pathway indicating any exit. Evidently, over the years, weather and/or landslides had eroded the opening to cause it to fill in. There were several broken wagon wheels and two just perfect ones. Those, of course, we snaked up by rope as well as the bed on our trip back out. In the half loft of the barn was a mirror top of a non-existent dresser; it too in perfect shape and hand carved design across the top. That too rode the rope to the surface. Since it bore no glass I could put my arm through the frame and be ascended together. That frame lives with me on my dresser to this day 35 years later. The last find could come up in a pocket. While in that hen house, we took a stick to poke in the nest boxes as fingers could get bitten by some resident in there. It turned up a glass egg. Other than being dirty, it was perfect, not even a crack. How many years had that egg been through all kinds of weather and critters looking for shelter. Amazing.

Once out, we stood in awe of that venture and mused repeatedly of who ever lived there, where had they come from, gone to and how had they survived. Reluctantly, we walked away and felt as though we left friends behind. It is a strange reaction, nothing tangible to connect to.

After a quick clean up from the water jugs, the sandwiches, fruit and coffee thermoses were made short work of. This day would live in memory. We passed an old cemetery in an area near our campsite and felt the urge to prowl about but turned up not even a name still visible on the eight wooden crosses. Although each of us inquired of everyone we met from Havre, Malta, Lodgepole, Landusky or even the museum, no one had a clue about our little hidden valley or its inhabitants.

This job was winding down to a close, time for preparations for what was to come next. As yet, we had not been contacted, so we enjoyed a few weeks at home. I needed to finish my canning, clear out garden and flower beds, get down the storm windows, which I loathed washing and be sure our "ready box" was fully prepared. A ready box in our profession meant essentials to load the fifth wheel.

One of the highlights of the Zortman job was the wedding

of one of our crewmembers to a local girl. Surprising in the fact we had only been there eight months, not surprising in the fact that there was little to do for the men but play poker, pool, or whatever else the younger single guys do.

There were just the buildings for the residents, a huge garage hut and an ancient church up on the hill just outside of town. It had no electricity and half logs for benches. There was a building that tripled over for a bar, a restaurant of sorts, a pool hall, general meeting house and local watering hole.

The entire town, our camp employees and anyone invited, attended that wedding. More excitement than Zortman had seen since gold rush days I can imagine. The entourage went up the hill to the little church for the wedding and down the hill to the afore mentioned building. Several men had pushed the pool table over against the wall, the women all had prepared tasty dishes, pies, a wedding cake, provided candles and an assortment of festive items for decorations and made do with what was on hand.

One resident of eighty plus years still had linen tablecloths and napkins, so another put down a base of newspapers first, then the linens on the pool table. There was enough food for a small army arranged on the table or in the table as it has a raised edge. That was good to keep little fingers from exploring the food also. I never saw so many people or children in this little town, but then there was no cause for all the inhabitants to congregate before, either.

Once the food and merriment was over and cleared away, the men moved the pool table out on the board sidewalk and a variety of instruments appeared from who knows where, and music came forth for dancing or listening while others sat or milled about.

Clarice and Troy left for a three-day honeymoon to an undisclosed destination and I, for one, did not blame them for that. These people still believed in a shiveree and the other young fellows just loved pranks and jokes pulled on each other.

Jess went hunting, got an elk which he butchered and sent to quick freeze, did some fishing, also for the freezer as well as table use, put up the storm windows and put away the hoses, lawn furniture and in general readied for a minutes notice departure. The one funny thing I didn't mention and we still do not, is that prior to his hunting trip he took me out to a thicket a few miles from town and asked if I knew how to flush game – flush? Visions of a commode flashed through my head. No, I did not.

"Well, you see that area to the right where the smaller trees are?"

"Yes."

"Well, go over there and pretend you see a deer, clean over there to the left. Now, ease up quiet to spook it out towards me and I kin shoot it." That didn't seem too outlandish, so I trotted off. Now, I was wearing jeans and and RED shirt – one does not hide well wearing red you see- but I started towards my imaginary deer. About two thirds of distance gained on my trek, a big brown pick up stopped out on the road with a logo of some sort on the door.

The driver got out and approached Jess with a hearty, "Hello there, you got car trouble?" I was out of sight, sort of, but was about to pop up when the man spotted me. You ok over there? I was about to announce my excursion in "flushing" when Jess nearly yelled, "you know when nature calls, you don't ignore it." That was an odd remark under the circumstances, I thought. The men shook hands and the pick up drove on. I wiggled my way out of the brush and emerged just a few feet from my dear spouse who seemed all shook up, as the song says.

"Whew, that was a dang close call." He said, and lifted that greasy old hat off his head to wipe his face.

"What was?" I ask in total innocence. "That was the game warden." He said as he sheepishly grinned and shook his head.

"So?" I ask.

"Well, Sooky –it's against the law to flush out wild game."

"Oh." Says I, who felt like I didn't have the brain God gave to geese.

The next job presented itself the following week. We were summoned to Dayton, Nevada, an area east of Carson City to a place that contained a twelve-space trailer park named Little Lake (of which there really was one there in the desert) with approximately too hundred people, plus or minus, and an assortment of dogs, cats, ducks, chickens, owls and a goat who thought he was a person. Marie Long ran the park and her hubby was the local plumber. We became good friends over the extended stay there. I stopped to see Marie a couple of years later while on my way to pick up the fifthwheel in storage while Jess was in the Middle East. However, during my spare time, which was plentiful, I could scarcely wait for my husband to leave for work so I could go explore. One of the first things I found was three families living in tent-like accommodations down on the river. Naturally I wanted to know why, when there was ample housing. After all, Dayton was nearly a ghost town. It seemed they had been living there some three years and were gold miners that worked the river panning for gold. I spent one entire day with them. A life I would not recommend to the weak of heart but such fun.

Next, I set out for the old cemeteries, my fetish. On a hilltop northwest of town was quite a large cemetery for a small town, so off I went with my little dog Hitchy. I would guess that little dog saw places in his life that even God had forgotten about. Dirt roads, abandoned buildings, paths to seemingly nowhere and cemeteries seemed a magnet to me, the little "sissy" dog always at my heels.

The first time up the steep hill to that cemetery, I took stock of the odd layout of head stones. That was cause for deeper investigation. I soon learned it was divided off into distinct sections. At the far left corner were seven rows of Catholic souls. Across the aisle were Norwegians\. Down from them were Italians. Across from them seemed to be Polish and Hungarians names, each section bordered by a perimeter of rocks. An empty space about twenty by thirty feet and the markers began again. Off to the right, more or less, separated from those I was walking through, were ten or twelve individual family type enclosures forming a crib-like enclosure made of iron or pot metal stakes or pallets on all four sides, bearing an elaborate gate or entrance into these enclosures. If one wanted to read the inscriptions, dates and often poetry, you must open the gates. Most still creaked badly and needed a push, but did move. This one particular day, I had spent several hours of the morning gathering up the wooden head-markers that years of wind and neglect had deposited haphazardly along the wire outer fence, most intact. Some could even be read yet as the carving had not entirely been obliterated by sun or storm. After cleaning sandy mud off the surface, I placed them flat in the soil, in a row side by side and piled rocks in the center to better anchor them from the hellacious winds that a desert can produce.

On my way down the slope through to my car, I passed one of those enclosed grave sights. The weeds and growth nearly swallowed the stones and since one in particular stood three feet above the grass, I thought I'd just clean it up and see who was there. An amazing sight to see and more amazing results.

A large Manzanite bush was immediately to the left of the gate so once inside the crib, Hitchy went over to lay down in the shade. At that time being there only three days, I had not become aware that rattlesnakes also could have been under that bush. I started pulling chunks of grass and weeds, throwing them over the fence to the outside of the gate. It took an hour or more to work and weed my way back to the large stone. It was about five feet in height, twelve to fourteen inches square based and tapered to a peak at the top. Four-sided, it was quite a tribute compared to wooden markers, flat or slightly raised stones throughout the rest of the cemetery. The normal information of name and dates was plain to read although over 100 years old. The script alone in cursive was still readable and said:

"There is no longer a home to go to as the light of my life has now been extinguished. I will see you again one day, my dearest love."

I stood there and wept. As I progressed further along both sides of the marker, determined now to clear this resting place, I unearthed a small headstone on either side of the monument. Yet further along on the left was another stone only slightly larger than the two little ones. Once I could read all four of them it was plain to see the two little girls had died three days apart, their mother four days behind them and her mother six days later. He lost his whole family within two weeks. Since there were no others, one would assume he just went on with no longer a reason to remain. This so touched my heart I called Hitchy and pushed open the gate. But the gate would not open. Thinking it was the depth of weeds and debris I'd tossed over, I reached across and dislodged it, clearing a space to open the gate as it opened outward. As I stood up once again prepared to open the gate, a wind came up so fierce it pasted me to the gate like I was tied to it. The wind ceased just as suddenly, much to my utter surprise, not one blade of pulled grass seemed to have been disturbed and the dog was whining pitifully.

I gathered him up, opened the gate and turned to look once more at my handy work. I then proceeded on fifty feet or so toward the car. Stopping to put the dog down, I saluted that gravesite and out loud said, "Rest in peace, lady. Your husband must have really loved you." Not a breath of air stirred on that hillside at three P.M. that late October day, but the Manzanite bush waved back and forth three times. When the stupor I was in let my mind reenter reality, I hurriedly left that place. Once back to our fifthwheel, I sat to ponder this latest event and accept it as natural which, of course, it was not.

After a cup of coffee, I ventured over to Bob and Wendy Wilson trailer and rapped on her door. Her little ones were just awakening from a nap, so I sat down and told her of my day. She was incredulous and asked could we go back up. Of course, so I drove all of us back up the hill and parked outside the fence as near that grave site as I could get. We stepped out and I pointed to the place. As if on schedule, the bush shook. She was quite frightened and we left. I never approached that cemetery again.

Instead, the next day, I assembled my laundry, a grocery list and went into Carson City for the day. After the chores were done would be a good time to go gamble a little. Since I had about fifty dollars yet, there was some leeway in spending so I started on a nickel machine. Soon I won twenty-five dollars so I moved over to the quarter machine. When I was down to about three dollars left, I hit the oranges for fifty dollars. I was even money now and knew I should stop but, of course those machines are addictive and I moved up to the dollar machines. In about twenty minutes I had twenty nine hundred dollars.

Laundry, groceries, dog and I left. Then! When Jess came in at eight P.M. he asked what I'd gotten into that day. I said I'd been to town, etc, etc and when he got out of the shower I had the money piled on his plate at the table. The expression on his face was worth a million dollars. After a few seconds of silence, he reached for a beer in the refrigerator and sat down to count his plate of money after which he seriously said, "This is my last day on the job here." I whirled around and asked how that could be so soon. I knew since he was "the boss" he wasn't let go. So this serious-faced man of mine said, "I thought I'd just take it easy and let you support us at the casino".

The day after I won the money, Jess declared I was not to cook; we would eat out at the club where I had relieved them of my small cache. After playing a few machines and in general fooling around, we took the escalator to the second floor buffet. Since these places always start their plates out at the salad end, the plate is then full to capacity by the time you reach the meat at the other end. That does not suit my man Jesse AT ALL. Taking up his plate, he marched to the meat cutter and held out his plate. No one was in line at that very moment, so he got away with it.

The server stared at Jess like he was a buffoon or he himself could do with a bromide and asked, "Yes?" Jess shoved his plate at the baron of beef and grunted some vague reply, so the confused man cut a slice to deposit on the afore mentioned plate. Since neither the plate nor man even moved a muscle, the server looked up to see the plate pushed at him again. He obliged with another thin slice. The poor soul had under-estimated the tenacity involved here. Once more the plate did not move. People were now in line and the beef cutting was stalled.

"You want MORE?" asked the server, very irritated. Very calmly, Jess drawled out" Nah Sur, I jest want SOME. I don't know where you learned to slice tissue paper, but I paid for food." Whereupon twenty plus people took time to clap. Their appreciation was undeniable. Yours truly was at the end of the line and remained there while a dozen or so others went on before. The meat carver possibly figured this little guy in a big Stetson had arrived from the bowels of hell just to harass him.

After an hour of food and fun, it was time to let the dog out of the car first and then head home.

We had an unsettling thing occur the next evening there at the park. There were maybe twenty ducks on the lake, a mixture of Mallard, Pekin and combinations of integration among them. But for over a week they were ever quacking, hissing and on the move. Marie mentioned it seemed a few went missing and laid it up to coyotes, which we could hear often at night. Since all of us came and went daily and most of us had two vehicles, no one paid attention to who was or wasn't there,

I had just put Hitchy out on his leash when he put up such a fit like I never had seen and actually frightened me. I hurried back out to see if he had been attacked only to see an old black Toyota pickup speeding in reverse down our driveway. About ten feet from the road lay a dead duck. I walked down to pick it up when I saw the small piles of corn. Those men evidently had taken out enough of the floor to entice the ducks under the truck to get to the corn, then grab them, wring their necks and have a good meal. What scum we have among us.

A day of ironing, cooking, baking and cleaning shortened the week. With necessary things completed, it was scavenger time again but this time I thought I'd prowl about in the remnants of this old town. I had gleaned quite a bit of history along the way and learned that Dayton was the oldest city in Nevada, not Silverton or Virginia City, as is usually claimed. There were still a few residents year round who worked in the clubs or businesses in Carson City or were old-timers retired and not willing to move into a newer way of life. The main street consisted of four closed-up buildings, a novelty shop that doubled for the Post Office, souvenir store and two room residences of its own. A red brick house in remarkably good condition sat at the end of the one block long town and even had a few flowers and a rose bush.

As I wandered along poking my nose into anything vaguely interesting, I saw an ancient-looking lady sitting on a plastic chair in the side yard of this brick house, so I moseyed over and asked her if she lived here a long time. Much to my surprise, her voice was strong and young sounding. The desert does a hardship to ones skin! She invited me to come in and sit with her, which I did. She began to reminisce and oh I wished I'd had a tape recorder. However, I was so enthralled. I recall most of it quite vividly.

Her name was Ida Loucinda McFee. She was ninty one years old and had lived there since her wedding at age thirteen years to Aaron Lucas McFee. Her father had been a gold miner and McFee a railroad man and was some twenty years her senior. There was no town to speak of anywhere near but the gold camps supplied poker games, knitting bees, home schooling, if any existed and other bits and pieces of life in those times. McFee won the last poker hand and gained a wife thirteen years old. There was a wild party; they jumped a broom handle near the campfire and Ida Lou was a married woman.

She bore thirteen children before Mick died and she had outlived most of them. Her house was tidy and full to the roof of life-long living. I saw her nearly every day until we left for that next chapter of our lives.

How I loved our life style. No one at home in Kauai believed one word I ever told them. It was outrageous to them. Little do they know?

We next returned to Hawaii for a visit and to collect things left in storage. The Bonners and Wilsons had purchased properties up on Puget Sound north of Seattle and spent spare time building and clearing space for trailers and vehicles. Gib and Mary had established roots in the San Diego area. Chuck and Thelma Grable had built a lovely log home near Bothell, Washington. The Griffins had settled in Arkansas. Chuck and Gladys Hand had gone to Tennessee. Bud and Alice Nelson were also in Tennessee. The troublemaker was back in Idabell, Oklahoma. The Chastines had divorced; she returned to Germany and Bill remarried again to his sister-in-law whose marriage he had broken up to get her. More the pity for Patty.

The Hawaii job reassembled most of us and introduced me to several new couples I'd only heard mentioned. The St Germains were just swell folks, Edith a saint in character. Their son and wife were there but newlyweds and thirty years younger than us so they stayed mostly to themselves. Our neighbors were Phyllis and Paul Everett. He met her on a job in Australia and brought her like a trophy. His nephew lived with them. The first night all had arrived was on Jess' birthday, December fifth, so there was a LOUD party at our place until midnight when the hotel manager informed us it was over. From then on 10 P.M. was *go home* time.

All in all, it was a good job, good times, good fun and good money. In February, we got a call from the California office ordering Jess to go put out a gas fire in the Sacramento slews Baldwin Island, and he had to be there in twenty four hours. By now I had become adjusted to this on-the-spot moving and settled into it rather remarkably. If you had known me, you would realize I'm a planner, every hair in place and organized to the point of boredom type of person. We do have split personalities. I can attest to it.

The phone call came to the hotel desk, so I needed to go find Jess on the job someplace. At about twenty miles out I located him running a big green Buckeye Ditcher, dredging a trough for gas lines. When he saw me, he figured the worst as is natural of human creatures and became alarmed. Never had I approached a job site. You just don't do that.

I said he better come with me and call the California office for details, I could not repeat for lack of vocabulary. They have terminology understood only by themselves. The upshot was I was to leave within the hour, take the ready box and make the switch of clothes and any necessary items needed for California. Then I had to repack and leave our Hawaii clothes in storage in Honolulu, get plane reservations on the next available flight, regardless of airline and call him as soon as I got off the plane. He would finish the paperwork, grab his suitcase and join me on the 6 P.M. flight from Kauai to Honolulu. Just be there. I did it and even had time to get a tooth filled, stop to see Fran, borrow her car to get finished with all the back and forth trips to be ready at 6 P.M.

We left at 7:30, arrived in Sacramento near midnight, dog and all, rented a car, found a motel and collapsed. By 6 A.M. my tired husband was headed for the jobsite some 30 miles away and I didn't see him again for 19 hours. One wonders at times how easy it would be to be deserted. For five day we lived at that motel, doing my best to hide a three-pound Pomeranian and finding ways to fill the hours. After locating a thrift store, I purchased a coffee percolator pot, an electric skillet, two plates, two cups, a couple cooking utensils and silverware. No space for anything else at all, so made do. I had blankets, towels, soap and essentials in the ready box.

The fifth day Jess came in all smiles and said, "Clean up and clear out. I found a place to move to." Oh, happy days. A quick meal at a drive thru and we were headed toward the job out on the Island. I kept after him to tell me what and where, but the only answer was, "Surprise, surprise" in a happy mood. After up the road and down the road three times, I said, "What are we looking for?" A cabin on the river was the reply but with far less enthusiasm that was noticeable at first. Why men just will not ask directions I do not know, but finally it was getting dusk and we needed a roof over our head. I said, "We have passed that little store repeatedly. Why don't you go ask where this cabin is?" It was non-existent as far as I could tell.

After much hemming and hawing and a scowl to sour sweet milk, my spouse succumbed to my scowls and went in the store. In short order he returned to just sit behind the wheel with his head in his hands and the silence was deafening. Several minutes burned off the clock, when I said, "It is getting dark. What have you learned? Where is this place?"

He jabbed his thumb out the window under my nose and grunted. I saw absolutely nothing. "What? There! Where? Look!" Interesting conversation. We got out of the car and looked over the embankment, down to the water. Nothing but a rope railing to hold while one descended some wooden steps, two missing, and a platform below. Now on this platform sat a chicken coop about 30 feet square, also held in place by some hefty ropes.

Anyone in their right mind would have fled the scene and raced back to the motel, but it was a challenge I could not let slip by. "You get the ready box and pass it down then the three bags of stuff accumulated and the dog and let's get on with it." This from an enthusiastic me, speaking to a very grim man.

Once all items were alight on our 'deck', I asked for a key to the sliding glass door. No Key, only one half of the door opens and the other doesn't lock. No screen and mosquitoes in a drove. After manipulating this fine entryway, we searched for a light switch. Good luck. It is now dark. Jess located it hanging on a bulb suspended from some suspicious looking wire dangling from the ceiling, which was also the roof.

There was a table, 1913 vintage, two unmatched chairs, no stove or sink, but two buckets and a refrigerator the likes of which neither of us had made acquaintance with in our lifetime. It was a curious sight to behold, indeed. An oblong metal box, with a handle, was standing up 18 inches or so off the floor. It had a contraption on top that, at best, resembled a sad layer cake and sounded as if it might self-destruct at any minute now. I opened it expecting to see a raccoon nest or some such, only to find it shiny clean and cold. Hooray! The first sign of hope had arrived.

Since we had presence of mind enough to have purchased some groceries on the way, we started putting them .... somewhere. Eggs, bacon, milk, butter, bread, potatoes, onions and hamburger went in this blessed refrigerator that actually worked. Will wonders never cease? I already had purchased coffee, so we made some once we located a water faucet in the bathroom sink. We sat down to contemplate our fate while the coffee perked and decided it would suffice.

Next came showers, but where? Oh, look at this now. There is a door outside from inside the bathroom. Jess opened to investigate this strange set of conditions and lets out a curse heard in the state of Maine. Since he never swears, I rushed over to see what was the cause of such a disaster. Oh, well. It seems the toilet and sink are inside this bungalow, but the shower is out on the porch. One learned to bathe in the dark or by starlight and in a hurry due to frostbite or mosquitoes with a ferocious appetite. It is now November and the idea has occurred that we will soon entertain winter.

With our light bulb we discovered two beds. One with no legs and the other a double bed looked fairly reasonable. Once into PJ's, Jess crawled in first and disappeared before my eyes. He looked somewhat like a deserted puppy living in a heap on the floor inside the bed framework. I couldn't stop laughing while he scrambled out and many new syllables were added to that bed's reputation.

After an investigation again, we decided that the box spring sagged. The mattress was one of ancient vintage when, many years before, there was a fad going around that the latest thing in mattress-land was a two-fold idea. One half firm, the other half soft or softer, so each person could take his or her choice. This particular mattress had gone to its demise some forty years earlier and how it survived a trip to this final destination was quite a wonder.

"So, now what? Do you want a divorce?" I cracked up. "Look, why don't we take the single mattress off the legless bed and stuff it under this soft side? Lift the joker up and wedge the box spring under both mattresses?" That accomplished, we had the semblance of a bed. The first one climbs in and hootches up to the next level about six inches higher and the other fellow has the newly arranged furniture for the rest of the night. That was a pun if you don't recognize it. The rest of the night meaning hours long. The rest of the night meaning hope to God you sleep. Once covered with our own blankets and exhaustion, we achieved exemplary slumber. The lower half gets trampled if nature calls.

Not too worse for wear, we awoke to birds on the deck railing, Hitchy yapping to get-out and the culinary arts awaiting with breakfast in mind. So how will this take place? To begin with, you unplug the refrigerator to plug in the coffee pot. While the coffee is in progress, you peel potatoes, prepare eggs and open the bacon. Once the coffee is done, you unplug the electric cord and plug in the electric skillet. This means you move the table to the side of the refrigerator so the cord will reach. You fry the bacon and potatoes at the same time and scoot it into the lid while you cook the eggs. Now toast with bread and butter was here long before toasters. You do dishes in the buckets; also your socks and hand wash. Not the same water, of course.

Once father Black has gone, it is now time to really take stock of this situation. Really, not too shabby. The chest of drawers had four drawers when it was first born, but now has three with fronts and the top one with no front. Okay. So if I pull it half out, now I have a desk that can be shoved back in out of the way. Our meager supplies are stowed and the bed is made up to look like a bed with no one there but us to know otherwise.

So now the imagination button kicks in and it's time to start figuring out how and or what to cook and, pray tell, *how* was the next question. That little store at the top of the ladder was a treasure. No use for a pan. There was no stove, so that day's supper was spaghetti. We go through the refrigerator plug in and unplug scene several more times, but you can make meatballs with bacon grease. Add some Ragu to it, cook the spaghetti in the coffee pot and add to the meat sauce. I made jello in our coffee cups and purchased some Diego Red for liquid. The bed wasn't such a disaster after two glasses of wine each.

The next morning was a variation of the day before and off to work he went. Now to figure out the next meal; hamburger patties and milk gravy in the skillet, boiled potatoes in the coffee pot. The newly purchased thermos held the coffee. I had ample bacon fat, so I thought I'd try biscuits and gravy. You can bake baking powder biscuits with self-rising flour in an electric skillet, and put them in the lid covered with a towel to keep them warm while the gravy cooks. It was satisfactory, not wonderful, but okay. I scrounged up a bowl from the city dump, it held salad makings and we ate straight out of it. No harm, no foul.

I used to take Hitchy and go for walks all over the small island and at one end I discovered English walnut trees, many of them. The ground was littered with nuts. That evening, I excitedly asked could Jess find me some gunnysacks. "For curtains?" he asks. "No, I have a surprise." That makes his blood run cold. He had seen my surprises before. But, he never told me *no* about anything and he had the patience of Job in the Bible.

The next day four-gunny sacks arrived along with him. The following morning Hitchy and I scrambled up our stairway and headed for the nut trees. I filled two, each half full as too heavy to drag when full. It was easier to make more trips with less product. It became a real workout, but I had two full bags on the platform when he got in that evening.

"Now what in blazes are you going to do with those?" was

the only comment.

"We are going to send your family each a sack full for Christmas. If you can wangle up some wire to close the bags, I'll make tags and take them to the bus station."

"Waall, I'll be!" the next comment. *Waall I'll be* was a common phrase for most anything with Jess, my quiet partner. The bags full of nuts and delivered in early December had arrived at the Greyhound bus terminal in Cleburne, Texas all intact, picked up by Jess' only sister, Emma, who I dearly loved. She took them to mamas until distribution time. It went over well.

While I tangled with my dilemmas, Jess had a job no one would envy and hardly anyone else could have done anyway. When we arrived, he went early to see what was the main problem he had been sent for. It seems a gas line had either broken or ruptured and flames were shooting thirty feet in the air from the crack in the ground. I shall never know how on earth they ever even got that big machinery onto that island. It was so shallow, it went up and down with the tide and actually tipped slightly with the weight of the machinery. It was for him to dig a lateral line eighteen inches deep and a certain width across the surface to a given point to tie in the broken area. He did it slowly and precisely, just eyeballing it in which in itself is an award-winning task. He got the fire out, the line in and no one else I knew was capable at all. When it came to his work, he was as well known as Abraham Lincoln.

Once he repaired a broken axle on a truck out in the middle of nowhere while another worker went miles for the parts. He met them coming back as he had it running again. This job had been dangerous too. One day the Uke dropped from the island. The driver was fished out, but the Uke is on the bottom of the Sacramento River. There were other near misses, but that's the pipeline work. You never quite got used to it yet it never changed a thing.

We left for a line beginning in Burley, Idaho shortly

330

thereafter. Jess came in one evening and wanted to talk to me about trading fifthwheels. He told of one that was absolutely gorgeous, in a storage lot near Reno. It seems another couple had purchased it thinking to do some traveling. They had arrived in Florida for a few weeks and started back to Nevada only to have him not feeling well. He had a heart attack and died at the wheel. The poor lady had to guide the big rig off to the roadside and from there I don't know the story, except someone drove the truck and trailer back, put it in storage and put it up for sale at a preposterously reasonable price.

We bought it nearly sight unseen. What a joy it was from the smaller trailer. Of course, I started building and changing it. I put in a microwave, added a doorframe closet, bought a small organ, made new curtains and other insignificant things that made life easier. But we had a beautiful trailer to start the new job.

We went from Burley to Twin Falls. My son came to visit over Mothers Day and to explore the possibility of a new career in law enforcement in the Hagerman Valley area. We had gone to dinner and had a lovely day, but upon return, after 2 P.M., there was a phone message on our door to go to the office immediately.

Jess was to call this Texas phone number left from the caller. He started to the phone, stopped and came back to me and said, "I can't. You call". He was deadly gray in color and I was sure he figured his mother had died. I held out my hand for the slip of paper with the phone number and nodded my head toward Jake to stay with Jess. The unspoken message was accepted through our eyes.

The phone was in the Cleburne hospital. Emma, Jess's sister, answered on the first ring. She said Melinda was on life support but it was useless. A kick in the stomach could not be worse. Melinda is our tiny love bug of a redheaded daughter, pretty as a picture and kind and sweet natured, just like Jess and just as gentle.

She had made a cake to take to her husband Paul's family for Mothers Day dinner and potato salad to take to Grandma Black's for lunch, so they could be with both families. Paul had five year old Harold with him out at the new home, putting up the yard fence, as their new mobile home was to be delivered the next day. Melinda had the cards signed, kitchen cleaned up, the new seven-week-old baby girl SueAnn down for her nap and had gone to the bathroom to shower and be ready when Paul and Harold returned.

That's where Paul found her on the floor. She died instantly of a brain aneurysm at age 29. Our world fell apart. Jess left immediately for Texas and I remained in Utah with my son until Jess came home. Nothing was right for a long, long time as I had been on the outs with my other daughter for some time and Jess begged me to correct that as truly it had been mostly my fault, we did not see eye to eye on much of anything, she and I.

We got through the sorrow, both of us being baptized in the little United Brethren Church across the road that we had attended since arriving in Twin Falls. I found a job for a while to keep busy and Jess slowly accepted the fact that Melinda was gone but I could see the suffering in his eyes. A few months later Jess's brother, Keith's youngest son, Joe, was killed in an accident the day before his wedding and Emma's daughter, Bonnie, lost twin girls in a raging fire because no one could get to them. A very, very difficult time it was. The next year, my foster daughter died of a burst appendix and it seemed there was no end of heartbreak. The new trailer lost its luster for a time.

As in all of life, time heals but leaves scars. The next segment of the job progressed further west and required us moving along to a small town called Glenns Ferry, a place I would like to live even now. We were back with crew people we had worked with before and old friends were good to see. The Grey's had a motor home next to us, the Bonner's three spaces down from them. The three ladies of us looked through the town and discovered many points of interest; an art gallery that was quite well appointed, several boutiques, ordinary stores, gas stations, some bars, four churches, one being my own denomination and we went the first Sunday there. Within three weeks, I was doing the special music, as I sing quite often for different functions and enjoy my music. I also put out the Sunday bulletin and joined a Sunday school class.

The men were working around the clock to beat the weather, as their job was on schedule yet. They had to divert the river and dig under the river to put in a culvert to carry natural gas lines across the state of Idaho. I fell in love with that valley and the people. There was a small park at the west side of town that had a Buffalo bull and cow that had produced a calf earlier that spring.

I was so amazed to see that the babies are orange in color and play like a calf or lamb. Our little Hitchy loved to run along the fence on the outside and the baby buffalo would follow on the inside. They could play for an hour at a time if I would stay that long. They would touch noses through the fence and back away like they were frightened, but then do it all over again, then run and jump along the fence line. I called them the Papa Lo, Mama Lo and Baby Lo. Hitchy learned that nearly on the spot. I would ask him if he wanted to go see the Baby Lo and he was out the door. Many good times there.

The group we chummed with had a birthday party for me. I'm sure my sweet guy arranged that although he pled innocent. About twenty were there and we had a memorable time, Ray and Mae Wilson joined us on that job, like old times.

At one time Glenns Ferry had been known as Three Island Crossing, and in August of each year, community volunteers re-enact the famous Snake River crossing made by pioneers over one hundred years ago. The Opera Theatre is also a fascinating place to see. The winery lets you always sample the estate-grown and bottled wines of their award-winning vintage. Then there is the Glenns Ferry Museum, on the historic registry. It has a fabulous display of the Oregon Short Line Railroad, which later became the Union Pacific Railroad.

If you're so inclined, there is jet boat and skiing on the Snake River. In the fall, pheasant hunting prevails with always-beautiful scenery of spectacular fall colors. Native Americans encountered this area 150 years ago. Next came the Oregon Trail and its history well preserved. There is an Educational Center with exhibits, a library and upper-level viewing of the Three Island Crossing on the Snake River.

But soon we had to move on further west. That move took us to Onterio, which is on the border of Idaho and Oregon. The railroad tracks divide the town; each side has its own post office and address, Onterio, Oregon and Onterio, Idaho. We arrived in Onterio, Idaho by way of Mountain Home and Caldwell. Since we had friends in both towns, it was good to spend a night in each place. Clara Penworth had a new cake recipe she insisted I try. It was called a Friendship cake and consisted of fermented fruit. For one thing, you used the liquor from the fruit juice in the batter. Living in a house with fermented fruit is possible. In an eight wide RV it *is* impossible. The voice of experience here!

While in Onterio, we heard of an old town up a steep mountain road. It still had a few permanent residences, although the road was impassable during the winter. I coaxed Jess into going one Sunday and we took two other couples with us. By one hour on that steep rutted dirt road, I wish I'd kept quiet. We did make it and all of us were glad to see the town, but what a gem of a place. The old houses still had furniture, the bar had a mirror 16' wide, lovely old chandeliers and the artwork, dishes and needle work were wonders to behold. To think all that had been pulled up there by horse and wagon and not broken. I could have spent a week there and still not be satisfied I'd seen it all. But Jess said we needed to get back down that God-awful road before dark. We all agreed to that. We stopped at a Mexican restaurant for dinner, which was very tasty. We enjoy Mexican food.

Now from time to time Jess mixes up his words. Often they are so silly, I'm inclined to think he does it on purpose. When the waitress brought our orders, she forgot the tortillas, but he asked her, "Where are the tarpaulins?" which brought down the house. Come to think of it, they do the same job now don't they?

Another time, he came on home all bent out of shape because his paycheck was incorrect. He said, "Here now, Sooky. You look this over and see what's wrong." I couldn't see that anything was, but he insisted it wasn't correct.

"What did they tell you?" I asked.

"Well, I don't know exactly. Something about our pay being radioactive."

I did not dare laugh because he seemed serious so I said,

"Are you sure you didn't hear them say retro-active?"

"Something like that, yeah. Why?" I explained the situation, but to this day I'm not sure that wasn't his humor spilling over.

We had been on this job over a year and were ready to head home. He was ordered to Saudi Arabia, so I stayed home. Jess was very concerned and walked the floor. "You will be in zero weather, alone. What will you do to keep from going bonkers with no garden or flower beds to busy yourself with?"

"Oh, I don't know. I may start a restaurant."

"A RESTAURANT? Well, where?"

"I'll figure it out, don't worry."

He was as upset as when I asked for a lathe and workshop for Christmas that first year. Of course, I got it too. I was spoiled and loved it, but I loved him too and found a thousand ways to show it. I'm not so good at saying it. I cannot ever remember my mother or Grandmother ever telling me they loved me, hugged me or held me on their lap. They were wonderful good people, just not emotional. I vowed never to hand that down to my children, yet I did sometimes. We all have regrets. It's natural.

He left for Saudi and I cried at the airport. He would be gone fourteen months. He nearly turned back, but I said no, I'll be just fine and I'll write every day. And I did, too.

The first year we had the gray house, I met a neighbor who owned a thrift store, she and the banker's wife. Ethel suggested I volunteer at the store and meet people. I did and still have friends there 30 years later. One lady in her 70's came in each day and quietly walked around looking and feeling many items. One day, I asked her if she was looking for any particular thing. She said yes, any small pieces of cotton as she made hand-made quilts. Since I sorted out the new donations each time I was there, I started saving her dresses, aprons, curtains, etc, that were stained, torn or in some way not suitable to sell. If it were being disposed of anyway, she might as well get what good she could out of them. We formed a close bond that summer that remained until she died at 101 years of age.

Her name was Dora Ellen Jones. The similarity in our lives was quite astonishing. My Grandmother was Nora Ellen. Her daughter, who died at 13, was named Dora Julie. My cousin is Donna Julie. Her wedding to Tom was my anniversary date with Jess. Her daughter and I were born the same year. And so it went. I adopted her for a mother and she enriched my life beyond any bounds one could expect.

The first time I needed to go to Great Falls looking for items for this restaurant I had in mind to establish, I called her to see if she would like to ride along. "Yes, I would. I'll be ready in twenty minutes and don't be late. I can't stand tardiness."

That was my introduction to my new mother. But what a joy in my life, gruffness and all. She traveled with me for several years and what a pleasure. She was quite well learned, much to my surprise and would point out such things as different strata in the rocky hillsides along the road or name every tree in sight. There was a song she used to sing in her gravel gerty voice she said her pa taught her. It had twenty verses and was called *Gasoline Gus and His Jitney Bus.* Many times I wished I'd written it down.

One fall day my phone rang at 7:30 A.M. It was Mrs. Jones just short of having a hissy fit. Once I learned what the trouble was, I said I'd be right there, hung up the phone and sat there laughing until my side ached. The old house where she lived had been turned into four apartments, two up a dark stairway and two on the ground level. The one bathroom was upstairs at the end of the hall.

Because she was an early riser, she always went to her bath early to avoid the other tenants. This was November and as she opened the bathroom door, she was dumfounded to see a deer in the bathtub. At least it hadn't been poached or shot out of season, but had been dumped in the tub quite unceremoniously to cool out. Why in God's name any one would do such an unthinkable act is quite beyond me, but there it was.

I drove over and questioned the other residents until I learned the deer belonged to the brother of one of them. I suggested the deer would be a good gift to the old age home to help with their menu if it was not out of there in less than an hour. It was removed shortly thereafter. However, Dora fussed and sputtered about that deer for two years. She cleaned, scrubbed, scoured and disinfected that tub until it was surprising there was any enamel left on its surface.

Eventually by pulling a few strings and inventing a story about her apartment being closed off because, to continue to heat the upstairs hall and stairwell (not so) would not be profitable so she was forced to move to the new complex that had been built for seniors. Fortunately, she got a studio on the second floor next to the elevator, which was a blessing and it had a wonderful view of the river.

After that, we traveled a great deal, which she enjoyed. One particular trip we took was back to Ohio to attend a reunion. There were many stops along the way, some turning out to be nearly hilarious. We pulled into a city park in a small Missouri town, as it had been advertised along the road as a Historical replica of years gone by. There was even an old out house with a quarter moon in the door.

She had a news paper and wanted to read it, but the wind made it difficult. I stepped over to a flowerbed to see if there were any I didn't recognize, but when I turned around, she was nowhere in sight. After several minutes, I saw her sitting in the outhouse with the door open reading her paper.

"What's up?" I ask.

"Well, the wind doesn't rattle the paper here and no one wants in here, I'm sure." Typical humor.

We stopped at Herbert Hoover's home and went through the buildings. There was even a blacksmith shop working on horseshoes. She had quite a conversation then and there. It reminded her of her childhood years on a Kansas farm. On along our progress were many points of interest. One in particular everyone should see is the Corn Palace in Mitchel, South Dakota. Every wall inside is constructed of shelled corn and even the exterior is covered with cornstalks, husks and kernels. The amazing thing is they change it each year. Well worth seeing!

We went on to Chicago for an over night stay and hotel accommodations out of the August heat. She got in the tub but couldn't get out. Did you ever try to lift 165 pounds of dead weight, and one who is wet and slippery? It's a fiasco. Thank goodness one end of the tub was open so I could get my arms under her to lift, but I couldn't hold it long. Both were exhausted by the time she was out again.

I had worked some seminars and lectures into this trip, both for a break in travel and extra earning along the way. This particular time I had a speaking engagement at a mental health group meeting as Psychology is my background, I had performed a considerable amount of public speaking on related health topics in conjunction with psychological reactions to mentally disturbed persons.

I needed to be gone most of one day and left her to rest, eat, explore the huge hotel and otherwise entertain herself. Since she was going to the dinner with me the next evening, we went shopping that late afternoon for a new dress for her and shoes that would be far more appropriate attire than old slacks and a blouse with some age to it. She chose a pretty pink shirtwaist style and white string closer shoes. Since she had beautiful blue eyes and snow-white hair, it was a lovely choice. We noticed a thrift store or consignment shop in the next block from the hotel, tucked away in the corner of a bookstore. Since she loves books, I suggested that might be the next days adventure once she was ready.

Now let me explain Dora Ellen Jones! She was 72, quite alert of mind and body, a bit mischievous by nature, curious about everything and built rather stout. What Jess calls the heavy-duty truck and bus type woman. Not flattering, no, but somewhat descriptive never the less. She had wide hips with a bit of a shelf, no waistline that was noticeable and an absolutely non-existent bust line. Therefore, she never wore dresses. The hemline sagged in front and hiked up above her knees in the back. This new pink dress had a gathered skirt, which added fullness to hide the lack of waistline and the hemline was not so prominent.

I arrived back at the hotel around 2:30 P.M. and started preparing a short thank you speech to deliver at the dinner. Sitting on my bed with a clipboard, I paid little attention to much else at that point but my project at the time. After twenty minutes or so, Dora conveyed to me that she was going to take a shower, no tub this time, and get ready for going out. Grand idea says I and continued with my own preparations. After the water stopped running, I could hear her muttering around in the bathroom, sounding somewhat miffed about something. Not sure if she was talking to me or herself, I walked to the door to listen a minute. She was grumbling to her clothing about not finding some garment so I hurried back to sit on my bed before she openned the door and found me eavesdropping.

As I passed the foot of her bed, I noticed some odd-looking contraption just under the edge of the sheet. Stooping to take a closer look, I nearly squealed with pent up laughter. She had evidently gone to that second hand store, as this get up was a nursing bra stuffed with panty hose and pinned shut. It was about a size 44 and had some very outstanding features. I pulled the sheet back over it so as not to appear disturbed and sat back down with my clipboard.

About that same instant, she came out of the bath in her towel and slowly started looking on the dresser, night table, suitcase by the lamp and any other area available. I never even looked up, but she wandered over beside me and very calmly said, "Alright. What did you do with my tits?"

I nearly laughed myself into hiccups, but the bra worked well. It filled out the top of the dress so the hemline rose to meet the rear and she had a nicely fitting dress.

In the morning it was foggy but we needed to leave that day, as our time was shorter now to reach Ohio for the reunion. Usually I jogged each morning but had not for over a week. She said to go ahead while she got us packed up and ready to leave.

After taking inventory, I didn't see exactly how I could do this. No tennys, raincoat or hat, only heels or casual shoes, good jacket and a new hairdo. Now let's see. There was the big black leaf bag over the hanger-hung cloths which I lay flat on the backseat, not folded up in a case. So that could be a coat if I cut out a neck opening and slots on each side for arms. Now for a hat. The plastic bag from Dora's "sale" would do fine if I cut the handles on one side to tie under my chin. I t was August and warm, so bare feet would do just fine. They could be washed, no problem.

I went down the back elevator to the black top alleyway behind the hotel. Luckily, so far I hadn't seen anyone at 5:30 A.M. I trotted up and back, up and back several times and since no one was around I decided to include the other end of the alley also. After 20 minutes, I decided that was quite enough and headed back up the alley, but nothing looked right. That was not the hotel so back I went the other way. That didn't look right either. I saw a car coming and it stopped at the light, so I motioned for her to turn her window down. She did about three inches. I asked her which corner the mental health building was on near the hotel I was in. She looked so sad and said, "Oh, my dear. Just stay there and someone will come to find you soon."

After that startling remark, I realized how I was dressed. If it hadn't been so ridiculous, I'd have cried. What had occurred was I crossed into the next block in the fog. After reconnoitering, I backtracked and realized what had happened.

By the time I got back to the elevator there were many people busy with their shifts. I had shed the coat and hat, much to the amusement of my audience and hustled myself back upstairs. I did not relate my mornings outing. The rest of our trip was uneventful after that.

Upon our return to Montana, I continued to plan for this restaurant. I thought a family style would do well for late meals and Jeanne had a restaurant open from 6 A.M. until 2 P.M. The only other eatery in town was in a bar and had steep prices. As plans took form, I decided this was to be a fun project not pomp and ceremony with customary regulation. Together, Dora and I searched yard sales, thrift stores, going-out-of-business places, anywhere we could pick up plates, bowls, platters, cups and saucers, sugar and creamers, salt and pepper shakers and large pans and skillets.

After a months' scrounging, we had what surely would be enough. Now for tables and chairs. The Air Force base at Great Falls had recently put a new cafeteria in their building and was selling off the old furniture. This turned out to be a gold mine. Nice metal chairs and 48 x 48 metal tables for five dollars each, you haul.

Since I'd already rented a large house from some people in town, I know there were three rooms for dining areas. The main one I painted green. The two downstairs bedrooms were perfect as well because of large double-door openings. There were two bathrooms, one between those two bedrooms to the front and another off the green room nearer the kitchen. Just fine.

I had found red-flocked wallpaper on sale for one bedroom and blue paper for the other one. Since I know how to hang paper and make curtains, this was a treat, not a treatment. Once the tables and chairs were in place, I had trucked them up from Great Falls in Jess's blue Dodge truck that I detested; it was time to think about the front room to the left of the entry hall. It was used as a parlor years before. It was opened up for weddings, funerals, reunions and so forth, but otherwise closed off with huge double doors.

After consulting Jeanne about her clientele, we decided it would make a perfect waiting area for families to wait in. There was a fireplace, so I bought a used living room suit and end tables, two rockers that had seen better times and rented a piano. That was the best investment money could buy. Ranchers would come in late and wait for other rancher neighbors or friends and family, then get their ticket to dinner.

The menu changed each day but I maintained a regular service of two meat dishes, three vegetables, six salads and one dessert. You paid your $4.00 and sat where you pleased along the length of those tables placed end to end in two rows across the room. Linen tablecloths were covered with see-through plastic runners. No two plates were alike; neither were cups or saucers. New water glasses were turned upside down at the top of the plate to one side, the cup upside down in its odd saucer on the other side. Fork and knife were wrapped in paper napkins and placed across your salad plate that was sitting in your dinner plate. Spoons were in pint canning jars down the center of the tables. Sugar and cream packets were in their appropriate vessel, also down the middle of the table mixed in between salt and pepper shakers.

All of the salads were on the table at six when I opened, so anyone could choose a seat and help themselves. The other food was placed at the end of the tables nearest the kitchen and passed along, just as one would do at home. This was, after all, a family style kitchen. Once they were finished with salads, they took their salad plate to the rubber tub by the wall that held dirty dishes and utensils, and used the eight-inch plate for the main event. On a long table similar to an old-fashioned library table sat the dessert of the day and the six-inch paper plates. Help yourself when ready.

To avoid pandemonium with the wee folk, I had picked up child-size table and chairs and placed them along the wall in the green room. This kept people with tots in one place. The mess was less work as it was confined to one area. Above the kitchen door was a sign that said, *Take what you want-but eat what you take.* This turned out to be a threat from parents to kids to clean their plates. Quite an oxymoron.

Since Jess was in Saudi and I with the restaurant, it certainly filled up my time. I did all the cooking each day, no small task, but I loved it, from 7 A.M until often midnight with people still visiting and lingering in the big room with the fireplace. There were acres of seed planted, hay bales, cattle sold, sheep shorn, etc. from that parlor room. Some one would play the piano, others would sing and grandparents rocked the little people. Just a wonderful camaraderie by all.

The menu changed each day, but the cooking still required time. I did not bake. That is a disaster waiting to happen. Pies I can handle, but cakes? I can ruin a package cake mix; biscuits you can use for a baseball game and cookies turn to some flavored cardboard. My early attempts at piecrusts about aborted any further attempts. My first pie was a lemon meringue. It was a beautiful work of art, BUT when my husband went to cut it, he cut and cut and cut, finally getting a piece dislodged from the plate, he wanted to know why I hadn't taken the paper plate out first. That was that!

Our meat dishes were roasts, meat loaf, chicken in various ways, fish, steaks, pork chops, liver and onions, lamb chops all in various ways of preparation. The vegetables were the usual type, especially zucchini, which can be prepared thirty different ways, I learned. Desserts were pies, cakes, puddings, shortcakes, turnovers, upside down cake, blitz, crème puffs or an assortment of cookies. A friend did the baking and another neighbor made fresh rolls daily. The first weeks' income cleared the entire cost of opening and I had a wonderful time.

The one salad in particular that seemed the house favorite was my sauerkraut salad. Even the truck drivers stopped to eat that. Orange Jell-O with apricots and whip cream also disappeared quickly. Then there were old favorites too, potatoes, macaroni and coleslaw, which can be fixed in several different ways. The slaw with shredded carrots, sour cream and crushed pineapple was a favorite I soon learned.

Once a week, I'd make a pot of stew or goulash for those who didn't want a big meal. Soon there were requests for special occasions like Lions club, Kiwanis, church circle meetings, small groups of lunch people, PTA or other organizations. I had named the restaurant Mama's Kitchen and before long the kitchen was fairly well known.

The biggest problem I had was the blasted blue Dodge truck, which I christened the Blue Bitch. That truck hated me. I'm sure it sat all night dreaming up some other misery to bestow upon me. Everyone else could make it run with no problem, but just let me drive it down two blocks and it would simply stop running. Which meant I was to drift over to a curb and walk, then call the Dodge dealer and have him go get it AGAIN. It was such a common practice that if I walked into the Post Office, Mr. Evans would say, "Hello, there Julie. You walkin' or brought BB this time?" Usually the answer, of course, was yes to both. Everything that could be changed on the Dodge had been changed and often. After the snow started, I rarely used that truck. One morning I needed too, however, and when I went to turn the ignition, all the engine said was *Yer rumph* two or three times and then stopped talking.

I had a nice neighbor, Mr. Warner, who usually baled me out of trouble, so I called him. He said he'd be right over, and he was. He said it was just "froze up" and to call Cal down to the garage and tell him to bring the big fan to slide under the motor. I did as I was told. In a few minutes, Calvin and his fan arrived and miracles were supposed to happen.

After a time, he climbed in and it didn't start. He asked me if I had the heater on. Now what kind of stupidity was this? If the thing refused to start, how could I turn the heater on? I said I guessed not. After a few seconds he said, "Well you DO have a heater, don't you?" Another stupid question.

I said, "Well, of course. It's that black plug on the left side of the dashboard." For Pete's sake, this man works on vehicles in a garage?

"Oh, no." Says he of the stupid questions. "I mean a block heater."

Now there is an interesting thought. A cement block would never fit under the hood even if it were heated to cinders. I said as much in utter frustration. I thought he just might strangle as he laughed so hard tears came to his eyes. Once that fit was over, he wisely commented, "Oh, you're from Hawaii. No wonder this is confusing." And set about to explain to me the workings of extension cords and block heaters. This all taken care of within the hour, we next discovered the battery had frozen and split. No end to this blasted truck's ailments.

After another week, I just forgot it and walked. I had tried to drive the Lincoln out of the garage and promptly got stuck in the snow with the rear tires while the front ones rested quite comfortably inside the garage. I still cannot fathom why a 130-pound woman can walk through snow but a 1700-pound car cannot make tracks in the same snow.

By January, I was a wreck. Everywhere I could look was nothing but white, white, white; enough to blow your mind. One Sunday, I put papers down on the front room floor and dragged the lawn mower up the back walk from its home in the tool shed, placed it on the papers and talked to it. Soon a knock on my door produced a neighbor from next door who suspiciously spied my lawn mower with a wary eye and asked if I was handling the winter without Jess. I said I was doing OK but I was surely tired of the cold and snow.

That snow was up to the door handle when going down the street after the plowing. We visited a bit and Bob went home. Within the hour, the neighbor lady across the street rapped on the front door with a loaf of newly baked bread. I offered her some tea, which she graciously accepted and she tried her level best not to look at the lawn mower.

Once she departed, Chuck Carter just *happened* by, you bet, and came in to set a spell. Finally he asked why the lawn mower with five feet of snow and six below zero was in the room. "Well, the carpet is green and I'm sick of the snow, so it just looks encouraging to see the lawn mower."

"Oh." he sighed. "We thought you tripped your switch."

`Who is "we" I wanted to know since he and Marge lived about twelve blocks away. The coconut wireless had been put to use at the first viewing of the lawn mower, I suppose.

Here is a poem I wrote about winter.

WINTER

Hell is hot, so we are told
I know differently, tis the miserable cold.
Snow is lovely, so they say,
Until you're in it for months to stay
With the doors all closed against the wrath
Of wind and cold; winters breath.

The driveway? Yes, it's there no doubt.
You may get in, may not get out.
The pipes are frozen, there is no end
To the discomforts of winter, once it sets in.

You cannot then bathes yourself or the dog
Except from a bucket that sends up a fog
Of steam, in a shivering room
As the heater turns off and on like a tune
I hear it now, "Near my GOD to thee"
One more "winter" and that's where I'll be.

The faucets must drip or freeze up tight
Driving you nuts both day and night.
Conserve energy – that's all we hear
While the furnace roars in your ear

The heat tapes work at ninety per
Before you can leave the engine must whirr
For about twenty minutes and burn up the gas
Enough to have taken you there and back.

Extension cords strung all over the place
To keep the motor hot enough to race
Two sets of shoes the vehicles need
Two sets of clothes for me, yes indeed
You wear out those clothes from the inside first
Taking them off and on, but what's worse
Is the hauling about of the extra footwear
So the next stopping place you can change the pair.

The puddle of water from the melting snow
To clean up after where'ere you go
That snowy mess I surely deplore
As it constantly ruins my nice shiny floor
There is no end to the laundry required
Provided the pipes are not then retired
To ice at the time, and then in such case
You have wet rugs all over the place.

To get to the Laundromat, now that's some fun
Slipping and sliding while on the run
Shovel and sweep times with out end
So on the morrow you can start over again.

What else? Oh, well the heater goes out
The fuel runs low and without any doubt
The fuel truck is stuck twenty miles out of town
And sits there waiting to get towed around
The electric bills soar and batteries die
While gasoline pours like rain from the sky

You bundle all up and look like a clown
To avoid pneumonia, to just go to town
Doors and windows shut and rooms closed off
You're there in your cage, and if that's not enough
Not a breath of fresh air that does not cause
Your nose to turn red as old Santa Claus.

The gasoline tank requires canned heat
The dog can't go___ without frost bitten feet
I've been stuck in the snow and shoveled it out
Hauled wood in, the ashes back out
The car block has its own heater, oh such a muddle
As my mind is in as I stand in my puddle.
If this is "winter', I've had all I need
As I gaze out my window, I wish it GOD SPEED
It has its own beauty, this I know
But mercy, I do hate the snow.

By the end of February, I closed the restaurant, packed what I needed, Dora Jones and Hitchy boy. It was time to head for Nevada, pick up the fifthwheel and get to California to meet Jess when he got in from Saudi, which couldn't be too soon for me. We had wonderful friends in Quartz Hill, California who had a quarter acre of land with their house, and a good place to drop the trailer while going to the airport.

Of course, the BB stopped every couple hundred miles and there we sat along the road for half an hour or so when it decided to start again. It took a while to get from Montana to Nevada. Along the route once again everything that could be changed, was changed, including a whole new wiring harness at $225.00. Forty minutes down the road it stopped again. This for six hundred miles.

We stopped at Dayton to see Marie and I told her of this Damned truck I would gladly blow up if I dared. She said,

"See that little shop off to the right by the pasture?
Well, walk over there and ask Eddy what's the matter with it."
I was incredulous. A kid and a shade tree machanic would tell me what was the matter with it! What did I have to lose? I trotted across the field and caught him just as he was leaving. I explained the dilemma and that Marie had sent me.

"Oh, sure, yeah. I know. Follow me into town in the morning." So I did. What other option did I have, really?

By morning, he changed his mind and said he would follow me in case it stopped again. At the intersection, he yelled out to me to turn right three blocks because there was a Marathon station on the left and to go in and tell Alex to get you a cellinoid. Off he went and off I went. Within twenty minutes, I had a $3.47 cellinoid and never again was there a problem with the Dodge after $700 or $800 repair bills over the winter. So do you laugh, cry, cuss or just shoot the damn thing.

We proceeded on to California and put the fifthwheel in Tucker's back yard. Tucker and Marie Parkins for 60 years have been friends through everything imaginable. Since their two daughters lived 50 miles away, one in Lancaster, the other in Palmdale, I decided to see them the same day I went to Jeanne and Jerry Boyde, also in Palmdale. So I called Celia, saying I was on my way, could she call Maryanne to let her know and we could all meet in Palmdale, as I had not seen the girls in several years. Dora stayed at Marie's. She was wearing down with so much "going" as we were doing. It was about 11 A.M. and a hot day, up in the 80's already. Thank goodness for air-conditioned cars.

About half way between Palmdale and Lancaster, there was a blue station wagon showing signs of wear and age with washed out paint. I had followed it for several miles when all at once it started to jerk and slow down. Figuring I'd better stay behind, I slowed down also. After a few more spasms it coasted over to the side of the road and rolled to a stop. Now if it was a woman driver, I would stop' if a man, I'd take description and license then tell the first cop I saw to go get help.

As it turned out, it was two nuns, so I pulled ahead and stopped then went back to see if I could help. "Did they know the problem?" No they had no clue. "Well, I'm going into Palmdale and I'll take one of you, but I'd suggest the other stay with the car and lock yourself in. If you abandon it, you will not have even the steering wheel left by the time you get back."

While deciding who would go and who would stay, a big tanker truck came by and seeing three women along a deserted stretch of highway in 90-degree heat, he pulled over and stopped also. Walking back to us, he wanted to know what was the problem. I said "not the first clue" and related the events up to that point. The truck driver said his name was Tim and he had a pretty good handle on mechanics, so let's see if I can figure out a problem here.

After pulling, poking, prodding, shaking and tapping on every exposed part, he said nothing visible seemed out of order, so where are the keys and he would see if it would start. The nun who had been driving held them forth and Tim stepped in the van. The engine sent forth a trill of sorts, with no other response. After a look at the dashboard, Tim announced the van was out of gasoline.

I told them not worry as I had about 2-3 gallons in a gas container in the trunk of my car, but I doubted the broken end of the spout would fit in the tank opening. The truck driver said he had 872 gallons of gas on his truck, but his hose had a 10-inch long nozzle, far too large to be of use unless you have a funnel. I recalled seeing Jess make a funnel from a newspaper once. He can improvise most anything, so I asked the ladies if they had a newspaper. No they did not. Neither did I, nor did the driver, Tim.

I asked what was in the van. The driving nun explained that they had supplies going to the medical clinic in Palmdale. They had just come from the Lancaster Hospital and who on earth would give a car with no gas to two women in the first place and on such a hot day out in the desert to boot? We went to see what really was in the van and learned it was bandages, tongue depressors, cotton swabs, Q-tips and other items in the same category. The only other thing in there was a vintage area granite bedpan. We spoke of it in a rather amused tone but Tim wanted to see the bedpan. That came as an unusual request, but said bedpan was handed over for inspection.

"Well, if one of you can hold open this flap on the gas tank let's see if we can pour the gas in the pan and hope enough will go in the hole and not on the ground."

To my surprise, approximately six tablespoons full just accidentally went into the tank, the rest on the ground. Tim went to his truck and came back dragging his huge gas hose saying for us to steady the pan, be sure the aperture was open and he turned his hose on. Gasoline poured like rain from the sky. After two minutes or so, he announced that must have about nearly a gallon in the tank and six more on the ground, a bit exaggerated I hoped, and he must get on his way. He had a schedule after all. The nuns implored him to take pay, which he declined and climbed back in the truck once the hose was again secured.

Walking back to their van, they said to me that there was about a cup or more of gasoline in the bottom of that bedpan and did I think we could splash it in the tank. "No." I said." I really doubt it." As I was speaking, a dirty brown Ford pick up pulled up behind us and a cocky little man about five feet, four inches in height, wearing dirty clothes, a cowboy-style hat and boots worn over at the heels, descended and walked over to where we were and asked what he could do to help.

"Oh, nothing sir," piped in the smaller of the two nuns. "You see, we had run out of gas, but the Lord provided our needs and we are about to go on our way." The little bow-legged guy in the cowboy hat just simply stood dead still and stared, first at the bedpan, then each of us in turn.

Abruptly, he doffed his hat, scratched his head with his thumb and drawled out, "Uh huh, yeah, waaalll OK," but with one last glance at the bedpan with its thin sheen of gasoline, he said, "I see yer folks of faith and all, but if you think that old car is gonna run on piss, good luck." Still scratching his head, he retreated to the safety of his Ford, as I am sure he thought we were escapees from some nearby institution. We laughed so hard; we ached as he drove on out of sight, then we got to the business of starting their van. After pumping the accelerator many times it coughed, sputtered and belched blue smoke and they were off. I followed them to be sure they ever saw that medical center. They did and I proceeded to Marianne's house.

Since I had been occupied with my gasoline people, I was over a half hour later than they had expected, so they had gone ahead with lunch preparation instead of our eating out to save the girls the trouble. After an hour, I begged off because I wanted to stop off to see Jeanne and Jerry Boyde, my dear friends from Holland originally. He was really a rocket scientist and had retired from JPL in Silicone Valley. Jet Propulsion Laboratories held many Government secret works and IQ's the numbers of which would break the bank.

Jerry had worked for the Red Cross during WWII, been captured by the Germans, put in a train for Auschwitz concentration camp and by convincing the people crammed in that boxcar to switch the saliva in their mouths until they had a goodly amount of what appeared to be foam escaping from their lips. Since Jerry had a Red Cross arm band, they yanked him off and wondered what was wrong with these people swaying on their feet, some moaning and all frothing at the mouth. He said they all had hydrophobia and it was deadly. Their boxcar was let loose on a sidetrack and they were locked in, supposedly to die with their contagious disease. It took some time and I never learned how, but one way or another, they either found a way to get the door opened or a passer-by let them out. His life story would make one fantastic movie.

Once my short visit with them was complete, it was time to start back to Marie and Tuckers. We were waiting one day at a time for Jess's phone call when he arrived. Three more days passed when the call came. I was elated. Marie rode with me, as I did not know how to find LAX airport form Quarts Hill. We were ahead of time for arrival so had a hot coffee and settled down. As the passengers came off the plane, Jess was toward the front and I met him at the gate. But, oh my, he had lost weight and looked so very worn and tired. I was glad we did not need to be in a hurry to be anywhere.

For a few days, Jess rested and told of the job and events, some of which were just hilarious. It seems there was a young man, perhaps in his early 20's, known only as Big Sid. He was not retarded, but had a mental disability of some kind. Jess said it was just phenomenal the things he could do that others would not even consider, like run his hand and arm down a snake hole or any nest of varmint or vermin and never get bitten, go pick up an Ocelot cub and never get a scratch, pick up snakes and actually play with them among other unbelievable tales.

He was also full of the very devil, loved playing tricks on people or daring to do outlandish things. Jess told of one hop-plane trip (hold 4-6 people) from the job sight to field headquarters with five members of the working crew that were going into a large city. The fellows just wanted to get away for the day and the company men went for supplies. They would meet a larger sixteen-passenger plane at the company airstrip to change over.

This particular day, there were six elderly ladies waiting for the same plane as they had missed their designated connection and were hitching a ride to the National Airport. Unbeknownst to anyone, Big Sid had purchased four little bottles of Near Beer, which comes in a green bottle about the size of a large baby food jar. Each bottle resembles a small keg. He had slipped them in his pockets and gotten on the plane with everyone else. At take-off, the stewardess went through the customary ritual of do's and don'ts, pointed out the oxygen masks, the barf bags in the pocket of the seat in front of you and offered juice, etc.; the standard fare of short flight trips.

The ladies were seated midway two by two on the left side of the aisle. Jess and another man were directly behind them where he could see across the aisle to where Big Sid was seated. There was something suspicious going on there. As he watched from his peripheral vision, he could see Sid opening his hidden brew and emptying them into his barf bag. Soon after that, he held up the bag and pretended to vomit, causing some sick-looking faces among the other passengers. Once he wiped away the spittle from his mouth with the back of his hand, he tipped up his beer and drank it down. Three elderly ladies fainted, pandemonium set in and the pilot forbad him ever to ride on that plane again. Indeed, they would not even let him fly back. He needed to find his own way back anyway he could at anytime he could.

Two days later, Sid turned up on another plane wearing a new blue suit cut off at the knees, sleeves removed and a gaudy pink tie that hung halfway to his knees. With greetings to all, he shouted, "Hey guys. Looky........Ain't I pretty?" Typical!

Another of his antics was a Friday night out to the bar. There were no empty stools and he wanted to sit there so he threw himself down and proceeded to imitate a fit or seizure. People left their stools to help him up and see to his state of health. He brushed himself off, said "Gee fellows, thanks a lot." He then picked an empty stool of his choice.

There were many more stories and leisure time with the Perkin's before starting to Montana. Since we owned thirty acres three miles south of Wendal, California, we decided to take a detour past our property, as we had not been there in four years. Not much had happened there. It was on a black top road that went through to Pyramid Lake on the Nevada side and fairly well used, but also just off the range of the Herlong

Army Depot. We had some fanciful plans for that acreage. It never came to fruition due to several factors, but it was a good idea at the time.

There is a great deal of history connected to that area. It is referred to as the Valley of the Moon, and has a shallow water area about a half-mile across by name of Honey Lake. The ranchers can drive cattle across the ice in winter and save going around the lake. There are two very interesting stories connected to this valley; one being there is the remnant of a basement and partial wall of the first school there and it had been built by the Lewis and Clark party. We even found an old green-backed primer under some rubble in one corner of the collapsed basement.

The other is not a work of fiction either as one can verify with a jaunt to the valley. The wagon trains going through the mountain passes were headed for the Oregon Trail but one group was too far south, but not realizing it. They came upon this beautiful valley with a small lake for water and grass as high as the belly on a horse. Since there were sixteen families they decided to settle there and called the newly formed town Rosemead.

It was the month of May, so they were busy clearing, building and planting. Several wagons had starts of grapevines; others had pear and apple trees. Yet others had wild rose starts and vegetable seeds, onion sets and tools. By fall, the gardens had produced, animals bore new life, little trees thrived, and wells were dug, as water was so close you could dig a three foot hole and it would fill with water from natural underground springs. This kept the lake supplied as well.

But in late October, a herd of some two hundred cattle and their drover, crew and cook of chuck wagon showed up on the scene and were just unreasonably furious.

"Who the hell are ya and where the hell did ya come from. How did ya git here," and so on. The head of the cattle drive told the towns' choice for a mayor they had been driving cattle to this valley for winter forage for years and they could pack up and GIT!

"No!" says the mayor. They had already staked a claim in the town of Susanville (once they knew of it) and were stationary, like it or lump it. This went on for a week, when the tempers flew.

The drover and mayor had a shoot out. One report was ever heard from the guns and both dropped dead in the street. After much to do and threats, the cattle crew and towns-people decided to join forces and all stay put in peace. They took the newly deceased about a half-mile north of town, dug one grave, rolled them both in it, and placed a marker there that reads, *This here town woodin hold them, but this here grave duz;* with names and date of 1867. It is there to this day, enclosed by a cyclone fence put up by the historical society to keep away vandals should any aspire to such things. It is still very sparsely populated and unless someone tells you where it is, it remains unharmed and safe.

A few other interesting facts of that Valley are equally interesting. A German man living in Ohio had ventured out that way in the late 1940's or early 50's and found rich fertile soil. He started Hybrid seed corn by planting acres of it and detassled every other row to re-pollinate creating a new variety of seed corn for farmers. His name is Brumel or Brumle, I can't say which.

JJ Horatitz of Hollywood fame came by and the remoteness was a magnet. He and his wife started a dude ranch. There were still wild horses then and an Indian family, by the name of Hightower, started breaking horses for profit, not just to sell to the dude ranch but also prospective buyers.

A dentist from Long Beach, California had traveled up there to go hunting, discovered a repairable log cabin, purchase ten acres and decided to plant onions. His market was Campbell Soup Company. They purchased the entire crop as is and did the harvesting. This turned a good profit for six years. The seventh year, the good Doctor decided to hang on to the crops as long as possible believing it would be one of the last available, but the frost got the entire crop and that was the end of onion ranching. However, you can find wild onions all over the valley floor; same with the pear trees. Some exist and have huge Bartlett pears that the neighbors around pick every fall. If you get up on a hillside so you can see down into the valley, you will find deteriorating cabins about every mile and quite a few wild roses where homes used to be. If only that valley could talk, what a wonderful thing that would be.

Another story about that valley is when Jess went for an eight-month job in the Middle East. I decided to take our camp trailer and go see Rachel and Jonesy in Susanville. I had known her for years and we were best of friends. Her life story also would make a wonderful movie.

Since I had the dog, Hitchy with me, I drove out to the acres and thought I'd stay a week. I had supplies in the camper except for only a one-gallon tank of propane. The little refrigerator ran on propane also. I just hoped it would last out the week. I had gone out on a Sunday afternoon, stopped to see the Fillapelli family and the Gordons and set the jacks under the trailer by 8 P. M. I fixed a sandwich, made coffee and prepared to sit out in a folding lawn chair to watch the moon rise and get a full view of the stars, as it is black dark out there. About 10 P.M., I got the dog in as I heard coyotes and I locked us up for the night. It was so quite and peaceful, I just did a good job of nothing the next two days.

However, Tuesday night a mountain lion and a coyote fought each other to the death along about 2 A.M. and on Wednesday I pulled the camper over into Clarence and Alzora's barnyard and told my pity-party story. I asked if I could please stay there a couple days and would love to leave the trailer there for the winter. If they wanted to use it, that would be fine, even as a bedroom for guests as they had only a one-bedroom section house by the tracks. Clarence was a railroad man. He ran the Depot and other related businesses. The dearest people you could ever know.

On Wednesday night, I slept in my little Chalet the best I could. The switch engines started moving cars at 11 P.M. The locomotive pushed cars from one set of tracks to the siding. When the cars collided and connected at the "buckles", it would wake the dead. The ground shook and the noise even frightened the poor little dog who dove under the covers with me. The mattress shook like the St. Vitus dance. It was after 2 A.M. before it was nearly quiet. I say nearly as the coyotes were after the chickens; so between the coyotes barking and yapping and the squawking of the chickens, it somewhat resembled a freaky nightmare.

About 9:30 A.M., I wandered over to Clarence and Alzora to beg a cup of coffee. She asked what I had been doing so long this morning. I stared at her in disbelief. "I just *woke up?*" I said. "Oh, no, no Julie. The switch engines work from 11 until 2, but we don't even hear them."

A grain of salt would turn to a pillar before I believed that. However, she was quite amused and related it to Clarence when he came in at 11 for lunch. It seems his workday begins at 5 A.M. Horrors!

Thursday night came and bedtime arrived at 9 P.M. for them, so I retreated to my tiny dwelling of 12 feet and read awhile. Once I was all settled in by 10 or 10:15, it was quiet as a tomb, dark as tar and I happily snuggled down for the night.

WHAM! Up I shot. Oh, no. The switch engines. Now that's it. I jumped out of bed wearing my white cotton pajamas, pulled on my white terrycloth slippers, wrapped my long black hair inside a white bath towel, securing it with two clothespins and waited. Once the man with his lantern had walked forward toward the next car rolling its clacking way, down to join the last car, I scooted across the tracks and hid behind the outside corner of that first car they had just dropped off.

Here he comes, I thought, wig-wagging that lantern up and down –pause- back and forth-pause-in a circle-pause-and started the procedure all over again. Signals of some sort obviously. How far, how fast, distances, what ever it specified, I had no idea, but when he was within a cars length of me, I jumped out from that car shielding me from view, ran up on the tracks, waved my arms up and down like wings and ran toward him with a healthy woooo, woooo shrill woooo, woooo and drug out the last wooooooooooo.

That lantern flew 20 feet toward me, but lit in a broken heap on the stones next to the tracks and with a yelp to compete with the coyotes; he sailed forth down the tracks toward the engine in a very big rush. The impression fleet of foot entered my mind.

I could hear him yelling all the distance to the locomotive. "Git the HELL out a here!" He repeated as fast as one could speak. I went back to bed and slept quite well until 7:30 A.M. When I was dressed and had let Hitchy out for his morning constitutional, I slowly drifted over to the Bowens' house. I was quite surprised to see six men lined up along the kitchen wall in tipped-back kitchen chairs. All seemed in a somber mood that I studied while helping myself to Alzora's major coffee pot. It never was empty, you see.

Clarence was seated at the end of the long kitchen table with toast, eggs and coffee. He casually said to me, "Need tah ax ya bout something twas goin on during the night."

"Oh," says I with appropriate interest.

"Yea, uh hum, well ya see, Grady here attests to the fact he was run after by a spirit or ghost and won't change his tune. We called a meeting this morning to figure it out cuz he ain't gonna work nights no more and we dint get no one that will, neither." With that said, a boisterous clatter rose that would dull your senses. Grady got in good form then and out yelled everyone to declare that By God it was him what got chased and only him what knowed the story. So for the umpteenth time, he was telling it again, gyrations and all, much to the interest of his audience and the delight of me.

"This here thang jest tore down the track on wheels and shrieking like a Banshee, with wings that flapped after me and horns on its head, all white and nigh onto my own height." With explicit detail, he exploded with indignation at the skeptical looks he received.

I drank my coffee with elbows braced on the table and took in this tirade with clenched teeth. The piece about fire pouring out of its mouth nearly made me choke. Wheels, of course, were the motion of my running feet. Horns I assume were the two clothespins. Wings, hardly, but flapping arms would be a close substitute. So, I innocently voiced my opinion that nowhere had I seen or heard any such thing at all. Well, I hadn't, not that story.

As Friday was Alzoras birthday, her crippled brother, Walter and I drove into Susanville to get a cake and ice cream. As we approached the State Highway Patrol office, I remarked that I needed to learn of a short cut through to Montana. As soon as I entered, I inquired about an alternate route, not going through Alturas.

"Oh, yes. 395 to 12 and cut east out of Idaho. Where you from, lady?"

I said I'd visited the Bowen's at Wendell station, but needed to head home the next day.

"Really. Bowen's huh? What do you know of the spook on the tracks?"

Mercy, gossip does move right along! I said I was sure I had not seen anything with such a description and with a thank you for the information; I ducked out as soon as I could before further questions caught up with me.

Walter and I did our shopping, procured a lovely bouquet at the florists and headed back to Wendell. Friday dawned hot, dry and humid. Clarence had called the Fillapolis's, Bell's, a few other scattered friends out on the valley floor and all assembled around 5 P.M. He asked Alzora to take the day off and let me cook the venison steaks and prepare the meal.

So I agreed and we talked of many things, including the spook, while potatoes boiled, corn was prepared by Walter for roasting ears, bread slowly rose, salads were cut up, gravy makings were ready for the frying pan and nearly all was ready by 6 P.M. Clarence said grace and we each tucked into our food. Cake and ice cream climaxed an eventful day but the ghost seemed to be the topic of choice.

Walter and I cleared the table and started on the dish washing. The wilder the story advanced, the harder it was for me to keep any composure. My head was getting closer to the dishpan as the minutes went by, hiding a face about to creak up with laughter. As I reached to put a freshly washed plate in the drain rack, I realized it was full so evidently Walt was not wiping the dishes.

I looked up to see him standing there staring at me. With a sheepish grin, he cleared his throat too loudly and said, "Attention all, I think there is someone in this room a bit more informed about this spook than has told the truth."

Well that did it. I grabbed a chair and fell in it, laughing out of control. I relayed the events that led up to this wild story to a rather stunned audience. No one suspected me, of all people. Women just didn't DO those things and once the image soaked in you never heard such noise. A gaggle of geese could do little to improve the racket. Poor Bob just doubled over, his hair hanging in the gravy bowl at the edge of his plate. Nellie Fillapoli laughed until she had tears squeezing from her eyes. After Clarence re-adjusted his wits to fit the moment, he pounded the table and hooted. So it went around the table.

I left on Saturday morning for Montana, leaving the camper with Alzora and suggesting Walter use it for a "room" he did not have in this one bedroom house. He slept on the sofa-no privacy.

Stopping for late breakfast with Rachel and Jonsey was

the next on my itinerary and fixing Hitchy's food, water and blanket on the back seat floor, we were northern bound on a glorious fall day. I needed to be home in the grey house and stocking up again as I'd emptied the refrigerator before I left. Jess would be due to arrive in less than two weeks. Believe me arms, hugs and kisses mixed with a few tears were welcome for each of us. I rather wanted him to myself a few days, but that was a pipe dream.

The Decker family next door, Powers from across the street, Carters from the lawn mower escapade and then relating that story to him, Tomas's coming in from the farm and his chum and fishing buddy, Duncan, soon were like attached to a swinging door. I really didn't mind, as I was so proud of him and love to hear his exploits, as did the others. We did take a couple days to go up to Calgary to see the Hoorhees friends, Mike and Evie. He was from Alaska and she was from Hawaii (my chum) then settled in Canada. Some cultural shock there, you can bet on it.

Since we had purchased a 50 foot by 16 foot mobile home a few years before, we thought this winter, during time off, we would drive through to Casa Grande (please pronounce this correctly Casa *Grah n dee*, not like the word *grand*) Arizona and spend a few months in our mobile home poking and puttering around, visiting the old Casa ruin, look through stores, visit local interests, thrift stores, our favorite past-time, and visit with John and Sonja Hill, who lived across the street and had been the instigators of our purchase there.

John, at one time, had worked for Jess and a mutual bond of friendship had formed. This year Jess repaired things he could around the property and I made kitchen curtains, and bought self-adhesive tiles to put down new floor surfaces in both kitchen and bath. We washed down walls and put wainscoting in the kitchen. This done, we sent Mrs. Dora Jones a plane ticket to come down for a month. She was delighted and so were we.

Then I had another Crohns attack that just wiped me out for ten days. Once back to our normal slaphappy way of life, we explored other areas, planted flowers, slept late, ate too much and, in general, relaxed. This was a good time for my Jesse. He is possibly the hardest working man I've ever known and with not a first complaint about it. He thrives on work, fishing and hunting. Well, I fit in there too, somewhere.

In mid December, we sent Dora to Montana. She had enough desert heat and sand. She loved Montana with the snow country and the riverbanks laden with many varieties of trees. Her second floor apartment, at the head of the elevator, allowed her this view and many times she spoke of the elk or deer on the riverbanks or coyote pups playing on the mounds. This was her joy.

If you like a descriptive lifestyle, you could have had a delightful life following us around. W e were thinking Christmas in Texas again as it had been three years already since our last Texas trip. We drove through Dove Creek, California, the Pinto bean capital of the USA. Jess said how about beans for the families this year with a brochure to accommodate the package. That sounded pretty cool to me, so we bought two 20-lb bags and stowed them in the trunk. As it was early yet, we could have driven on, but decided a motel, hot showers, good meals and a stint in the swimming pool sounded just right.

There was a truck stop near by and as Jess always comments concerning restaurants, usually the larger truck stops have great food and reasonable prices. He was correct, as always. Our meal was more than ample and quite tasty. During our dessert there were three car-carrier trucks that came in and parked. These I understand are referred to as Drive-aways.

Each driver had a pet with him, we overheard. A Gate city carrier had a weasel, the Commercial carrier driver had a small yappy dog and the Decatur driver had a parrot. Weasel and dog stayed in the truck cab but the parrot came riding in on a massive shoulder. He deposited it on the coat rack at the end of the booth and all three sat down. Such a riotous group: happy fellows laughing, telling jokes and in general, very good-natured men. The waitress took their order and brought coffee.

The traffic light at this corner was a trip light. For those who are not familiar with the term, it is due to wiring under the paving that trips the light from red to green, etc. The reason being that should only one vehicle approach the intersection and the light being red, the wheels crossing the trip wire would cause it to turn green. If two approached nearly at the same time, whoever arrived first would get the green light, often allowing the red one to remain red until another car tripped it from the other direction. All well and good most of the time; however, when there are several in a row, that light flips red, green, red, green often so swiftly, one cannot get through the light before it turns again.

This particular evening there were many trucks and tourists stopping for dinnertime and the light was causing some squealing brakes and hot tempers. One truck having to catch the green light was nearly there, approximately 30 feet from passing through, when it flipped red and he slammed the brakes, squealing tires and clattering the parts he was carrying. Out of the blue, his parrot jumps up and down and screams out 'fuckin women drivers, fuckin woman drivers'. The owner snatched that bird and dove for the door never more to be seen that day. The startled patrons were dead silent for 60 seconds or so when pandemonium broke loose and people nearly collapsed with sidesplitting laughter. What one encounter along the routes of our country can be quite amazing and/or amusing. It's in the eye (ear) of the beholder. This was a new story to pass along the line.

In the morning we drank our complimentary coffee at the motel and started on towards Texas. We had a new Lincoln hardtop convertible, silver with black leather roof and magenta colored upholstery. A dream of a car I truly loved. Jess had a black Lincoln at the time we married and I had a two-toned green Lemans. It stayed in Hawaii in storage should we be reassigned there.

The car purred right along nearly putting you to sleep, but we made good time and were in New Mexico by nightfall. A similar routine of motel and restaurants again but this one was Mexican food which I loved and ate quite often. It had turned quite chilly and Jess said it would snow. I thought that a ridiculous prediction as I was in shorts, sandals and thin blouse.

I've learned over the years to not be too opinionated about such things as weather, in particular. I've never known him to be wrong, the same as with people. We would meet someone and, as always, he would ask what I thought of the person or couple. I would always say "How can I draw any accurate opinion since I didn't know them from Adam", but he would quietly assess their characters and share his thoughts. In all our married life I never knew Jess to be wrong about another person in his life.

True to the night's prediction, there was six inches of snow in the morning. There was a real scramble among luggage to locate anything at all appropriate to wear. The car heater was a Godsend. Once we left Deming, it would only be a seven-hour drive, more or less, on into mamas. Nothing in the way of projects this year was in the plans but now facing those 120 miles of nothing from El Paso to Van Horn was not relished by any means. A self-respecting jackrabbit would not be caught out there without a knapsack.

By late afternoon, we were near Sweetwater and called ahead to see if Hank and Gwen were home or out on a job. They were dear friends and part of our wedding party. She was one of my bridesmaids. They had saved and spent earnings wisely. It showed in their new home (paid for) which was filled with gracious living, artifacts and momentums of jobs over the years. A painting purchased at Glenns Ferry was a duplicate of my own treasure from there. Their standard poodle had left this world but not the property. His headstone read *Pompedeau, the joy of our hearts* with dates engraved as well. He was there to stay.

They implored us to stay over a day with promise of chili and beans, Texas style. It didn't do a lot for me as I am not much impressed with chili, but the other three licked their lips and rolled their eyes. Now I know what chili is, of course. You cook up the hamburger with onions. When cooked, you add tomatoes and sauce, a bit of catsup, Worcestershire sauce, chili powder and let it simmer for half a day or so.

When we sat down to eat, things surely didn't look like a pot of chili, help yourself. We had a plate with an empty bowl in it, a cereal type bowl to the right and salad plate to the left. I took this in with a questionable smile and waited. Here came Hank with a tureen, ladle and all, to pass around. I just mimicked the others, as I really did not know how one went about building chili.

The tureen held a red broth with weeds in it from the look of things. One puts this in your bowl. Next was a pot of kidney beans and rice. This went in the plate to the right. Next came chunks of cornbread or Johnnycake that went on the salad plate. Now you are served and you manipulate this array around until you put the beans and rice, by spoonfuls, into your red broth or gravy, as it is called, by dipping your spoon of bean concoction into the gravy and eating it one spoonful at a time. I'm here to explain, once and for all, that this "gravy" is NOT chili to taste. It is hot enough to remove the varnish from your teeth and bring tears to your eyes. I was certain no chili powder remained in Texas, or any place at all.

You next break off chunks of Johnny cake and dip it in this gravy from hell and sort of suck on it first and bite it off second. It must have been noticeable that I was not accustomed to such delicacies, so I commented that Texas was a LONG way from Kauai, Hawaii. But my husband said I was game and patted my head. The hot gravy reminded me of eating salsa with Tucker and Marie. Once you open your mouth to take in the food it is on, the fumes cause you to choke. Tuckers only comment was "Eat it Junko. You never get no worms!"

We had a lovely visit with the Springs and bid them farewell. We would attempt to see them on a return trip one day. It had taken me a while to digest their Christian names. His was Hankworth and hers was Gwendolyn. It didn't spoil two families. Sweeter people you could never hope to meet.

On Saturday late, we arrived at Mamas. We had not set a time of arrival as both of us have wandering feet and never know for certain where or when we will surface. She was alone and we did not announce our arrival so we brought in the beans and explained our "gift". Not a word she spoke, just got a saucepan and four big paper grocery bags with handles and said to get started. Jess lugged them to the kitchen and opened them. We dumped them in an eight-pound washtub and mama set about dividing them, pan full by pan full one each to the bags, equally distributed and ready as a present.

Christmas we all had gathered at Mamas when Jess said to Roy, the youngest brother. "How would you like to go to Hawaii?" Without hesitation, he said it would be great except he had Nancy and their three rug rats, Robert, Betsy and Josh. A silent moment and Jess added, "As I recall, you were always so gassy, I just thought with ten pounds of beans on hand you could go sit on the edge of the ocean and putt, putt, putt your way across." He, Ha. He, Ha. He. Ha. So pleased he was with his own joke.

That afternoon, some of the Doss family were there. Mama was a Doss and had six sisters and one brother, Uncle Leon, who I adored. Since the Hawaiian language is nearly archaic, you seldom hear it spoken except by those of us who lived with it and unthinkingly revert back to words or phrases. One of the aunts has a bit of a caustic tongue and sweetly remarked that she was surprised I could teach school when I could not speak proper English. I never missed a beat and told her, "Oh, well, when you speak several different languages, and I speak five of them, words oftentimes collide in a sentence, but besides grammar, our people are taught good manners also and try not to be offensive.

We just went on with the topic at hand, which was explaining about the Wood rose, an odd plant vine of flowers that has two lives in one season. It blooms first as a bright yellow Morning Glory and closes up tight when finished blooming. However, unlike a domestic Morning Glory, it flowers and drops off the spent flower. The Wood rose just stays in place. Three months later the dead flower unfolds itself and opens as a beautiful, beautiful brown rose that you would swear was carved from wood, its center being one large seed about the size of a white hickory nut. The most gorgeous flower arrangements can be made of these.

Soon after that the aunt left and others departed as well. When no one was left but Mama, Jess and I, Mama sat at her kitchen table and slapped her hand down hard and started to chortle away. She looked at my husband and declared, "Jesse, Jesse. This Julie of yours can tell people to go to the devil so kindly they say *Thank you.*" Then she laughed out right. His reply was, "You never know what's next with her, but she is mine and a keeper."

On Christmas day each family had their own family Christmas as all had been at mamas on Christmas Eve. We knew Keith and Betty had their water heater burn out and now the stovetop burners were going from heating water in three-gallon buckets. So we bought them a new water heater for Christmas. We delivered it that afternoon and Keith, the boys Don and Jim and a neighbor, Doyle Watson along with Jess all proceeded to oust the old and hook up the new. We shall not discuss that job. Suffice it to say the air was smoky blue for a number of hours. However, it worked, much to everyone's delight.

Betty and the oldest daughter, Joyce, started our evening

meal while the men were outside with chores and palaver, in general. Since we had been asked to stay over and pleased to do so, I busied myself sorting through a few pieces of wearing apparel among our soiled clothes from the past five days on the road. We always carried a duffle bag for several purposes, this trip a dirty clothesbasket.

An automatic washer and dryer put us back to average in less than an hour while we all sat around the kitchen reminiscing over people, highlights of our lives and the usual family chatter. Betty is an excellent cook and there was such an amount of dinner left over, we occasionally picked at it since it was left there for that purpose. Eventually it got around to Hawaiian foods as it usually did and the remark mama had made on my first visit to Texas.

While preparing a pot of vegetable soup, I cleaned the carrots and saved the parings, chopped celery, saving the leaves, shredded the cabbage, saving the outer leaves, and also the potato peelings, turnip and rutabaga skins. I had them piled in a pan when mama came by the sink. She reached to throw them out.

"No, please. I want them." I said. She just walked over to the pot and poured hot water into her instant coffee. Once the stew pot was steaming away, I added water to my parings and set them to simmer. The three of us, Jess, mama and I were sitting around the table when Emma popped in the back door.

"Um. Smells good in here," she quipped with a big smile.

"You want to stay?" I ask.

"Oh, no, but thank you. I have my four kids and hubby to feed. I'll take a rain check, OK? I brought over some fresh okra I just picked from my garden."

Bless her heart. She remembered I'd never before tasted or heard of okra and I just loved it. I stood up and pulled off my peelings from the stove and looked for a strainer.

"What's that, Julie?" Emma asked, but before I could reply,

mama piped up with her version.

"That's the garbage she is cooking up." This with raised eyebrows.

"Really?" from Emma in a too high voice. Jess is sitting there with his elbows on the table, his hands cupped over his mouth, I felt sure to hide a smile as he well knew what I was cooking up.

"Is there a need for cooked garbage?" Emma asked, rather incredulously.

"Well, yes." This from me. "All the vitamins are in the skins of vegetables plus there is still a certain amount of meat left on all parings. Once they are cooked down to a mush on the bottom of the pan, I strain it, freeze it and next time I make stew or gravy, I put it to use."

"Never heard of any such thing. Hmmm, hmmm, learn something new all the time. Well I guess I better get a move on, kids are alone, teen age is as bad as pre-schooler sometimes."

Once it was just us three again, mama slapped the table again, her way to emphasize her point, and she said, "Well, Jesse. I'll tell you. This is a new idea. Some people they are economical and some are frugal, but this one," pointing at me, "she is just plain cheap."

"Uh, huh, um, huh, yes I know, but she can stretch money farther than anyone I ever knew." He said. "She built our home and it's paid for too. All the furniture is hers from out of storage and we have added to it some. She may be a cheapskate, but she is mine and it's OK with me."

From mama, "Jesse, I'm really proud of you both." With that, mama got up to make her famous buns to go with our soup.

We related that story around Betty's table and decided to call it a day. That was the biggest error in judgment any of us had that day. All in all, it had been a very *good* day. Jess put the sofa bed down in the living room, Don and Jim headed upstairs to bed and Keith and Betty started down the hall to their front bedroom. All was quiet and dark as pitch.

From the front bedroom, we could hear the conversation going on in there, even though spoken softly. It had been a long day and they were tired, but Betty reminded Keith that the skunk was still getting her chickens and had anyone remembered to slide the door shut on the small opening to the egg nests and roosts. The answer to that was an, "I don't know". Silence prevailed. Not for long however. In about twenty minutes or so, as everyone was drifting off to sleep, the hens in the coop started up a clamor to set a cemetery afoot.

"Keith, Keith, get your gun. I bet the skunk is in there and maybe you can kill it this time." Obediently, Keith arose, stomped into his boots and shirt. Since he had his long johns on already, he just snatched up a flashlight along with the shotgun and hurried through the kitchen and screened-in back porch on his journey to the hen house, some 300 yards from the house. He did not saunter but slowly approached the building, holding the flashlight along the barrel of the gun. By now, Jess had joined him to see what, if anything, he could do to be of any help.

Flashlight in hand, Keith crouched down to better see in that 10" x 14" doorway. He could see the skunk under the roosts. It hesitated at the sight of a sudden illumination. Just as Keith was ready to pull the trigger, the skunk ran out. Simultaneously, Humphrey the big liver spotted hunting hound, who no one had seen, showed up and poked his cold, wet nose up against Keith's bare backside, as the trap door on his long johns had popped open due to the strain on the fabric while in his squatting position.

The gun jerked up, the dog ran off, the skunk went on its way and Jess nearly choked laughing. Keith was not laughing and we shall dispense with his comments. By now, Jim, Don and I were all out to see the commotion. It was midnight, near thirty two degrees, but no snow yet, just cold.

Eight windows' glass was blown out of the frame and seven

dead chickens was the final count of night. Now nothing to do but start heating water. Butcher and clean chickens and start on our new day at 1 A.M. All pitched in and by 2 A.M. chickens were in the freezer, feathers in the trash, chicken feet, heads and guts were dispatched to the garbage. Kitchen cleaning was going on while the men cleared away the foul mess. That's a pun! And by 2:30, all were full of black coffee, had stopped laughing and were bedded down once more. Good nights were heard throughout the house. Even after soap and water, our hands still smelled of butchered chickens.

Within ten minutes, a shriek from hell lifted everyone off their mattresses and a scramble down the hall to the front bedroom. Betty, in her nightgown was standing between the bed and the window jumping up and down and gurgling something in a frantic panic. Keith had tripped over the bedclothes and was sprawled on the floor on his side of the bed nearest the door to the hallway. He didn't seem able to collect his wits and with jaw sagging, finally said, "Well now, hell Betty! What in tarnation is the matter with you?"

All were collected in their bedroom by now and Don, seeing the results of the latest fiasco said, "What in hell is going on NOW?"

This brought common sense back to Keith, who patted his six-foot tall son. Betty started to cry and calmly said, "Don. Do not swear. It's unseemly."

We nearly collapsed in a fit of laughter. She was concerned about Don's upbringing and vocabulary right in the middle of pandemonium. I'd have laughed if he threatened to shoot me. Jess headed for a beer, Jim went back upstairs to bed and I sat down on a chair and said, "Well, what in Gods name IS the matter?"

Finally we got a coherent story from Betty. After she was back in bed evidently Keith had flopped his left arm out to find a more comfortable position. It landed across Betty's body, just below her breast. This was nothing new to her, so she slowly reached down to lift the arm back up and off her to tuck it down along his side. But when she picked up the "arm" it was fur and warm and she screamed bloody murder. In her mind the skunk had gotten in the house.

As a matter of fact, what had really occurred was during the woeful circumstances in the barnyard, the screen door to the back porch had been left open. The big black barn cat, not permitted in the house, had taken advantage of the open door, no broom after him and curiosity set in. Once we started back inside with headless naked chickens, there was no escape so he hid in the farthest place possible; that being, obviously, under the bed in the bedroom where Betty and Keith slept. Once it was quiet, the cat must have set about looking for an escape route. Since the window seemed a hole in the wall, the cat tried to jump out, hit the glass and streaked across to land on Betty. Once there, it must've hesitated just long enough for her to reach down and get a handful of cat. She grabbed that poor cat and flung him across the room, up against the wall and between its screeching and her screaming, it was bedlam in the first degree. If anyone ever got to sleep the rest of that night, I'm unaware of it. By 4 A.M. it was nearly time to get up and do chores.

After a big breakfast, we went through the customary hugs and kisses, handshakes and good wishes, then we were on our way back to mamas with a story to tell her that she just might not believe.

With Christmas over, there were still things to do at mamas; cleaning away winter out around the buildings, mulch pile to relocate, trees to trim back, a new hand rail at front porch steps, windows to wash and various other tasks to fill up the day. We said our goodbye, which is always difficult and drove back to Casa Grande and warmer weather the next day.

Once ensconced in our mobile home there were chores there also that needed attention plus Domino's with John and Sonja, some fishing and side trips to investigate. Then I became quite ill. Once again, we were unable to fund a cause. Not until several years later was it diagnosed as Crohns. Since there is no medical answer, no pills, treatment or surgery to correct it, one suffers through it until the present attack runs its course. You have no warning and it's completely unknown what triggers it once it is dormant for a time. Like all other cancers, it will get you in time. It's just a matter of time.

At the end of March, it was time to think Montana and check with the Company office about our next location. I always say "our" location as if he is in the USA. Jess does not leave me behind. I enjoy the jobs, people and places. Travel is in my blood and I love it.

We stopped in Raton, New Mexico, the first night out from Texas to find a motel and go to dinner. As we passed a pet store while walking back from dinner, I could see it was open and wanted to go in and see the animals. Well, that was a mistake. Right there in the first cage was a little brown skunk. A domesticated skunk is brown with a light tan streak down its back and tail. It was just a month old, had been de-scented and adorable. "Oh please. Can I have it," I begged and held the tiny thing in one hand. Even Jess was a sucker for the little skunk. It left the store with us. I named her Rosita Malia and what a little troublemaker she was. Just a precious, little bundle, but she made a raccoon's curiosity look like a Sunday school class.

She had a collar and a string for a strap, was hands down, the most highly intelligent animal I'd ever even heard of. You teach her once and that's enough. She learned to heel like a dog in about 15 minutes and I'd take her everywhere I went. We sent out baby invitations to all the families advertising the fact that Jess and Julie were the proud parents of a new baby girl weighing in at 12 ounces, had brown eyes and hair, her name and size, etc and that she was an adorable little stinker

Almost in the return mail my sister-in-law, Nancy, sent a hand knitted pink blanket one-foot square. I have that blanket yet, although Rosita does not live with us any longer. She did everything she was not supposed to do, like tearing wallpaper loose, emptying Kleenex boxes, tearing open loaves of bread, knocking plants off windowsills and chasing Hitchy, among a few hundred other mischief making things. One day she got out of her collar while I was washing down storm windows so Jess could put them back in the attic of the garage, when I noticed she wasn't with me. I looked and looked and looked. We both went on a search party to no avail. The next day I began again, going through the neighbor's yards, in garages or doghouses. Anywhere I could think of.

The third day I cried and felt dreadful, realizing some dog had possibly killed her or she was shot laying some place. At noon the phone rang asking if Rosita was cocoa colored. I said yes. The neighbor caller said they thought she was in their basement about four doors down. I ran over there nearly forgetting to hang up the phone. Sure enough, there she was sitting in the inside on the windowsill. Ethel said she was afraid to pick her up and wondered if she bites. I told her no and that she was also odorless. Once home she curled up in her basket after eating four dog biscuits and half a jar of water.

She would stand on the palm of my hand with her hind feet and I would put the other hand in front of her with index finger and middle finger spread open. She would hold the index finger with those tiny paws and I'd push her head down between my fingers and repeat, *Say your prayers*. It took four times and that was memorized. I'd hold up my fingers and say, *one, two, three*, while holding each finger. After a few more times, I'd say *three* or which ever digit I intended and she would reach over and grasp the correct finger.

I taught her other tricks as well; such a little scamp, but so much fun. She used a potty box, slept in a shoebox and ate dog food- no trouble except what she could find to shred with those ten little fingers.

Easter came and Jess asked what I would like to have. I said nothing really. I want for nothing. He didn't have any desires either, so I decided on lawn furniture. When Max and Vi stopped by that weekend, she said, "Oh, new lawn furniture for the patio. That's so nice."

Jess, jokingly said, "Yes, that's my new Easter outfit". I nodded my head and said yes it was, and it went over so well. I'd decided next year to buy him a new dress. That caused some chuckles.

Summer was just around the corner as the old expression

quotes but we had been raking that carpet of fallen leaves for days. It seemed they had been headed for an endless winter while we were gone. Reports of 20 below did nothing for the heart I can tell you. The wind was still shaking the trees mid April. The days were longer now and the sunset's made shadows reaching greedy fingers along the view from the garden side of the house. Despite inclement weather in Montana, I never ran dry of the means to cope with anything life dealt out. God's unlimited resources are free for the asking without stinting.

I was wondering about the garden. Would we be here? Where? Still waiting for word from headquarters. Not for long as it came the next day. We were due in Wyoming in four days.

That is no longer a problem to load needs and procure other things after you set up. Jess had a mechanic go over that BB truck and I made 50 trips back and forth, or so it seemed, filling the refrigerator and freezer, and packing two sets of clothes because you can't predict weather or afford to buy unnecessarily either. In the early morning, Jess hooked up the fifthwheel, I stuffed the Lincoln with dog, cat and skunk and their paraphernalia and by 6 A.M. we were Wyoming bound.

I had called the insurance company to be sure our policy was in order or not due in two weeks or some other disaster, only to get a question and answer session. Of insurance companies I have decided they are not supposed to be understood because no insurance company wants the outside world to know what's going on.

This job looked like a short run. Looks can be deceiving. Our main headquarters would be Cheyenne. The other end of the line was Laramie, 50 miles northwest across the mountain pass. It is 712 miles from home to Cheyenne, not a great distance and because of leaving one day early we were a day and a half ahead of schedule and trying to locate a trailer space to park. Forget that! We drove in the car, as I had followed the fifthwheel all over town but located nothing, then started to the outskirts of town and up on the higher levels.

There was one area that seemed to be a mobile home sub-division with one corner lot approximately 50 x 100 that was unoccupied. Jess drove to the office to inquire about its availability and learned the lot was owned by a man who had the month before moved his mobile home and family to another state and the space was for sale. We asked permission to park there overnight until we could contact the party who owned the lot to see if we could rent it for six months or until it sold, which ever came first.

The next afternoon, the man contacted the mobile park office and agreed for us to rent it for $100 a month. Under the conditions we found ourselves in, it was a bargain and Jess proceeded to get us set up. The next day I located a nursery and purchased some marigolds, petunias and lobelia plants. Anyplace I've ever live in my adult life I've left flowers behind once we moved on. Before I married Jess, it was the same. Half the soil, in my view is turned into flowerbeds.

It took most of the day to dig, clear and plant the outer perimeter along the existing sidewalk and along the carport as well. It was a good day. Once dinner was over and he had a chance to just sit, I asked about the job, the fellow workers – were any of the old crew there, any unusual sights to see and so on. He told of what he had time to see. It was a treacherous job over the top of a steep mountain pass, detoured out over solid rock with no barrier at the edge of the detour. If you slipped, you went some 500-feet down in the bottom of the flatland. There was already a Greyhound bus down there sitting upright on the chassis – no wheels. Not much is known about it otherwise.

We had been there two months when one evening sitting in folding lawn chairs, Jess looked up at the sky and said, "Sooky, do you know what to do in a tornado?" No I didn't as no one ever heard of such a thing in Hawaii. "You find the nearest depression you can and lay face down as close to a surface as possible. Even just along a curb in the street." Then he explained to me about tornados. I do believe the man is psychic or a 7th sense came with him at birth. Before the week was out, Cheyenne had its first tornado in history. If it hadn't been so tragic, I could see the humor in the after events.

It was on a Thursday afternoon around 2 P.M. I was sitting at the table writing to Wilma Lee, Jess's cousin in Amarillo. She always enjoyed letters so much explaining where we were and what it looked like. It seemed to be getting dark already and I thought that odd and looked at my watch. 2:10 P.M! My watch must have stopped! I got up to look at the clock. 2:10 P.M! Now how strange! I opened the backdoor to better see the sky. The sprinklers were on; watering the marigolds, lawn chairs where they always were, sky was blue but smoky. Off to the northwest the sky had a huge dark smoky cloud, but I gave it no thought at all as there is a school for United Airline pilots over there and smoke in the air from jet fuel most of the time.

I pulled the hose around to another section of plants and walked back in through the front door. I had just sat down when I remembered I had not turned the water hose back on after moving it, so went back out the rear door to correct this error in judgment. But when I stepped out a refrigerator door went sailing over my head and bits of other debris accompanied the refrigerator door. Here was something to worry about and it seems women are genetically programmed to worry anyway, but this was off the wall strange.

I stood there and looked back over to the left at that cloud. It resembled an enormous mix master churning around ever so slowly but full of stuff- not air. It took less than 60 seconds to realize that must be a tornado from Jess' description. I tore back through the trailer, grabbed the dog, threw a blanket over the cat so she couldn't scratch me and actually threw them in the car, slamming the doors shut and locking us in. Then I backed out of the driveway and started down to the intersection where

I could drive off into the field across the street, as it was lower than the street. With accelerator to the floor, I was doing 12 mph. The windshield was sucked out and gone. I went head first over the field edge and came to rest among ten or more other vehicles. Once the roar stopped, I realized my camera was on the seat beside me and snatching it up I took a picture of that monstrous thing and its whipping tail. Pretty unnerved, I just sat there.

The other vehicles started to move so I tried the Lincoln as it had stalled when I came to such an abrupt stop. Thanks to God's good grace it started up and I eased forward to turn and follow a pickup ahead of me. We were back on the street at the first driveway and I went back to the trailer. It was standing there as if nothing had transpired just moments before. It took a few hours before I realized the big blue house on the other side of the fence was no longer there. Jess's boat I had towed over was sitting along the fence on our side not disturbed in the slightest. The water was still sprinkling away.

I unwrapped a very unhappy cat and a cowering dog and set things right. Not until I went to look at the non-windshield did I realize the top was gone on the car. I had what is called a hardtop convertible. This is just an ordinary car with a vinyl top glued to the roof to appear like it could be folded down. Once that sight shook me up I thought I'd look along the fence. Nothing! Just ground up houses with here and there a garage or part of a room, some upturned cars and wiped out trees. Devastation everywhere. It was unbelievable.

I walked along the sidewalk to the end of the block where police cars, ambulances, fire trucks and every assorted emergency vehicle in town had assembled in one place or another. I'd seen the aftermath of earthquakes but not a candle to this. Dogs were howling and pulling their doghouses behind while trying to walk or run. Dazed people emerged from basements or just arrived from work down in the city. Just indescribable.

People looked deathly, felt likely to become part of the membership beyond the grave. One woman was hysterically screaming for her son who was a paperboy on his bicycle. It turned out he had been swept up by the wind and carried four miles from town only to be set back down so he rode back to town. Unbelievable stories flew for weeks.

By 4:30, things had settled down somewhat. How much can a disaster really settle? No more screams at last, just zombie-looking people walking this way and that. I went back to the fifthwheel and started thinking of dinner when I heard that blue Dodge screaming up the hill. I ran out in the street to meet Jess as he came around that intersection on two wheels. He came to a stop halfway home, put his head down on the steering wheel and nearly collapsed. I did not see tears but God as my witness, I know they were there.

He was shaking when he drove on up to the trailer. He never said a word just held me and trembled. I said, "Just look at the car". He couldn't have cared less.

He had been several miles from the rest of the crew using a dozer when one of the men heading back to town spotted him and flagged him down. Yelling at Jess, he asked "Isn't your rig up on Buffalo Ridge?" Jess said yes, and why? "Nothing left; a tornado took the entire ridge. It's gone.

Jess jumped off the dozer, hitched a ride back to his truck and the rest is part of our history. God's mercy is what saved us. Thirty feet away a two-story house looked like toothpicks. The entire street both directions was a shambles of wood, stone, plaster, brick, splintered pieces of furniture and thin lengths of just nothing. The cement was as clean as if it had been swept. The most pitiful were people looking for pets. Amazing as it seemed, we had not heard of one fatality.

The next morning after Jess left for work, I called the insurance company. Was I ever glad I had contacted them before we left, to be sure all was in order and up-to-date. They told me to find a shop, get the glass repaired and then find an upholstery shop or maintenance place to get a new top put back on. It took over a week due to a hundred or more other casualties of the tornado. In fact, we were lucky to get anything done.

I was so eternally grateful to God that we had been spared that I hunted down the Red Cross office and offered to help anyway I could. They were being bombarded with donations and the gym at the school looked like an enormous Goodwill. A lady from Myrtle Point, Oregon was in charge and directed me to a desk and told me to give out vouchers for what people needed. Once I got the hang of it, it was not only rewarding but also informative. Now years since, how I wish I had recorded their stories as they came through. Some I can recount verbatim.

One lady needed dishes and kitchen things as she had found shelter in a tent set up in someone's backyard and had a camp stove. Another told of being in the basement with her children and the dog when it took their house. Eventually they cleaned a way up the stairs and pushed aside the splintered door to see absolutely nothing, but her crock-pot on the cement all in tact, spaghetti sauce still hot, but the electric plug was driven two inches deep into the cement floor.

Another told of coming up from her basement with everything seemingly in pretty good shape. She set about cleaning up and opened the refrigerator to take out food for their dinner, but instead, was looking at the grass lawn. It had cut the house in half, but the eggs were still in the refrigerator door, not broken.

Yet another lady had been back several times needing bedding, underwear and shoes. I asked her if she had gotten some elsewhere, but she said she didn't know, as she could not see well. That was a revelation. I asked if she needed to see an optometrist, but she said she had; that was the trouble, she didn't have her glasses on.

A sweet little woman came in to help and I heard her story

while she was sorting clothing. Their house also had a slice off its side. The front room and stairs seemed pretty solid until she thought of going upstairs looking for her cat. The steps wobbled and she decided to wait for her son-in-law. She asked if he could please go up to search for her cat. He very gingerly went one step at a time, as there was no house on the other side of the stairway wall. He could see the roof was gone and everything caved in on top of the bed. She handed up a plastic bag and said if he found the cat to just put it in the bag and she did NOT care to see the poor thing.

After what seemed hours, the son-in-law started back down the stairs with a cat draped over his shoulder. She started to cry and asked why he did that, as she hadn't wanted to see her dead cat. He pulled the cat off and handed it to her with a wide grin and said maybe after three days under a slab of drywall, the cat might possibly be very hungry. Why didn't she concentrate on that?

A week later, one couple drove back up to the empty lot where the house had been. As they pulled in they saw two blue eyes in the car lights. Their little poodle had been under the bushes for a week.

On and on they came. But the most surprising of all was one thirty-something lady who came in all smiles and floating so happy we could have scraped her off the ceiling. Her story was fabulous. Her divorce was due to be final the day of the tornado but when the ex-hubby learned of it and what area of the town had all but been obliterated, he flew in and found her. They were getting back together and looking for a place to live, as her house was no more.

Finding lodging also had become one of my tasks. I called every realtor anywhere I could and asked about anything at all, even houses for sale and empty. It is amazing how hearts open during tragic times. Basement family rooms, spare bedrooms with kitchen privileges, unused upstairs rooms, and older people alone who would love to have someone in the house became available. The surprises seemed endless. What a rewarding job it was. I stayed 108 hours and have an award signed by the Governor of Wyoming to prove it.

One day I talked Jess into taking Hitchy to work with him since he would be shut in for ten hours. He growled and fussed so much I thought he wouldn't do it, but in the morning he grudgingly stuffed my little fuzzy darling under his left arm, gathered his hard hat and banged it on his head making the little 3-lb dog flinch. He picked up his keys, his lunch pail and extra shirt all in one swoop, leaned over to peck me on the cheek and as he went out the door, I heard him say, "You fuzzy little shit. If you get me into any trouble you're a goner."

A few weeks later while meeting some other work crew and wives for a BBQ I had a young man come over to me and slyly ask if my dog was okay.

"Oh, yes thank you. How did you know I had a little dog?"

He could scarcely talk for trying not to laugh. He said, "Well, Jess handed me this little tyke and said you're not oiling today. I'll pay your wages if you just watch after this little bastard. Don't you let anything happen to one hair on its head or I'll be headed for the divorce court and I like my home just the way it is. Got that?"

"I didn't see Jess until quitting time. You know, that is a pretty neat little dog really, for a sissy." I bit my lip.

On Sunday, Jess said to load up, as he wanted to show me something. Off we went out toward the job. Nearly twenty miles out, he took a detour to somewhere out across a field. He asked if I had my camera and, of course, I did, as I seldom went anyplace without it. We came to what appeared to be a pyramid in the middle of a Wyoming plain. Not another thing in view within eyesight.

How I loved these odd mysteries. We parked the truck and walked over to this monument. It was approximately twelve feet tall at the peak and twenty square at the base. Two-thirds of the way to the top was a bronze plaque with the face of one man to the east and the west side bore the likeness of another man.

We read the story on the plaque that told the events. There were two brothers who had purchased a sizeable acreage at this time in history that the railroad was being built across country. Their vision was that the railway would come through this wide-open place so along with other progressive minded people; they decided to build a town here. For a couple of years they thrived fairly well, but the railroad built several miles away and within another year or so, the town, such as it was, died away. But with great anticipation, the brothers erected this pyramid, dedicated to themselves, pictures and all, to proclaim that they had been the founders of this town to the many generations to come. So there it stands in all its glory, fifty miles from anyplace with no trace of a living existence.

I remarked that it would be nice if at least the historical society would place it on the list of Points of Interest or the Railroad would have some mention of the place in their memorabilia. I did try to find any such information even in the local library, but none was available.

We walked around and looked for signs of any former life and how I wished for a metal detector. Jess bought us one soon after that. My new toy was a wonderful investment. Many hours of fun and entertainment resulted from that purchase.

Once this job was finished, we started back to the grey house in Montana. It was early fall so once again time to get out the storm windows as we knew not when we would be on the road again.

Jess propped the windows up against the trunk of the lovely big Elm in our backyard. It stood about three feet from the iron railing of the patio; oftentimes the birds would sit on the rail and sing, clean themselves or just hop along for the joy of living, I guess. While looking up in the tree to see if he should prune it back, he saw a robin's nest and called to me in the house, "Sooky. Come out here. Got something you should see."

Up there twelve feet or more was the bird nest with every color in the rainbow and then more. We stared at it a while and I started to laugh. Well, I'll be darned. Last year while we were home I used to sit out here working on my quilt. As I came to the end of the thread in my needle, I'd drop the two or three inch length left over, usually in a place where I could easily gather them up when I went in the house.

The birds building their nest found easy pickings for filler material. I ran for the camera, thinking one day I'd enter that picture in a contest of some type, perhaps titled *The Bird Nest Quilt* or a short story being sure to include the many-colored blanket for the bird babies. Just using my imagination, you know.

Not having anything in particular to do and not hunting season yet, my restless Jesse was constantly underfoot. The man did not know how NOT to work and the idle time was hard for him. One day he came in and announced he was going to work. That was a startling piece of news. "When and where" I wanted to know.

"Well, I went down to the Gold Medal Company to see if they needed a driver and got hired. I'll drive a Refer (refrigerated truck) to the flour mill with a load of wheat and bring fresh produce back to the grocers here."

Now here was a new wrinkle in our lives. He perked up considerably once he had something to do. Off he went to Great Falls to get his big 18-wheeler and a new venture. He never could really predict a time of arrival back home for a day, and this made a difficult schedule for me, as I am punctual to the death and very organized.

After the third trip out and gone a few days at a time,

he called home to say he wouldn't get in that night so don't be alarmed. Again? I said, in not too pleasant a tone of voice. "Sorry," was the reply.

When he did get home the next day, he said, "How would you like to go along on the next trip?" I said I would love it and, wow, what a trip. First you unload the wheat, and then begin the route to pick up lettuce, other vegetables, potatoes, onions, squash, beans and a multitude of things. All night long we went from field, barn to warehouse. Did the man never sleep?

We stopped frequently for coffee, a sandwich, and pie or just to stretch our legs. Once a man in a diner asked Jess if I helped drive.

He said, "No, but she sings all the time to keep me awake and now and then I join in."

"How did you get away with her as a passenger if she doesn't drive?" the fellow wanted to know.

"I just asked the office if I could take my wife on one trip," and they said yes, after some consideration. I said, "thanks" on the way out the door, hesitating only long enough to add, "and her fuzzy dog too" before closing the door against any repercussion there. So that's how I got to come along.

During the next trip out we received the phone call that we had been waiting for. I needed to call Jess but he had already left the terminal. I asked for the phone numbers to the weigh stations along the freeway but I missed him at two stations and called the third one next. Good, he hadn't gotten there yet. I left a message he was to call home as soon as he pulled into that weigh station, which he did rather anxiously. No, nothing is wrong. I just needed to let you know Whittier called and to be ready to leave January 1st for Ecuador I told him. This cancelled any more truck assignments for now.

That caused a flurry of things to do at home and I flew into action. One of the first things was to find a home for this very bad girl called Rosita. What a calamity she could cause and in such a hurry too. I placed an ad in the Great Falls paper to the effect that a rambunctious pet skunk was for sale and be prepared for a mischief-maker. The ad went in on Saturday and by 8 A.M. we had over twenty calls. Yes, she was descented. No, she doesn't bite. Yes, she is house broken. Yes, she gets along with dogs and cats. No, she isn't dangerous. Yes, she eats dry dog food, sleeps in a shoebox and no, she doesn't chew up her little blanket. Yes, she has had shots. Yes, she walks with a leash. Yes, she likes to ride. Yes, she climbs on the furniture. No, she doesn't eat fruit and so it went.

About 8:15 A.M. I received a call from a woman who rather frantically inquired if we had sold the skunk yet. No, but we've had many calls. "We are stationed at the Air Force base in Great Falls and we have a domestic male skunk. Do Not Sell her before we can get there."

"We want $100 for her," I explained sympathetically, thinking maybe Air Force pay did not allow extravagant spending on non-essentials.

"Oh, that's fine, just don't sell her."

In about an hour they arrived with a dog and two small children. I called Rosita from wherever she was playing and she crawled up on my lap with those little hands working at anything she could find. I put her through her paces, much to the delight of her new owners. They said her antics made their Buster look like a dunce and after some tears from me, hearty handshakes between the men and gathering up shoebox bed, toys, food and dishes; they were off to Rosita's new home.

We kept in contact for over a year and as things usually happen, the correspondence grew less and less. They moved to a new base and we moved on along the job line.

However, we did receive a notice that Rosy, as they called her, had become a mother of three little stinkers which made us laugh. We too, had announced her as our little stinker. Since we had paid $25 for that skunk and sold her for $100, Jess thought I should go into the skunk business. Not on your life-one skunk per family was all the experience one needed, I told him.

Over the years we had a varied assortment of pets. My flowerbeds and pets are the highlights of my life. I must say, as I have grown older, I like animals far better than I do most people. From the time there were still children around, I'd help nurture cats by the dozens, dogs, rabbits, cockatiels, guppies, parakeets, canaries, horny toads, gold fish, hamsters, a turtle that ate grapes and sparerib bones, of all things, a monkey, three raccoons at different times, the skunk and even a cheetah once. That used to set peoples nerves on edge.

Once on the road again, we stopped off to see old friends if not too far out of the way. Jess had an Uncle Leon and Aunt Minnie in Amarillo that he was exceptionally fond of. Their only child Winnie, Jess's cousin, lived next door so we pulled in their large front yard for a couple of days to visit as we had not seen them in about three years.

Wilma and James had an old dog of some questionable ancestry, named Quawna. I set Hitchy down in the yard and the big dog proceeded to grab him by the back and shake him like a rat. This meant a veterinary and a big expense. Hitchy had a drain tube through the holes in his back for over two weeks. Thank goodness, we were way ahead of schedule to allow us time for stops along the way. The Vet said Hitchy was a spoiled brat.

While we were there with James and Wilma, they told of the latest escapade that they had heard of. There is a small town called Tulia, Texas south of them that had had a very strange thing going on. There are no train tracks in Tulia, yet for some reason at around 2 A.M. there was a train whistle heard night after night. It spooked some folks so badly they moved away. After months of this oddity, one person got up the gumption to venture down town at 2 A.M. to see where or how that was happening. Before long there came a big 18-wheeler traveling through with several others. It had a horn that sounded like a train tooting and he thought it quite a hilarious joke to pull on a sleepy little town with no train. Once the discovery was announced, nerves settled down but tempers flared too. The man was reported to his company but whatever came of that we never heard.

At Sweetwater, we learned Hank and Gwen would also be on this location, which pleased me no end. They were good people and our friends. As we began to assemble in Texas awaiting our orders, we also learned a rather undesirable couple would also be along. He was abusive to his wife, a drinker and womanizer, in general. This was not good news but you take the good with the bad and make the best of it. We left the truck and fifthwheel at mamas and joined the rest of our crew in Dallas to fly out to Ecuador.

Home in Montana after 18 months found us back in the little grey house. We spent little enough time in Montana but it was always a good sight to see when we pulled all the vehicles in the back drive and opened the door to a contented life.

My next project was soon in view and once again I was told "go build your house, don't bother me with it," which suited me just fine. There was a cedar sided house by the river that was over 100 years old. The lady who owned it had recently left this earth with only two grandsons as heirs. They lived in California and could not be bothered to even come to Montana to sign papers and handle the estate let alone be concerned with this behemoth of a house.

In its original setting and time, it had been a prime figure of wealth and modern living. It had three bedrooms and a bath. Bathrooms were not in the wilderness. It had a huge kitchen and buttery that would in time be known as a pantry. Also there was a living room of some 30 feet in length, a storm hall and mudroom at rear entrance where one left boots, coats and other items not to invade the kitchen. To my utter surprise it also had a huge basement. Some forethought went into that planning.

This town of 700 or so souls had seen much history. It had been a fort 90 years before and actually it was part of Montana territory, as this area was not a state yet. The riverboats came up from St Louis and the history of those boats is a fabulous story in itself. There were elderly persons who well recalled the house in its prime and the tales told are fascinating.

However, my first encounter with the property set a new precedent for the town itself. When the title was transferred and surveying completed, much to everyone's amazement we learned that particular piece of land was missing lot 13. It read lots 11-12-14-15, corner of Front and River Street. There were five lots 50' wide but only four were recorded. This entailed the re-recording of said property to which there seemed no end of red tape and paperwork involved.

First it had to be corrected to read lots 11-12-13-14-15 added to Amando Township, Choteau County, city of Benton in the state of Montana, each step done separately and through a court system. The final paper was declaring that the state of Montana now had a 50' x 100' strip of land hither to not proclaimed on record. Thank the powers that be, I was not expected to pay back taxes on said property, as it was 110 years old from start of homesteading.

One more weird experience. When all this unfolded and I sat down with the papers to explain it to a husband who "just don't want to be bothered," his only comment was, "Well, I'll be!"

After combing his hair with his fingers, the shock of hair looked as if it just might stubbornly resist a comb. He was, as he said, "Jest plain flummoxed about it all."

It took three months to renovate or update, lower ceilings, build a stairway up to the attic and transform that cavernous place into another bedroom, wallpaper all seven rooms, change that pantry into a bathroom by moving the pantry door to the opposite wall so entry was from the dining room end of the living room, install new light fixtures, put in modern cabinets, build an island and bar for eating purpose, add a built-in range over a partial wall to accommodate a refrigerator, open up the plastered-over chimney to install a free standing Ben Franklin fire place then carpet and paint. Those three months kept me out of my mister's hair and netted us $30,000.

I cannot knit or crochet, do fancy embroidery, fix my own hair and to use make-up is a joke of gigantic proportions but if you give me my tools and a project, I'll turn out some pretty good work. I can ruin a boxed cake mix but know how to trawl cement and grind valves in an engine. You raise five boys, you learn things, you know.

Now I have time to reflect on all these accomplishments and still look so healthy it is indecent. I live in a small town where gossip is the main industry, have a twenty pound cat and my flower beds, time to write of so many things, continue my poetry, still sing a great deal and am older now and I realize that when you are young, now is forever and tomorrow doesn't matter. Our bodies rebel at the thoughts of winter, which somehow seem endless once it sets in. One believes Mother Nature has forgotten there ever was such a thing as summer, so you endure and remain thankful to our God that we have lived this long.

In our case, the memory bank is overflowing with dividends that are priceless. No dollar and cents value can be placed on love or laughter. As we age, we seem never to run dry of the means to cope with anything life and its troubles throw our way. Often times we find nothing more painful than to live ones own contradictions; it lacerates our intelligence and our feelings.

Thank goodness both of us are relatively uncomplicated people without too many layers and most thoughts lie close to the surface. After a life of high-octane vigor these few years, which are welcomed, for fishing, visits with old cronies. We realize life has arrived. The long unmeasured pulse of time moves everything forward. That includes Jesse and me.

Epilogue

This story is built on factual locations and in many instances, the people depicted are real. Their names changed for privacy reasons, of course.

Although a work of fiction, most incidents are based on a real life experience, in areas mentioned and in the correct time span.

Life was good for Jesse and me.

Memories of the Author

Printed in the United States
142343LV00004B/23/P